Harmonious Souls
A Broken Souls Novel: Book 4

ELLA SHAWN

Copyright

Ebook:
ISBN: 978-1-7370141-6-4
Print:
ISBN: 978-1-7370141-5-7

Any references to historical events, real people, or real places are used fictitiously. Names, characters, and places are products of the author's imagination.

Front cover image by Ellen Shawn.
Book design by Ella Shawn.

https://www.ellashawn.com

Dedication

For my twin flame. The only soul who could convince me it's worth it, every time we incarnate. Thank you for your unconditional acceptance, compassion, forgiveness, and most importantly... thank you for loving the whole of me without condition or expectation. I fall in love with myself a little more each day because of the way you love me. I hope my love does the same for you. Let's see what the next thirty years bring.

Author's Note

Where do I even start?

No, seriously, I don't know how or where to start this note. I've gone back and read the previous three notes written in the first three books of this series, no help. So, I guess I'll start this note by telling you how absolutely proud and excited and sad and uncomfortable I am to be finished with my first book series. I'm all over the damn place. Mixed feelings aside, I am proud and excited.

If you've read the first three books, you already know that my writing style is not for the faint of heart. I don't write for everybody because not every story is meant to heal or resonate with everyone. I had to accept this as a truth a long time ago.

There will always be trigger warnings in any book, story or poem I write. My mom always asks, "Baby, why you gotta use so many cuss words and talk about all that nasty stuff in your books?" I have to remember that she doesn't see me as a writer so, she probably thinks I'm in to all the things I write about. Knowing this, I still inform her why I write.

My intentions are based in the medical definition of the word. In terms of medicine, intentions mean the healing process of a wound; in other words, how a wound heals.

For me, writing is part of the healing process of the wounds that afflict Black Womanhood as a Collective. I write about Southern Black Women because our stories don't even make the news. If the villain in the story is family member or family friend... They're not even our stories, anymore. They're transformed into bullets named liar and demon. Bullets shot to riddle our sense of self-esteem and our right to say no, with holes big enough to bleeds us out. Sometimes, our stories are transformed into nooses made of blame and tightened with embarrassment. Ready to hang us at the first mention of the pain we've endured at the hands of daddy, uncle, pastor, older cousin... etc.

The forbidden and unheard stories of Southern Black Women are not pretty. They are not easy. How could they be? One of my favorite

—

4

writers is Zora Neale Hurston. There is a quote from Their Eyes Were Watching God, that perfectly illustrates this. Janie's Nanny is talking with her about the way of the world, explaining where her place is, and where it isn't.

Nanny says, So de white man throw down de load and tell de nigger man tuh pick it up. He pick it up because he have to, but he don't tote it. He hand it to his womenfolks. <u>De nigger woman is de mule uh de world so fur as Ah can see</u>. Ah been prayin 'fuh it tuh be different wid you. Lawd, Lawd, Lawd.

I'm not the first Southern Black writer whose writing is part of the healing process of the afflicting wounds of Black Womanhood as a Collective.

I won't be the last.

I'm in good company so fur as Ah can see.

What do you need to know about Harmonious Souls?

There is no cliffhanger

Valery and Collin are more prominently featured, which means Valery and her g-dropping, profanity riddled speech patterns are more present, too. The way she speaks is not a reflection of her intelligence or her importance. Her speech patterns are indicative of her role in the DID system—nothing more, nothing less.

Vera is more prominent in this final book and if you don't already love her, you will after reading Harmonious Souls. Her personality really comes through.

John and Vivian give me a reason to believe in Twin Flames and everlasting love. They also make me want to start practicing Tantric BDSM.

Secrets are revealed.

Acceptance occurs.

Love is found and supported.

The entire story ends where it began.

Thank you for supporting The Broken Souls series. It's been a pleasure and a burden writing it. I've learned so much about myself as a woman, wife, mother and of course, as a writer. It's been more like therapy than anything.

—

I'm not sure what my next adventure will be, but I know whatever and wherever it takes me; the Broken Souls series will always be with me. In a jar on my shelf, waiting for the moment I need it to remind me that I did write four cohesive, full-length novels and I can do it again.

Make sure you check out my website, I'm starting a Member's Only section for fans to hang out with me and the characters from this series, and every other book I write. It will be a wild and exciting ride. Join us, you'll be glad you did. (Available March 2023)

<u>Trigger Warning</u>

Harmonious Souls contains explicit sexual content, profanity as well as incidences of childhood SA, marital rape, and gun violence.

Part I

t's amazing to know in the truest heart of oneself, though part of a collective system, the highest aspect of self belongs to the individual. It affirms that I, Vivian Bruno Ellis, do indeed exist separate and apart from Vera, Valery, and Valeria.

~Vivian Ellis

1

John

While driving home from work, flashes of my wife's body submerged in our soaking tub on New Year's Eve have me gripping the steering wheel a bit tighter than is necessary. She wanted us to be more intentional with new year rituals.

Usually, we attended a few parties where we both networked, drank, and left in time to watch Dick Clark count America out of one year and into another. By the time the ball dropped in Time Square, I was already balls-deep inside my wife. I shake my head thinking about the look she gave me when she told me her plans for us

"John, instead of going to parties with people we don't like to drink wine we would never buy; I'd like to stay in. We can take a tantric bath to reconnect, and make love until the sun comes up or, until we pass out." She looked so damn beautiful. So innocent and vulnerable, how was I supposed to say no? I couldn't, even though I'd argued the best way for us to reconnect would be for me to tie her up to the brand-new St. Andrews cross in our newly remodeled playroom.

One look into those summer-sunshine eyes and, needless to say, while everyone else was partying and drunk off their asses, Viv and I sat in some oily water, surrounded by a floating fruit salad and sea salt crystals the size of small diamonds digging into our butt cheeks. With all the humming, massaging, journaling, and deep-eye-connecting; I was so ready for Vivian, I damn near came as soon as I felt her soft lips around my cockhead It was one of the compassionate, selfless gifts she's ever given to me.

I admit, I'm not opposed to bringing in another year like that.

It's after seven in the evening, and the Carolina sun dips behind the horizon just as I cross over *Malfunction Junction*. It's the one thing about winter that drives me out of my mind. Fall back an

—

hour... for what? The agricultural industry is not dependent of day-light-savings time in 2003.

But, what the hell do I know? I'm not a farmer.

My thoughts are all over the place and it feels like it's taking forever to make this forty-five minute drive home. I'm anxious about whatever is going on with Cole and the Order, but there's something else bothering me. It feels like earth worms tunneling through my brain, moving granules of memories around while depositing their desiccated waste. I want to believe that Viv and I are getting back to something resembling normalcy but honestly, I'm pretty sure we've never had a real sense of normal to begin with. So, I guess we're settling into our new normal.

There is a new, deeper intimacy within our relationship that has nothing to do with sex, communication or anything I can readily pinpoint. Maybe it's that I've learned to trust myself more, and no longer need the kind of validation that fueled my insecurities. Or, perhaps it's that she trusts herself more and is no longer willing to sacrifice her needs for a false sense of safety. It definitely has something to do with our newfound ability to trust ourselves, which is odd because I always thought trust issues stemmed from having difficulty trusting other people.

Whatever is happening, I'm glad we're finally in the same damn book; even if we're not on the same page.

Finally, I pull into our driveway and the motion-sensor lights illuminate the front of our house like someone inside flipped a switch to see who just pulled up.

Can't be too careful when your friends become your enemies and attempt to burn down your entire world.

"Vivian." I call because I still don't have a garage opener and have no way of knowing if she's home or not.

Need to get that rectified like yesterday.

—

"Hey, Viv!" I leave my shoes in the cubby before walking into the kitchen where I usually find her this time in the evening. But the kitchen is empty.

Where the hell is she?

I check my phone for a message but there aren't any. I poke my head out to check the empty garage, confirming what I already know is true. After securing the door, I go back into the kitchen to see if she left anything in the fridge for tonight.

Least I can do is get dinner started for us.

I pull the vegan hamburger-less macaroni and cheese casserole from the fridge and place it on the counter to preheat the oven to 345 degrees. While I dig through the everything-but-kitchen-sink drawer for the wine opener, the door bursts open with a flurry of what may be my wife or a wild animal... I'm not sure which, at the moment.

"John, you won't believe who I ran into." Vivian blows into the kitchen like some kind of Autumn woodland nymph; flowing scarves in muted reds, bright oranges and deep purples cascade around her lithe body until she comes to a stop in front of the small island. Her multihued locs of ginger, cinnamon and blonde hang down her back like Medusa's powerful coils waiting for the perfect time to exact their vengeance on unsuspecting and deserving males.

"Viv... hey, lovely slow down. Here, give those to me."

"John! did you hear what I just said? Thanks," she hands the grocery over to me as she continues talking. "... there's fresh fruit in one of those bags. Be careful. So, anyway..."

"Vivian."

"... wasn't even looking where I was going when I bumped in..."

"Vivian!" Her head snaps up and she stops her frenetic movements long enough to realize she's standing in the middle of our kitchen. She looks like she has no idea how she ended up here. "Take a breath and calm down. Damn." But I know this woman and I know that look. Resigned, I give her what I hope is a look of patience, instead of the weariness crawling up my spine, turning my shoulders into heavy boulders.

"I went to the market on Rosewood—Tammie had extra coupons—to pick up some Castile soap. I was so busy reading the ingredients on the back of the bottle, I wasn't looking in front of me and ran right into none other than Cole Whitman." Expressive eyes are stretched wide as she tries to convey some unspoken message to me, but I'm as lost as I am shocked.

What the fuck is going on?

"Cole. Coleman Whitman. My friend from college—*Cole*?"

"Yes. The one you were whipping on that horrible video. The one you said you *couldn't* get in touch with. Coleman Whitman."

"What did he say to you?"

"Nothing," She places the casserole into the oven before turning around to lean her butt against the counter beside the double wall ovens. "Thanks for taking this out. No, I didn't say one word. I turned around before he saw me; I dropped all my Castile soap and got out of there." She mumbles something about still needing to get her soap before her coupons expire. "What, why are you staring at me like I did something to you?"

"W-What do you mean... you *actually* ran. From *Cole*?" Her beautiful summer-sunshine eyes darken with indignant confusion as she watches me like she's looking for a hint of what I might be thinking or accusing her of. In a bid to salvage this conversation, I ask a better question. "Why didn't you just say—I don't know, excuse me. Oh, it's you. Hi Cole—and tell him I was looking for his ass?" I sound exasperated and pissed. It's not her fault, but why would she just... "You just ran away. You know I've been searching for this bastard since those men broke into our home?"

"Okay? But if you've been looking for him in connection with the men who broke into our house and cost us another child, why would you think for a minute that I'd be comfortable confronting *your friend*? When he's been avoiding you like he gave you an STD?" She flounces around the kitchen until she stands in front of the refrigerator.

I stare holes into the back of her head because I know she can't see me. Until she snaps, "Stop looking at me like I'm one the bastards who hired those men to come into our home."

As always, this woman calls me on my bullshit and doesn't give me a chance to scrape it off before dealing with the stink of it.

"I apologize, Viv. It's just..."

"That sigh... the one that sounds like you've traded places with Sisyphus. What's up, what aren't you telling me about the Cole Whitman situation, John?"

"I wish I could tell you everything. I can't and still, I need you to trust me with this."

"Tell me what you can."

"Cole's been working both sides of field in regards to The Order and the government, I think. But that's just it, lovely."

"What? You don't know if you can trust Cole or if he's involved in whatever The Order has going on?" It's amazing, how clear she sees what's going on, when I'm either too close or too far from the situation to gain any sort of clarity.

"It's not that I'm not sure, as much as I'm not certain—"

"John, you're splitting hairs at the follicular level when you'd do better to trim it from the ends."

"I'm not bullshitting you, Viv. You asked me a question and I'm trying to answer it to the best of my ability." I don't know why she's pushing me, knowing I can only tell her so much.

She comes right back at me without missing a beat. "I never said you were bullshitting me, John. What I said, is that you're getting bogged down in the minutia and factoids which are being fed to you, instead of looking at the bigger picture." That stops my mouth from opening in defense and my position because she's right. I'm definitely nit-picking and trying to figure out the how and why of all these false facts coming in as intel.

"You're right. Of course, you are." I open my eyes when I feel her arms slink around my waist and her head on my chest. I wrap myself around her and we stay like that for long moments.

"I need to get that." She whispers against my chest, her warm breath passing through the fine cotton/silk blend of my dress shirt to kiss the skin over my heart. I release her with some reluctance because nothing feels better than having my wife in my arms. Especially, when it feels like I'm slowly losing my grip on everything that matters.

"You know," I start as she pulls our dinner from the oven to rest it on a trivet while it cools. I wait until she turns back around to face me before I tell her what I've been loath to say. "... I don't know if I can get us out of this. The Order, it's—"

"An organization made up of human beings. They're only flesh and blood, John. The moment you decide you no longer want them to be a part of your reality—stop giving them your attention and energy—they're ability to determine how you choose to live the rest of your life will end."

Viv's words hang in the air like the stench of old, sweaty jock straps in a middle school locker room. I expect to see reticence in her honeyed gaze, but I don't. I see her resolve and hard-won belief in what she's said. I can't just blindly go where she wants me to, even though I wish like hell I could. Vivian is the most unencumbered woman I know—with all the shit she deals with on the daily—and it's because of her ability to detach from the nonsense and focus on what matters to her.

I toss her a smirk that doesn't reach my eyes and say so low in the back of my throat that she only hears the sounds and not my words. "New year, same shit."

"If I were you, I wouldn't stay in it too long."

"Stay in what, too long?"

"The same shit... because the longer you stay sitting in it, the less odious is starts to smell. Pretty soon, you won't be able to smell it at all. Which means—"

"Stop wallowing and clean this shit up because something tells me that even if I stop smelling it, my wife sure as hell won't be sticking around pretending she doesn't."

"You're smarter than most people give you credit for."

"And you're an even bigger brat than you realize, lovely."

"Your brat."

"And aren't I a lucky bastard that you say so?"

"Luck has nothing to do with it. We are inevitable—we would've happened regardless of the how or the when."

"I love you."

"Of course, you do. I'll pour the wine; you fix the plates. I'm hungry."

2

Vivian

John is a quiet, judgmental wolf gnawing on the bones of probability, while making tentative calculations on what the next move needs to be. In moments like this, I adopt Bill Clinton's policy on homosexuals in the military; I don't ask. He doesn't tell. When I made the decision to let go and let John, I didn't realize it would be so difficult to actually do it.

It wasn't until I chose myself over his happiness and peace of mind, that I understood how toxic and co-dependent our relationship was. I'm still grappling with forgiving myself for the part I played in creating an environment where that kind of toxicity was encouraged and allowed to flourish. The truth is, I had to come to this understanding on my own, and John will have to do the same thing.

Here's what I know for sure: I am not responsible for my husband's happiness; I can only change my own circumstances and how I respond to others accordingly and before anyone and anything... me first.

John's low rumble cuts into my musings as he jokes, "You look like you're writing you womanifesto over there, lovely." The twinkle in his dark eyes glitter like gold leaf on a gilded frame. The attempt to bring levity to the post-dinner lull is sweet, but unnecessary. There's a lot between us and I'm not here to spot clean and hope no one lifts the potted plant and discovers our stains.

"No, not my womanifesto, as much as reflecting on the three ah-ha moments I've had over the last year or so." I meet his gaze with an unwavering one of my own.

"And I assume these *moments* concern me in some way."

"You know what people say about those who assume don't you, John."

"Yes. Since we've already established, I'm an asshole of epic proportions, I'll keep right on assuming your ah-ha moments came about because of me."

I take a hearty gulp of my red wine, to buy myself a little time. Another mouthful before deciding how to best say what I know needs to be said, but John is having none of it.

The impatience rings clear when he all but challenges, "Come on, Viv. Out with it."

"You already know how over the moon I was for you when we first got together. How I wanted to take the shadows from your eyes... be the reason you felt joy and happiness." He nods his head, once but otherwise doesn't move or speak. The breath I need to finish spilling more of my secrets to this man, is trapped in my chest.

"Why do you look so nervous? It's you and me having a conversation over a glass of wine."

I down the last sip of liquid courage and will my voice to be as steady as John's gaze. "I willingly sacrificed myself, my happiness, my peace of mind and my soul for you."

He shifts forward in his chair, and I hurry on before he can interrupt me.

"I don't regret it."

To that, John presses his full lips together until only the seam is visible and cuts me a look that says I'm a dirty-two-faced-liar and he aims to prove it. And then he speaks in that black-velvet voice that leaves my panties wet.

"You say you don't regret it and still, you have three *ah-ha moments* from being so *giving*." The way he emphasizes specific words sends apathetic horripilation down my arms.

I rally my gumption and counter, "Wisdom isn't the same as regret, John. I've simply learned that I'm not responsible for you or your happi—"

"I never asked you to be responsible for me or my goddamned happiness, Vivian. I didn't ask you to gift me your... your s-sanity. You,"

John rises from his seat and walks over to the fridge and pulls a bottle of beer from the middle shelf before striding back over to the table to stand behind his discarded seat. I wait for him to finish, but he just twists the cap from his beer bottle and starts to knuckle roll it while he stares me down like I owe him money.

"Me, what?"

He takes a pull from the bottle and of course, my stomach tightens in response to the way his mouth seals over the lip of the bottle—a perfect kiss; possession, suction with finesse—and the how his throat works on that swallow. Watching a man drink from a beer bottle shouldn't make me this horny, but then again, my husband isn't just any man.

When he finally answers my question, I barely remember what we're talking about.

That is until he points out, "You gave freely. Willingly. Yes, I may be an asshole for taking it, definitely an asshole for redeeming them but I never once asked you for a goddamned thing Vivian. Nothing except for your love, submission and your fucking loyalty."

Another pull, another gush of wetness soaks into the gusset of my panties.

"I'm not accusing you of asking me for anything," I reach for my wine glass, only to find it's empty. With nothing better to do, I run my index finger around the rim several times before I attempt to speak again. "I was telling you—before you interrupted me—that my selfless acts of sacrifice weren't so selfless, after all." It's taken a lot for me to be able to face what made me feel ashamed for years, and I'm determined to get through to my husband why these ah-ha moments are so important to me.

"Fine, Vivian, you're not accusing me, but you blame me all the same for all the shit I've done to you. How could you not?"

"I don't blame you for anything, maybe it's you who's point accusatory fingers at yourself. These moments aren't about me blaming you or anyone else, they're about growth... my growth. And yours, too."

"Mine? What the hell does your *gotcha* moments have to do with my growth?"

" First of all, they're not called—you know what, never mind. You're obviously not in the right head space to have this conversation. I'm sure it has everything to do with my announcement about running into Cole. We can talk about this lat—"

"You don't get to decide what I can and can't talk about, Viv. Now you brought these moments up for a reason, I would like to know what that reason is."

"Please don't interrupt me—let me finish getting it all out before you barge in with your own perspective."

He nods his head and takes the last pull from that damn beer bottle, before he runs the tip of his tongue across his bottom lip, pulling the flesh into his mouth as he blinks heavily lashed lids open to find me staring at him like he's the last drop of water and I haven't drank in months.

"Everything all right, lovely?"

"Hmm?"

"Are you all right? You look a little..."

"Oh, yeah. I'm fine... was just thinking—what I wanted to say earlier, was that I realize every time I would sacrifice any part of myself for you, that I was acting from a place of fear. I was afraid if I didn't give everything—even though you never asked me to—that you'd leave me. That I'd be on my own again—"

"I would nev—"

—

18

"I know that now, John. I understand that you love me the same way I love you, but I didn't—couldn't even fathom your unconditional love as a reality back then."

He stares into me as his shoulders relax. His face is calm and open.

Thank you, sweet Black baby Jesus born to white people in the desert.

He plays with the paper label on his bottle, but his eyes don't stray away from my face for even one second.

"Anyway," I clear my throat before admitting, "the most important ah-ha moment was realizing that every time I tried to keep you from experiencing pain or sorrow, I was really keeping you from opportunities to grow."

"How did you come to that conclusion?"

"Have you ever heard of the Universal Law of Magnetic Affinity?"

"I may have read something about it in an article of quantum physics I read in Scientific America. It sounds vaguely familiar. Why?"

"This law states that before each incarnation, the soul establishes exactly what it wants to experience in a particular life cycle. Magnetic Affinity asserts that nothing that happens within a person's life is a coincidence; it's all predetermined before the soul is born. So, the tests and trials we face, are the ones we planned for ourselves. It's all about creating balance and paying back karmic debt and showing what has been learned in previous incarnations."

"Let me get this straight—"

"Look, John, you don't have to believe in the law to understand what I'm telling you. I only wanted you to know where I'm coming from when I say that my need to jump in and make your life easier and your experiences less painful, probably did more harm than good—to you—that is."

—

"I never sought the favor of a sacrificial lamb. I have and will always just need you. Your love. Your submission in our bedroom. Your loyalty in all things. And I think you may be right."

"Wait, what? You think I may be right about hindering your... g-growth?"

"Yes. Why do you sound so surprised? Honestly, I walked around thinking my shit smelled like roses, no wonder I had no problem sitting in the middle of it for as long as I did."

"Throwing my words back at me, huh?"

" Not really, just realizing how appropriate they are in this moment. You know, I never thought about my actions or why I did half the shit I did. Not saying it's your fault, but I think maybe because your opinion seemed so high of me... I never saw a reason to check myself."

"Ah-ha!"

"Ah-ha, what and why the hell are you slamming your palm down on the island like you just won some big court case?" There's no heat behind his words, and the wrinkles between his brows tells me he's a little embarrassed he flinched.

"Because you see the value in these ah-ha moments where you and I are concerned." He wraps his long fingers around my hand, as we take a deep breath and share this eudaemonic moment.

~3~

Vivian

John steps into our room fresh from the shower, just as I return from checking on our Maine Coon, Lady Bertha in her whelping box. I draw to a stop in the middle of the bedroom floor. He angles his head to the side in a silent question, while tying the drawstring of his gray sweatpants. My mouth goes dry, while another set of lips become decidedly wet. *My Lord, my strength and my condemner*. I swallow the whimper threatening to give me away before John can hear it.

I swear watching him tie those sweats up is comparable to witnessing the creation and destruction of the world, happening in unison. My husband is a source of harmonized chaos; too powerful to be harnessed and too remarkable to be unleashed. Yet for me. he willingly gentles himself.

"You see something you like, lovely?"

Cocky bastard.

I withhold the pleasure of my response and revel in my womanhood as he tracks my path to our bathroom.

"Perhaps you would like... *something else* to do with that beautiful mouth." His soft chuckle tightens my lower belly.

By the time I start the shower, I'm a collection of coiled need and craving. That he can do this to me without even the slightest touch, is a testament to the power he wields over me. Knowing he's waiting for an invitation that won't come, is a testament to the power I have over him.

While water beats down on my shoulders and the slow drip of arousal infiltrates my bloodstream, I send gratitude into the universe for the practice of sacred sexuality. John and I have been stoking this particular fire for the last four days, and we won't be ready to bask in its inferno for another two or three. Slow and steady is our new favorite speed. In the beginning, he complained and grumbled about

---

21

not being in control like he needs to be but now, he's fully on board with being—what he calls—a tantric Dom.

The room is dim, but it doesn't obscure the view of John laying on top of the covers with his right leg straightened, and the left bent at a forty-five degree angle. I take my time and peruse his bare chest, noting that his right fingertips are just inside the waistband of his gray sweats.

God, he looks like my favorite faded fantasy pulled from an old photo album.

I covet him like he doesn't already belong to me. Like having his entire heart and soul as my secret enchanted garden isn't enough to assuage this insistent need for him.

"To answer your implied question from earlier," I cross over to our bed and observe the curious amusement that dances in his darkening eyes. I love how he waits for me to elaborate before seeking the answers he wants.

Patience is another benefit of our sacred practice.

I lock eyes with him before admitting, "Yes. When I was in the shower... I thought about the weight and girth of your shaft the moment it touches my tongue. The preliminary suggestion of how intensely your need for me is, just before I take you deeper. How I relinquish my need for breath in deference to my need to hear that vulnerable sound you make in the back of your throat when I swallow you whole."

I climb into bed beside him, sidle up next to him to lay my ear against his chest and press my naked torso against his.

One, two, three breaths and the heat of desire quiets down to something more manageable.

"Thank you for answering my question, lovely."

"Of course."

"Did you take care of—"

"No. I wouldn't do that."

"Just making sure I don't need to work a punishment into our next play date."

"Sounds more like you're looking for a reason to add one."

So, please consider doing something—anything, really—that could earn you one."

"I don't plan to, but you know what a brat I become when we push our limits. You'll probably get your wish, and I won't even mean to fulfill it."

On a soft huff of hope, he squeezes me closer to him, even as he places a chaste kiss on the crown of my head. "I checked on Bertha while you were in the shower; she looks fucking miserable."

"She is but she doesn't have much longer before she delivers. I'm so nervous about the whole ordeal."

"I imagine you are, considering."

"Considering, what?"

"Don't do that, Viv. I know you're thinking about our previous pregnancies; I for damn sure am. I want it to be easy for her."

"You know I didn't even realize that's where all this anxiety was coming from. It's like I blocked out the fact that both of our pregnancies ended tragically."

"Sometimes, denial is more than a river in Egypt."

I giggle, which is exactly why he made the corny joke. The low flame of arousal burns a little hotter as love and appreciation for this man warms my heart.

"She's close?" It's the quiver in John's voice that makes me turn my head to look into his face. I smile and study him for a couple of beats. When I think he's done, he adds in a protective voice, "if you want me to go over there and sit with her... for a while, I will. I know you're tired and I have some reports to read so, I'll be up for a while anyway."

"Would you mind? I don't think *she* wants to be alone. I have the low-wattage bulb on but she's pretty uncomfortable from what I can see." I don't know what he sees in my face, but it softens his features into an expression filled with love and concern.

"You know she's going to be fine, don't you, Viv?"

"I—I want her to—I hope so."

"I know. Neither of us have reason to believe her pregnancy will be normal, or the expected outcome will take place, but—"

"But we can't project onto Lady Bertha. I know. I need to meditate and journal so, thanks for doing this."

He stands and crosses to his dresser to get a shirt. The smile he gives me before pulling a white tee over his head is filled with promises that have nothing to do with what hangs beautifully between his thighs.

~4~

John

I have no idea where the fuck Coleman Whitman is hiding, and I'm starting to think maybe Vivian was mistaken. I've been meaning to ask her about it several times since she mentioned it last week, but she's been so busy with preparations for the artist coming in from South America; I haven't been able to touch base with her. I'm tempted to set up a stakeout at the Rosewood Market to see if his country ass shows up there again.

What the hell am I talking about... stakeout?

"Mr. Ellis," Amanda pops her head into my office without so much as a knock on my closed door. She flashes me her all-American-girl-smile full of straight white teeth and a side of fuck you. The hair on the back of my neck and down both arms stands at attention.

"Yes." I keep my voice calm, even as I try to read the uncertainty filtering through her eyes. I also note the way her bottom lip trembles just a little, like she's fighting hard not to break down in tears. She's chewed all of the dark, wine-colored lipstick as well as some of the skin away in her nervousness. *Who in the hell could make her this nervous?*

"Um. Mr. Ellis... ur, there is... um, that—uh... um—"

"What the hell, Amanda. Either shit or get your ass off the goddamn pot." It's not only her mouth that trembles, but her entire frame is vibrating. As soon as I realize who's in my waiting area, I hear a high-pitched squeal and a horrible thud.

I kneel in my doorway beside Amanda's crumpled body, trying to play connect the dots. It feels like I went to concessions in the middle of *Lord of the Rings*—when Aragorn fell from the cliff and

---

25

was presumed dead—and when I get back in the theatre, his ass is running through Helm's Deep to warn of the impending battle.

Coleman-motherfucking-Whitman.

"Mr. MBA"

My body falls into stasis; air, blood and thoughts cease to flow. The moment stretches into the infinitesimal microseconds of eternity. I become the rotation and revolution of time and space. My conscious mind catalogues every aspect of this moment right down to the minutia of the dry cracked skin hanging off the dead man's bottom lip. Strangely, that skin isn't less or more important than the Desert Eagle with a silencer screwed into the barrel, which is pointing at my chest. Somehow, my mind makes them both important and impotent in equal measure.

"Cole, I knew you were slick as an alley cat but damn, just how many lives do you have left?" A flash of his sharp incisors is his only response so far. His eyes track my movements as I stand to my full height and step across the felled woman in my doorway. Placing my body between hers and Cole's. Warmth and something that looks like brotherly love, softens the hard plains of his stoic face. I don't trust him. He doesn't trust me, and still, we stand facing each other with smiles and a loaded gun between us.

"You lettin 'me in, *John*?"

"Do I have a choice, *Cole*?"

"We always have choices. Even when facing the barrel of a loaded gun—so, yes or no—see, choices."

I stoop back down, not taking my eyes from my old friend, to lift my assistant from the floor. Her hair is in disarray; instead of the bouncy layered-bob she's so proud of. Her rich cinnamon-brown skin is the color of an old, worn saddle.

Amanda's large doe eyes are mostly black as a result of her blown pupils, leaving none of the sticky sweet caramel visible. *I'm going to fucking kill Cole for making my office a war zone.*

"Right now, Cole," I pause and escort Amanda from my doorway into her adjacent office. I collect her bag, put her coat, hat and scarf on her shaking body and walk her to her door.

Cole barks from his position just inside my office. "What do you think you're doing, John?"

"I'm helping my assistant walk out of a situation that has fuck all to do with her."

"No, the fuck you ain't, brother."

"Then, *brother,* you're going to have to shoot me. Otherwise—" I don't bother finishing as I whisper explicit instructions to Amanda. "... nod if you understand."

Her head bobs up and down like she's sitting on the dashboard of a diehard sports fan, along with the rest of the team's immortalized bobblehead statues.

"... good. Don't return to work until I call you. Take a vacation, use the expense account. Have a great time." I push the elevator and feel only slightly better when Felix, my building's security, is standing inside to escort Amanda safely to her car.

He stretches his eyes at me. With a small shake of my head, I assure him, "I'm good. Just a late meeting and I'll be on my way. Thanks for seeing to Amanda. Have a good night, Felix."

"Yes, sir, Mr. Ellis. I'm working the late shift tonight... so, I'll be around if you need me to pick up dinner or anything." I flash him a smile that says thanks, but get your ass out of here, right-the-fuck-now. He gets the message; I watch the elevator doors close. Leaving me alone with a goddamn gun-slinging Coleman Whitman. *All right, fucker, what game are we playing tonight.*

"Always the fuckin 'gentleman, ain't that right, John?"

"Call your man downstairs; tell him if he follows them, I'll be sure to hand deliver his feet to his wife or whore. If one hair is

—

27

further harmed on her goddamn head... Cole," I move away from him before I finish with my warning, "... don't fucking test me."

"Guess you wanna see what I sent." I watch as he hits a button on his phone. I lock Amanda's door from the inside. My back to him, the entire time. My hands are itching to feel his bones breaking against their crushing blows, but I'm still curious and decide to hear him out.

"You fuckin 'that little secretary, John?"

"Put the goddamn gun away, Cole." I walk into my office, not sparing a glance for the asshole still standing just outside my door. I want to go to the bar and poor an entire bottle of Scotch down my throat, but I need to keep a clear head. I smell bullshit on the bottom of Cole's military grade combat boots—I'll be damn if he leaves one crumb of it with me when I kick his ass out of here.

"Fine, John." I hear him put the safety on before he slides it into a customized holster made to accommodate the silencer.

Stupid asshole.

"You ever wondered why The Order selected your black ass?"

I don't respond. Just let my gaze move around his face like I'm trying to find the weakest place to strike. I am, but not in the way he assumes I will.

"Yeah, well... there was a lot of talk about you back home."

I walk around my desk to retake my seat like I couldn't care less about whatever bullshit he's spouting. My left foot presses a hidden button that turns on my internal surveillance system and sends the feed to an offsite terminal.

"Okay." I finally reward his country ass with a response.

Who the hell does Cole think he's talking to? I invented the game he's trying to play with me.

"My family heard a lotta 'bout how you and your almost white Momma was livin 'like well-off white folk up in Georgetown."

That tantric thing happens again. I see Cole Whitman, but in a way, I've never seen him before. He's familiar because I know him from undergrad... also because I fucking hated him—an older, meaner, more depraved and fucked-up version of him—since the day he walked into my grandfather's house as my mom's new husband. My eyes glaze over as Cole morphs from the twenty-seven-year-old white-presenting biracial man I've called my brother for the last ten years, into a middle-aged, poor-white-trash lump of anarchy and moral decay. He hated everything about my mother and me but still, he married her.

I time travel back to roughly twenty years ago and see me standing in my childhood kitchen. I'm looking at a white man who thinks he's somebody important. My mother's thick chestnut waves fall down her back like pulled salt-water taffy. Her buttermilk-colored skin is glowing with pride and happiness as she introduces her blue-chip Black son to an inelegant white man from. *Fucking. Alabama.*

"Jonny, this here's Earl Friendly. His people come from Alabama, but he move to Georgetown to get a fresh start." She's looking at me with her big blue-green eyes that shine like galaxy marbles. Why is she talking like we live in Faulkner's Yoknapatawpha County, and have a recurring role as the negro mother and son in one of his books?

My mind crawls back through the sludge of memory to spit my consciousness into the present moment, where the spawn of white-America sits across from me. Whatever he sees in my eyes, causes him to flinch.

There. Found the weak spot on your fucking face.

"You figure it out?"

"What do you want?"

"Did you figure out who my family is?"

"What. Do. You. Want?"

"Acknowledge my fuckin 'family, John."

"Malachi Dodson, Francis O'Leary, Garrett Browne, and me."

"Fuck you, cunt. I'm not fuckin' 'round with you. Goddammit, you will acknowledge my family right fuckin 'now. You goddamn motherfuckin 'porch-monkey!"

I fight the smile that pulls both corners of my mouth up. He is well and truly pissed, and even more stupid than his ass-backwards relative who died at my hands.

Let's see where this rabbit hole takes us, Alice.

"Why did The Order select me, Cole?" He doesn't remember asking the question. They should have sent someone more fucked-up than I am to do this shit.

~5~

John

"Wh-What?"

"Why did your family select my family, Cole?"

"Because you had no right livin 'better than us. You had no right to have an almost white Momma when ours wasn't."

The fuck?

"Did I kill your daddy, Cole? What happened to you and Carla's mother?" He is out of his chair reaching for his gun before he registers what he's doing.

I don't attempt to move or defend myself; The Order doesn't want me dead, maimed or hurt. I sit back and watch Cole pace around my office, while he points the gun at his own temple. Mumbling shit about uppity n-words and getting what they deserve. He stops abruptly and spins on his right foot.

"How's it feel knowin 'you've been friends with the man whose father was responsible for killing your mom, hmm?"

"I imagine it feels a lot like being friends with the man who's responsible for *killing* your dad, hmm?"

Rage seeps from every pore on his body. He shakes with it, while I sit behind my desk like butter wouldn't melt on my tongue.

"How did I not see the resemblance before now?" I mumble to myself as I continue to watch him lose his shit.

Cause your ignorant ass didn't want to see the goddamn truth, boy. Of-fucking-course, Earl would pop into my head while the runoff from his ball sack stands in my office having a fucking meltdown.

"Fuck you, John." He throws his butt-hurt emotions across my office like they're some kind of gauntlet.

"Cole." His name is the crack of a bull whip. When he turns to face me; I bear witness as a wraith of sanity drifts through his eyes like it's hunting for its next victim. "Good." I reward him with the praise I know he craves, and I take a moment to center my breathing. Acknowledge and accept my surroundings.

I'm in my office.

I'm Jonathan R. Ellis.

I am safe.

I am in control.

I create my own reality.

"Let's stop all the bullshitting and get to the reason you're in my office giving this Oscar-worthy performance." I extend the invitation like he didn't just pull a gun on me. His less than confident stride back to my desk would deceive anyone who doesn't know how deadly Cole is; but I'm not just anyone, so I keep my guard up and visible.

"Fine, John, fuck. Fuck. Fuck. Fuckin 'fuck." Each explicative is another audio bullet that boomerangs off the floor-to-ceiling windows, only to return back to him.

My stillness is louder than his outburst. So much so, he cups his hands over his ears like he needs to protect them from the absence of my verbal response.

Am I fucking high right now? Maybe this is a fever dream.

"Cole, you need a drink. Maybe something to take the edge off..."

He walks over to the bar and pours himself two fingers of my top shelf whiskey and downs the entire thing in one go. After he slams the tumbler back onto the bar, he devolves into a coagulated lump of conscious sin.

"John—I." He tries to breathe, but a pitiful sob falls from his throat, instead. With a disbelieving shake of his shaggy head he admits, "I've fucked everything up to hell and back."

"How?"

"In all the fuckin 'ways imaginable, man." He moves like a slug, but eventually makes it to the chair in front of my desk, again. As he takes a seat he groans, "From listenin 'to my uncles and cousins to followin 'in the footsteps of my family's legacy with The Order. I fucked it all!"

That could be his epitaph; immortal last words stamped on his tombstone when he finally dies.

I. Fucked. It. All.

"Start from the top; Earl's really your dad."

"Yes. He beat and raped our Black momma until she couldn't take it anymore. She loved us with all she had, but—"

I interrupt, "She killed herself or died at his hands."

"Suicide. Her note said she'd planned to take us with her, but I had a peewee football game and Carla was with my auntie." He belts out a laugh that sounds like broken promises and missed birthdays. "I thought she was just goin 'somewhere to run an errand. I didn't want to miss my first peewee football game, so I went with my uncle instead."

"Seems like peewee football saved your life." I check the recording indicator to ensure the equipment is working. It is.

"Yeah. We were 'bout five when she did it. Earl didn't show his face at her funeral. Didn't put a flower on her grave." Cole balls his face up into something reminiscent of a small defiant toddler before he shares, "My uncle, her brother, came to our house and packed all our shit up and took us to live with him, his white wife, and my three cousins."

That shocks me into asking, "Where the fuck was this uncle when Earl was beating the shit out of your mom?"

"She never told, and he never asked." Sad eyes glare at me like I told his mom not to tell her brother. He continues, "Carla and me were too scared to say shit to anybody. You know how it goes in the

33

South... keep people who don't pay bills in your house out of house business."

"Keeping house business in the house only protects the guilty, while leaving every other family member vulnerable to destruction. Now as adults, some of us choose to pretend like we didn't have to keep family secrets; like we aren't victims of prolonged childhood trauma. And others are so fucked up because of the secrets they kept, that as adults they continue to perpetuate a legacy of protecting the guilty and keeping secrets. Which one are you?" I hold his gaze and my opinion darkens my eyes.

"The thing is, all my life I knew I had a daddy somewhere who didn't care about me, my sister or Momma." His eyes are as open and honest as I've ever seen them, but it still doesn't mean shit to me. I let him see that, as well.

"Okay, so what's any of that have to do with all your machinations over the past months, Cole?" Instead of answering my question, he starts telling me about how his daddy ended up married to my mom.

"Earl crawled his way up here."

He stops talking like I give a fuck about his goddamned white-trash daddy. He must read the hurry-the-hell-up look plastered across my face because he abandons that line of nonsense.

" Fine. You don't want to hear about Earl but if I don't tell you about all of this, then what I really need to tell you won't make alickasense." With a shake of his shaggy head he continues, "I was fourteen the first time Earl contacted me. He'd been gone for about nine years by then. He started telling me about his new life. How he remarried a pretty white woman in Georgetown and how he just had to figure out how to get rid of her *stupid kid* before he could bring me home with him." Cole's checking for a reaction. I don't have one. I know exactly the kind of evil bastard Earl was, so nothing surprises me about him.

34

"We started talkin 'everyday; we talked about so much shit. I felt like I was gettin 'a second chance with my dad. I knew what kind of house you lived in. The sports you played and excelled at. He even told me your favorite foods and flavor of soda. Said... I needed to be able to slide right into your slot, so his pretty white wife wouldn't notice." I'm looking into the face of a man I've gone through hell with and would've—up until a few months ago—gone through hell for, but I don't know if I should pity him or murder his ass. I'm leaning toward violence.

"So, Earl planned to kill me, bring you in as my replacement, and live happily ever after while dancing over my dead body in the woods?" I lean up and place my elbows on top of my desk and ask, "What about Carla?"

"Basically. He said he didn't want to have nothin 'to do with her. She looks just like mom."

"Let me get this straight, Earl's grand plan was to kill me, replace me with you—a *white* boy—live happily-fucking-ever-after with my pretty *white* mom who wasn't even white or half white." I laugh my ass off. My stomach is tight with the hilarity of this bullshit. With tears running down my face, I question, "What the fuck was Earl smoking to come up with this plan?"

Cole doesn't spare a second before he responds. "The sad part is I wanted it to work. I fuckin 'hated you. Hated that you had my father and your pretty white—not even white—mom. I wanted what you had. The two-story house on motherfuckin 'tree lined streets with sidewalks. The friends you played basketball and baseball with. I wanted it because Earl told me it should've been mine to begin with. Said, *shit musta 'got fucked up and we ended up with the Alabama life instead of the Carolina life.* But he found a way to fix it..."

"Cole look," I scrape the shit eating grin from my face and attempt to level with him. The sense of entitlement still settles

—

35

around his shoulders like a royal cloak. "... if it's any consolation, life with Earl was horrible. He did the same thing to my mom that he did to yours, except my mom was too stubborn to kill herself. Earl was the beginning of every nightmarish story in Pat McKissack's *The Dark Thirty*. Your daddy was a misogynistic bigoted pedophile, who hated anyone and anything that represented what he could never be.

"In short, Earl Friendly was one of the most sadistic motherfuckers I've ever known. You and Carla got off lucky, because if Earl had gotten his filthy depraved hands on you..." I don't finish the sentence. He's trying to work through everything I've said about his father.

"H-he... he *touch* you."

"Yes. Started about a month or so after he got there. I was eight. Kept at me until I was big enough to knock him on his ass. Maybe eleven or twelve. There was absolutely nothing human about Earl Friendly. He was more akin to reanimated human waste—without a hint of a soul or conscience. Believe me, you and Carla were much better off without him.

"He never told me any of that. He said this marriage was perfect—that *she* was perfect."

"If by perfect he meant he beat her breakfast lunch and dinner, while raping her for his three designated snack times. Or if he meant he got her hooked on drugs and alcohol and turned her into a crack whore, then they did have the perfect marriage." Cole looks like he's about to throw-up onto his lap, but I refuse to give him a moment to find a breath because I want him to know exactly what kind of animal his dad was.

"When he finally bashed my mom's head in with my old baseball bat—the same one I would eventually use on him—she was seventy-five pounds, baldheaded, missing teeth and smelled like she had already decayed on the inside." I kept my gaze locked on his. He tried to look away, but I wouldn't let him.

His father had told him he deserved to have what I had; surprisingly, I agree with Earl one hundred and fifty percent. Cole *does* deserve to experience a hint of what his sire ushered into my life.

To choke on the stench of depravity that suffocated the harmonious tranquility out of my mom.

"How can you sit there and talk about this shit and not feel... pissed the fuck off? He took a crap and dumped it right in the middle of your life and then he went and killed your momma!"

I bark in retaliation, "Yeah, and he made your mom kill herself, but that provided you with the chance for a better life. It was better, wasn't it... Living with your uncle?"

"In retrospect, and in light of what you've shared with me," Cole licks at the dry cracked skin of his bottom lip before admitting, "I was fuckin 'lucky to have Momma's brother take me in. He was a member of The Order and as his adopted son, I was a—"

"Legacy. Wait, how was her brother a member of The Order?"

"He wasn't her real brother... he was a foster brother who'd been raised by my granny from the age of twelve. She never adopted him and when he turned eighteen; he went into the military so he could go to college on Uncle Sam. Granny and Momma was the only family he ever known."

"So, your uncle made you a legacy and as a legacy, you got to choose one person you wanted in your pledge class."

"My uncle had four girls. He didn't have anyone to pass the legacy to until Earl drove my mom to kill herself. He trained me from an early age to be ready to join The Order."

Well, isn't this just fucking convenient?

"You chose me because you wanted to fuck my life up? You've been playing the long game Cole. Is this my day of reckoning?"

"You sure are an arrogant motherfucker John. Sittin 'with a man holdin 'the power to ruin your entire fuckin 'life."

He's not incorrect in his observation. And I feel inclined to let him know just how arrogant of a motherfucker I really am.

"Man, short of killing Vivian, there is nothing you can take from me that I can't get back. I never needed The Order to become the man I am, but if I could gain some advantage from joining some old white man's organization, I was going to. So, what are you supposed to be doing now Coleman Whitman?"

He leans forward in his chair and without blinking or swallowing, he rattles off his assignment like a goddamn shopping list. "I'm supposed to plant two hundred and fifty million dollars in a few offshore accounts in your name, create a line connecting the funds to the underworld and frame you for being the washer."

The smile on my face feels like the one Jack Nicholson wore as *The Joker*. "So, where's this money coming from and who's footing the bill?"

"The money is legit from the underworld and has been washed by several members of The Order. It does reside in offshore accounts."

"What aren't you telling me?"

"I scanned, didn't detect any surveillance equipment. Is your office still secure from the last time I secured it?"

"Yes, of course. Speak freely. It goes no further than this room and you and me."

With a deep inhale, he sings like a choir boy on Easter Sunday. "The FBI is aware of the subversive tactics of The Order and tapped me as an operative. I've been working for them for the past five years. They wanted me to identify the chief players and those who simply got selected and don't really participate. Of the eight hundred members still alive, only one has refrained from using The Order's influence."

~6~

"Let me guess, me."

"Bingo! The higher ups in The Order need a scapegoat, and only one person's name came up."

"Mine."

"Give this man a prize. The Order knew about my history with you, even though *you* had no idea. They wanted me to use it to trip you up and get what I needed to frame you for the washing job."

"So, why are you telling me this now? You playing both sides of the board, or are you still trying to avenge your father's death?"

"Fuck no John. From the moment we met, I knew Earl was full of shit, and I also knew you were a good man. My uncle vetted you and vouched for my choice. You couldn't have made it through selection without a vote from a standing member. When I call you, *brother*, I fuckin 'mean that shit."

"Fine, why all the crazy when you first got up here?"

"I had ears and eyes on me. Up until about forty-five minutes ago... Before you ask why not now, they want plausible deniability. If they don't hear and see what happens, they won't have to lie about not knowin 'what happened."

"I can't trust you, Coleman Whitman, but I will hear you out. What's your deal with the FBI?"

"You are the golden fleece, John. The only squeaky-clean nail they have to hammer into the coffin of The Order. Brother, I need you and Vivian to disappear."

"I'm going to need more than that to make your little request a reality. Vivian has a new artist in residence coming into town next week, not to mention Val—" What the fuck, I can't mention Valery.

But she does have shit going on, too. "No, I'm going to need to speak with an FBI agent if you want my cooperation. Excuse me for not taking you at your word, *brother*."

"I knew you would say that. Give me a minute to make a phone call." He reaches inside his jacket pocket but before he can pull out whatever he's reaching for, I have his ass crushed face first across my desk.

"Fuck, I forgot how crazy fast you are. Dude. I'm just going for my burner."

"Where is it?"

"Left inside pocket."

"Nothing funny; I don't want to kill you. And I can't believe a single word you've said since you stopped talking like the crazy fucker you've always been." I slip my hand into the pocket and pull out a generic burner phone. Holding it up for him to see, I ask, "How do I make contact?"

"And you're still the same paranoid motherfucker you've always been."

"Keep friends who turn into enemies close, and all that shit. How do I make contact?"

"There's only one number programmed into that phone. Open the call app and press star-one."

"What's your contact code?"

"Fuckin 'hell John, if I didn't know better, I'd think you've been down this road a time or two. Bravo. Sam. Five-eight-three. Nancy." I follow his direction and wait for the call to connect, while leaning all my weight across his back. He doesn't struggle because he knows he doesn't have a snowball's chance in hell of breaking this fucking hold.

"Bravo. Sam. Five-eight-three. Nancy." I repeat the code. I feel Cole's hands twitch where they're clasped behind his back under my forearm. "Bravo. Sam. Five-eight-three. Nancy. This is Jonathan Raynard Ellis. You sent an operative into my office wielding a Desert Eagle, and now he's incapacitated and I'm talking on his burner phone. Who the fuck is this and what the hell do you want from me?"

"Ellis. Glad Cole was able to get to you before someone else did." I look at Cole because I need to know what the protocol is when his FBI contact answers.

"Three-five-eight-Sam-Nancy-Bravo." Coal's voice is nonexistent, but I hear him clearly. With his eyes stretched wide, he wants to know if there was a breech in protocol.

I have a choice to make. Tell him this man didn't not reply properly or see who the fuck I'm talking with. The latter is looking like the right choice for me. Letting Cole stand up, I walk away from him and over to the wall of windows facing the State House.

Such a beautiful city.

"Yes, sir. It's clear you all have been working overtime to secure what you need." I don't know what they fucking need, nor do I care. I just want to keep this shit stain on the line long enough for my guy to trace it to a name and location.

"Cole explained you're the only one on the registry of The Order who hasn't participated in their more illicit undertakings."

"Is there a question in there, sir?"

"What kept you from getting your nose dirty and who's been protecting you from being tapped to *earn your pin*?"

This guy must be stupid or, maybe he just thinks that I am. He just gave himself away as a member of The Order.

I look at Cole, who's about ten different shades of what-the-fuck. I shake my head and point at the phone that's pressed against my left ear. Moving away from the window, I point to my executive bathroom and start making my way there.

———

He's bleached-flour white, gray eyes as big as mercury in retrograde. I'd laugh if I didn't know why. He was telling the truth, and realizes he's been compromised, and that his handler is probably dead.

"Those are interesting questions, agent—"

"Agent Garrett Francis."

Garrett Francis, What the fuck is going on here?

"Agent Garrett Francis," I repeat what he says for Cole's benefit. His eyes connect with mine and a million words pass between us in the time it takes either of us to blink. I turn my attention back to the tool on the burner. "Does it matter why I chose to refrain from deepening my association with The Order, as long as I kept my oath to uphold The Order's anonymity?"

"That ain't my goddamn handler!" Cole whisper-screams at me while pulling out another fancier phone.

The fake agent growls down the line, "It matters because it means you've known all along criminal activities were afoot, and you failed to report it to the Federal Bureau of Investigations."

"I'm a Black man, born and raised in South Carolina. My stepfather was a sadistic son-of-a-bitch saltine-cracker, who hated Black people. Do you think I would be the one to turn on the most powerful, *white* men in the country?" I give him a minute to choke down the saltine-crackers before continuing, "I was born at night, Agent Francis, not tonight, though."

He clears his throat and tries another tactic, but before he can peel the words away from his tongue, what sounds like a wet tennis ball hitting a brick wall cuts into the call. Then all hell breaks loose. On his end.

"Hang up the phone, now!" Cole yells from across the room, while barking orders to whoever he's talking to on his double-o-seven spy phone. "Compromised, my ass. Find him and get him to cover."

"Cole."

"One minute, John."

"No! Not another second, Cole. Answer every question in my goddamn head or I'm killing you just like I killed your white-trash daddy. Start talking, motherfucker."

"John, it's not whatever you're thinkin'. I don't know how they got to—"

"Who the fuck are *they*, Cole?"

"The Order. The goddamned Order, John. They're runnin 'scared like damn cockroaches when the lights come on. I didn't lie to you. You're the only one they can pin a shit-ton of work on because you haven't shown up on anybody's radar. I gave the FBI your name and information because I knew... I fuckin 'knew they would be gunnin ' for you."

"Why?"

"Because they knew why I brought you into The Order to begin with."

"Are you telling me that The-fucking-Order has a goddamn hard on for me because of you and your fucking daddy issues? Cole, Jesus H. Christ... please. Earl fucked up my childhood and I killed him. That fucker's been dead for years, but he's still fucking shit up for me. Know this is not acceptable. I didn't sign up for any of this bullshit. Whatever fucking games you rich, white boys are playing; I'm out. I am no longer a pawn in this dick-swinging-sink-my-battleship game."

"It's not that simple. John, they've got so much power. They could bury you and you'd never see the light of day. I'm tryin 'to—"

"Cole?"

"... get you from under this avalanche of shit, but—"

"Cole?"

—

"... your name, they find a way to block it. I can't even depend on th—"

"Cole?" He finally stops speed talking long enough to look at me. *Good.* "Do I look worried or pressed? I watch him rake his eyes over my face like he's a cyborg trying to see if I'm on his kill list. I don't put on a mask or change my expression. Both my demons and my light are present, and it feels fucking fantastic to let both sides out to play.

"N-No. You look like you know somethin 'I don't know."

"Bingo, Cole. You need to worry about yourself. Thank you for telling me who you are and why I was selected to become a part of The Order. You have always been a friend to me—"

"But..."

"This is where our friendship ends. If you ever show up in my life after tonight, I will kill you."

"John, I'm only tryin 'to undo the wrong I did before I knew you. You are my best friend—in a way—we *are* brothers."

"I don't have a brother, Cole. I'm my mother and father's only child. Your father married, destroyed and killed my whole world and now I've built another one. I'm not going to give another Friendly motherfucker the chance to destroy this one. We are not brothers because we happened to survive the same goddamned disease."

"John, let me help y—"

"If I see you again, Cole, I will kill you." I open his phone, remove the sim card, break the phone in half and give it back to him. "Take care of yourself. Our class is gunning for you, *brother*."

~7~

Vivian

"Collin!" The receiver is pressed between my shoulder and my left ear, while I'm typing a response to an email from another artist who's interested in securing a spot in our April showcase of Southern minority women artists. I've been on hold for the last ten minutes, but I know the moment I hang up, I'll hear someone come on the line. "Collin?"

"Quit your caterwauling, woman!" Molten silver eyes dance with slight irritation and a little concern. He's been a pissy something for the last two weeks and I know why, but I still don't know what to do about creating space for him and Val to explore their personal relationship. I know he wants to take it further... and she's already threatened to hijack the body and take Collin for a ride.

I can't say I blame her.

"I'm sorry, it's just that I... Yes. This is Vivian Ellis; owner of La Magnolia Noir and I've been holding for the last ten minutes—what? No, please don't place me..." The horrible music starts up again, "...on hold again." I pull the receiver away from my ear, looking at it like it just stabbed me in the back.

"You just what, Vivian?"

"When did you get in here? You know what, it doesn't matter because I'm losing my damn mind. I can't seem to get things moving the way I need them to."

"What do you need?" With four simple words Collin slows down the hands of time and gives me the moment I've been searching for. The moment I need to take a breath and refocus.

45

"Thank you." My lids flutter over my tired eyes. The pressure that's been sitting in the middle of my face all day suddenly melts away. The oxygen filling my lungs is sweeter than any breath I've taken before this one. By the time I exhale, I'm myself again.

"You been running around like a rocket and you're no closer to getting it all done than a bawhair is to becoming a damn toupee."

"What the hell does that mean? It doesn't matter... I think I get the gist of it. I've been holding for the insurance company for the last twenty years of my life but if I don't have everything in place before Milla gets here—"

"Then you'll have to get it in place after she's here. What's going on with you, Viv. This isn't like you." He walks fully into my office, ensuring my door is closed before he crosses over to the chair in front of my desk.

"Collin. Have you ever had that feeling when nothing was going wrong, but nothing really felt right, either?" I watch his gorgeous face as he processes my words. Over the last several months, Collin has become something like a brother to me. His honesty and willingness to accept people and circumstances for what they are until they prove to be something else, is refreshing. His talent and eye *for* talent is the sexiest thing about him... that and that damn man-bun he can't seem to complete a day without his hair ending up in. He takes his time when considering my question because he knows how complicated my life is.

"Is there something going on with Vera or Val... maybe?"

"There's always something going on with us. That's not what... this isn't coming from inside. I can't put my finger on why I feel like I need to shore up my walls, but it feels like a storm is brewing and heading straight for me."

"What's John got going on?" Boom! That's exactly what this feeling is. What *does* John have going on?

"Good question. I don't know because he hasn't talked to me about anything in the last week or so. He works late and leaves early. I only know he comes home because I feel him get into bed after he showers."

"Well, lass, I think you just found the source of your weird. But Vivian," Collin clears his throat and levels me with a look of pure determination before he says, "he's a grown ass man. Let him handle his shit and you take care of what belongs to you. Speaking of..." I know what he won't lend his whiskey roughened voice to, because the loquacious woman he wants to ask about, refuses to shut up about it.

"I know, Collin. I haven't had a chance to talk with John about this, but he's acknowledged there's something between you two. I didn't expect him to notice or even be willing to see Val as her own person separate from me."

"Why does this decision have to go through John?"

"If you were in his shoes, how would you want this to be handled?"

"He doesn't own the body. For fuck's sake, he doesn't own the women in the goddamned body, either. He has nothing to do with Valery and me. Nothing to do with what we do with each other."

"I can see how you think that's true... but Collin, up until a year and some months ago, John has had exclusive rights to this body and the only woman he knew occupying it." I bring the receiver back up to my ear because I think someone's saying something, but it was just the shitty song playing. I place the receiver back in the cradle after pressing the speaker button and muting the sound.

No one needs to hear this conversation.

"I get that, Vivian, but he still has no right to keep two people apart who obviously want to be with each other."

"No. He doesn't, and he won't. Tell me something, Collin," I take a seat behind my desk because I'm probably going to be on hold

—

until the middle of next week. "How do you see this thing playing out... you and Valery? John and me?"

"Fuck, Vivian, I don't have a fucking clue. All I do know is I miss Valery when I can't pick up a fucking phone and talk to her. When I can't go to her home and spend time with her... or bring her over to mine. I love her banter and watching her smile those sweet shy smiles I know she only has for me. I need time with her. We need time together."

"Shit. What the hell am I supposed to say to that?"

"We work together two days a week already." I see the wheels in his head turning and spinning. Trying to find a way to build some kind of relationship with Val. One that will stand the test of time.

I hope he comes up with something viable.

"Yes, and..."

"On the days we work together, how about Val and I just spend the entire day and night together. I bring her back here and you get to change into your fancy designer clothes, work and head back home to John. I mean... what, with Val and I working Mondays and Wednesdays. That's only two days and nights without you."

I bark out the most unlady-like laugh and can't seem to stop it from bubbling up my throat. All I can hear is Valery yelling at me about Collin and John working out some kind of *co-pussy custody agreement*. Tears leak from my eyes remembering the incredulous look on her livid face. Val was so pissed with me and the situation, it was comical. And also, horrible.

They deserve a chance to be together.

"Lass?"

"God, I'm sorry. I'm not laughing at your expense, but your suggestion reminded me of a conversation I had with Valery about how things would look when you and her got together. She was less than impressed and asked one of her typical take-no-prisoner questions." I flash another quick grin and manage to keep the laughter at bay.

"What'd my girl, ask to make you smile and laugh like you do?" *His girl*. God, Collin, you're goddamn killing me.

"The short version was her asking if you and John were supposed to come to some kind of *co-pussy custody* agreement, giving the pussy only one day to herself." I watch as his eyes twinkle with mirth. He's doing his best to fight the grin and the laughter causing a tickle in his throat, but he knows it's no use. Another twitch of his beautiful mouth and we both burst into obnoxious howls of pent-up frustrated confusion that choose to masquerade as excessive moments of joy.

Its sad belly dragging the bottom of the floor like the useless primordial pouches of an old fat cat. It serves no purpose and yet, it's always present. Just in case we find ourselves flat on our backs with our opponent trying to rip out our soft vulnerable middle. There are no opponents, and no one is coming for the soft parts because there are no soft parts left. Not in me and not in him.

The empty full-belly laughs have quieted down to a few whisps of air and an errant tear. The only truth in this entire conversation just fell from my chin onto my Kelly-green corduroy pants. Leaving a small, dark circle as a reminder for anyone paying attention. A reminder to always be honest with yourself, first, and everybody else, afterwards.

"Sounds like something she'd say." I pretend I don't see him wiping the forlorn cravings away with the edge of his large, calloused thumb. He pretends he doesn't see me staring at the dark circle on my pretty, Kelly-green cords.

"Today is Tuesday, Collin."

"Yes, I know."

"Why don't you drive my truck back to our house tomorrow after you and Val are done here. John will cook dinner for you guys. And you..." I watch that bitch named hope sift into Collin's soul like cigarette smoke corrupting a newborn's lungs. He inhales. Holds his breath. Becomes high with just one hit of her seductive flavor. When he exhales and opens his eyes, his pupils are blown wide-open, and he's completely blissed out.

"Will I wake up with Val?"

"Unless Vera gets curious about white men, yes. I won't come out until she says so."

"Will Vera... come out?"

"Doubt it. Vera pretty much stays away from people with boy-bits. The only man she can tolerate is John and that's because he treats her like a goddamn baby. And she needs him to."

"Needs him to...?"

"Treat her like a baby. John is very protective of Vera. He dotes on her when she does come around. Always buying her books of poetry, journals, and expensive pens. Whenever he discovers some new thing she's fallen in love with, he makes sure to get it and wrap it up in the most ostentatious paper and silk bows. He spoils her and she needs it. It makes her feel safe."

"That doesn't sound like John."

"Like all of us, John is a multilayered human. Don't write him off as a total caveman, Collin. You're going to have to build a friendship with him if you want this relationship with Valery to work out."

"Fuck!"

"Indeed."

"Does he like Scotch?"

"Collin. I think you're going to be all right." I say this with a reassuring smile. I grab my favorite pen to scribble down the name of John's favorite Scotch and pass it over to Collin, just as the insurance adjuster I've been holding for, breaks into the pop music with his crisp, efficient salutation. *Fucking finally.*" Yes, this is

—

50

Vivian Ellis..."

~8~

Vivian

Shortly after securing the last bit of provisional insurance for Milla and making sure Collin's good to go for tomorrow; I pack up early to get home and cook John a special dinner. He promised not to stay late at the office.

I have never been reluctant to talk with John about anything. He's been more open during our conversations concerning Val and Collin, but I don't know if he's ready to give them space to explore their relationship—fully.

All of my concerns float away as I pull into the parking space in front of the market on Rosewood. A sleek little Dodge Viper pulls in next to me. What are the odds that this is a coincidence. "Think, Vivian." I mumble to myself while I way my options. Stay in the car and wait for him to go in before leaving or, get out and go in like I don't know who's parked beside me.

And because my secretive husband hasn't said two words about his friend, I don't know how to approach Cole one way or the other. I tap my clear-varnished nails in a nervous rhythm against the leather steering wheel. I take a few deep breaths. Nope, not enough to calm my fraying nerves. Certainly not enough to keep my eyes from slanting to the left.

Oh-Give-me-liberty-and-great-wealth, I need John to call me right now.

My rambling pleas die a quick death when the green light indicating an incoming call, flashes like a warning to Gatsby that he doesn't have a chance in hell to be with Daisy. I'm so relieved, I don't even look at the caller ID to see who it is before I answer.

"Hello, John?"

"No, it's me... Jessa. What's going on? You sound... *stressed?*"

"Shit, Jessa. Listen, I need you to call John. Tell him I'm at Rosewood Market and Cole is parked beside me. Tell him I'm going into the store. Okay?"

"Vivian, what's going on with y—"

"Dammit, Jessa! I don't have time to fill you in. Just... please, call John and relay the message for me. Okay? I promise to tell you everything later. Just... just, hurry and call him. Okay? And um, bye." I hang up and grab my purse from the backseat. After tossing my phone inside, I pull the key from the ignition and take another series of deep breaths. I sneak a peek at the Viper and whisper to myself, "Okay, Cole Whitman, let's see why you're really here."

I don't make direct eye contact with the driver because I don't want him to know that I know whose driving such a fancy car to a natural food market. Once I'm on the sidewalk, I lock my doors and drop the keys into my purse. It's feels like my vision and hearing have become ten times sharper.

Adrenaline and cortisol with a healthy dose of endorphins. Calm down, you're safe and in control.

I grab a handcart and smile at the petit girl standing behind the register. She must work here afterschool; she can't be older than sixteen. Seventeen at the oldest.

What the hell do I care how old that girl is? Focus, Vivian.

Um... Everything's all right, yeah? Vera breaks into my rambling thoughts.

It's not a good time. I need to be present. Please go back and tell Val to stay inside until I say otherwise. I'm fine. We are not in danger.

When I come back to awareness, I realize I'm groping eggplants like some kind of pervert with a vegetable fetish. At least she's gone into her room, and I can focus on what's going on around me. I choose the two smallest eggplants and place them into the handcart.

———

Apparently my reactions are moving on CP time, because Cole calls my name before I even realize he's standing next to me.

"*Vivian*? Vivian Ellis, as I live and breathe." I turn around like I'm on the laziest Susan ever invented. Guarded and a little confused. I haven't seen Cole since John and I got married, so he may believe my antics.

"Yes, I am Vivian Ellis. It seems you have me at a disadvantage because I don't—" As expected, he cuts me off before I finish my bold-face lie.

"Don't break my old foolish heart and tell me you don't remember me, Viv." He's pulling out the big guns, using my nickname. And that smile. How many hearts has this man broken with his smile alone? I run my eyes over his handsome face, cataloguing every detail just in case I need to give a description.

Just for shits and giggles, I screw up my lips, narrow my eyes, and tilt my head to the left before blurting out, "Oh, my go-tell-it-on-the-mountain!" I beam a large, toothy grin at him as I watch what looks like genuine relief brighten his empyreal eyes. "Coleman Whitman, how have you been?" I lean in and give him a side hug and step away from him just as he starts to wrap both of his heavily muscled arms around me. "I'm sorry I didn't recognize you at first. It's been... what? Almost six—"

"Since you and J-John got married, yeah. It's been a long damn time, but there ain't no way in hell I could forget your beautiful face, darlin'." I flash him a brief show of teeth with a dimple. Still studying him, I realize he's doing the same to me. "You look good, Viv."

"You sound surprised. What did you expect me to look like?" I sass and step away from the eggplants. He follows me over to the long beans.

They're on sale for two-ninety-nine a pound. That's a good deal, and they're locally grown.

"Oh, I don't know..." The deep rumble of his voice pulls my attention back to the man who seems to be shopping with me. After clearing his throat he continues, "I mean the married women I know gain a shit-ton of weight for every year they stay with the poor bastard. Then they start dressin 'like lesbian gym teachers who never go to the gym."

A crack of laughter ricochets off the refrigerated produce and lands back in my chest. How could I forget how funny Cole is? "I shouldn't have to remind you," I turn to face him once I've placed my beans in the cart. I smirk and deadpan, "but I will just in case you've forgotten..."

"Forgotten what?" His eyes are flashing with delight and it's hard to hold on to my discomfort because he looks so damn happy simply because we're talking.

"That well-loved and cared for Black won't ever crack. I'll look this good until they put me in a grave." I watch him while he looks his fill. Expressive gray eyes rake over me from the crochet beanie pulled over my locs to the pointed toe of my over the knee leather boots, wrapped in silver chains. I felt... exposed and not in a bad way.

He brings his gaze back to my face and says in that deep Alabama accent, "No, darlin', I'd never forget somethin 'so important as that. So, where's that husband of yours? I can't remember a time I've seen you without him sniffin' 'round behind you?" He was doing such a good job of keeping the strain from his voice prior to asking about John.

Cole seems to be the same goofy guy he was back in undergrad. What's changed?

I pull my thoughts back to the man standing in front of me and answer his question. "He's probably still at the office, Cole. I dipped out of the gallery early; I wanted to surprise him with a special, home-cooked meal." I figure it's easier to look calm and unaffected when I'm telling the truth. I study Cole's face and he looks like he wants to invite himself over to our house for dinner but knows his buddy would kick his ass before feeding him scraps.

I'm starting to feel a little anxious so, before I make a huge mistake, I pull the handcart closer to my midline and explain, "My Maine Coon just had kittens. At first, John hated her, but now he's a doting big-grand-cat-papa." I giggle a little because this too, is the truth. "He's been so great with my girl and her brood; he deserves a special treat.

"This dinner is just to whet his appetite." I have the good grace to look away demurely as I step around his back to look at the rest of the produce. I choose a large English cucumber and mumble, "... if you know what I mean." I offer another shy smile, for good measure.

"I don't think you're goin 'to need to cook a special meal to whet John's appetite, Vivian." His voice is a little rougher than it did before.

I look up to find his gaze fixated on my right hand. It's not until my own gaze lands where his is, that I realize I'm giving the cucumber a damn hand job in the middle of the produce section of Rosewood Market.

Filthy-mother-father-stop-beating-your-kids.

I throw the offending fruit back onto the pile and almost trip over my own feet to get away from the scene of my lewd produce assault.

Cole chuckles and says, "That boy's had it bad for you ever since I met him. You could save yourself some trouble and pick u—"

"Coleman Whitman. Fancy seeing you in the market, speaking with my wife. Especially after our last conversation." I watch as Cole's face blanches white. He doesn't take his eyes from John's, even as John leans down to drop a hard, quick kiss against my temple. He snakes his arm around my waist and rests a possessive hand against my left hip.

I don't need to see his face to know it's made of storm clouds and deadly lightening.

Cole finally finds his balls and addresses my husband. "John. I just asked Viv about you. She thought you were at the office; you got a trackin 'device on her or some shit?" I can't tell if Cole is trying to be funny but the way John's hand flexes against my hip, tells me he is not amused.

"I told Cole how amazing you've been with Bertha..." I trail off because there is nowhere for this comment to go. I'm anxious and the girls are picking up on my discomfort. It takes everything I have to keep them inside. Val's nails scratch around my belly. She wants to come out and protect me and the body. *I've got this Val. Promise. John's here with me. Relax.*

When I check back in, John is saying something to Cole and from the look on Cole's face, it's not the invitation to dinner he hoped for.

"... accosting my wife at the grocery store. I told you what would happen the next time I saw you. When have you known me not to be a man of my word?"

"John, this isn't what it looks like. I live around the corner. I come here 'bout once or twice a week."

"And you just happened to need something from the local organic market—when your country ass can't even boil water —*today*?"

"Yes—and I can do a hellavuh lot more than boil a pot of water—because I'm cookin 'dinner for this woman I met down at... You know what? Answer me this, Magnum PI, how the hell would I know Viv was comin 'here when she said she took off work early to surprise your paranoid ass with some special dinner for takin 'such good care of her fuckin 'pussy."

The tiny lady with the black-framed bifocals stops looking at the butternut squash. She whips her head around toward our trio and her beautiful, silver-blue hair sails across the small distance like a flying geriatric squirrel. For some insane reason, Cole lifts his arms and catches the wig before it settles on the floor.

That's when reality floods back into my consciousness and I'm already doubled over with laughter. John attempts to pull me out of my fit, but he's laughing harder than me.

I almost have myself under control when I hear Cole's rich Alabama accent...

"Ma'am, I caught your toupee."

I nearly fall on my ass and my giggles start all over again.

I caught your toupee.

I. Am. Done.

~9~

John

Un-fucking-believable! None of this makes any sense and why would it? It is Cole's conniving ass I'm dealing with. All joviality left me as the reality of who was walking back toward us sank into the marrow of my bones.

Earl Friendly's spawn.

Vivian finally finds her spine as she too, realizes how incredibly fucked up this situation is. Her eyes dart up to mine and just like that, the sands of time slow down as they descend toward the neck of the hourglass. Vivian and I are suspended in animation as every thought and emotion she feels in this eternal moment plays out across her beautiful features. I watch her mouth as it spreads into a devastating smile that lights up her summer sunshine eyes and reminds me of what's most important.

She blinks.

The sand slips through the thin neck and time returns to its normal fast pace.

"Eh, Vivian, I'm sorry if I scared you; although, you didn't seem to be scared of me when we were catchin 'up."

"No, Cole. Of course, I wasn't... I mean, what reason would I have to be afraid of you?"

"No reason. None other than your cave-man husband and his goddamned conspiracy theories. *John...*" Cole turns my way and something about the way he says my name makes me pause.

"Don't you have shopping to do for your date?"

"Brother, you know there ain't never gonna be a pussy more important than fixin 'whatever I broke between you and me."

Vivian cuts through the tension with a whispered, "John, I'm going to finish shopping and get home. If you and Cole go out, please be home in time for dinner. It's... *important.*" I tear my eyes

---

59

away from Cole to give my full attention to the woman who made me cancel every goddamn meeting I had on for this afternoon. The way she says, *important* makes my balls itch.

"Lovely."

"Really, John. It's nothing you need to be concerned with." She stretches her eyes as if she's trying to convey some age-old wisdom with her gesture. "I need to run somethings by you about Collin and the artist he's been working with." Another eye stretch and my pulse ticks up into racehorse speed, because I already goddamn know what she wants to talk about. I nod my head before bending down to take her mouth in a filthy, possessive kiss.

We're all tongues, teeth, lips, and slurps. This kiss is so damn dirty, my dick swells more and more each time she sucks on my tongue. Or makes that little helpless noise in the back of her throat when her sex clamps down on itself.

If I don't end this right now, that little old baldheaded lady will really see how well I take care of Vivian's pussy.

With a soft peck on her swollen lips, I send her on her way. I watch as her tall, svelte body garners attention from everyone in this little market. She's a goddamn queen who carries her invisible crown atop her head like everyone else can see it.

Cole clears his throat to bring my attention back to him and the shit eating grin spreading across his scruffy face. I keep my eyes glued to her until she rounds the corner into the can goods isles. It's only when I can no longer see her, that I give Cole the attention he seeks. I know he staged this fucking run in with Vivian to get me here and now I'm curious.

"Okay Cole, you wanted me. I'm here."

"John, first of all, I honestly had no idea Viv would be here. Secondly, there's a lot of shit you don't know about and the only way I can tell you is to get you out of your normal places. Shit is fucked up and I wasn't lying to you when I told you what I told you last week."

"Fine Cole, let's go for a drive."

"Mine or yours, brother?"

"I'm not folding myself into that tiny ass arachnid you call a car. We'll take my truck."

"S'not a motherfuckin 'spider you cave dwelling neanderthal. I drive a fuckin 'Viper. As in bad ass venomous snake. Get that shit right."

"I don't give a fuck what you drive or that you need it to compensate for your... ur, shortcomings. I'm not riding in your tiny-dick-mobile."

"Fuck you, John. I've got your tiny dick right between my harry thighs."

"I know, Cole. That's what I just said... that you have a tiny dick. Catch up, Opie. Let's go, my girl's cooking me a special dinner for taking such great care of her *fuckin 'pussy* and I don't plan to be late for dessert."

Somehow, Cole and I walk out of that pretentious little market grinning like we were still students at Carolina with the rest of our lives to figure shit out. I still don't trust his ass, especially since his breeding papers check out. But Cole has always been on the up and up with me. I'll hear what he has to say and if I don't like it, he may get to live with his father after all.

***

The house smells like a proper Mexican restaurant and my mouth waters as the scents permeate my olfactory system.

Of course, she's pulling out all the stops for this talk.

"Vivian, je suis à la maison. Ça sent bon putain ici, bébé." (Vivian, I'm home. It smells fucking amazing in here, baby. *Where the hell is she?* I walk into the kitchen to see the Mexican fiesta laid out on the large island, to include her deadly margaritas, but what I don't see is Vivian. "Viv, where the hell are you?" And then I remember Bertha has been home all day with a fucking cat doula and Vivian is probably upstairs babying her *pussy*. I take the stairs two at a time and find Viv exactly where I thought she'd be.

"Lovely, how's she doing?" I've already taken my shoes off downstairs. I use the hand sanitizer Viv placed just inside the door before stepping fully into Valeria's old room. It's so strange knowing I won't get to know the little girl who stepped in and saved Vera from a world of hurt, because she decided she was done. *Scariest shit I ever heard.*

"She did so good today, John. Macy said she's nursing like a pro, and she's already identified the runt of the litter and makes sure he's the first one on, and the last kitten off during feedings." Vivian is so in love with this damn cat, it's bewildering.

"That's good. You said she'd be a great mother, and if anyone knows Lady Bertha, it's you." She looks up from where she's holding one of the larger kittens, this one has a dark purple ribbon around his neck. All of his siblings are wearing dark purple ribbons, except the smallest one. She's wearing a soft teal one made of velvet. It has a small bell and fits perfectly beneath her dainty head. She's the only one who looks like Bea and the only one Vivian will want to keep.

"So, how did things go with you and Cole?" Straight to the head, no pregame and probably no chaser.

"It's all..." I don't even know what to say to her. This shit is fucked, and I'm fucked because I'm associated with fucked-up people. Which means Vivian's fucked because she was stupid enough to fall in love with and marry me. How the hell do I tell her how deep this rabbit hole goes without her losing her shit and leaving my black ass?

"It's all... what, John? Talk to me. You haven't said a word about Cole since I told you I saw him the first time at Rosewood Market, which is why when Jessa called me, I had her call you." She looks frustrated and a little pissed. She has every right to be both.

"The Order is under investigation." There, I put the umbrella up, now I need to find my balls and tell her this is all the protection we have against the shit storm heading our way.

"What does that have to do with you? You're not that active and you never rose in the ranks..." She pays attention to everything I say and files that shit away like a super-computer.

"That's just it, Viv. I'm the only member of The Order with clean hands. I've never gotten a loan from any bank because I've always had my own capital.

"I've never needed them to clean up my dirty shit because I have my own people to do that. The one time I called on them, it was so minor, my regional director never even logged it in their books. So... according to the DEA, FBI and the NSA, I haven't participated in anything."

"Okay, so what does the investigation have to do with you and where does Cole fit in?" Before I can give her an answer, she places one slender finger over her pursed lips and stands to her feet like a prima ballerina. My heart slams against my ribs trying to get to her. I acknowledge her directive with a quick nod and turn to leave Bertha's sanctuary. I'm sure that's why we're moving this conversation elsewhere. No negative energy or low vibrations allowed around Bertha and her four kittens.

I get it. I respect it, even.

John

"I hope you're hungry, I made enough food just in case you brought Cole home with you." Vivian must've showered when she got home. She's in one of her favorite things to lounge around the house in, her velour track suit and fluffy socks.

"After that kiss, I'm starving. I guess I should eat... before I take good care of my wife's *fucking pussy*." We share a smile. I make a show of looking around the island and praise, "You've outdone yourself, lovely. Should I be concerned about this important thing you want to talk about?"

"No. But before we get to that, I want to hear the rest of whatever is going on with you, Cole and The Order. Don't shut me out, John. You left me vulnerable today. I didn't like or appreciate it." She's right. I did leave her in a weakened position because I still don't trust her love for me enough to let her see all the darkness in my life.

"No, yeah, you're right, Viv. I fucked up when I didn't keep you abreast of what's been going on since you saw Cole. I'm sorry and I apologize. I'll do better."

"What fresh hell is this?" I watch her shaking her magnificent ass around the kitchen as she makes her way over to the large island where I'm waiting. The smile on her face is worth all the humble pie I just shoved down my throat. Her eyes are alight with amusement and the lingering lust of our filthy kiss.

She is the most beautiful destruction I've ever endured.

"Surely, my ears are deceiving me."

"You heard me correctly, lovely. Now stop being a brat and get your ass over here so we can eat and talk. I have a feeling I'm going to need to fuck you afterwards for a long time. Maybe the whole night." The peals of laughter spill from her and she looks like a little girl playing dress up in her mother's expensive clothing. No makeup on. For some reason, her hair is in two ponytails with pink ribbons that match her velour track suit. Looking at her gives me a toothache. I can't wait to taste her sweet magenta flesh tonight.

The sooner we hash this shit out, the sooner I'll have her in my mouth.

"I'm almost sure you're going to need to bend me over quite a few surfaces after I tell you what's going on. I've already used the lubricating suppository for my backdoor."

Fuck me. Jughead just sprung wood so fast, I'm lightheaded. Holy shit, most of me doesn't want to hear what she has to tell me, but Jughead is on board with anything she says as long as he can get inside of Viv's ass tonight.

"Okay, first we eat, then we talk." I sound like I've been swallowing charred charcoal straight from the grill.

"Then we will remind each other who I belong to."

My heart drops to my knees and tries to bounce back up into my chest cavity, but it fails. The poor fucker only makes it as far as my stomach. *I do not want to deal with this shit.*

"Is there any meat in any of these damn dishes, lovely?" I know my frustration and dour mood are misplaced, but what the hell am I supposed to do with it. I knew this was coming. I've been talking to Oscar about it since Viv started bringing it up.

Somethings are inevitable, John. regardless of if we want to accept them or not. You've accepted your wife's mental exceptionality—I fucking love that term, by the way—which means, you accept that each identity is an individual with the same rights as your Vivian.

"... didn't use meat—John?"

"Damn baby. I'm sorry, what were you saying?"

—

65

"Let's just get this over with because obviously, you know what I want to talk about and it's not sitting well with you."

No shit, Sherlock.

How the hell is knowing that some big, Scottish motherfucker wants to plant his goddamned flag in my plot of soil supposed to fucking *sit* with me? Of course, I don't say any of this to her. It's not her fought or anyone who's still alive. *Sorry, sons-and-daughters-of-bitches.*

"Hmm." I say instead of ruining the rest of our evening.

"That bad, huh?" Viv looks so conflicted; it makes me want to try to be a bigger person. Someone more accepting. Easy.

I throw her a bone, "I—I want to be evolved enough to be happy for Val and Collin..."

"But—"

She knows me too damn well. I can't lie and I don't want to. "But... I'm the only man you ever shared that body with—of your own will—because you fell in love with me, and I with you. I can't reconcile that the body I've loved and worshiped, and almost destroyed... belongs to two other women. Lovely, what the fuck am I supposed to do with that?"

Way to be an asshole, Ellis. She shouldn't be responsible for blowing sunshine up my ass.

"John," The determination in her voice makes me pay closer attention as she continues, "I'd be lying if I told you that I don't feel uneasy about this entire situation. Because I definitely do. I've had cart blanche with this body since making the decision that JR Eli was a better devil than the one we were living with." I flinch at her words. No child should have to choose between two rapists and feel grateful to the motherfucker she chose.

What the fuck kind of world do we live in?

66

"Okay," I place a little bit of everything she's cooked on my plate and pile a heaping serving of rice and beans to buy myself some time.

I'm still not ready to talk so, I scoop a spoonful of rice and beans with spicy vegetables into my mouth and it feels like Satan just came in my mouth. "Goddamn, you went heavy on the fucking peppers, didn't you?" I pour water down my throat and scowl in Vivian's general direction because I can't see shit with tears streaming from my eyes.

I hear her silly ass snickering. Trying and failing not to crack the hell up. Walking over to stand in front of where I think she's sitting, I stick out my tongue like a five-year-old and ask, "Did I fucking burn all of my taste buds off?"

I know I'm being ridiculous, but at least the tension is broken.

We collapse into the quiet suffering of bruised hearts. We wear our laughter as mirrored masks to hide each other in beautiful lies. We seek refuge from a reality that warns us we no longer have exclusive rights to defile and consecrate each other as we see fit.

Vivian stands from her stool and walks toward me. Once we're only inches apart, she places her hands on either side of my face. Her knowing fingers run through my beard.

Gentling me.

Soothing herself.

Those goddamn summer sunshine eyes are as bright as I've ever seen them. She doesn't look away from me. Doesn't say a word. Just holds my gaze as we slip into dormiveglia. I don't know how she gets us to this space that stretches out like the beginning of a perfect night, but every time she does; I fall more in love with her.

I've lost track of how long we've been dipping into and out of each other, but when she places her soft mouth on top of mine, it's like waking from a great night's sleep but no time has passed at all.

—

Without preamble she announces, "Valery works with Collin tomorrow." Her words whisper against my lips. A single tear slips down her right cheek, blessing us in salty melancholy.

"I know, same as every week." No idea why I felt the need to say that. Maybe to feel my lips moving against hers.

"Collin will drive Valery home in the evening. They'll have my car." Another blessing splashes. This time, her words scrape the skin, pulling dry ribbons from my lips.

Fuck my life.

"Okay."

Four letters.

Two fucking syllables.

They could mean anything from... *I understand* to, *are you fucking with me.* Whatever I mean, saying it depletes the air in my lungs.

Viv's tears no longer crash, one at a time because they've become a tidal wave of healing, battering against our fortified mouths. Mixing with my own heartbreak to form a tsunami.

"He." That one word is thick with her love for us, and who we are together. I experience the gift of her palate as she licks her lips to catch some of our mingled fear. I reciprocate. Our tongues touch— barely—we suck in a quick tandem breath. "Collin will spend the night with Valery, John. In her room. Alone."

She's breaking.

Earth quaking shutters bend her toned shoulders. Desperation twists those elegant fingers into painful grappling hooks. I don't know if she's trying to hold me together or keep herself from flying apart. Either way, it feels like the first time someone called me a nigger—with the hard *e and r*.

"All right," I grunt into her mouth before continuing, "We are all right, lovely."

A sob crawls from her clenched throat and falls onto my covetous mouth. In our effort to hold on to each other, our mutual need tears us apart.

I eat at her mouth.

Thrust my tongue deep into its warm depths.

Vivian can't catch her breath.

And still, I don't stop...

I can't.

Neither can she.

"Authenticate me as yours. Conceal me inside our love so nothing that happens outside of us can touch me."

"Goddammit, Vivian. Don't say shit like that, or I won't be held responsible for the carnage you'll find when you come back home to me."

"Please, John. I need them both to recognize that *I* belong to *you*. That the part of me that makes me who I am, it belongs to us. *Show them*."

The need threading through the last two words clear the mist causing my mind to relax and forces me to pay attention to the empty spaces between each letter and breath used to speak them. I pull her away from me and stare into her eyes for a brief lifetime. She wears her acceptance of Collin and Val like a crown of thorns. I know what she needs from me and as her Dom, I'm obliged to give it to her. However undeserving of it I believe her.

"Sub. Do not attempt to top from the bottom. It is not your place to direct us into play."

Her body melts into mine as the relief of her submission sluices through her like a favorite drug. She slurs, "I'm sorry, Sir."

"What is your frame of mind?"

"I am completely cognizant, Sir."

"And... your *needs*?"

"Sir, may I speak freely?" I run the tip of my nose against hers because I need to touch her.

"Please, lovely."

~*11*~

Vivian

I am the mouthpiece of my soul's desire to be in harmony with its other half.

John continues to lick at the seam of my mouth, coaxing my own to join in this carnal game. The feel of his hands, clutching at my hips like he can't help himself. His need to consume me drives his body without his conscious consent.

"Vivian, you asked to speak freely... so, speak."

"I love you. Regardless of all we've been through—and *because* of it—I trust you with my life. I endeavor to be honest and sincere in my actions and speech." I take the breath he gives to me, because my body's autonomic functions no longer seem to work.

I touch John's bearded cheek in an effort to quell my response to the sexual energy zipping through my body. Instead, my mouth touches every surface available on his face, hoping to transfer this throbbing vivacity to him; maybe he'll be able to transmute it into something more useful.

"Slow down, lovely. You're moving too fast, talking too fast. Slow. Down... Just—let's just breathe." After seconds or minutes, my mind settles. My breathing returns to something between hyperventilating and running for my life.

"Thank you, Sir."

"Of, course. Whatever you need."

"I want you to know that it doesn't matter what happens between Valery and Collin. No part of *me* will be there. This body is just like a car, John. That's how we see it, anyway. I'm not always going to be in the driver's seat. Adopting this perspective has been integral in my spiritual growth."

"How's that?"

"Well, Sir, once I was able to view my flesh and blood body as only a vehicle that I use to move my consciousness... the part of me that makes me separate from the two or more persons sharing this car, I—"

"You realized the most important part isn't the car, but what drives it."

"Yes, Sir. Just... it's like Collin is going for a romantic ride in a beautiful car, it's only special to him when Valery is the one driving it. Just like... it's only special to *you* when I'm the driver."

"I love you, Vivian. Little sub, why here?"

"Because I know you'd have a harder time if he took her to his place. You may not care for Valery... that much, but you do care about Vera and me. I thought it would make it easier for you if they were here, and you knew you could protect our body if we needed you to, Sir."

"You are my entire fucking world, lovely. *You.* Not your body, your cunt, not even your goddamned heart. You, Vivian Ellis are the only reason I take breaths every day. I will be right-fucking-here when you come home to me on Wednesday morning."

"Sir?" I watch his nostrils flare at the same time I feel a consistent flow of arousal slick my panties.

Does he... *smell me?*

"Get your ass downstairs. Assume the position. No hard limits tonight, sub."

"Okay, Sir."

"Oh, and Viv?" I lock my eyes on his feral gaze and my pussy clenches down hard, reminding me how empty she is when the god standing in front of me isn't pounding into her. "Tell the girls if they try and fuck shit up for us tonight..." He doesn't have to finish his sentence because we're on the same damn page.

***

I've been waiting down in our playroom for about five minutes pass eternity. When I think I can't hold on to my sanity another minute longer, the energy shifts in the room.

It becomes denser.

Darker.

Electricity pings off my skin like acid rain bouncing off heated asphalt. Like steam is rising from each individual pore. When finally. Finally, I watch his elegant feet as they carry him around the room. He touches several spaces, but none of them near me. None of them close enough that I feel the rush of anticipation when he reaches out to touch any part of me.

Is that me, panting like a bitch in heat? Embarrassing.

My white cotton panties are soaked. The evidence of my arousal is coating the inside of my spread thighs. And still... he hasn't said a word. Hasn't even come close to touching me. I swear with the way my internal walls are contracting and releasing, I'm going to come.

I'm so deep inside my head, the rumble of his voice startles a squeak from me.

"I smell that sweet pussy, lovely. How close is she to giving it up?"

Swallowing pass the globe of lust in the back of my throat feels like a Sisyphean feat. It's audible when I finally manage to make it happen.

"What happens if you come without my permission, sub?"

"Punishment, Sir"

"I suggest you don't earn one, lovely. Not with the way my demons are riding me after that conversation." I don't bother answering him because I'm already prepared for a rough night. We both need it if we're to survive the next forty-eight hours. "Answer me."

"Yes, Sir." The lie feels like sandpaper against my tongue. I know he hears it, too, if the quick intake of breath is anything to go by. He doesn't acknowledge it, just gives me my first directive.

"Crawl to the bondage chair." I do as he says. It's only a few feet away, but my thighs are shaking so bad, I'm barely able to get them to move, one in front of the other. Once I finally reach him, he's already undone his belt and the top button on his button-fly jeans. His long, heavy phallus that leads to that thick, flared cockhead is clearly outlined against the inside of his left thigh; the sight of it causes saliva to pool in my mouth.

"What are you waiting for, lovely?"

I come up on my knees, my hands interlaced behind my back. I expect him to finish unbuttoning his jeans and pull Jughead out for me to wrap my lips around, but he just stands there. Looking like a piece of forbidden fruit, waiting to be plucked.

"Take me out, Vivian."

I do as I'm told. There's so much liquid coating both sets of my lips, I would be embarrassed if it didn't turn John into an animal. I hold his length in my right hand. The vulnerable skin encasing his erection bears the rich color of pinot nior grapes at the peak of harvesting season. His taste is just as complex, tart cherries, sweet strawberries, grounding earthiness and decadent caramel. He is my favorite libation.

"What are you waiting for, lovely? He doesn't bite." He teases, but the tension in his voice belies the razor's edge he's riding. When he wants me this bad, I know how much it cost him to maintain this level of ataraxia. So much so, I expect him to guide my mouth onto him, but he just stands there. His large hands hang loosely at his side. The chiseled plains of his flat belly are vibrating with arousal.

"It isn't going to suck itself, sub. Don't make me repeat myself." A crackle of awareness dances down my spine, creating a volatile concoction of arousal, fear and anticipation.

"Yes, Sir." I lean forward and lick the weeping tip with the flat of my tongue. The first hit is salty. Earthy. Fucking delicious.

Part II

I trap the rest of my insecurities behind folded lips and clenched teeth. I hold them and chew on the thin skin until I drown they asses in my own filthy blood. I still ain't said shit and I don't think I'm gonna.

~Valery Danyal

~12~

Vivian

Once I've cleaned the pre-ejaculate from his large cockhead, I open my mouth and pull him into the back of my throat on the first hallowing of my jaws. The pleasure so complete, he rewards me with a sigh of great satisfaction. I don't gloat, avoiding the bratty behavior that would earn me a punishment. I let his length languish in my esophagus until tears form in the corner of my eyes. Until saliva spills from the sides of my mouth. Until John can't resist rolling his hips to screw himself deeper into my clenching throat.

"No one will ever fill you like I do... lovely-mine." I shake my head back and forth, letting my teeth run across the top of his soft skin. Reveling in the hiss that comes as a result of the abrasion. Finally, John pulls his hips back. Leaving only the leaking tip to hang off of my lip like a cigarette. A thick string of pre-cum and spit connects him to me. Tentative and fragile.

I lick my bottom lip, severing the tenuous bond, while I watch his belly go concave with his effort to remain in control.

Oh but John, I don't need your control tonight. I need you to be a filthy, depraved animal with me. Need you to fuck me like we were never introduced to civilization.

Or rules.

Or any of the bullshit that makes human beings turn sex into the most mundane thing they do.

John makes two ponytails of my locs—hands fisted at my roots—to use as handlebars as he starts to ride my face. I open my mouth as wide as I can and relax my throat. I am available for him to use and debase because he's the only man who respects me enough to seek my willing submission.

"That's it, lovely. Show me how much you love and worship my dick." He's completely unhinged. I'm the perfect cum slut for my

---

husband. I work my neck back and forth like a deranged chicken while I swallow him until he can no longer form coherent thoughts. I need him to feel the constriction of my throat closing in on him.

I open wider for him like my salary depends on how well I suck my husband's dick. Using the flat of my tongue, I drag his pre-cum back towards the tip, and because I know he's trying to maintain control, I push my tongue—covered in his pre-cum—into the leaking slit.

John's thighs shake.

His pulse pounds in the head of his dick.

John growls the filthiest nonsensical words, and still, he continues to hold himself back.

This won't do. I need him to destroy me.

I redouble my efforts. Swirling my tongue on each withdrawal. Scraping my teeth on every plunge. Humming Floetry's, *Say Yes,* in the back of my throat. Sending delicious vibrations along the bulbous head when pushed back into the depths of my mouth. I wanted him wild. Insane and out of his ever-loving mind.

"I know... fuck—ing know. What you're... Jesus-fucking-christ, lovely. T-there. R-r-right th—"

Most of him is in my mouth. Just the tip is resting inside the opening to my throat. I won't take him any further, and I don't stop humming the sexy little tune, either.

"Goddammit, sub! You t-think you w-want this, Viv."

"Mmhmm." He tightens his fingers in my hair until the pull turns into a painful burn that only makes my pussy weep more. I take a deep breath through my nose before slurping and slobbering around his length like my life depends on making this man come down my aching throat.

"You are not in control in this room." I suck him harder.

Longer.

Deeper.

"Fucking hell. Your throat... So, fuck. King. Tight, baby." *Come on, John. Let go. Please.*

I become the thing I need. Taking him all the way back down my throat, I moan for an eternity. More tears leak down my cheeks. More saliva puddles from the sides of my mouth. I'm a fucking mess. I love it. I'm almost out of breath. Almost out of energy. Almost out of my damn mind, but I refuse to let up until he takes charge of this runaway train.

White lights and grey fringe dance around my fading vision just before I rub my nose into his trimmed pubic hair. I drag my teeth side-to-side across the base of his cock.

"Ahhh. I d-don't want to h-hurt—"

Another moan. Another scrape of my teeth. I'm on the verge of passing out when I feel his hands relinquish their grip on my locs to wrap around the back of my head. John wrenches my mouth away from his groin and allows me to take in some much-needed oxygen.

"Is this what you want, little sub?" He growls so low I'm not sure if he's talking to me or himself. He falters a little when he spits out, "... topping from the goddamn bottom, lovely. You. Are. The. Fucking. Submissive." Each word is punctuated with rutting stabs of his hips

No mercy.

No finesse.

Only him forcing me to take what I begged for. I stare up at him and my chest cracks wide open with all the love, respect, and gratitude I feel for the god standing above me. Making me pay for sins I had no part in but are mine just the same. His anger is valid. His punishment, righteous and exacting. Only he can absolve me of my transgressions... and he will.

"... pushing me too motherfucking far, Viv." Every thrust causes my nose to connect with his pubic bone. My clit swells with an orgasm that will end my reality and I'm here for all of it. "Well," he

—

continues, "... it's me who's pushing this thick, long dick down your willing throat, now. Right?"

I don't know if he wants an answer and I'm not sure I could give him one with the way I'm choking on his length.

"Answer me, sub. Am I right?"

"Th...e... sss, Thl...ir." I attempt to answer while my mouth is still full of him. More drool spills from the tiny pockets of space not currently connected to his shaft, mixed with thick strings of John's pre-cum. I'm a hot ass mess. Tears stream down from my eyes like sacrificial holy water. He's still pounding into my face. Ensuring every time he pulls my mouth onto him, my nose is buried in his pelvic area.

He smells like every sin Eve was too timid to commit.

"You're going to swallow..." He doesn't even finish before thick ropes of his cum shoot down my throat; almost bypassing my tongue altogether. "Take it, sub. Every fucking drop belongs to you. Don't waste a single pearl."

John holds my nose to his groin, rumbling inhuman grunts and commands. Rotating his hip to screw his cock deeper down my throat.

"When he kisses her, he'll taste my come on her goddamned breath." The last couple of twitches reward me with thick, sweet cream down the center of my tongue. He pulls out of my mouth and runs the tip across my swollen lips. Painting them in my favorite shade of love.

"Get up, lovely. I'm fucking every hole you have tonight. And then, I'm going to fuck your tits and ass cheeks." I almost come from his words, alone.

"Where are you, Viv?"

"Green, Sir."

"Good girl. Here..." He reaches down and grabs me under my armpits to lift me into the bondage chair. The leather is the deepest

—

80

shade of admiral blue I've ever seen. Soft and supple, thanks to John's meticulous care, it feels like butter under my overheated skin. Before he gets me into position, he pulls a blade from somewhere and cuts my ruined underwear away from the wet flesh between my thighs.

"You..." He places the gusset into his hungry mouth and sucks my arousal from the cotton; making a show of satisfaction in swallowing my juices without having pleasured me to get them into his mouth. "... taste like fucking honeysuckle nectar and a fresh salty breeze. This goddamn pussy."

I can't say a thing because the pussy he's waxing poetically about, is clenching and sucking on emptiness like the action alone can conjure John's dick deep inside.

"You haven't come, yet. Have you, sub?"

"N-no, Sir."

John pushes me against the angled back of the chair. Ushering me to rest my head on the raised cushion before securing my forehead with the padded constraint.

John

"Place your arms on the arm rest, palms up." I watch as her arms float out from her body like the wings on a butterfly after breaking free of its cocoon. Vivian's submission has the same effect on my dick as her warm, wet mouth. "Good girl." I mumble because most of my blood has dropped back into my greedy cock. Like I didn't just have the mother of all orgasms. *Pipe down, Jughead, it's Vivian's turn to receive pleasure.*

I kneel between her spread legs, lifting first the left foot and then the right onto the leg supports. Her sex is on full display, and it's all I can do to stop myself from falling face first between her spread thighs. "You look like my favorite meal, Vivian."

I whisper against her smooth skin as I secure the leather constraints around her ankles, knees, and upper thighs, dragging my fingernails along the sensitive skin until I'm almost touching where she's wet and open for me. Her swollen inner labia pout their disapproval as they drip arousal down into her rosebud, which flexes in response. I'm momentarily transfixed on how sexual this beautiful cunt is without stimulation. With only the heat of my gaze—she weeps with anticipation and the insatiable need to be licked and fucked—this perfect pussy is primed to come all over whatever I choose to give it.

"How close?"

"Almost there, Sir."

"That doesn't tell me a goddamned thing, lovely. How close is my pussy to coming undone?"

"If you touch me—anywhere—I'm going to come, S-Sir." The words are barely audible through the thick notes of desire playing through her vocal cords.

"You don't have permission to come." I whisper in her ear, my lips brushing the sensitive area just beneath her lobe. I watch as a distinct shiver works through her body. "Sub." There she is. I knew she'd go off like a firecracker if I startled her at the right moment. The most beautiful thing I've seen is a spontaneous orgasm move through Vivian's body like flood waters lifting Noah's Arc to salvation. It's just as holy and divine as that bible story; only more so because I get to experience the miracle first-hand.

"Mmm."

I watch as her elegant and dexterous pointer fingers and thumbs pluck and squeeze her hardened nipples, milking them like her lush mouth milked my dick only minutes before. I can almost see the lust working through her Vega nerve straight into her sopping, greedy sex. I stand between her spread legs to watch the thick, frothy cream of her release flow from her spread folds and puddle onto the floor beneath the chair.

"Fuck, yes. So good, John. Feels so good."

I'm about a second away from dropping to my knees to lap at her essence on the floor, but more than that, I want to punish her for coming without permission. She's dipped two fingers into her cunt, pumping in and out like it's her first day on a new job and she's working to impress the new boss.

If it were, I'd have to give her ass a raise.

I walk away from the most erotic acts I've seen Viv perform in a long time. I can't fucking wait to bring her to heel.

She's working herself up to another orgasm when she never had permission to have the first one. She's goading me to punish her...

What my lovely wants, my lovely shall receive.

It's my fucking pleasure to give her the desires of her heart. My pleasure and my privilege.

—

"Enjoying yourself, lovely?" I inquire just as her loud moans and high-pitched screams from her second release settle into panting breaths and whispered nonsense words. I've sourced my favorite long spanking paddle from the hand painted, Chinese wedding armoire I keep in the comer behind the bookshelf. This is what turns Vivian on.

The unknown... the unsettling conjuring of her imagination.

"Answer me, lovely. Did you enjoy those orgasms?"

"Yes, Sir. T-thank you, Sir."

"So, fucking polite, little sub. But tell me, what have I done to earn your gratitude?" Her legs tense. Her breathing is shallow, at best. I'm standing beside her left arm, having already restrained the right, I complete the last buckle across her left wrist.

"Um, f-for allowing..." I see the exact moment realization sifts through her glazed eyes, that I never gave her permission to come the first time and certainly not the second.

"For allowing, what?"

"Um, Sir?"

"Yes. Lovely, lift your head as much as the restraint will *allow*. Good girl."

"Uh. I d-didn't realize I'd," She swallows audibly before she continues. "... be blindfolded, Sir."

"*No*?" She tries to shake her head in response. "Words, Viv. Use your mouth before I gag you with your wet panties."
"No, Sir. I didn't know your p-plan..."

"Why so nervous?"

"I'm... n-not, Sir. Not real... ly." She tries to move her head, but the restraint keeps her in place. "... Justin Timberlake, *Sir*?" She has no idea where I am. The blindfold, loud music and the post-orgasmic endorphins have her feeling off kilter. Not to mention, she's still unsure if she had permission to come or not. *Perfect, lovely. Just how I need you for the next part of our scene.*

"Do you like it?" I move between her spread legs, the ergonomic handle of the midnight-blue, leather spanking paddle rests in my right hand.

Patient.

Silent.

An unassuming thing to those who don't know how to wield its power.

To me, it's a tool designed to ring the most mesmerizing cries of decadent pleasure from unsuspecting subs, like my beautiful wife, Vivian. "Red. Green. Yellow."

"Huh... Sir?"

"Where are you? Red, green, or yellow."

"Green, Sir?"

"Are you not sure?"

"Green, Sir."

"Good girl." Without a second's hesitation, I pull my right arm back and revel in the whistle of the long paddle as it cuts through space and time to land on Vivian's wet, vulnerable cunt with such a satisfying smack, I nearly come in my pants.

"Fucking-Jesus Christ-on-a-block-of-government-cheese!" She screams a string of curses I've never heard her use before. I'll laugh about it when we're done in here. *Maybe.*

"Color, Viv."

"G-green, S—" She doesn't get to finish because her pussy is on fire once again with the aid of blue lightening. "Jesus-fuck! Joh—" Another hard slap of the paddle has her weeping; pussy juice and tears feed my inner beast. He roars in triumph when Vivian gives up a sweet little whimper of hard-won surrender. I drop the paddle on

—

the floor. My hands shake with the adrenalin and anticipation of what awaits me once I get these damn jeans unbuttoned.

Lovely is a blubbering mess. She has never looked more beautiful. Try as I may, I can't stop myself from looking upon the puffy lips of her sex. All deep purples, bright pinks surrounded by an angry shade of magenta. Fuck, I can't wait to sink into her swollen heat and lose the rest of my goddamn mind.

"Vivian." She tries to take a deep breath and fails. Instead, a watery sob burbles from the depths of her soul. I examine her to make sure I didn't take things too far. I don't want to bruise or mark her. Just bring the blood to the surface and make her clit swell with it.

She's fine. Just breaking in the best way possible. The way she needed to be broken.

"S-Sir." Vivian's soft voice yanks me from my concerns and back into the scene. My pants are neatly folded and rest atop the small table to the right of the bondage chair.

When the fuck did that happen?

"What is your color?" My dick's so hard right now, I'm not sure I'm comfortable pushing it inside Viv's body, but my unease won't stop me from doing what we both need.

"Y-yellow, Sir. May I p-please have a drink of w-water, Sir?" I don't answer her. I simply move to do her bidding. I know she's reeling with the reality of what will happen tomorrow, but she doesn't need my softness any more than I need her forgiveness for what I'm doing to her. After retrieving a small bamboo cup of room-temperature water with a slice of lime, cucumber and a pinch a sea salt, I stand beside her head.

"Open." She does with hesitation. I place the edge of the cup to her ruined mouth before tipping the swallow of electrolyte fluid onto her tongue. Her slender throat works hard on a loud sip that has my hips pushing forward of their own accord, in remembrance of the blowjob that started this scene. "Good. Red, yellow, or green."

"Green, Sir."

"Perfect." I'm back between her legs but decide at the last minute to change the angle I enter her by bending her legs and pulling them back, so her knees are almost touching her shoulders. This way, I have access to both entrances. And I already know I'll start in her pussy and come in her asshole. Pre-cum leaks from my tip at the thought. Without further preparation or warning, I step forward and sink my entire length into the only woman I will ever love.

"Ahhhh." She screams for a momentary eternity before she pants like a succubus being fucked to within an inch of her life. And loving every minute of it.

"What's that, lovely?" I pull back and slide inside again, only this time, I rotate my hips in a clockwise motion to screw myself deeper than I'd been before. My pubic bone rocks against the distended bundle of nerves with just the right amount of pressure to remind her of the spanking she just received at my hands. "You want more." Vivian's head is secure, as are her limbs, which means she can only absorb the excessive stimulation.

"Yes, Sir. Please and t-thank you, Sir."

There she is. My girl has come out to play.

"You're so fucking sweet, lovely." I pull all the way out, leaving only the tip inside her greedy, sucking lips while my thumbs play her clit like a kalimba. Poor Viv's hips are bucking and twitching as much as her restraints allow and it's driving me goddamn crazy knowing she's going to come, and I get to join her. "Are you ready to come on my cock, sub?"

"God, yes, Sir? Please? Puh-lease, let me come. *Master*." That's it. This little vixen knows me well. I've been at her for about forty-five minutes. Giving her slow and thorough strokes. Hitting the end of her, stimulating the tip of her sensitive cervix with my cockhead.

———

Screwing so deep into her, I'm sure I've fucked her soul. *She has the nerve to whisper, Master.*

I reach up to remove the blindfold and watch as she blinks into the dim, blue light. She finds and holds my gaze with blown pupils surrounded by a golden ring of summer sunshine. Her eyes emit enough warmth and comfort to sooth the savage beast lurking just beneath my civilized flesh.

"Welcome back, lovely. Give yourself over to me. Now, lovely. Give it up to me."

Our eyes lock: our hearts, minds and souls mirror the sacred act. Only when we are as connected as two separate beings can be, do I surrender to the need to slide into her silken walls. Prepared to die and be resurrected as harmonious souls.

"Sir?"

"I've got you, lovely. I'm going to take care of you. You trust me... to know what you need." I pull from her creamy center and push back inside with shallow strokes, just enough to take her mind off of what I hold in my hand.

"That's it, lovely. Let me in."

"Yes, S-oh, my god!"

"There. It's done, now breathe through it." I blow a stream of cool air over her clit as the bejeweled clamp winks up at me like an exploding star. She cries out from the intensity. The tight bud goes from flamingo pink to blood-red in no time. I surge forward, letting the heavy weight of my dick carry me to the opening of her womb. My groin hits her tortured nub over and over again. Still, our eyes remain locked on each other. In that way, I feel what she feels and vice versa.

Fucking tantric sex.

"What belongs to me, lovely?"

"Everything." She slurs her response.

"Baby. When you gift me this much submission..." Words falter when I slide my index finger into her ass. She told me she'd already used a lubricating suppository before I got home, but that doesn't stop me from lubing up my dick and running the tip between the crack of her ass cheeks. "Fuck, Viv. Keep your eyes open and on me." I place the tip against the tight ring of muscle just to let the idea soak into her mind. Her breathing increases to short puffs of air. Through our connection, my breath follows suit. I add the necessary pressure to break through the sphincter ring. She's warm, wet, and tight as fuck.

"You're amazing, lovely. I surge forward and don't stop until I bottom out. I know this is going to be quick. "I'm going to fuck your ass; you have permission to come as many times as you can." I don't wait for an answer before I pull out and start thrusting back into my demon's idea of heaven. It's only been about five or six strokes when I hear the high-pitched keening of an animal giving up its will to fight against what's happening to it. I reach up to remove the clamp from Viv's clit and... I am not fucking prepared.

~14~

Vivian

I am shattered. No longer a corporeal sentient being, I exist as microscopic points of luminescence. Attached to nothing yet connected to it all.

I am tomorrow, the day Collin and Valery fall into each other. It fills me with a light brighter than the sun. As that day, I give myself to them... allowing them to luxuriate in each other for the entirety of my lifetime.

I am without condition as I acknowledge, accept, give compassion to, and forgive all I'm connected with. No judgement or shame.

Wave after wave of energy in motion moves me along the river of choices and consequence, until I'm years into a future. I experience many lifetimes in mere seconds.

Slowly, my essence solidifies into what feels like... a *prison*. Before I am fully formed, I realize I've retained memories of moments waiting to happen. It's disconcerting to know what *will* be, while not being sure of exactly *how*.

This trammeling, uncouth version of self, is heavy in its assumption of importance. I immediately miss the freedom of fluidity. The right to move as neflebata do; from cloud to dream and from dream to anoesis. After several seconds or an entire lifetime, I open my eyes to a rich golden-brown gaze filled with wonder and gratitude. *John*.

"Welcome back, beautiful." He's the breeze off the lake on a perfect spring day. Smooth on the surface and teaming with life and unsettled currents below. His smile tells me he's satisfied with himself and the experience he gave us in our playroom tonight. The lines at the corners of his eyes tell me he's more than a little concerned because of my *response*.

"Hey, baby. How long have I been under?"

"Long enough for me to bring you upstairs, after your bath, and rehydration aftercare. Long enough for me to have a shower and check on Bertha and the kittens."

"That sounds like a long damn time," I inject levity into my voice, hoping to cover the growing anxiety chewing at my trembling insides. "How long?"

"Almost an hour, lovely. But you weren't unconscious, as much as you were in between here and wherever you went."

"That's a great way to describe it." I offer him a wan smile. I'm tired as hell but also filled with a sort of buzzing, frenetic energy. I'm a living, breathing, walking dichotomy.

"Can you get up, are do you want to just go back to sleep. It's pretty late. I was just waiting for you to come to, before turning in for the night."

"No, I'm good to go to sleep. How was Bertha and the kittens when you checked on them?"

"Fine. Bertha is a great cat-mom."

"And you're a wonderful grand-*cat-daddy*."

"You stay with the jokes, don't you? I got your cat-daddy hanging between my legs." The air becomes denser as the last vestige of joviality is sucked away with the realization that tomorrow is now, today.

"John?"

"I've made my peace with it. Maybe Collin is exactly what Valery needs to keep her from behaving like a stupid, selfish bitch. And if he can do that, then who the hell am I to begrudge their relationship?"

"I love you, baby. So, so much."

"I love you. Now, shut up and let's get some sleep. The sooner today starts," He moves around the room turning off lights and fixing curtains before sliding into bed beside me. He pulls my back to his front, wraps his heavy arms around my middle and drops a hard, fast kiss to the top of my head and declares, "The sooner it will be over. Good night, lovely. Dream of me."

Always.

"Night, John. Thanks for taking such good care of my *fuckin ' pussy*." We both crack up before John groans something under his breath like, *stupid and country ass Cole,* then tells me to go to sleep.

I do.

Without a heavy thought or emotion flitting through my soul. I know that this is the only way forward and I'm damn happy that John is evolved enough in his manhood to support this reality.

I'm dosing off when John's sleepy voice interrupts the sandman and his sprinkling of moon dust, to ask a question so dumb, I can't do anything but laugh at him.

"Viv, I'm not going to wake up with Valery's ass pressed against my morning wood, am I?" Laughter is my only response.

~15~

"So, what you sayin, is John surly ass knows what's about to go down and he all right with this shit? Get the fuck outta here, Viv. That possessive mothafucka ain't bout to let Collin fuck me under his goddamn roof and you know I'm tellin the damn truth."

Valery, if he weren't on board with everything, why would I tell you and Collin it was fine for him to come over and stay with you?

"Cause your crazy ass got some kind of death wish or some shit. Maybe you the masochist of this fuckin system. What... you lookin to give John a reason to beat your ass raw? I don't know, when the fuck did you decide... wait one goddamn, mothafuckin minute. Who the hell gave your meddling ass the right to decide any-fuckin-thing where me and Collin is concerned.

Stay in your goddamned lane. Just cause you always drivin this bitch, don't make you the master of this shit. When Collin and me decide—for our damn selves—that it's time for us to fuck like rabbits, you won't have fuck-all to say about shit we do."

I didn't decide it was time for you two to... fuck like rabbits, as you so ineloquently phrased it. Collin came to me to air his grievances and I don't know. I felt bad for him and for you, too. It's obviously something more between you guys. You know? Other than art and crazy chemistry.

"What if I let him fuck me tonight and then," For the first time in my whole damn life, I have doubts about fuckin somebody. I'm so damn gone over this boy, it ain't even a little bit funny.

And then what, Valery?

"And then he start treatin me like John and Harry did. Like I ain't nothin but a collection of goddamn wet holes to be filled with his fuckin cock or fingers or hands or tongue or toys or..." I don't know where these goddamned feelins comin from, but what I do know is I don't fuckin like how these fuckas feel.

Look, Valery. I don't pretend to know what's inside Collin's heart, but I know what I see in his eyes when he talks about you. Or when he stares at a piece of your art. Or when I tell him something funny or insightful you've said.

Collin is in love with you. Even John saw it when he played Captain Cave-man that one time. If he didn't know for sure that Collin was the real deal, there's no way in hell he'd be all right with this arrangement.

" Yeah?" I fuckin hate how needy I sound. I slide my new, human-hair wig into place and make sure the bondin glue is securin this bitch to the stockin cap, while I wait for more of Vivian's sunshine to warm up my asshole.

I was letting Vera know what was going on today. What'd you say?

Tired of playin the goddamn victim, I give the front of my wig a harsh tug—enjoyin the bite of pain—before I sigh, "Fuck it. Either Collin gonna be like every mothafucka out there who just wanna get his dick wet or," I need to concentrate to get these damn lashes on or I ain't seein shit today. Not tryin to look like some kinda caterpillar is livin on top of my fuckin eye.

Tricky little shits. Things I do in the name of goddamn beauty. Valery!

"What, bitch. Quit callin my name like you got some authority over me or some shit. What the fuck you want?"

You know damn-well, I'd never let you get so deep with Collin if I thought he would bugger off after a dalliance with you. You know him better than me, and he's not like that.

"Shit, girl. You spend more time with my man than me. He even got your cornbread-eatin-country-fried-steak-ass usin them stupid British words." *Bugger.* I roll my eyes so damn hard at her

—

94

foolishness, makes me glad my boo can't see my black ass right now. "Anyway, I don't think I'm gonna let him fuck me. At least not tonight."

What?

"What? You act like I'm just a walkin pussy who happens to know how to paint. Like all me and a man can do when we alone is fuck and suck each other until one or both of us finds a happy-fuckin-endin." I look at my clothes and feel good I ain't choose the other outfit I was thinkin about wearin today. I mean, it's already fuckin hard to look like an average goddamn woman with this fuckin body and these juicy tits. But black skin-tight jeans, see-through button-up and this sexy as fuck lace bra are about as demure as a bitch gonna get.

I didn't say a word about what you two do. I just thought that maybe... Yes, Vera, I'll be inside shortly. Val's still getting dress—

Valery.

"Oh, for fuck's sake. What the fuck you want, big country?" I'm fuckin lovin this new shade of lipstick, this shit make my lips look almost as kissable as the pouty lips of my wet ass pussy. *Shiny mothafuckas.*

First of all, you don't have a reason to talk to me like that. Secondly, I just wanted to say I'm happy for you and Collin and I hope he is who he present himself to be. You deserve someone to treat you kind, yeah?

Shit, what the fuck am I supposed to say to that. Vera make me so goddamned sick when she treat me all nice. I feel like I gotta be nice right back.

Fuck my slit sideways when I'm walkin to church!

"Um. Yeah. I guess, Vera." What the hell, can't I just say fuckin thank you and I'm sorry I'm such a ragin slunt?

Of course, I fuckin cannot.

—

Yeah, well, okay then. Vivian said enjoy yourself and um.
Whatever you do decide, don't do it because you feel scared of losing
him, yeah?

"Yeah, Vera. Um. Th-thanks. Now, get the fuck outta here before
Collin fine ass come in here to get me. Don't try to peek in on what
the fuck we do, either. Feel me?" There. That's more like fuckin
normal. Shit, I'm not tryin to turn into one of their goddamn *sissies*
or some shit.

I can respect you need to protect yourself, yeah? And don't worry,
I don't want to know what you and the pasty, white man get up to
when y'all together. Nasty and nastier.

"Bitch."

I've been called worse by worse people, yeah. So, your words
mean little to me. And don't bother trying to come back at me, I'm
going inside. Be safe and take care of our body, yeah?

Who the fuck told her slow-moving ass to get a goddamned
backbone?"

What-the-fuck-ever.

"All right, ladies of the Internal House." I'm loud as fuck cause I
wanna make sure them bitches can hear me as I announce, "Close
your fuckin doors. Plug your fuckin ears. Whatever's about to go
down with this body is only for the mothafuckin grown and the
goddamn sexy folks." No reply. The slight lift of my right shoulder
felt like somethin someone else would do in a moment like this. But
at the same time, it feels so like my dizzy ass not to give a fuck
about what the hell them two broads think about me.

One last look in this fancy ass mirror and I'm ready—as ready as
I'm gonna be—to meet my boo and get this paintin in.

"Collin, where the fuck you at?" I walk around the corner where
we usually meet but he ain't standin in his usual spot.

What the hell he playin at?

"Okay. I'm gonna get started then, I guess." I say to the goddamn empty space where his fine ass usually be standin. I walk into the room Viv gave me to work in... Oh, my fuckin god. This mothafucka done lost his damn mind or my crazy ass is havin some kind of wet-dream, or he really standin in front of a black tarp. Naked as fuck. Thick and long. So goddamn hard, my cunt throbbin from the sight of that thing hangin between his spread muscular thighs. No man-bun today. Shit, he's my filthy fantasy come true. And a little too fuckin *cheeky* for my likin.

"Hi, lass. You look like you thinkin 'about either killin 'me or beatin 'my ass. Neither of which I was hopin 'to inspire with my surprise."

That damn accent. His rumbly voice. Shivers flow through my body and kiss my nipples and clit with long confident licks. It's hard to remember why I'm so goddamn pissed off in the first place, but when I'm pissed, that shit has to be handled before every-fuckin-thing.

"Why the fuck you naked, Collin? We get the green light to see where these fuckin feelins might take us and the first goddamn thought your horny ass has is to fuck. Of-fuckin-course, that's the first thing you want—probably the only damn thing you want from me. You got a dick, right?" I smile but it don't feel like it belong on my fuckin face.

I don't know if this fire in my chest is anger or pain. What I know is that if I don't get my ass outta this room, I'm gonna burn this mothafucka down with me and him in it. I turn to walk back to Vivian's office. I'm gonna let myself sink into the safety of the Internal House; only large, calloused hands stop me from marchin off.

"What the fuck is wrong wid ye, lass. I was hopin 'to git ye to paint me, lass. What'd ye..." He turns me to face him, but I keep my eyes on my shoes.

97

Thank fuck I'm black as tar, I'm so shame-faced. Goddammit-all-to-hell.

"Talk to me, Valery. What's that all about?" A self-defeated huff of air is all I can offer his ass. Fuck, he sound as sad and lost as I felt when I saw his goddamn dick swingin in the wind.

Oh. That's just me bein a fuckin insecure slunt.

"I. You..." Shit, why the fuck is this so damn hard? I pull on a pair of Vera's big-girl drawers and finally meet his metallic gaze. Fuckin big mistake. "Collin. I."

"Ye whoot? Ye say ye want time paintin 'male figures. Woorkin ' wid nude models... no way in hell or heaven was I goonna let some other bloke stand in front ye wid his dick swingin 'all aboot." God, he so damn worked up he ain't even speakin English no more. Poor bastard.

"Fuck. I'm too stupid to... I'm sorry." I apologize and reveal, "I guess I was feelin too... *exposed?*"

"Exposed? How, lass, I'm the one wid my dick and bollocks hangin 'out." He pushes his sexy ass smile into his words, and they pull the corner of my lips up. "There's my bonny lass. Talk to me. You're nervous."

"Yeah, and don't have a fuckin clue what I'm nervous about. You know?"

"No, because I barely got any sleep last night my damn self. I'm nervous and scared as fuck that I'm goin to do somethin 'to fuck us up. And considerin 'I've been beggin 'every damn god and ghost and fairy to make this day happen, I can't for the life of me figure out why I feel like I'm goin 'to vomit any minute now." His shoulders relax a little but he still lookin at me like I can save his fuckin soul.

The tension ain't so bad around my chest. I take a deep breath and stare right back at his pretty ass. We two goofy, fucked-up fools standin here in an empty ass gallery too scared of what might happen, yet not willin to do nothin.

"I thought you were waitin with your dick out cause you wanted to fuck me and then—" I trap the rest of my insecurities behind folded lips and clenched teeth. I hold them and chew on the thin skin until I drown they asses in my own filthy blood. I still ain't said shit and I don't think I'm gonna.

"Fuck you and then... *what*? Tell you to fuck right off?" Collin's voice is a low, cool breeze blowin across a muddy, rollin river. Not enough to calm the waters, so it just get caught up in the rip tide and carried out to sea.

"Yeah."

"How could you think that lass? I had no plans of fuckin 'you today or tonight. I just want to spend some uninterrupted time wid ye. Time we can talk, eat and cuddle up together. Like the couple I want us to be. You're more than a goddamn fuck-toy to me, Valery. I thought I'd made my feelins for ye clear. I guess I didn't do such a good fuckin 'job, did I, lass." Collin head hangin so low, it look like he prayin to them little fairies he always talkin bout.

I ain't gonna let him take the blame for the shit stains in my funky ass carpet. They belong to me, and he don't have to clean them bitches up. But he need to know about them, so he don't track any back to his own damn carpet.

"You did, and you do." I start lettin him know he ain't the blame for my hurt. I continue, "It's me. I got a shit-ton of baggage, Collin. So much, I don't even know if I'm aware of what's been packed away." I chance a look at him and instead of seein pity or sympathy, I see understandin. If I recognized how love looked, maybe I see that too. He scrub the rough pad of his thumb across my bottom lip with enough weight to smear my lipstick. My lip pulls to the right with the movement.

—

"You are a perfect realization of impossibilities. I know shit won't be easy—for more reasons than our baggage—and I don't need it to be, Val. Listen lass, just so you know because there can't be any uncertainty where this shit's concerned, I fuckin 'love you. All the fuckin 'amazin 'parts I know and everything I goddamn still have to explore; I adore you. Your sense of humor. The way you own your sexuality. The demonic way you bleed your soul onto a canvas. The way you smile when I give you a well-deserved compliment. There isn't a damn thing about you that doesn't make me want to love you"

I can't. Is this man for-fuckin-real or am I stuck inside dreamin about my perfect other half?

"Col. Lin. I—"

" I'm committed to you and me bein 'an—us, lass. If you want me, I intend to love you into a soul affirming healing, baby." When he ain't upset or scared shitless, he only drop the endins of a few words. He sound more American when he calm.

I throw myself into his naked chest. The feel of his arms around my middle is every-fuckin-thing I never knew I goddamn wanted. How he's able to accept a ride on my crazy train, I don't know and don't have a fuck to give. All I do know is he's on board.

"I don't know what love is," I step away and drop into the silver whirlpools of his intense gaze. I baptize myself in the perfectin turbulence of acceptance I find there. Power slides through my goddamn veins—like a hit of heroin—even though he know how much I'm lackin. But with him, I feel like a whole mothafuckin beast. "... Collin, but I wanna be more; I want to mean more than any-fuckin-body else ever goddamn meant to your gorgeous Scottish ass. I want to talk with you, cook with you, sleep—not fuck—but sleep with you. I'm the saddest, mopiest bitch around when we don't talk for days. It hurts. Like a mothafucka when we ain't together.

"I wake the fuck up with you on my mind and fall the fuck to sleep with your name on my lips. I ain't never been loved by a man, and I don't know how to goddamn love a man, but I want you to love me, Collin. Can you teach me how... to *love* you."

He sound like chewed gravel and broken dreams when he says, "Fuck, lass! Ye make my dick hard with them bonny words and that raw honesty." His chuckles is foreplay even if the last thing he said makes me feel some kind of way. He reaches out and grabs my hand before I can storm off and says in a low, growly voice, "... and it has not to do wid me wanting to fuck ye into another time zone.

This erection is filled with goddamn cave-man tendencies; the need to beat my hands against my chest and piss a circle around you. Let every other bastard know that you belong to me. That you are mine to protect, provide and care for. To make sure you have everything you need in this world so, all you have to do is be the brilliant co-creator of a world for you and me. You. Are. Not. A goddamned fuck-toy, Valery. You're an entire universe wrapped in an enchanting cloak of wondrous mysticism."

"Okay, that was fuckin sexy as hell. If you want to fuck me, you can. That last shit you just said, got my pussy gushin like a damn geyser, fuck. We get this first time outta the way, and then I'll paint that glorious dick you got swingin between your thighs." At first, he look like he's gonna take me up on my offer before he bends his fine ass over and laughs like the lunatic he is. When he comes up, he still laughin, but he grabs me around the waist, and I start laughin with his looney ass.

"Oh, gods. You're so fucking funny. Get your ass into the room. We got painting to do. But—" He pulls me into his arms. Holds my head between his clutchin hands and angles it the way he wants it before sayin, "Give me a filthy kiss."

Hell-fuckin-yes.

Collin seals his full lips over my fuller lips and sucks on them like he's between my thighs. Just light pulls that make my lower belly heat up like I drank some of John's Scotch. That thought makes me smile cause Collin is better than any bottle of Scotch John has in his office.

"What has you smiling, lass?" He whisper the sing-songy words across my puffy lips.

"Tell you later. Kiss me." He does. No more preamble. Just his thick, sweet tongue pushin through the seam of my lips. Make me wanna feel the thick, mushroom head of his cock push through another set of lips.

Shit, I want that to happen.

Our tongues slide against each other. Wet. Sweet and tart. My mouth is full of him. I moan in the back of my throat as I suck on his organ like I want to be suckin on his big, long dick. My thighs clench. A little growl scrambles up my throat and I sound like some kind of lioness bein fucked in the grasslands by the king of the mothafuckin jungle and his barbed dick.

Mmmmm, that's hot as hell.

Collin fucks my mouth like he gonna get a goddamn bonus for doin so. If his tongue was longer, his ass would be throat fuckin me with it. This is a filthy ass kiss. I crave it.

I don't know whose drool dribbles from the sides of my mouth, nor do I give a shit.

It's ours.

Everythin, we make while we're makin *us*, is ours.

We're slow to pull our mouths away from each other. When we do, a thick line of spit stretches between us like a dirty version of spaghetti noodle from Lady and the Tramp. It makes me smile and frown because I don't know where I know that story from, but I know I used to watch it.

Hmm, somethin to write about in Seekin Wonderland.

~16~

John

I've been absolutely worthless all day. I knew staying at home waiting for Valery and Collin to come stumbling through the door while hanging all over each other, would not end well for them, so I went to work. Dragging ass like I'd been working on somebody's chain-gang all night. Could be the soul-binding eroticism we found in our playroom.

Fuck, she was so open. She gave as good as she got.

It's after six, there's no reason to be in my office, but I can't seem to make myself get up from my chair.

No phone calls to make.

No goddamn meetings to take.

"Get your ass up, John. You promised Viv you'd be there for them." *Wait, did I just say that shit out loud?* Another look around my empty office before I collect my satchel and put on my coat. I'm in the hallway walking toward the elevators when my cell rings. I set this ringtone for one person. I wasn't hoping to hear from him so soon after our last conversation. *What's this fucker want, now?* I take the call, but I don't utter a goddamn word. I'm patient, but only when it serves my purpose.

"John?" I hold the line.

"Okay, sorry 'bout the lag. I'm lookin 'into some shit with The Order. Your name's all over some highly classified financial documents." I still haven't so much as taken an audible breath, I can't trust Cole.

"Fuck, John! Can you at least say somethin', brother? Lick them damn soup-coolers and let me know I ain't talkin 'to my damn self. Jesus-fuck, you sure know how to hold a motherfuckin 'grudge. Shit." His exasperation makes me smile, a little.

"Listening." That's as much as I'll give to him.

"Have you ever... a holdin 'company by ... name of Eme—Isles Holdin', Inc? list you. ... chief fin—cial ...ficer. ... an—ng. ... you?"

"Cole, send me the documents." I hang up the phone and get into the elevator. Even with Cole's call cutting out, I know exactly who owns that company and I also know I've never had anything to do with him or *that particular* company. This shit gets messier the further down the rabbit hole I go. "If you want to play," I mumble as the doors open on the garage level, "let's fucking play." My thoughts tumble around my brain like bingo balls. So many opportunities to win the jackpot, it all depends how the numbers fall.

I fucking hate the game of bingo.

***

"Hello! Is anyone here?" I'm hoping like hell that Val and Collin are out having a real date and will take their evening back to his place.

"John?" *No such luck.* I walk into the kitchen to find Collin's big, highlander ass standing in front of our stove with a fucking apron tied around his waist.

"Valery. Collin." It's all I can grit out between my teeth. I take a minute to look at her. She's wearing a pair of tight, low-rise jeans, a black long-sleeve turtleneck that looks like it's been painted onto her svelt torso. She's paired it with a long, fringed crochet vest. She stands beside him in her sock-feet and has her straight, black wig pulled up into a high ponytail with full bangs framing her angular face.

She looks so different; I can't even find my beautiful wife in the woman standing in front of me.

"Aye, John. We're just finishing up dinner. You welcome to join us." Valery cuts her whiskey-colored eyes over to Collin and I'm surprised his head doesn't burst into flames from the scathing look she gives him. I chuckle to myself.

"The fuck you laughin at, John?" *Okay, maybe not so much to myself, then.*

"You and that, I'll-kill-you-dead-look you just gave Collin." I snicker, again and hear Collin huff out a short laugh of his own. At least he knows his girl is bat-shit-crazy. "Don't worry, Val. I have no plans to impose on your evening. I'm going to get a shower, and get some work done in my office."

"Oh." Now she's looking at me like there's a giant dick sticking from my forehead.

"What, Valery?"

"Why you bein so goddamn chill about this shit? You plannin something, ain't you? Don't try to fuck this up for me, I know where your monkey-ass lay your goddamn head down at night, mothafucka."

"Did Vivian leave me something to eat in the fridge?" I don't entertain Val's crazy, and Collin seems impressed. Not that I care to impress his ass. He means as much to me as Valery does.

"Aye. Big glass container with your name on a sticky note. I can pop it in the oven for ye while ye go get cleaned up." I honestly have no fucking clue what he just said but I say thanks on my way up the stairs anyway.

"What the fuck Vivian do to his surly ass..."

"Maybe he's just coming round to the idea of us, baby."

"We betta lock the mothafuckin door, he gonna stab one of us. Either that, or he gonna cut that dick off before I get a chance to feel it inside me."

"Fuck, Val. Don't say shit like that when my dick's near an open flame."

I hear them laughing and kissing as I go into Lady Bea's room. She and her kittens are doing exceptionally well. I take care of the litter boxes, refill their food and water bowls, before sitting on the floor and playing with the five felines for a while.

"Vivian will be back tomorrow, girl." Bertha lets out a low deep purr, as I rub that special spot behind her ears. One of the kittens crawls over my ankle and chews on the toe of my fucking Brioni oxford. The little shit is so damn cute, I don't try to stop him. How anything can find so much contentment in chewing on a piece of goddamned leather, is beyond me.

"Hey, John..." I look up to find Val standing just inside the door looking at me like she's never seen me before.

"Hmm."

"Um, you good with Collin stayin over tonight, right?"

"Yes, why?"

"You not gonna stab him or some shit?" A bark of laughter tumbles from me that makes the little kitten run for protection under all that black and silver fur covering its mother's body.

"Hell no, Val. Look. I get it, okay. Just... be respectful. To the girls, the body, and my relationship with Viv."

"She threaten you didn't she?" Smiling—more to myself then at her—because what the fuck?

"No. We've been working on this shit for a while. I'm just glad you were patient. Gave me a chance to wrap my mind around you and him as a couple."

"Okay. So," She steps further into the room and Bertha hisses a little in her direction.

I fucking love this damn cat.

Val shoots our girl a stink eye and hisses back at her. "Calm your tits, you hairy ass pussy. Anyway, you good with this, then."

"Yes."

"Okay. Well, Collin put your food in the oven. We gonna eat in the dinin room and probably head up to bed. So."

"Good night, Val. Make sure you say your goodbyes to Collin before Vivian takes over."

"Of-fuckin-course. I don't want her uppity ass wakin up with my man any more than you do."

"Good to know. Oh, and Val—"

"Yep."

"If you don't feel safe or need me for any reason, I'll be in the downstairs master's."

"Okay." She's gone before I can get up from the floor. I don't think I've ever heard her so polite. Maybe Collin is good for her. *Hope I don't have to kill his ass.*

"All right, Lady Bea. I'll check on you before I turn in for the night. I'm going to shower and get some shit done in my office. Mommy will be back in the morning. She's taking a much-needed break from everything. Visiting with Auntie Vera." I leave the night light on for the cats and cross the hall to get myself sorted for the evening.

I stroll into the kitchen to find my baked ziti with broccoli and cauliflower sitting on the small island with a bottle of decanted Malbec, accompanied by a cabernet wine glass. *Nice.* I take what was left for me into my office and sit in my favorite Chesterfield, pour a healthy amount of wine, remove the top from my vegetable pasta and take a deep grateful inhale. "Well Viv. This isn't as bad as I thought it would be. I miss you, though. Love you, see you in the morning." I eat and drink while Nina Simone serenades me with *Don't Smoke in Bed* from the built-in speakers. *It's a good night.*

~17~

Valery

It feel like I ain't ever slept with a man before. I'm so fuckin nervous about havin Collin stay over with me tonight. I spent a good portion of the mornin cleanin my damn room. Changed the bedding. Organized my damn closets. Put away all my fuckin toys. We just finished eatin and now he's ready for bed. *Why the fuck I feel like a virgin?*

"You all right, Val?"

"Mmhmm. *You?*"

"Fine. Listen, I don't have expectations for tonight. I'm genuinely so fucking happy to be spending the night with you, sleeping beside you is more than I dared to dream."

"I don't know why I'm so fuckin nervous. It ain't like I'm Vera." I look into his howlin-at-the-moon eyes and feel a little better. Less unsure.

"Baby. How about we take a shower. Let me wash you and then we can go from there, okay."

"I want to fuck, Collin. But I don't want to be fucked over, you know?"

"Lass, I got you. Trust me to take care of you."

"You don't feel... weird?"

"Fuck no! Why would I?"

"Every other time I fucked; it was... wrong. The wrong reasons or the wrong goddamn person."

"And this time?"

"This time is," I look at Collin's face and my breath sticks to the inside of my lungs, like I'm sufferin from tuberculosis. I wet my lips and try again, "... is more. Means more to me. John, Vivian, even Vera's stupid-actin ass said to do what I want with you."

"That scares you, lass." He already know the answer. Why he makin me say it, kinda pisses me off. Before I can throw shit his way, he whispers against my neck. "I want to hear your thoughts, lass. Need to know you and I are on the same goddamned page."

"*You* mean more. We... what we do together. It all means more than all the shit I ever done." His whispered words become sweet, wet kisses along my jaw line. Goosebumps crawl all over my skin and turn me into a puddle of need and tightened belly.

"Come. Show me." That's it. Fire scorches up my spine and settles in my mind. I'm blazin with thoughts of Collin and me. Us, rollin around in my bed. His golden skin, rubbin against my darker mahogany hues. So fuckin sexy, the thought of it makes my pussy weep with arousal. I reach back with my right hand and grab him. The strength in his left hand pulls a goddamn whimper from my horny ass.

I hope he chokes me with that much strength.

"Let's go. No turnin back, Collin. Don't get up here and be a pussy when I tell you what the fuck I want from your cheeky ass." His laughter breaks the tension across my shoulders and reminds me how much goddamn fun we are together.

"Same goes for you, Valery. Don't back down when this monster cock is only seconds from impaling your luscious cunt."

"Shit, Collin. I almost came. Get your ass up these stairs. I got plans for that gorgeous face. Ooooh, and those big hands wrapped around my neck, yes Lord. I intend to be choked—one way or the other."

"Fuck, lass. I'm hard."

"Good. Because that's exactly how I want you, *lad*." We laugh all the way up the stairs and into my room.

The moment we shut the door to my room, I'm on Collin's ass like white on rice. He scoops me into his arms and carries me to my bed, only to drop me like a fuckin hot potato. I bounce onto my elbows and watch him stride over to lock the door. I'm damn near tearin my clothes, I'm so goddamned hot for this man.

"Why are you just standin there." I swear to goddamn Bob, Collin looks like he just sucked a demon up his ass and is bein ridden hard. No lube. I watch his chest rise and fall like he ran a marathon to get his cock in the same place as my pussy. "Dude."

"On your knees."

That's it. Three words. Three words and my panties are fuckin soaked. My lower lips are swollen and sensitive. I never felt this close to comin without havin someone or somethin touchin my clit before.

"On. Your. Fucking knees, baby."

I suck my bottom lip into my mouth and look up at him through my lashes. Slow—like a slug creepin across the back porch steps—I slide from my bed and land on the floor. I deepen the arch in my back, and crawl to him on my hands and knees.

Nina Simone's *I Put a Spell on You* bleeds into my room from wherever John is listenin to it. The filthy timbre of her voice makes my cunt tremble. Thousands of images of fingers playin my clit like the ones makin all them instruments fuckin whine, leaves me breathless.

Weak.

"I'm here, Collin. What you gonna do with me, now?" I refuse to straighten my ass up. If he want me to suck him off, he better figure out how to get that shit down my damn throat.

"I said, on yer knees; not yer fecking hands and knees, Valery."

Oh my, fuckin god. I barely know what the fuck he sayin, his Scottish accent is so damn thick. His voice is all whiskey and brimstone. Darkness. Filled with sin and the promise of reckonin. I obey him before I realize it.

" That's it. Better."

God, my own fuckin Scottish demon.

"Release me."

I'm shakin like this is the first time I'm ever seein a dick in my life.

Fuck, calm your ass down, Val.

Collin's jeans look like he picked them up at the local Goodwill, from the clearance rack. Light blue denim, army-green canvas sewn around the top where a normal waistband should be. The only special thing about these damn pants is the leather crotch currently cuppin his growin bulge. I have his belt buckle undone; I reach under the flap to pull his zipper teeth apart, but I only find a row of wooden buttons.

"What the fuck, Collin?" A strong hand around my throat makes me pay attention as he tips my head up by pushin his thumb under my quiverin chin. His eyes are liquid steel. They feed his thoughts into my mind like he speakin words from his scowlin mouth. Without sound, he tells me to get on with it and stop pussyfootin around before he snaps my goddamned neck.

I pull one side of his shit-kicker jeans, and the whole row of buttons fall apart: deliverin one monster of a cock.

Commando. Fuckin yes, I'll take that shit.

"It won't *sook* itself, lass."

I lick my dry lips before stickin my tongue in his weapin slit at the tip of his flared cockhead. The taste of peaches, beer, and Collin explode on my tongue and breaks the trance I been in. I pull the head into my mouth. All suction, no teeth or tongue. Just mouthin him like I'm suckin on my mamma's nipple. He's quiet. Testin me to see how hard I'm willin to work to hear the rumble of his pleasure like God's voice from the mountaintop.

Pretty fuckin hard, you bastard.

I keep my hands behind my back and let my neck do all the work. I take a deep breath in through my nose, hold on to that bitch and swallow Collin's gorgeous cock in one slick swallow.

"Mother. Fucker." The two words carve their way from his belly. Fire and ice bank behind the silver gaze focused on my spread lips as I rub my nose in his neatly shaved pubic hair. "Suck it, Val. Make me fecking come, lassie."

I do. I take a big swallow and let Collin feel his dick on the palm of his hand that's wrapped around my throat. It's like he's gettin a hand-job and a blowjob at the same time.

"Shit. Fuck. Jesus-fucking-Christ."

God, I love to hear him growlin and spewin all kinds of filth from his mouth. I gyrate my hips to the push and pull of my mouth on Collin's dick. I'm goin to come with nothin but him in my mouth.

"Mmhmm." I hum and take him all the way to the back of my throat. He keeps squirtin thick cream on my tongue. Sweet like condensed milk. Shit, but he tastes so fuckin good. I need him to goddamn come, already. Pullin almost all the way off, I lick the angry, purple head. Just lickin that bitch like my own personal ice cream cone. So much pre-cum dribbles from his tip, it's like the messiest frozen treat ever served.

"That's it, baby. Keep doing... that. Fuck, yes." Collin releases my throat and wraps his hands around my head. Holdin me just how he want me; my head tipped back a little and my mouth wide open with my tongue stickin out over my bottom lip. "Don't counter, aye? Keep that fucking mouth open for me, lassie. So fucking bonnie."

I nod my head, while he paints my face with his arousal. I'm so turned-on I know I'm gonna come when he does.

"Ready, Valery?"

The way he calls my name is a drug slidin through my veins.

He pushes the fat cockhead into my open mouth and keeps right on pushin until his groin is smashed against my face. I can't fuckin breathe. My nose is full of his scent and my throat is full of his goddamn shaft. Filthy, depraved words cut through the fog and white noise buzzin around in my oxygen deprived brain. I'm humpin the air like I'm ridin Collin's dick. Just when the black dots dance in my vision, he pulls my head back and wipes the drool from my mouth.

"Take a fucking breath, Val." I do and then he's right back in my throat. This time, he doesn't stay in there like he did before. No, this time, Collin is plungin in and out my mouth like he's punishin me. Like my throat owes him money.

"Take it, Val. Don't back away from me..."

His words are cut short because I scrape my teeth along his aggressive cock. Large fingers tighten around my head, pre-cum dribbles from his tip, and just when I think I can't take anymore; he announces. "Tha mi a'tighinn. I-I'm coming, Val. I'm a'tighinn!" I seal my lips around the base of his dick and suction that mothafucka like an industrial Hoover. He probably won't have a goddamned scrap of skin left on this bitch, but he'll sleep like a baby when I'm done with his ass. I suck a few more squirts of cum from his tight balls and swallow him down as a sacrament. So fuckin good for me. I wonder if bein baptized in Collin's jizz feels the same as findin salvation in church on Sunday mornin.

"You have a dirty fuckin mouth, Collin Duguid." I lick the corners of my own dirty mouth and meet his lazy gaze. He looks well and truly satisfied.

Why the hell does that make me happy?

"And you, bonnie girl, have a very *fuckable* mouth. And a very fuckable cunt and a decidedly fuckable asshole." He reaches down, hooks his hands under my arms and lifts me to my feet. My legs are a pincushion full of needles; some with only enough thread to sew a button back on and others with enough to mend a hole the size of a large bruise. He holds me to his chest until I get the feelin back in my lower half. The whole time, he's kissin and whisperin how much he appreciates me and my *fuckable mouth*. How he's gonna return the favor a hundred times over because he 'feckin loves watchin 'me come.

"Let's get you naked, lassie."

"Okay. Shower with me?"

"Of course, after I've fucked you seven ways to Sunday."

"No."

"*No?*"

"No. I want to shower with you and crawl into bed—naked and warm and sleepy—with you, and just be..."

"Let me guess, with me." He gifts me with a confused and beautiful smile. I know he's tryin to figure out what the fuck is goin on in my head. I'll tell him once we're clean and cozy under the covers.

Shit, I never had anyone stay the night with me.

***

Collin took his time undressin first me and then himself. Said he was goin to move in here just to use my shower. I know plenty of men who are willin to help me get filthy, but Collin is the only one to ever enjoy cleanin me up just as much. We laughed when he had to use my shampoo and conditioner because he forgot to bring his.

His corny, white ass had jokes. *So, if I use this shite tonight, will I wake up the morrow with a big ass afro?* I sprayed his simi hard dick with ice-cold water and watched it shrivel up like a cocktail wiener—if cocktail wieners were the size of foot-long state fair corndogs.

"Why don't you let me pleasure you, lassie?" I hear some of the insecurity in his voice. Fear that maybe I'm still weird about us fuckin because I share this body with other people.

"It's not that."

"It's not what, baby?"

"Not what you thinkin it is. It's not that. I can't wait to feel you slide into all my fuckable places, Collin," He chuckles, and his minty breath blows across my cheek, leavin his affection along its path. "I—re. Remember when I said what we do means..."

114

"More? Yes, of course I do, lassie."

"I don't have a lot of backstory, Collin. Not like Viv, Vera, and Valeria. At least, none that I can remember."

"I get that and it's the freedom from the confines of a history that makes you so goddamned amazing in every way that truly matters." I squeeze the arm he has wrapped around my middle. His left hand holds my right one like he has a mortgage on that bitch. It's comfortin.

"Only you can make the most fucked-up shit sound so goddamned sweet I develop sugar diabetes." I feel his smile against my neck because his scruffy cheek is pressed against it.

"It's not fucked-up. Tell me why, Val."

"I more than like you, Collin. It's more than lust. I want to discover who the fuck I am, and I want to do it with you. I have to believe it's more to me than my... my fuckable places." *Shit.* I barely get the words pass the thick lump of self-hatred sittin in my throat before the backs of my eyes start burnin.

Now for the fuckin waterworks.

"Baby." More tears coast across my nose into my other eye and down into my hair. *Fuck my fuckin goddamned fucked-up life.* "You are so much more than your *fuckable places*. If that's all you were to me, I'd want to fuck Vivian, and we both know that's not ever been a thought in my goddamn head."

"When you first met her stuck-up ass, you didn't want to fuck her? Collin, I'm callin bullshit. I know how goddamn sexy and beautiful that haughty bitch is." His body shakes as he squeezes me tighter and kicks out a little laugh.

"Okay, I'll admit it, but fuck, Valery. Don't go getting yourself all out of sorts over what I'm about to say and for the love of art, don't go telling Vivian or John—especially John's cave-man ass—any of it." Now I'm laughin at his scary ass. How can he be a mountain sized man and still be afraid of Viv's skinny ass.

"I'm listenin, Scottie." My tears dry up as fast as they came. *We must be gettin ready to get our fuckin period. I'm stayin my black ass in the house for the next week.*

"Where'd you go?"

"Just thinkin maybe we're gettin ready to start our period. I'm all over the place. So, tell me how bad you wanted to fuck Vivian's..."

"What the hell did I just hear you say, Valery?" John's voice shakes the hinges on the door or maybe it was his fist.

Oh, deliver me from saggy tits. It's John.

Collin jumps up from the bed with his dick hangin out, his wild-man hair swingin all around his head, and those sexy ass tattoos on full display. Not to mention that damn Prince Albert piercin twinklin on his big dong.

"Collin," I giggle-whisper-yell at him. "What the hell? Get your naked ass back to bed." But I'm too late. Collin pulls the bedroom door open to an unimpressed, six-four, two-hundred-twenty-five pounds of pissed-off Black man, holdin a cup of tea and Vivian's sleepin bonnet and her pillow. *Poor bastard.*

"John! I didn't know you would be walking by. Val and I were talking about..." Every word sounds like Collin has never spoken American English in his life.

I can't catch my breath as I replay his heavily Scottish accented words in my mind. *Au don't knoo yood bee wookin by.* Oh, my fuckin god.

"What the hell did you just say, and why is Valery losing her damn mind? You two aren't doing drugs in here, I know." The vein in the middle of John's forehead pulses with every quick beat of his heart; I hope he don't stroke out or some shit like that.

"Feck, no! John. Please calm your tits, man."

"*Calm my fucking tits*? Get your clothes on and get the hell outta my damn house, you overgrown-highlander-motherfu—."

"I'm not goin 'to be too many more of them highlanders, John. Nobody was sayin 'anythin 'disrespectful about your wife. And Val," Collin looks over his shoulder to find me rollin around under the covers, screechin and cacklin like a wild hyena. And that's when I see the first crack. It starts in his eyes. Then a small twitch of his mouth. Then all hell breaks loose. "Man, John..." Laughs and hoots and yells pour from us. Collin's dick is bouncin all over the place and he still can't stop. I point at it and pull the covers over my mouth to stifle my own laughter. When Collin realizes what I'm pointin at, he crumples to the floor in a pile of demented joy.

"I'm going downstairs; I don't care what you two do, keep Vivian's name out of your conversations." I hear the reluctant smile in John's voice, and I have to sprint from my bed to the bathroom before I piss myself.

"Get it right, Valery. Don't piss the sheets, lassie." Collin calls after me and I barely make it on the toilet. Still snickerin and feelin so goddamn happy I don't think I'll ever feel any other way. I hear the door close, and the lock clicks into place.

I'm dryin my hands and pattin my face dry when Collin steps into the bathroom. He lifts the toilet seat, takes a loud piss, shakes himself dry and comes to stand beside me at the vanity. His six-five, lean muscled body covered in golden skin, tattoos, and just the right amount of well-groomed pubes to make me come when I rub against his pubic bone.

Me; five-nine, big titties, little waist, big ass—that's how I see myself when I look in the mirror. My skin glows in the soft light of the bathroom. Gold and mahogany create such a harmonious portrait, I wonder what we'd look like on canvas.

———

"I did fancy a shag with her when I first saw her, but after that first meal," He's whisperin in my ear like he's tellin all of his country's military secrets. It's quiet. Cocooned in this crazy ass bubble where only Collin and Valery exist. Warm, wet, and safe. "... I don't see her as anythin 'other than a great woman, an amazing gallery owner and hopefully a good friend." He licks the shell of my ear and kisses my temple.

"And what about..."

"The first time I saw you?" I lock eyes with him in the mirror and nod my head. "The first goddamn time I laid eyes on you, was on a six foot canvas and my eyes welled up with tears. It felt like somebody had shot me in the center of my chest, Valery."

I shake my head because I don't. I can't let my stupid heart believe him.

He reads me like a book. "You think I'm lying to ye? Ask Vivian what my reaction was to your self-portrait, then. It wasn't even close to being finished, and still," He turns me around to face him.

Now, we can't hide from each other's eyes. I don't think it's ever been so fuckin quiet in the house. This feels like confessional. Like after he says this thing, every part of us will be changed. Different. *Whole?*

He breaks the silence and admits, "I said to Vivian—while still gawking at your painting—I'm gonna marry this woman. Whoever the fuck she is, I'm going to marry her and fill her with my babies."

"Collin." He kiss me with soft lips and light suction. Just enough to remind me that I ain't come tonight, but not enough to distract me from sayin what I'm almost too chicken-shit to say. "I don't know what love feels like," He tries to interrupt me, but I shake my head before he can. I'm squeezin his hands like I'm pushin one of them babies he wants to put inside me, out. "I only know what hurt, fear, and wantin feel like." I watch emotion collect in his eyes and then it's fallin over his high cheekbones.

Baby, your eyes are Mercury in retrograde. I can't believe you look at me and find any kind of beauty.

I tell him, "And I know it'll hurt me—heart and fuckin soul—if we don't make this work between us. I know I'm gonna wake up in the middle of the night screamin and cryin because I'm so goddamned scared you're not real... and we don't really feel what we say we feel for each other." I let my own tears stain my warm cheeks. We're two contradictions revealin a universal truth. I sniff and finish, "Most of all, I know that I will never want nobody, or no things more than I want you to..."

"I fucking love you, Val. So goddamn much it makes sense that what you feel for me hurts you. Scares the living shit outta you. And leaves you wanting more and more of that feeling."

"I love—no, that's not the right word—it feels bigger and heavier but still so light I can carry it everywhere I go. You know what I mean?" I search my brain for better words, smart words. But the only thing that comes to mind make me cringe. I can't sing for shit, but I open my mouth and belt out, "You giving me a heart attack, but it's the kind I like." I sing the worse lyrics ever sung in a damn song. But they somehow express perfectly what I feel for this man.

"What the ever-loving-fuck? *Cameo*, Valery? You hate that red-plastic-codpiece-wearing freak!" We burst into tearful laughter. *Maybe love is a heart attack.*

~18~

Vivian

The reason for her flight landing at butt-crack-o'clock is well above my pay grade, and it's too early to ask anyone who makes enough to answer the question. Sitting in the baggage claim area at the CAE airport at four-thirty on a Friday morning is not how I wanted to start my weekend. At least I had all day Tuesday and a good chunk of Wednesday inside the Internal House. It's always refreshing to take time away from the busy hum-drum of living. I think this *co-pussy-custody* plan is going to work out well for everyone involved.

"Flight A234 from Chili by way of Atlanta, GA head to the baggage claim to await your luggage. Welcome to Columbia, South Carolina. Home of smiling faces and beautiful places. Enjoy your stay." The disembodied voice pulls me away from my thoughts.

Finally, it's about damn time. I stand from the most uncomfortable chair ever created and amble over to the large crowd of gathering people who look as unhappy to be awake at four-thirty in the morning as I am. I lift my large white cardboard placard with CAMILLA (MILLA) FAZZINI written in bold black letters.

After ten or fifteen minutes, I see a petite, olive skinned woman with a pile of dirty-blonde and golden waves twisted into a top-knot on her head. Black leggings, black turtleneck sweater, black boots, and an oversized orange and cream jacket completes her ensemble. She turns toward me and a devastating smile breaks across her wind burned face. I return her smile and wave the cardboard around like an idiot.

"¡Hola chica! Me alegro de que lo hayas hecho de una sola pieza." She throws herself at me and I'm forced to drop the cardboard or be knocked over by this tiny ball of energy. I return her hug and laugh at her childlike exuberance.

"Hi." Milla practically screams as she disentangles herself from me and pushes the long whisps of hair away from her face, only to have them flop back where they were before the effort. "I'm so happy to see friendly face. You come alone, no?" I'm enchanted by the way her accent curls around the basic English words, painting them in soft notes of blush rose and buttery yellow.

"Yes, I'm alone. My husband is actually out of town on business—some sort of emergency—and won't be back until Sunday. Which bodes well for you because your apartment isn't ready until Monday after twelve, noon. So, if you don't mind, you'll be staying with me and Bertha until then." We walk over to the luggage wheel of doom and wait for her bags to be regurgitated from the bowels of wherever they store luggage while people fly.

"I didn't know you spoke English, Milla. If I did, I would've been speaking it with you." I slide my eyes over to see what her face may give away and find a little devil glinting in her dark gray gaze. The slight frown of her smiling mouth lends an odd sense of irony to her expression.

"No. I never tell you I speak English. Mostly, I want to see if you speak Spanish for real or just enough to hold basic conversation." She cracks an unapologetic smile and reaches down to grab two extra-large army duffels with pink and cranberry polka-dot-ribbon bows tied to the handles.

As she lifts them from the metal surface, jingle-bells ring so loud, the couple next to us start at the sound. "This way, no one take my luggage. I put big bells and bright ribbon to identify my shit." She shakes her head as if someone had asked her why the hell she did what she did. Seemingly pleased with her explanation, she turns away from the spinning luggage and strides back in the direction she saw me standing, like she's been to this airport a hundred times.

"Camilla!" I start to jog to catch up with her turbo-charged little legs before asking, "Do you know where you're going?" Finally, she stops, drops her bags, and turns around to look up at me with such a befuddled look on her face, I burst into loud peals of laughter. I hear her join in my madness and I know people are wary of two women finding joy within each other... and in the middle of baggage claim, no less. This is post 911; I know we need to get our giddy asses out of here and head to my house.

"Dio, mio. I don't have any idea of where to go. It's so early. Most of my brain is back home and what is here, is hungover from the drinks I had on the plane."

I shake my head and take a good look at her. Sure enough, her lids are heavy and low, little red capillaries form delicate lace patterns across her nose and in the whites of her eyes.

Who the hell gets drunk on a flight to meet their new employer?

I bend down to lift one of her bags before I say, "Come on, chica. Let's get you to a warm bath and a warmer bed."

"Gracias. I'm sleepy and I think my period is coming. Dio, I'm a whole hot mess." She chuffs out a little laugh before picking up her other bag to follow me out of the airport. "You know, Vivian." I turn my head over my shoulder to look down at her struggling behind me and wait for her to finish. "You are one tall bitch. How tall..." Her bag drops from her small hands and she almost face-plants as she trips over the cumbersome thing. *Get a damn suitcase.*

"Camilla, please get yourself together. I'm all for having a good laugh, but this falling down drunk business is not a good look for you." I chide and disappointment drips into my eyes.

She lifts her head up to see my face and whatever look I'm wearing; makes her pick her butt up from the floor. She grabs her bag and starts moving with a purpose.

It's either too late or too early for this nonsense.

"I'm so embarrassed. I'm afraid to fly and need something to take the edge away." I don't respond. If she remembers this excuse in the morning when she's sober, then we can talk about it. Until then, I'm going with what she chose to show me about herself. I learned a long time ago when folk show you who they are, it's in your best interest to believe them. Usually, that's the only truth you'll get from them.

"Come on, Camilla. It's cold and I'm tired. My car is parked out front." After that, I don't say another word to my new artist-in-residence. Not when we place her bags into the trunk. Not when we're driving back across twenty-six to get to my house. Not even when I show her to her room and around the kitchen.

After I make sure John's office is locked, I go upstairs and check on Bea and her brood. They're all tucked in for the night... *morning?* I don't even know what time it is. All I know is I will send her drunk ass back to Chili if this is going to be a problem. John didn't want any drunk ass babies running around and I don't want any drunk ass artists running around, either. The thought brings an ache to the middle of my chest for the two little souls who tried it and found this life lacking. "Maybe next lifetime." I mumble to myself as I take off my winter gear and climb into bed.

Before long, I feel the bed depress with a weight too light to be John. *If this little drunk woman is crawling in my bed...* I look over my shoulder to see my girl, Bertha, laying where John usually rest his head. "Did you need a break from your four kittens, Lady Bea?" I ask as I turn over and run my hand over her large head. She purrs so deep; it sounds like a lion cub. With a quick nibble to my wrist and a lick to my palm; she stands, turns around about four times, and lays down to make biscuits on John's pillow before dozing off to sleep. "I wish your daddy were home, girlie. I miss him and can't help wondering what he and Cole are up to."

Take your silly ass to sleep. Your thinkin is wakin me up and I don't give a fuck what John and Cole is up to. But they probably fuckin each other up the ass as we speak.

"Valery! Why would you say something like that?"

Because you already thinkin that shit. I'm just bold enough to give voice to it, bitch. Now take your goofy ass to sleep. I want to be well-rested before I meet Ms. Thing in the mornin.

"This is not a confrontation, Val. Calm your tits."

Have you seen my mothafuckin tits, Viv? These shits don't ever calm they asses down, ask Collin how excited these girls get for him.

"No. I will not ask him anything and I don't want *you* to tell me anything. I don't tell you what John and I do, so have the same courtesy for me, please."

See, I don't care if you told me every fuckin thing John did to your stuck up ass. I'll probably use it in my spank-bank to get myself off. You don't want to know about the fuckery me and Collin get up to 'cause you scared he a better fuck than John.

"Are you out of your mind, Valery? You know what, don't answer that. Just go back to bed."

I been with John and Harry. And now, I'm with Collin. I can tell you who the best fuck is of the three. You wanna know?

"Not really. *No?*"

But you ain't gonna stop me if I tell you, right?

"I can't control what comes out of your mouth, Valery."

I hate to say it, Viv, but—

"But... what?"

John still the best fuck I ever had. So, you don't have to worry about what you might be missin out on. If you want some deposits for your own spank-bank, I'll be happy to tell you all about the way Collin like to eat my asshole out.

I bark out a laugh and forgive myself for wanting to know what kind of lover Collin is. That man is beautiful and looks like he might be dominant in the bedroom. That's really what I want to know. So, I ask, "Val, is Collin a Dominant... with a capital 'D'?"

What the fuck would I be doin with a man who couldn't dominate my ass when we fuckin? Hell yes, he so cold, Viv. I can't get enough of the way his voice drop so low down into the earth, it sound like he got gravel in his throat. Sometime he sound more a part of nature than humanity. So fuckin sexy when he turn feral and lose control. Said, he was gonna be the one to finally tame me. I laugh at him, but you know what, Viv?

"What?"

I think he already got my ass under his control, and we ain't even fuck, yet.

"I thought you guys had sex on Tuesday night. John said Collin answered the door butt-ass-naked and when you ran from the bed to pee, you were naked too."

Yeah, we was naked. We both prefer to sleep that way. I wasn't bout to change my sleepin habits because his fine ass was sleepin over. But no. We didn't fuck. I gave him the blowjob to end all blowjobs and he removed everybody's touch from me with his mouth. Fuckin worshiped my pussy, ass, and breasts. But he worshiped everything in between, too. So fuckin good, Viv.

"This is the first time we've been able to talk about our guys with each other. Is it weird?."

And here you go, fuckin shit up with your bullshit Kum-by-yah nonsense. I'm goin to bed. Night, whore.

"Night, Val." I feel her move into her room. Laying back down, I notice Lady Bertha is fast asleep. I smile at the turn of events and find my comfort in the dark abyss of slumber.

~19~

John

"It's me, lovely." I whisper in her ear as I crawl into bed behind her. She's all sleep rumpled and warm and just what I need to forget about the clusterfuck of meetings I've been in.

"*John?*"

"Better be." Her soft chuckle feels like my grandma's cornbread dressing and collard greens, the day after Thanksgiving.

"John," She turns over to face me before asking, "what are you doing home, it's... wait, is it Saturday?"

"It is. What time did you get back after dropping your artist off at the hotel?" I lean in and kiss her forehead, letting my lips linger while I take in her sweet jasmine scent.

"Um, about that."

Vivian pulls herself up to sitting before turning her head to face me.

"What do you mean... um, about that? Did she not show up or something?"

"No, she showed up. I just... since you were going to be away until Sunday, I thought it would be good to have her stay the weekend—" Her husky morning voice trails off and I already know the next words I hear are going to piss me off. "Here."

"She's here. In our home. Right now?"

"Yes. She was pissy drunk this morning when I collected her from the airport."

"But you'd already planned for her to stay the weekend here."

"Yes, but the fact that she was drunk, made it more important that I didn't leave her on her own."

"When will her apartment be ready?"

126

"Monday."

"Did you say, Monday?"

"After twelve."

"Do you have any idea of the shit Cole and I have to work through this weekend, Viv?"

"No, and I thought you guys were going to work it out away from *our* home."

"We were. I mean, we are but we needed to get the hell out of there..."

"Out of where?"

"Don't worry about it, Viv. This shit is on a need-to-know basis."

"Meaning?"

"Meaning, you don't need to know shit about what's going on. Now leave it alone."

"I will not leave it alone. Not when whatever is going on had me running into our panic room because armed men broke into my home, John. I will not goddamn leave it alone."

"Vivian."

"John."

"Later. I promise. We'll discuss it later. I just wanted to crawl into bed with you this morning. Hold you a minute before showering and heading back out."

"Back out... where; with Cole?"

"Yes and don't worry about where."

"But John. I need to kno—"

"Shhh, it's for your own protection. Trust me, lovely. Please."

"Are you in danger?"

"A little, but nothing I can't handle."

"John, you're not some Rambo-traipsing-through-the-jungle-special-ops jarhead, what do you mean it's," She lowers her voice to imitate my deeper register before repeating, *"nothing you can't handle?"*

"Lovely, trust me. I'm not going to let anything happen to you and in order to do that, I can't let anything happen to me either. Now, come here." I open my arms to invite her to slide across the bed and snuggle into my embrace. The moment she rests her head on my chest, the tension that's been riding me like the boo-hag, melts away into nothing. I feel her soft sigh and realize she needs this as much as I do.

"Baby, I need us to be easy with each other." Viv wraps her right arm across my belly, her hand snakes up and she caresses my beard. It feels so good, I damn-near fall asleep. "John?"

"Mmhmm,"

"Baby, I—"

"I heard you. Just. Let's be easy like Sunday mornings. Please, lovely. I need this."

"Okay." She reaches up and blesses me with the soft press of her lips on the underside of my jaw before whispering, "I trust you and it's okay."

***

Turns out being easy was exactly what Viv and I needed to start this Saturday off. After a few minutes of quiet cuddles—Viv's words, not mine—we got our asses up, showered, dressed, and went downstairs. Vivian's artist was still asleep, which was good for me. I wasn't in the right frame of mind to entertain anyone, especially a temperamental, hungover artist.

"Hey, Viv?"

"Hmm."

"Are you sure it's a good time to bring the whelping box and kittens down?"

"Yes. Bertha came into our room this morning. She's tired of being sequestered and the kittens need more room to run around before they leave."

"How many are we keeping, again?"

"Just the one, why?"

"Just asking. The owner of the king..."

"He receives one and we sell the other two."

"You're not putting Bea through this shit again, are you?"

"No. She's already scheduled to be spayed. I can't believe how much you've come to love her. The first time you met her, you told me she had to go, now you dote on my cat as much as I do." I hear the smile in her voice, it makes me shake my head because she's not even exaggerating.

"*Our* cat, Vivian. Lady Bertha belongs to both of us,"

"Fine, our cat. So, are you planning to tell me what you and Cole were doing?"

"Speaking of Cole, did I ever tell you Cole had a twin sister?"

"No."

"Yeah, his sister looks more like their mother and Cole takes after his *f-father*."

"Okay, and you're telling me this... why?"

"Cole has been working with the FBI to bring down The Order, who was planning to set me up for laundering mob money because I'm the only one who hasn't taken part in their illegal dealings." Vivian had been moving around the kitchen until I said the last couple of words.

"I couldn't have heard correctly, John?"

"Yeah, Cole came to my office a few weeks ago. He started telling me a bunch of shit about Earl,"

"Your mom's husband?"

" Stop interrupting me and let me finish. Yes. He wouldn't shut up about how he *tapped* me to be in The Order because he was a legacy."

"John, if you're trying to confuse me so I'll stop asking questions, you're doing a hell of a job. I don't know what you're talking about."

"Listen, Viv. I'm not trying to confuse you—hell, I'm more confused than I was before all this shit started. I haven't been able to make heads or tails of the intel I've received, but what I can tell you is that you are never to be alone with Cole. You see his ass, turn in the other direction. Oh, and you now have a security detail."

"What?! John, I—"

"No, Vivian. I'm not taking any chances with you. You and the girls will have security detail. You won't even notice they're around. I pay them to be invisible."

"Why are you helping him if you don't trust him?"

"What?"

"If you can't trust Cole, then why continue to work with him?"

"Keep your enemies closer..."

She walks over to where I stand at the double French doors, looks out over the backyard and wraps her arms around my middle. On her tip-toes, she gives me a soft kiss on the back of my neck and lays her head between my shoulder blades. When she holds me, it's better than any drug available on the market to reduce my anxiety.

"I don't like you playing James Bond."

"Fuck James Bond. Who the hell wants to be some uptight, British dude, when I can fucking be Isaac Hayes. Living on blood money and borrowed time as, *Big Mack Truck Turner*?" Her soft laughter makes me smile. She doesn't need to worry about any of this shit. *I'm not the one in danger.*

"John?"

Like a damn dog with a bone. She should have been an investigative reporter.

"Lovely. I'm good. I would never do anything that would place me in jeopardy. I'm too fucking jealous to leave your fine ass here for someone else to make a move on." I turn around and drop my mouth onto hers. It's a slow, deliberate kiss. Light suction and soft nibbles. She's so goddamned beautiful, my chest hurts.

"Kiss me, like you live and breathe for me."

"I do," I whisper into her mouth before licking the seam between her pillowy lips. "I live for your smiles." Kiss. "Your laughter." Swipe of my tongue across her bottom lip. "Your sweet, fearless heart." I move to her high cheekbone. "I live for your beautiful summer-sunshine eyes, when they go soft and dreamy as I push into that sacred space between your thighs." I kiss both her eyelids. "I live in you. Because of you." I rub my lips against hers, just feeling their softness. She gives me a low whimper that makes me want to possess her in every way.

"I need more, please."

"Anything you want, lovely." I seal my lips over hers and push my tongue into the wet heat of her mouth. Kissing her is akin to sitting on the front porch eating watermelon while watching the sky crack and flash its fury, leaving electricity skittering over my skin from its residual rage. Viv feeds her tongue into my mouth, licking my gums and teeth and the inside of my cheeks. Like she wants to crawl into my body and fuse our beings together. "Fuck, lovely." I delve back into the heaven of our kiss and things go from sweet and loving to carnal and savage in zero-point-two seconds.

We eat at each other's mouths with needy nibbles that make me hard as stone. Viv's nipples are furled pebbles against my chest, I can smell how wet she is right now. I want to strip her ass naked, and tongue-fuck her until she floods my mouth with her release.

131

"Hmmm, baby. John. I need..." She dives right back in and sucks on my tongue, I feel it along the length of my cock.

Holy hell, how'd we get here.

I'm grinding my groin against her belly, the tip dribbles pre-cum in a steady stream. Staining my goddamn pants and her shirt. I grab the back of Vivian's right thigh and rest it on my hip, to get closer to the heat radiating from her wet center. Grinding my erection against the warmth of her soaked pussy is a fantasy I never even knew I had, I want more.

"Lovely," I don't recognize the desperate ache riding roughshod over my words, but Vivian must like how it sounds. She digs her nails into my neck and meets my thrust with sensual rolls of her hips. "Baby, I'm going to fuck you in our kitchen if you... shit—"

"I did not know I got sexy performance for breakfast. Please don't stop, I'm so close..."

We pull away from each other. We're both breathing hard. I right Viv's clothes and she does the same for me. I watch as the combustible passion morphs into thermonuclear indignation on my wife's lovely face. Her swollen lips are in a straight, tight line. Solar storms flare in her eyes, and I feel sorry for the little Chilean artist standing behind us.

"Camilla." Vivian's voice is a flame of rational insanity. The sound causes jughead to flex, needing to get closer to its intensity. I turn away from the interloper to shove myself back into my pants. I pull my shirt down a little.

Camilla's going to have to take her ass to a goddamn hotel.

"Buenos días, Vivian. Cuando el marido no está, la mujer juega." (Good morning, Vivian. When the husband is away, the wife will play.) Camilla teases Vivian like that shit is funny and acceptable.

What the fuck is wrong with this woman?

"El único hombre con el que Vivian jugará alguna vez, Camilla, es su maldito marido. Jonathan Ellis." (The only man Vivian will ever play with is her fucking husband. Jonathan Ellis.) Her eyes are saucers with cracked cups. Large, dark gray orbs filled with fear and surprise. The flicker of excitement reveals her deviancy. "You didn't think Vivian was the only one who spoke Spanish, did you?"

"¡Mierda!" Camilla exclaims.

I kiss Viv on her temple and whisper a filthy promise in her ear that causes her to squeeze my forearm for balance.

Passing by our weekend cock-blocker on the way to my office, I extend my right hand to shake hers. As soon as she wraps her small hand around mine, I mumble under my breath, but loud enough for her to hear me. "Si no hubieras interrumpido, estos dedos estarían mojados con el jugo del coño de Vivian." (If you hadn't interrupted, these fingers would be wet with Vivian's pussy juice.) She pulled her hands from my clasp like she could feel Viv's essence on my fingers. I throw a dirty smile over my shoulder and my wife looks bemused and a little horrified.

"Camilla. It would've been nice if you announced yourself. We're not used to having people... and don't mind my husband. He's—"

"Fucking filthy. Lucky for you."

"I'm in my office, lovely. Cole's coming over at eleven. I'll let him in."

"We're not done—t"

"Tongue fucking? No, we most certainly are not." I swagger back to my office and hear Vivian's unimpressed tones as she tells Camilla what a jackass I am. It's fine, I'll be a jackass as long as Vivian is my jenny. The thought makes me smile because Vivian would kick my ass if I called her, a fucking *jenny*. The last thing I hear is the little artist telling my wife how hot I am.

"¡Ay Dios mío! Es tan sexy, Vivian." (Oh, my God! He's so hot, Vivian."

~20~

Vivian

Camilla stumbles toward my kitchen still wearing the clothes she slept in. I stop her before she enters with a little smile and a lot of where-do-you-think-you're-going-with-that-dirty-face energy.

"Good morning, Milla. It's good to see you mostly upright," I deadpan. "... so, have you washed up from your flight?" She scrunches up her nose and looks up at my face like I'm the one who smells like two days of travel, and a distillery.

"No, chica. Primero necesito café y luego me limpiaré." (No, girl. First I need coffee and then I'll clean myself.) She tries to step around me, and I widen my stance. She huffs out a breath that fries the fine hairs inside my nose before asking, "What fuck, hueon?" I have no idea what the last word means, but I get the gist of her thickly accented, *what fuck*.

"Look, I don't know what your morning routine looks like when you're in your place. But in my home, no one steps foot in my kitchen wearing what they slept in. And certainly not with a dirty face. Her bleary eyes scratch across my body, slicing through skin and fat and muscle seeking entry into my brain. The gray is all but washed out in the sea of red and coffee-stained white. Whatever she needed to see, she must have glimpsed it because her noticeably cooler with a lot more edge.

"¿Hablai en serio, Vivian? Pásame la wea? Mierda." (Are you serious, Vivian? Pass me that.) She lifts her rounded chin towards the coffee station with a disgruntled sniff and flounces back into the hallway, the rank scent of travel and embarrassment wrap around her like a shroud of righteous indignation. I look where she just stood, the ghostly imprint of the woman I all but begged to come in as artist in residence in my gallery, and I am disparaged by her broken energy.

After I fix her coffee, I straighten my shoulders, lift my chin and walk over to where she stands with her arms folded over her flat chest. Her pinched mouth, a puckered sneer, droops a little at the corners. She lifts dark gray eyes once she realizes I'm in front of her.

"Camilla."

"Sugar?"

"Yes."

"Bacán." She takes the large mug between her doll-like hands and inhales so deep; it looks like she's getting high.

"What does that... *bacán*, mean?"

"Chileno... how you say, modismo... sl-ang. Slang. It means, cool or whatever."

I nod my head and debate my next words to her. Before I figure out what I want to say, she speaks.

"You are rude to house guests."

I flinch a little, but don't defend myself.

She continues, "Apology would be nice, cachai?"

"Camilla, I'll admit my delivery was less than hospitable but that's as far as I will go. You don't know my husband, and you bounce into my kitchen wearing almost nothing..."

"You said he was away. I would never do. I don't want him."

"You're right, I did say he'd be away, and I know you're not interested in John. I apologize for the way I spoke to you and how I—treated you about entering my kitchen." I give her a cursory look and admit, "I'm not used to having people in our space. I'm protective of it and the energy we cultivate h..."

"You could've take me to a hotel. I don't need to be a guest, Vivian."

"At five-thirty in the morning, you wanted me to drive you around Columbia, and get you situated in a hotel? If you had kept the flight plans I made for you, you wouldn't be here before your apartment was ready." I try and fail to keep the ire from my voice.

"I had to—" Her voice trails off and she looks down into the mug of black coffee as if it will give her good news about her future.

"You had to, *what*?"

"Nada. No lo sé... (Nothing. I don't know...) She trails off and takes the first sip of the bittersweet liquid. Her eyes are so damn sad and confused. Mist of sorrow and cracks of fear turn into a bleak winter storm. It plays out so perfectly in her expressive eyes.

Artist are the only people I will ever trust to tell the world what's really happening. There is a part of them that stays connected to the divine creative energy; that part is powerful enough to keep them from lying or pretending or trying to fit in. I make a mental note to journal about artists and integrity before asking, "What's going on, Camilla? I can't help you if I don't know?"

"It's." She scrubs the big toe on her right foot into the hardwood floor as she mumbles, "It's nothing to worry with. I'm such a mess. But it won't affect my work with..."

"Go get cleaned up," I interrupt her with a smile in my voice and tell her, "I'll make us breakfast. Oh, and give me that nasty coffee. I'll a make a fresh pot of the good stuff and we can sit and ease into this cold Saturday morning." I give her a smile as she places the warm ceramic cup into my outstretched hands, before turning and walking back down the hall.

****

I knock on John's office door just in case he let Cole in through the outside entryway.

"Come in, lovely." I plaster a smile on my face to hide the leftover confusing sense of worry from earlier about Camilla. I don't need John going all caveman-save-my-woman on the poor girl. *Something has her frazzled.*

136

"Hey, baby. I brought you some fresh coffee and a warm breakfast." I walk inside his sanctuary. I don't see Cole, so I guess he hasn't shown up, yet. After placing his food and coffee on the table in front of his Chesterfield, I walk over to where he stands by the window and wrap my arms around the solidity of his body.

"Hmmm. What's this for?"

"Nothing. Just wanted to be close to you for a minute."

"Everything all right, lovely?" In four words, he conveys he knows something has happened and that something upset me. *So perceptive.*

"Yes. It's fine. Any idea what time Cole will be coming over?"

"*It* may be fine, but how is my wife doing?"

"I'm fine. *Cole?*"

"Why are you so concerned with Cole, Vivian?" I smirk into his neck, knowing he'll hear it in my voice.

"Put your little cave-man back into his cave. I just wanted to know if I needed to keep breakfast warming or just leave it out."

"Oh."

"Yes, oh. His—your *little* cave-man—services are not needed this morning."

"First of all, my cave-man is not *little*. Secondly, his services are always needed when he has a woman who looks like you."

"Awwww, baby. That's sweet in a weird, cave-manish kind of way."

He tightens his arms around me and breathes me in. I know we're both wearing happy grins, and it dawns on me how in sync we've become.

"Viv?"

"Yes, John."

"Are you sure everything's all right?"

137

"Give me another kiss like the one you gave me earlier, and it will be." He steps back just enough to lift my face and capture my lips in a searing kiss. A warm, firm mouth presses into my own. He nibbles at my bottom lip for a few seconds before licking the seam. I open for him; he wastes no time dipping his tongue into me. John wraps his hand around the back of my neck and pulls me in. My hands curl into his sweater as I clamor to get closer to him. Always closer.

"Fuck, Vivian. I'm right back where I was this morning." He speaks against my open mouth. Licking my lips and tongue; feeding me his words.

"Where is that?" My whispered breaths and hot tongue caress his working mouth.

"Hard as fuck and needing inside your wet cunt for a few hours, lovely."

After that, there's no more talking. Only the fluid glide of our mouths against one another. The slide of our tongues as we imbibe our combined flavor. Our teeth wage war with clicks, scrapes and heavy knocks. We're back to groping clothed body parts like horny teenagers; dry-fucking our commitment to our passion into this undying moment.

He's an ebony obelisk.

I'm a seething hot spring.

The collective energy is a living, powerful presence; it wraps around us like bronze armor. Its masculine energy is a protective insulation for the erotic energy battering our resistance... making it almost impossible to stay dressed and separate.

"We can't, John." I half-heartedly protest.

"Why the fuck can't we, Viv?"

"Because—" Just then, the doorbell rings and John bites my bottom lip. Hard. I smile and finish my thought. "... Cole is here, and my artist is a whole-hot-ass-mess."

He pecks me on my forehead before licking the drop of blood he drew with his nip, and whispers against my temple, "Raincheck."

"Of course. You'll get the door?"

"Yes, I told that fucker to come around to the side door."

"You know Cole... I guess this makes sense to him."

"I'll walk you out. If you need some help with the drunk girl, holler. You know you're always my first priority." We breach the threshold and step into the hallway, where we find a showered and dressed Camilla just leaving her room.

"Good morning. I'm ashamed... about earlier. I'm not usually so fucked in the head, never with the likes of Vivian." Red creeps up her neck but doesn't make it further than that. John doesn't respond, just kisses me on my left temple as the doorbell trills again.

"If you need me—for anything, lovely—you know where to find me."

"I'll bring you guys some lunch a little later."

"Thanks." And then he's off to collect Cole and get into whatever they have going on.

~21~

Vivian

I pass Milla as I walk into the kitchen, I'm not sure if she follows me and most of me doesn't care. She pissed me off earlier; I didn't handle it well. It is what it is. Artists. So damn temperamental.

Hey, Vivian, that artist here, yeah?

"Yes, why?"

Just asking. Um...

"What, Vera?"

What she like? I mean, she nice, yeah?

"Right now, I don't know what to tell you. As first impressions go, I'm not bowled over, but everyone gets the benefit of the doubt. Maybe she was just having an off day—night? Or whatever."

"Vivian, be the bigger one. Everybody on their own healing journey, yeah?

"I know... you're right. I'm tired and cranky and I don't like being around falling-down-pissy-drunk people."

She. Is... was. Drunk?

"When I picked her up from the airport," I pull a plate from the upper cabinet and mumble, "and still impaired when she stumbled on John and I kissing in the kitchen earlier this morning; I don't know." I trail off because I don't know what else is really bothering me about Camilla's behavior. I tune back into Vera, feeling her sadness and what feels like disappointment. "Anyway... I didn't like. She was too comfortable with my husband."

You worried about John going after Camilla, yeah?

"Hell no. Why would I need to worry? No, her behavior just left the taste of dirt and shame in my mouth. Or maybe it was her energy. There is a darkness. It... she feels... like she's wrapped in centuries of despair. And lies and secrets and... silence."

Camilla steps into the kitchen, but halts when she hears me speaking aloud. I don't have time to tell her what's going on because Vera is yammering away.

Oh, that something entirely different, yeah? Just. It... I feel like she might need to be here. Need it like every part of me need every part of you. She lost, Vivian, looking for sanctuary. Somewhere she can swim in her own creativity.

"Did she say something to you when you spoke with her?" My mind is buzzing like a hive of male worker bees wondering what Vera's alluding to.

No, not really. No. It was just something about her tone. The words she use, but mostly the words she didn't use, yeah? The ones she tried to keep bitten between her teeth and cheek.

"Okay. I'll bear that in mind. What are you, a *clairvoyant*, now?" I say with humor because what the actual hell?

I always pick up on things most other people don't, yeah? I just don't say nothing because I don't want no more attention given to me than necessary.

"Hmm, we can talk about this with Jessa. I mean when you're ready, of course." I look at Milla who's eyes frost over like a union of quicksilver and aluminum, the invisible vapors make them appear too special and active in her artless face.

Yeah, okay. You go on and... ur. Deal with your guest, yeah?

"Mmhmm. You want to see what she looks like."

It felt too weird to ask, especially since you know I prefer women over men, yeah?

"Take a look and don't ever be ashamed of your sexuality, Vera. How your love expresses itself is as beautiful as you. If and when you're ready, you can come out and talk with her, okay?" I turn around and drape my eyes over Camilla, who is standing beside the large island wearing a pair of tight, faded jeans and an oversized men's sweater with leather patches on the elbows. Her hair is pulled back in a loose ponytail that's leaning a little to the left, like she's naturally off-center. No makeup and a pair of thick, black plastic cat-eyed glasses finish her lazy Saturday look.

Gawd, Vivian. She so damn beautiful. Just like her voice on the phone, yeah? Be kind. Gentle and with a mother's care, she crave it, yeah?

"Vera says you're beautiful just like your voice was on the phone." I tell Camilla whose eyes stretch wide with understanding.

Vivian. Why'd you do that? You trying to embarrass me, yeah? I'm going to my room, time to work out, anyway. Bye, Viv.

"Talk with you later, Vera." I give into the smile pulling my lips up because I think Vera may have her first girl-crush. Of course, she'd fall for a troubled artist who probably isn't even into women. Milla moves deeper into the kitchen, holding her empty coffee cup like it's a shield of protection from the angry gods. She hasn't uttered so much as a peep. She folds her lips into a mouth stuffed full-to-bursting with so many syllables they're pushing against her cheeks, weighing down her tongue. I wait her out because I'm interested in which words will escape first.

"Entonces, hablas en voz alta con tus alters." (So, you speak aloud with your alters.) She doesn't phrase it as a question, so I don't respond.

I'm fixing my breakfast of grits, eggs, and eggplant bacon. "You always..." She moves toward the coffee and pours another cup. We keep the sugar and nondairy creamer beside the coffee maker for convenience. She busies herself with correcting her coffee while awaiting my answer.

"No. Not always. It wasn't until we found ourselves on our own that we started communicating in this way."

"What you mean, *found* yourselves on your own?" She stirs her coffee with a wooden spoon and takes a tentative sip before adding more sugar and cream.

"My husband left me—and doing so, subsequently left *us*—alone for three months last year. He returned home in November. While he was away, we took time to build a stronger, better functioning DID system. Everything kind of emerged organically from there."

Taking a seat at the smaller island, I lift my hand to stop her next question. I inform, "When I eat, I don't engage in conversation. I need to be present for my meal. Save your questions for after breakfast. Feel free to help yourself." With that, I eat my food. Tuning out everything except what's on my plate, my breath, and the act of chewing and swallowing.

Camilla joins me at the island with a full plate. I take a moment to watch her. Confusion etches lines and wrinkles across her forehead. I smile and nod my head at her in encouragement. Grits are a funny thing. You either love them or loathe them. Sometimes it depends on who cooks them.

I make mine the way John taught me but with a vegetarian twist. Nondairy milk, vegan cheddar cheese, nutritional yeast flakes, salt and pepper to taste, and olive oil. I watch as she places a tentative forkful in her mouth. First her brow wrinkles even more than before. Then her lips pucker like she's waiting for a kiss from a small child. After she swallows the grits—which for so many of us who grew up brown and neglected meant *I love you and I want you to be safe,* when someone took the time to cook them—her face breaks into a delighted grin.

It's always an experience to see people discover Southern food. To hold space for their pleasure. Joy blooms in my heart because Milla's expressive visage says she's a newly converted grits connoisseur. I return my attention to my food, and we continue to eat in silence.

***

"Camilla," I call while placing the last dish in the dishwasher before closing the door. "Let's take a walk to my office. We need to talk." The sounds of water whooshing around the dishwasher fill the quiet space that separates us. She stops by to fill her cup with more coffee before she follows me down the hall, around the corner and into my work space.

"Wow, Vivian. This is... It inspires."

"Thanks. It's exactly what I was going for." I smile and wave her into the room proper. She takes a seat in the wicker egg chair in the corner, a large banana plant in a terracotta pot sits to the left of it. Once she's comfortable with her legs crossed in half lotus, she turns her deep, luminous eyes my way. Camilla sits quietly. She makes herself almost invisible, taking up as little space as possible. Her eyes scan the room, but she doesn't allow them to move within their sockets. Yet, she sees everything. *Interesting.* Perhaps she's *Waiting for Godot.*

I smile remembering the first time I tried to discuss Beckett's Modernist play with John. *I hate that damn play. Beckett was talking out of his ass with all that existentialism bullshit. Of course, we have an innate nature—well, I don't know about them—Black people the world over are naturally connected to each other and the whole fucking universe.* I shake his words away and settle into my rattan lounge chair. I had it reupholstered in Tibetan sheepskin.

I jolt when I hear Milla's low voice break the silence. "I'm surprised," She nods her head at the sheepskin by way of explanation and continues, "... real animal fur."

"Why?"

"You're vegan, no?" That's it. She doesn't say anything else to make sense of her inquiry. I wonder at her loquaciousness over the phone.

"Yes."

"You don't eat meat. Why support the industry."

"That's a bold and often wrong misconception, Milla. Why don't you ask me what you really want to know and stop dancing around the campfire." Her eyes stretch so wide, they look like marbles in the bottom of a purple Crown Royal bag. "Well?"

"I knew... I expect you to be... cómo?"

"You can speak Spanish, Milla. I'm fine either way."

"Yes, but I want to work my English." She sinks further into the chair and brings her knees up to her chest and rests her chin on them. After a moment of contemplation, she continues. "Wealthy? I knew you had money. I didn't think you flash it around."

If she had called me a white-passing-sell-out, I still wouldn't be as shocked. I hope my poker face has improved. If it hasn't, I'm sure she can read the *what-the-fuck* expression causing my right eye to twitch like it's hooked up to an electrical pulse. But really... what the actual fuck would prompt her to say something so untoward?

Not wanting to come off as an entitled American bitch, I choose my words carefully. "Milla, I'm not sure I know what you mean by *flash it around*." I fail to keep the brick-red and shit-brown tones from coloring my words with sluggish anger. Milla flinches as they paint broad strokes of embarrassment across her cheeks and forehead, with flames of deep rose and splotchy-white fire.

"Not everyone has so *high* standard for manners. You made me feel like a filthy street stray."

I'm taken aback at the temper sparking from her. The fire licking high on her jutting cheekbones. Her gray eyes become a hole in a bright light.

"I didn't realize being clean and dressed for the day before coming into the kitchen, was a high standard but if it is then, yes I have high standards." I suck in a breath and inform her, "It has absolutely nothing to do with being wealthy, Camilla. When I was dirt poor, I still wouldn't go in the kitchen without washing my face, brushing my teeth and getting dressed. At least, not if we had running water and I had clean clothes to wear." Images from the last few months with Vera's father crawl through my mind like fat worms coming to the surface after a heavy rain. *I am Vivian Ellis. I am safe. I am home. I am safe.*

By the time I'm able to pay attention, Camilla is up and pacing around my office mumbling in a mixture of Spanish and English, her voice filled with violent affliction. "... nunca entiende what it's like ser despojado de la única voz I know how use. Vete a la mierda. Puta."

If I wasn't paying such close attention to her, I wouldn't have heard the jumbled thoughts flying from her chaotic brain.

But... I *am* paying attention.

And... I *did* hear those repugnant words.

Now I'm left with a sour taste of her ill intent.

"I don't know what happened to you," I enunciate every syllable because I need to make sure she understands what I'm about to tell her. I lean forward and advise, "But you will not stand in my house and curse me the way you just did. Either you sit your narrow ass down and tell me what the hell is going on with you, or I can put you and your bullshit back on a goddamn plane to Chili."

"I—I..." That's all she gets out before she crumples to the floor in a pile of broken breaths, mirroring her anguish, and consecrating her purpose for being here.

What the hell?

Just as I'm moving to help her up from the floor, raised voices infiltrate my office. My gut knows something wicked this way has come, while my brain has yet to register what it heard.

Vivian, you hear that, yeah?

"Of course, I did. Go back to your room, Vera."

John

Cole looks like a plate of death warmed over. I observe him as he paces around the perimeter of my office. He switches between pulling at his floppy hair and ringing his chapped hands like he's single-handedly responsible for finding and killing Osama Bin Laden. He's so worked up; his face is the color of an over-ripe tomato. It's been fifteen minutes since he stepped into my office, and he hasn't said one word. I don't know if it's pissing me off or scaring the shit out of me.

"Cole, sit your ass down, brother. You're wearing a hole in my heart-of-pine floors." He stops short. When he finally faces me, he doesn't look like he knows where he is, or how the hell he got here.

"John." My name in his mouth is a proclamation. Face still red and eyes too wide, he looks like he may be high on something. "Look, brother. There's some shit goin 'down. I don't know—I can't fuckin 'keep it's stink from blowin 'back on you." Adrenalin and anger seep through his pores, causing the air to ripen with the sickly sweet rot of it.

Viv's words float through my thoughts, and I realize this is my blue or red pill moment. I can either accept the reality Cole is feeding me or I can create the one I want for myself.

"Cole, listen." I stand up and walk into his personal space before finishing my thought. "I'm not involved with any of this Order nonsense, and I won't become a part of it, either. I've carved out a great life for myself, and for the first time in forever, I'm happy." His hard gray eyes bore into me like I'm standing on the wrong side of a sundown town's welcome sign. He can kiss my black ass if he thinks I'm getting involved with him and these wargames.

"Hey, brother, you don't goddamn have a fuckin 'choice. You're already in this thing. Up to your nuts and there's no gettin 'out of it, you *know* that."

"What I know is that life is about choices, Cole. In the grand scheme of things, making the right choice is simply being willing to accept the consequences of my decisions. I'm more than willing to do that." I know the price I'll pay for my decision is a bargain in comparison to what getting involved with this would cost me. He looks into my eyes, gauging my resolve. Tasting the air like a snake, picking out the smell of fear, confusion, or reservation.

You could lick inside my asshole, brother, and still not find what you're looking for.

"You don't know what they have in store for you. I can't protect you..."

"Cole, I don't need your protection, I never did. I'm more than capable of taking care of me and mine, but you already know this."

"You don't know these motherfuckers like I do. You *will* need my protection, *John*."

"No, I won't." I walk around him and clap my hand on his shoulder to guide him toward the side door. I live my life the way I choose, and I'll kill any asshole who tries to stop me.

"Brother, you don't know what you're doin'—"

"For the last time, I'm not interested in waging war with a bunch of old white men who enjoy playing sink my fucking battleship with the lives of real people." I push Cole through the side entry door and onto the driveway where his sleek little Viper is waiting. He turns toward me presumably to implore me again, but before he has a chance, his body jerks once and them slumps into a pile of shattered bones and staccato breaths.

It takes longer than it should for my brain to connect the dots of the last fifteen seconds. As soon as my mind catches up, a bullet grazes the skin of my left temple, leaving a scorched line of malevolence in its silent arc. I drop to my belly and reach for my phone to call 911. In the distance, I hear the pounding of heavy boots running away from my home.

"911, what's your emergency?"

"There were shots fired at my home, one person is down, and the assailant is on foot. I need police and EMS, immediately to my home address."

"Sir, are you hurt?"

"No. My friend's been shot. I'm not sure where, but he's still breathing."

"Is it safe for you to check on your friend?" I belly crawl over to Cole and turn his limp body over, so he's on his back.

"Jesus fuck! There's so much blood. I—I don't. I can't tell..."

"Sir."

"It's fucking everywhere. What..."

"Mr. Ellis. I need you to calm down and listen to me."

"Okay. Um, yes. Ur, I'm listening."

"Good. Can you see where the bullet entered his body?"

"No. It's... there's so much blood. It's every-damn-where."

"Okay. You're doing great, Mr. Ellis. The ambulance is only two or three minutes out. Do you have something you can use to press against his chest?"

I pull my shirt over my head, wad it up and press it against the center of Cole's chest. I apply as much pressure as I think is safe without breaking his ribs. I'm sweating and mumbling to Cole that I'd kill his ass if he so much as thinks about dying in my goddamn driveway.

"Sir? Are you applying pressure to—"

"Yes, but it's not. The bleeding is slowing down... I don't know if it's because of the pressure or..."

Cole, what the fuck did you do?

"Sir, you should be able to hear the sirens."

"Yes, thank you. I hear them." I watch the ambulance and firetruck pull into my driveway, and I exhale a breath I didn't know I'd been holding, before confirming with the operator, "They're pulling into my driveway now. Thank so much for staying on the line with me." I disconnect the call and lift my arms to direct the EMS workers over to where I'm crouching over Cole's body, with my blood soaked shirt pressed into his chest.

"Sir,"

"John?" Vivian's voice carries over the den of sirens and footsteps. I don't want her to see this shit.

"Vivian, get in the house. The shooter may still be out here."

"Shooter? What shooter. John, what's going on—is that Cole?" I hear her coming closer to me and all I want to do is stand up and drag her disobedient ass back into the safety of our home.

"Please, escort my wife into the house." I say to anyone in uniform whose within earshot and can carry out my request. I hear her protest and struggle to get to me, but right now, all my focus is on Cole and the two EMS workers who just placed an oxygen mask on his face. Once secured, they attempt to lift him onto a gurney. "Is he breathing?"

"Barely. The police are gonna wanna speak with you, but first you need to have that wound on your left temple checked out."

"It's nothing. A graze."

"Still, have it looked at. We're taking your friend to Richland Memorial."

"No, take him to Lex Med. It's closer."

"Yes, sir."

"I'll meet you there as soon as I'm done here."

"Mr. Ellis, follow me to my rig. We need to get that wound cleaned up."

"Yea, okay. That's fine." I allow him to guide me over to the EMS truck and take a seat on the open tailgate. As his pudgy fingers move over my temple, I think about the shit Cole shared with me about The Order..

Part III

Just because the cause of a thing is broken and dirty, doesn't mean the effect is worthless, yeah?

~Vera Bruno

~23~

Vivian

The detective and his partner just left. The forensic team is still out front and across the road from our house collecting evidence. Someone almost blew my husband's head off and managed to shoot his friend in the chest. We don't live in a low-income area where the sound of guns being fired are the norm. We live on Lake Murray in a million dollar home for fuck's sake. I don't say anything because what the hell is there to say.

The more I think about The Order, the more convinced I am John's keeping something from me. He steps into the kitchen; he looks like a pot of Thelma's oatmeal on Good Times. I push the words climbing up my throat back into my belly, but they will not be swallowed.

"What can you tell me?"

"Nothing. It's better you don't know."

"Why?"

"Plausible deniability."

"I won't be kept in the dark about this anymore. You are not protecting me, John. Ignorance is only bliss if your name happens to be Cypher."

"You and that goddamn movie." I share a small knowing smile with him as he holds out his right hand. Without hesitation, I place my left palm against his and allow him to pull me into the safety of his large body. The feel of my curves pressing against all his hard places, is like coming home. Wrapping my arms around his neck, I slot myself between his spread thighs, urging him to draw me closer. Together, we breathe each other in.

"Talk to me, please, baby." My breath whispers across his neck. Noticing the gooseflesh on his skin. It's not sexual, it's a sensual horripilation. A way of knowing what I need from him without me having to tell him.

"Everything within The Order is fucked to hell and back with gasoline drawers on, lovely." He stops abruptly and I know I'm not going to like what he says next. I give him the space he needs to gather his conviction. After another moment, he clears his throat and forces the words from his mouth. "I've been working with the FBI for the last year and a—"

"What the hell are y—?"

"... half, now and I wasn't sure I—"

". —ou talking about, working with the FB—"

"—was doing the right thing—wait, what did you say, lovely?"

"I?" I finally stop talking over John and try to piece together the parts of the conversation I missed. I give up and ask, "Did you say, the FBI?"

"When I left you for three months," I pull away from arms that feel less like home and look into troubled eyes that beg me to listen.

"Do you think finding out all that shit about Auntie was enough to make me walk away from you and my unborn child?" As my mind begins to comprehend John's words, my blood becomes boiling lava.

"Stop it, lovely." He snaps out like the arrogant bastard he is.

"Stop what, exactly, *Sir*?"

"Don't be a brat. Shut-the-hell-up and listen." I've completely removed myself from our little love bubble and now I stand away from him, arms crossed over my heaving chest, legs braced for the blow I know is coming.

" When the FBI needed me to go undercover, I wouldn't bring that shit to our home. Vera just happened to drop the bomb about Auntie at the perfect time. It gave me a viable reason to walk away from you." Those deep brown eyes with their golden-paper flecks have been staring into me this entire time. Full of honest love. My arms hang in surrender at my sides; made heavy by ambrosial words spoken moments ago.

"You didn't leave me." Sacred relief dribbles from my eyes. He places a soft kiss over each of my closed eyelids, just before he licks the suffering from my cheeks with the warm tip of his tongue. I am baptized in this moment. The sense of lightness that settles in my heart surprises me; I thought myself already freed from those shackles of self-doubt and hurt feelings.

"Baby, only death and the FBI could make me walk away from you. Nothing, absolutely nothing else in this world or the next, could pull me away from us." I throw my arms back around his neck; and if I didn't know I'd made the right decision taking my husband back, I damn sure know it now.

After an age, we disentangle ourselves from each other. Both our faces wet with the harmony that only truth can bring. I know I need to get back to Camilla, but John hasn't really told me anything. Not about his involvement with the FBI, what's going on with Cole and The Order, and not about the gunshots and why he's sporting a bandage just over his left ear. I'm about to launch into my interrogation when he raises his right hand to cup my cheek. I lean into the warmth of his palm and offer my lips up for a kiss. He obliges me before whispering his next words over my lips.

"Go take care of your artist. I promise we'll talk, and I'll tell you everything. I need to call my handler and set up a meeting."

I have a hard time stepping out of his embrace. For some strange reason, it feels as if I've just gotten him back this very minute. Like only his shadow returned to me four months ago and this—the moment when I kissed his palm—is his *real* homecoming.

He must see this in my face, because he pulls me back into his body and whispers into my temple, "I'm not going anywhere, lovely. You own me, body, mind, and soul. I'll be in my office." Before he can turn away from me, I reach up and press my lips against his. My intention is a soft confirmation of us, but the moment his tongue slides against the seam of my closed mouth, I open for him. Pull him between my lips and suck him like I'm on my knees with my hands behind my back. I feed him my tongue as a sacrifice and pray he accepts it as a proper offering.

He does.

In this moment we are air. Mist and vibrations. Riding against the weeping riffs of Santana's guitar as our love reaches a fever pitch. I feel John jerk against my stomach. Once. Twice. And a third time. The grown I swallow makes me wet and needy for him.

"Did you...?"

"I'll find you when I'm done, okay?"

"Yes." I murmur. My skin is coated in fearful joy and pained love. So much love, it makes me feel sick with its volatile concoction swirling in my heart. John wraps his large hands on either side of my head, his warm palms are familiar. He pulls me into his space and presses his lips against mine. The lightest pressure and a puff of his sweet breath are the only warning I get, and then he pries my lips apart to slip his tongue into my greedy mouth.

I open for him, of course I do. I wait for his tongue to seek my own before I start the dance that drags groans from each of our throats. Soft nibbles along my bottom lip. The tip of his tongue running across my front teeth. Uncertainty makes me ravenous as I start to eat at his mouth like I'm never going to have the chance to partake of this decadent meal again.

"Lovely." I don't let him say anything else. I dive back into his mouth. Deepening the kiss and sucking on his bottom lip; too consumed with my need for him to let any part of him escape my possessive tasting.

What if they take him from me, again?

"Baby, slow down. I'm n—" I bite down on that same bottom lip, drawing the honeyed, metallic flavor into my mouth. I shouldn't want it on my tongue, but I do. I suck on the wound and draw more of his life's blood into myself. Swallowing like some kind of vampiric succubus come to lay claim to his soul.

John pushes me away, but he doesn't let me go. His hands are still wrapped around my head. I feel his eyes look through me and I wonder why his form is a watery mirage. It's not until his voice cuts through the distorted noise in my head, that I realize I'm crying.

"Your lips are always so goddamned kissable when you cry, lovely"

"I-I'm s-scared. John. I'm s-so damn scared."

"There is no man, woman, beast, angel, or devil stronger than my love for you. Think about what had to occur for you and me to be in the Horseshoe at Carolina on the same day, at the same time on that September morning. We are an atemporal phenomenon. Time and space can't violate who and what we are destined to be for each other." John's words help me take the breath I haven't been able to since he mentioned the FBI. *I love... too much.* I place my forehead against his for a minute or an eternity. He lets me linger for as long as I need to. When I'm ready to move away, I do so with a soft kiss on his swollen lips. My apology for bruising him.

"I am we. My life belongs to you. That means your life is mine. Don't risk more than you're willing to lose."

"And that is exactly why I have to take this risk, lovely. I'm not willing to lose anything, especially you." He rubs his capable hands up and down my arms a few times to assess me. "Are we good?"

"If you're good, then we're great."

"I love you."

"I love you, too."

"Go on, lovely. I'll come find you when I'm done."

I don't respond because there's nothing to say. I turn on my heel and leave him to it. In the hallway, I run into Camilla.

"Hey, Milla. Look, I can't tell you what's going on, but please know you're safe in my home. I'm going to go lay down for a while. We'll talk later. If you see me—or someone who looks like me—walking around, it's probably one of the alters. If they seek you out, please interact with them as you would any new acquaintance. We don't like being treated like we're different aspects of the same person." I give her a tired smile.

"Are you and... your... ur, John... bacain?"

"John says we are, so we must be. Get some rest, You must still be suffering from jetlag. Better to deal with it now, than to suffer with it at the start of your first work week." I inject a little smile into my voice, and she gives me a small one in return. I'll take it.

~24~

John

I watch Vivian as she talks with her artist-in-residence. She looks so damn tired, I want to tuck her into bed with a good, long fuck. Make sure her dreams are pleasant, but there's no time to make it happen. I've got to get in touch with my contact. I cannot have this shit coming this close to my home again. Before I can escape from the kitchen, Camilla steps into the room.

"Hi."

"Hello. Look, I'm sorry all this shit went down..." I don't bother finishing because I don't owe her an explanation, nor do I have time to talk.

"No. It is... fine. Vivian, she tell me we are safe. Thank you."

"Okay, well..." I turn toward my office and throw a perfunctory wave her way and leave her standing beside the coffee maker.

***

"John is one of the nicest men I know, yeah?" I hear Vera's plantation-laced voice and wonder who the hell she's talking to.

"Claro. I mean, yes. He seems to be in love with Vivian."

"He a fool for that woman, just as much as she is for him. I love them together, yeah?"

"Hey Vera. Camilla. Vera, is Vivian with you or is she in her room?" I notice how Camilla's eyes follow each word as it leaves my mouth, like maybe they look different when I speak to Vera than when I'm speaking to Vivian. The little divot between her eyebrows makes her look like a confused kitten.

"Hey, John. No, she ain't with me. She said she was tired and went to her room to get some rest. Busy morning, yeah?"

"Yes. What made you decide to come out?"

"I knew that Miss Camilla—"

"Vera, I told you it is just Camilla or Milla."

"Right. I knew Camilla was on her own and wanted to keep her company, yeah?" I look at Vera a little closer. She's not wearing those clothes that look like they come from Hambrick's today. She has on a pair dark straight-leg jeans that almost fit the slim waistline of their body, a long-sleeve algae-green tee shirt, and a brown and green vertically striped cardigan. When she lifts from the bar height stool, she doesn't look like she's walking around herself anymore.

"Vera?"

"Hmm?" She stops and faces me. Her face is open. Large, bottomless gray-green eyes stare up at me. I smile.

"I hope I'm not overstepping, but have you been working out?" Immediately, Vera's eyes go wide and the shyest smile I've ever seen on anyone, has the audacity to grace her beautifully expressive gaze.

"John, stop teasing me." That shy smile has moved down to her full, wide mouth.

"I'm not teasing." I keep my voice in the playful, brotherly register because the last thing I want to do is make Vera think I see her differently.

"I've been doing Richard Simmons's, *Sweatin 'to the Oldies*, yeah?"

"Good for you. Well, Camilla, I'll leave you and Vera to it." I grab a beer from the fridge and make my way back to my office. Before I clear the kitchen, Vera calls to me.

"Anything you want me to tell Vivian when she wake up?"

"No, Vera. Thanks. Enjoy the rest of your evening. Oh, if you need to go somewhere, come and get me, *yeah*?" A small giggle is the only answer I receive for mocking her. Just as I pull the door shut behind me, the phone on my desk starts ringing.

"Yes."

"You stupid, stupid, motherfucker." I hold the line. There's an automatic trace alert set up on my office phone. They're getting desperate and that means they're getting sloppy, too. The voice sounds like it's coming through one of the drive-through speakers, distorted and kind of garbled. It doesn't matter who the fucker is on the other end, as long as he stays on long enough for the trace program to find his location.

"I'm going to need more than that if you're hoping for a specific response." I sound bored to tears, when in reality, my heart is beating a mile a minute and sweat is trickling down my spine into the crack of my ass.

"You ever wonder why you were chosen, *boy*?"

"No." If he thinks I'm going to lose my shit because he called me, *boy*, he must have me confused with himself.

"You didn't have the pedigree needed to be tapped for such an honor."

"All right."

"You were chosen as a sacrificial lamb, *boy*." The fact he's staying on the line as long as he is tells me they don't know I'm working with the Feds to bring their asses down. Thank fuck for small favors.

"And..."

"And. It's time to put your haughty black ass up on the auction block, boy. That's the, *and* you dumb fuck."

"Are we still speaking metaphorically, or do you expect me to bleed for The Order?" The quick intake of breath tells me more than any verbal response could. Why would he think I didn't know who was behind all the shit that's been going on?

"Normally, once you're done with the crucibles, that's all the blood required. But you are a special kind of stupid, Jonathan R. Ellis."

"Oh, yeah? What kind of stupid am I?" I get a text on my FBI issued cell letting me know they have a lock on the caller's location, but they want me to keep him talking for as long as I can.

"The kind that believes you have a right to hold the keys to the kingdom when you're not even fit to sweep the streets around the pearly white gates." I let him hear the shit-eating grin in my voice, so I over exaggerate the spread of my lips as I respond to this redundant asshole.

"Keys to the kingdom? Why the fuck would I need keys when I'm the architect and rightful owner. Get the fuck outta here, man." In my mind's eye, I see a short, baldheaded, fat as hell, middle management motherfucker turning the color of cooked lobster as he parses out what I just said.

"Don't bother going to sleep tonight, John. You or that whore you married. We didn't miss. We have y'all framed up so pretty, you could be hanging in that fancy art gallery your wife has." I don't care what he calls Vivian because why would I? But something about his choice of words has the hair on the back of my neck standing on end. I grab the cellphone and type a quick message to my contact because I'll be damned if something happens to Vivian's places of business, and I could've stopped it.

"Good. Good. My wife and I do make a striking image. Definitely worthy of being seen in her gallery. Tell me something," I pause as I await a reply confirming the dispatch to Viv's gallery and her artist's hub to come through.

Got it.

"Tell you what, *boy*?"

"Did you know that you and Cole had the same tastes in frames?"

"What the fuck are you talking about? Cole is dead. He's been dead for a couple of weeks now. You're the last of your class, *boy*."

Stupid, stupid asshole.

"Doesn't mean you all didn't share the same tastes in frames. Listen, I've enjoyed talking with you, but I have something important that's just come across my desk. It's time-sensitive, you understand, right?" I don't give him a chance to respond before hanging up and looking into my wife's summer sunshine gaze. It's filled with all sorts of questions that I can't even began to answer.

"Am I the time-sensitive important something that's just come across your desk?" Her eyes are alight with sensual mischief, and I wish like hell we had time to indulge. Still, I return her flirty smile while pushing her perfect ass from the corner of my desk.

"Yes you are. How was your nap?"

"Needed. Vera said you noticed she'd been working out."

"I noticed how her clothes fit better on the body, and the way she moves more than anything. I didn't upset her, did I?"

"No. She just didn't expect you to notice, and she was a little embarrassed because she had to admit she'd been sweatin 'to the oldies in front of Camilla."

"Camilla? Why would she be embarrassed about that. There's nothing wrong with working out."

"No, it's not that. Vera doesn't want Milla to think she's some kind of weird work-out freak."

"Lovely, help me out here. I don't understand. What's the big deal with Vera wanting to impress Camilla?"

"I think Vera has a crush on her."

"What, now?"

"I did tell you Vera's a lesbian, right?"

"I can't remember if you did. She has a crush on Milla—is Milla gay?"

"I don't know. What's going on with you?"

"Why don't you and Milla go to dinner, my treat." I'm hoping she'll just go with it, but I also know my wife.

"Why are you trying to get rid of me, John?"

"I'm not. Not really. Listen, I need you away from the house and I don't want you to go to your gallery or the studio, either. I need about an hour... two tops."

"You won't be dead when I get back?"

"Vivian."

"John."

"I love you. Now, go. I've got shit to do and you can't be here when I'm doing it. *Trust* me. This is about to be over. Promise."

"Famous last words, I love you, too."

~25~

Vivian

Milla and I are parked on the street in front of Diane's on Divine, it's Sunday which means we probably won't be able to get a table without a reservation. The parking area is full.

"What are we sitting here for?" Milla's face is free of makeup and her hair is carelessly floating around her narrow shoulders. She looks effortlessly beautiful. Even with the small crease forming a 'v ' between her heavy brows, she's a lovely woman.

"I'm texting my assistant from the gallery to see if she can get us a table for tonight. I wasn't planning on being out this weekend, but John offered to pay for dinner..." I leave it there as a message comes through on my phone. I smile and quickly type a thank you and I owe you to Tammie before turning to my companion with a smug smile.

"I take it, she get you a table."

"Was it the Cheshire grin on my face that gave it away?" I laugh until I see the horror splashing across Milla's expressive features. "What's that face for?"

"*Cheshire*?" I bark out a too loud laugh that makes her jump away from me, which only makes me laugh harder. As I try to get myself together, bright headlights catch my attention because they're stopped directly behind my parked car. *What the hell*? Before I'm able to explain Cheshire grin, there's a knock on my window. I lower the glass enough to hear the person bending down so his mouth is leveled with the crack.

"Mrs. Ellis, I'm Bradford Rosenburg with Addison Security," He places his ID and credentials up to the window for verification; I lower the glass a little more to get a good look at his face against the image as he continues. "You've been sitting here for more than fifteen minutes; your husband advised us to stay in the background unless we deemed it necessary to make our presence known. Are you and your companion all right or do you need some assistance?" *Of-fucking-course, John hired security and I chose to forget all about it.*

"No. We're fine. I was just waiting on confirmation from my assistant that there would be an available table for us in Diane's. Will you all be accompanying us into the restaurant?"

"You will not be able to see us. We will be discreet, but to answer your inquiry, yes ma'am. We'll continue to be with you everywhere you go for the foreseeable future."

"Okay, Mr. Rosenburg. Thank you." I raise the window back up, unbuckle my seatbelt, and prepare to step from my car, when a motorcycle moving too fast for the speed limit, passes by on the opposite side of the street. I'm immediately pushed back and down into my front seat as bullets pepper the concrete around my car. I reach up and yank Milla down onto the floor just as both our windows explode in shards of jagged, weaponized glass.

"Que mierda esta pasando?" (What the fuck is going on?)

"Mantén la cabeza baja, Milla!" (Keep your head down, Milla!)

"Que?" It's the last thing I hear before the street is filled with silence. Nothing is moving outside my car. I don't know if this means the shooters are gone, my security detail is dead, or if the bad guys are walking toward us right now. I take out my phone and press number one on speed dial.

"Baby, are you safe?"

"John..." That's all I can get pass the heavy lump in my throat before a pitiful sob paints its own macabre version of Edvard Munch's famous *Scream* across my own horror riddled face. I know John is saying something to me and I'm trying to pay attention, but Vera and Valery are yelling for me to come inside where it's safe. I know I need to stay with the body, but I'm so damn rattled; I just want to sank into the comfort of the Internal House. John's rough timbre brings me back to the present moment and I grab on to it because he is my lifeline.

"Everything is under control, Vivian. Rosenburg is coming to you right now. He is not going to harm you. You and..."

The tap on my windowless door causes Camilla and Me to yelp like wounded animals being kicked after a rough dog fight.

"It's Rosenburg, lovely."

He opens my door, sits down on his haunches and pulls the phone from my hand. I notice the passenger door is opening, but before I can lose my shit, Rosenburg tells me that his partner is assisting Ms. Fazzini into their armored vehicle. He also informs me that I should gather my things and come with him.

I don't even remember the ride home, or how long it took for us to get here. The only thing I want is to be wrapped in John's arms where I know I'm safe, cared for and loved.

"John."

"I've got you, lovely. I've got you." He wraps his strong arms around me, but I'm shaking so badly, my legs can't support me enough to walk into our home. John scoops me up bridal style; I fall into the strength of his body. Even while he gentles me with kisses on my forehead, he gives orders to the men in regard to Camilla and getting her settled, as well as securing the cars and property for the night.

John's heart is beating a slow and steady tempo in direct contradiction of my own out-of-control staccato rhythm. I try to match my breathing to his, because I sound like I've just run a marathon all uphill, wearing cement shoes.

"I'm so fucking sorry, Vivian. None of this was ever supposed to touch you." He whispers into my locs as he takes the stairs two at a time. All the while, holding me like I'm the most precious human alive. "I promise, I'm fixing this for us. You have to believe me, lovely." He continues to drop kisses onto my forehead, eyes, nose and cheeks where my silent tears are burning this anguished fear into my skin ad memoriam. I want to tell him that I believe and trust him. I want to return his kisses and assurances. I want to, but it's costing me everything I have to stay in the driver's seat. The girls are losing their minds, begging me to come inside where it's safe for me. They don't care about the body, they only care about me. And that only makes me cry harder.

"I've got you, Vivian. It's all going to be all right. I promise." I hear the shower running.

John has put me on the bathroom counter.

He's undressing me.

He starts with my shoes and socks.

Tells me to raise my arms and he removes my sweater, turtleneck and cami all in one fell swoop.

Next, he deftly unhooks the front enclosure and pulls the straps of my bra from my shoulders.

I'm naked from the waist up.

"Can you stand for me, lovely?"

I don't answer him.

I simply slide from the counter until my bare feet touch the heated tile floor of our master bathroom.

He tugs my belt open and pulls it through the loops around the narrow waistband of my Pepe jeans.

Another tug of the button.

A pull of the zipper.

John peels my jeans and underwear down my long, trembling legs.

He taps my right thigh.

I lift my right foot.

He repeats this on the left side.

This would be a sexy beginning to a filthy shower scene if the circumstances were different.

I'm completely naked, as I stand in front of my husband waiting for him to direct my feet. He disrobes faster than he usually does— when he's setting a scene--and guides me into our enormous walk-in shower.

The water is perfect.

I'm chilled to my soul with fear.

His soapy hands run all over my body, not because he's trying to get me clean, rather because he's trying to keep me present.

"Wash me, Vivian."

John gives me the soap.

I'm on autopilot as I form a lather between my freezing hands.

I give the soap back to him.

I wash his chest.

His shoulders.

His arms.

His flat belly.

"Enough."

He uses that sex god voice to give me short, simple directives; because he knows I would follow it through heaven just to burn in his hellish whispers.

"Turn around. Place your hands on the back tiled wall."

I do as he says.

I'm freezing.

My body quakes earn me a seven on the Richter scale.

"Vivian."

"Yes, Sir."

"I'm going to fuck you, now. If you don't want this..." He leaves it hanging between us like the steam rising from an enchanted lake.

"Green, Sir."

"Good girl. Spread your feet as wide as you can."

I comply.

How could I not, when he sounds like his sole purpose for having a cock is to service me? To bring me back from the brink of insanity with orgasms and pleasure.

"Bend forward."

I float like a ballerina into a cambre en avant; back perfectly arched and legs perfectly straight.

"Perfect, lovely. Red, yellow, or green."

"Green, Sir." It means so much that he continues to check in with me because he knows how fucked up I am right now. And like the amazing Dom he is, he also knows what I need to get through this latest trauma.

We call this, soul fucking.

"Brace yourself."

That's all the warning I get before he slams his entire length into me. No preamble or preparation. I'm not really wet or ready for his invasion, and the burn of his possession is exactly what I need right now. Something more painful than I just endured. Pain tempered with love and acceptance feels like a cooling balm over my battered mind. He stays seated deep inside me. Rigid and unmoving. He's reminding me of his love and devotion to me and our life together.

"You feel how deep I am inside this perfect cunt, Viv?" He runs his hands down my back from the base of my neck to the top of my behind. Then he wraps his left hand around my hip and drags his heavy erection through swollen and bruised tissue. Leaving enough pre-cum to make me wet for his next thrust. "Hold on, lovely."

"Yes, Sir." I feel like I'm miles away from John. I know he hears the desperation in my voice. Because I'm desperate for him to, "... fuck me like he paid for the privilege."

"Goddamn, Vivian."

Yes, you heard me.

"So... wet. Tight... the sweetest." He's not even speaking in complete sentences anymore, and I'm unable to speak at all.

" Made... to possess. Lovely. Fuck... Jughead."

Wet flesh slaps against wet flesh.

Hot water-pellets bombard writhing bodies.

Heavy grunts, mewls and whimpers fill the empty spaces between fear and oblivion.

"Need to hear... shit, yes. Need... you, lovely."

I don't know what he wants from me, but I have no words to offer.

Thwack

John's right hand lands on my wet butt cheek and it sounds like the window blowing out of my SUV. I clamp down around him so tight, he can hardly pull out to thrust back in.

"No, John."

Thwack

Thwack

Thwack

In my mind I'm back in my car. Bullets are flying all around me. "Get me out of here... What's... happening?"

ThwackThwackThwackThwackThwack.

"Please..."

"Stop fucking begging..."

ThwackThwackThwack.

The entire time he's whipping my ass, he powers into me like his life depends on how deeply he buries himself into my yielding body. The deeper he goes, the longer he gets to live. The harder he hits my ass, the better his life will be.

ThwackThwackThwackThwack.

"We do not fucking beg for our right to live." His voice is as incensed as the bullets whizzing by my head.

ThwackThwackThwack!

"Fuck you, motherfucker! You don't get... to. God, yes. John..."

"That's it, lovely. That's fucking it."

ThwackThwack.

~26~

John

I have to remind myself that this is not a scene. I can't afford to lose perspective because of how amazing it feels to be inside my wife. To have my hands on her like I do. No, this is about breaking into her mind to chip away at the past two or three hours, before they have a chance to take root in her soul.

"No! They don't have a right to... right there. Deeper, Sir. Harder, please, Sir." Vivian bounces on the balls of her feet, rubbing her glorious ass against my pubic bone. Driving me out of my mind with lust and love for her. Anger, fear, need and determination roll through her body like thunder over a turbulent ocean. "Break me, Sir. Please... need. Broken." *ThwackThwackThwack*

"What did I say, lovely."

Thwack

Thwack

"N-no b-beg. Begging." Her words squeeze through her clenched teeth as my balls slap the swollen flesh of her vulva.

Thwap

Thwap

Thwap

"That's it. Give it up to me, Viv. Now. Give it to me." On my command, and with one last crack of my palm against her burning ass, Vivian comes harder than she has in weeks. So hard, she pulls my orgasm from me, but I refuse to ejaculate.

This is for her healing, but fuck does it feel good. It takes every bit of my control to drag my attention back to the woman whose body is trying to milk come from my own, but I do it. She's broken two nails against the tile wall of our shower. The noises pouring from her are a siren's call to my demon's lust for her.

"Hmm. J-John." A sorrowful, keening cry wraps around my name; breaking off just as it touches the *n*.

I release her left hip and use both hands to rub soothing circles into her behind. I already feel the slight swelling and mentally run through the aftercare she'll need, as she starts to float back into her body.

"I've got you, lovely." I place small open-mouth kisses along her spine and on her bruised buttocks. Then I pull myself from the slick sheath of her body. Once I'm completely free, Vivian's knees buckle beneath her, but she's in my arms before any part of her touches the shower floor.

"Let me cherish you, lovely." I gather her up and carry her into our bedroom where a warm bath-sheet is laid out on our bed. I spritzed it with lavender-chamomile linen spray before I went down to meet security.

"Don't leave me, Sir."

"Baby. You're safe. I'm only going to heat some arnica oil and bring you some lemon-ginger tea. Relax, I'll be right back." I wrap my towel around my waist and will Jughead to deflate just in case I run into Camilla.

Wouldn't want to scare the poor lady any more than she already is.

The thought brings a little smile to my face.

I'm such a fucking child sometimes.

"Sir." Rosenburg is sitting at the large island with his laptop open. He doesn't look up from whatever has his attention on the screen. Before I cross the kitchen to look at the intel and get a quick report, I pour a fourth of a cup of arnica oil and five drops of comfrey into a small glass bowl. I pop it in the microwave for twenty seconds and flip the tea kettle on.

"How's our guest?"

"Gave her a sedative and sent her to bed with a glass of red."

174

"Okay. So..."

"Ran the plates and the fingerprints. Plates are registered to someone in Alabama, but all records indicate that the person is deceased."

The feeling that someone just walked over my grave, crawls up and down my spine.

"Earl Friendly."

"These tags are current and that's not all, John."

Of course, it isn't.

"Give me the shortest version, I've got to get back upstairs to Vivian."

"Someone has been keeping tabs on yours and your wife's every move. We found trackers on both vehicles, as well as spyware on your phones."

"We've been hacked?"

"Yes. We've sent the trackers off to be processed, downloaded the software and scrubbed your phones. Whoever is after you, has deep pockets and low friends in high places."

"Touch base with my contact and we'll meet in the morning in my office at 0600 hours."

"Good night, sir."

"Good job tonight, Rosenburg. Get some rest." I fix Viv's tea and grab the warm oil. Before I push the bedroom door open, I hear Vivian speaking to one or both of the alters.

"... I'm all right."

"Yes, it was scary, but I couldn't come inside with you guys." "Not brave, just responsible."

"Shut-up, Val. You would be the one to bring up the shower."

I hear the smile in her voice, and I'm struck by how much they depend on each other when shit goes sideways.

They really have come a long way.

"Knock-Knock." I call from the hallway like I'm interrupting something.

"John?" My name floats on a bubble of amusement. I'm glad to hear it in her voice, even though she still sounds like half of her is still stuck in the crossfire of bullets.

"Sorry it took a little longer to get everything together. I heard you talking with the girls, how are they?"

"Scared. Worried. Angry. Oh, and horny. Valery is the angry, horny one." She flashes me a small smile as she watches me place the tray on the bedside table. "Did you check in with Milla?"

"I spoke with Rosenburg. He gave her a sedative and a large glass of red." I relay as I pull on my black boxer briefs. I notice how ashy my legs are and walk into the bathroom to lotion up. Once I'm done, I return to the woman laying across the bed with a sore ass and wounded spirit.

"Oh, he's staying here?"

"He and his partner are in the other guest bedroom downstairs. There are also four other men and women on foot patrol outside."

"Is all of this necessary, John?"

"Yes." I walk out of the bathroom and over to our bed. "Scoot over, I need to sit beside you. How's your ass?"

"How much longer," She starts to ask as she tries to move over into the middle of the bed but finds she's too uncomfortable to get anywhere. "Ow. Help me, please?"

I lift her and place her where I want her. A silent tear leaks from her right eye and disappears into the towel beneath her face.

"Don't worry. We'll talk more tomorrow. For now, relax." I pour a little of the warm arnica-comfrey oil into my hands and rub them together before starting at her shoulders and working my way down.

"God, this is almost as good as what got me here in the first place." Viv sounds drunk. Loose-lipped and bleary-eyed.

"Good, because this next part will not be so pleasant, but you'll be thankful in the morning." Adding a little more oil, I start working the balm into her bruised cheeks. Her skin is so hot to my palms, I'm immediately hard. "I may have been too rough with you, lovely. I apologize if I was."

Shit, maybe I wasn't as in control as I thought myself to be after all.

"I needed... it." Viv's words are so slurred if they were written, they'd be italicized. "... just like."

I squeeze a particularly tender area on her lower right cheek.

"Hmm, that's amazing. I needed you to... be just. Like."

Another firm kneading of the same area.

"Hmm... that, John."

Yep, written in italics in some fancy ass font.

"I'll always give you what you need, lovely." I stand and get her a tee shirt and a pair of cotton sleep shorts. After dressing her, giving her some pain medicine, and letting her drink a few sips of her tea, I kiss her forehead and tuck her in for the night. "I love you, Vivian Anne Ellis. Don't ever doubt that."

"I love you, Jonathan Raynard Ellis. Don't ever *forget* that."

I throw on some sweats and an old Carolina tee shirt before heading downstairs to my office. I'm glad to find the house is quiet when I walk through on my final check. In my office, I pull out my encrypted phone and call the one person who can make heads or tails of this mess.

"Hello, motherfucker."

"Cole, where the fuck are you and how much longer are we doing this shit?"

"Until I shoot the biggest duck with the biggest bill."

"You're still out there hunting ducks?"

"Might be out here huntin 'a fuckin 'goose."

"That right? Canadian or white?"

"Fuckin 'fat, white goose."

"Will it be on the table for Easter Sunday?"

"I'm aimin 'to have his plump ass on the goddamn table for Superbowl Sunday. Boneless goose wing platter sound real good right about now, brother."

"Don't disappoint me, you know how seriously I take my Superbowl parties."

"I won't let you down, brother."

"You almost gave me a reason to fuck your shit up."

"I knew what I was doin'. Never would've hurt what's yours. Shootin 'blanks made sure of it."

"She's goin 'to kick my ass when she finds out."

"Better you than me. I gotta go, goose huntin 'ain't for the faint of heart."

"Keep your head down and your guard up."

"Ditto, brother. Ditto." After hanging up, I remove the sim card from the burner and crush them both beneath my feet. Now to send correspondence to my so-called contact with the FBI.

That the FBI has the audacity to assume they can dictate how I choose to move in my life, is laughable. It's a good thing I was born Black and Southern; I'm the embodiment of my ancestors 'wildest dreams. It's time to bring a few of them to fruition.

Vivian

"So... Milla, are you ready to see your home for the next three months?" I ask as we step into the elevator of the underground parking garage of her building.

"Yes. I'm excited to have my own space. No offensive, yours is a little *busy*, cachai?" An unintelligible sound slips through her uneasy smile.

"None taken. You're not wrong in your assessment. I would love to say it's not usually like that, but I'd be lying." I respond in an impassive tone because I refuse to be ashamed of any part of my life. My stomach dips a little as we climb up to the eighth floor where Collin is waiting for us.

"Well, maybe things will be calm soon." Milla clears her throat before asking, "Is Vera okay?"

Interesting.

"You mean after the shooting?"

"Mmhmm. I know from talks; she is un poquito... I call her, *birdie*. As a, how do you say... polola name."

Birdie? What in the fold-up-cup-kits has been going on under my roof?

"*Polola?*"

"Sí. Is like *novia* but not the exact same."

"Oh, like an endearment between *friends*?"

"Si." She laughs a little and then a shy smile settles on her mouth. "Because she feels shy sometime. Unsure but still brave, too. Cachai?"

Maybe Vera isn't the only one with a girl crush.

"Yes, she can be shy and unsure. Once again you're right in your assessment because she is also brave. Birdie is a perfect nickname for her. Thanks for asking, she's fine. A little shaken, but she's keeping it together." The elevator doors open to spit us out into a surprisingly crowded hallway. I look down into her open face and state, "You like her."

Before Milla responds, the two well-dressed men who look like rejects from the *Men in Black* movie, step towards us. I'm distracted, and almost miss Milla's voice as it floats away from her upturned mouth.

"I like her... well enough, yes. She's sweet." I split my attention between her and the two men, in black suits, trying to figure out who they are and if we're in danger. Milla reaches into the elevator to drag her two duffle bags out into the hall, but the door starts to close before she can escape. I reach for the button, but before my arm is even extended, one of the black suits has the doors opened and takes both bags away from her.

"Oh," It's only after they're walking down the hall to Milla's apartment, that I realize they're security. I mumble to the empty space they just left, "I didn't know y'all were accompanying us."

Milla and I follow them. She asks a million questions with one wide-eyed gaze.

Once we cross over the threshold, one of the suited men answers, "Yes, ma'am, Mr. Ellis doesn't want you to be inconvenienced in any way."

His partner stands just outside the door casing the hallway like the KKK will materialize from the ether.

"Well, I'll tell him what an awesome job you guys did; I didn't even know you were following us, thanks." I mumble as we move deeper into Milla's new home. I hear him before I see him.

"Aye, lass!" Collin's gregarious brogue greets from somewhere in the apartment. Milla almost jumps into my arms as the deep, smokey words filter into the living room.

"That would be," I explain while being engulfed in his familiar smell. "Collin, Val gave me a message for you." I whisper. His large body already shakes with laughter, and I haven't uttered a syllable of the tommyrot she made me memorize.

Valery is bat-shit crazy, and for some beautifully strange reason, Collin is completely smitten with her. I smile like a loon as I make my voice a little smokier and say, "Don't fucking think about looking at that bitch artist with a taco. You don't like Mexican food and I'm all the goddamn spice your Scottish ass need. I'll know if you give her the wrong attention. And Colli, you'll pay. With your blood and sweat. I'll bathe in the tears you cry."

Collin laughs so hard; he can barely catch his breath to speak. When he finally does, his words trickle out like a dirty limerick. "Mi heartbeat is a true nutter, isn't she, lass?"

I disentangle from his embrace and walk to the windows to check out the view. I smile over my shoulder and tell him, "Made me promise to give you that message as soon as I saw you. Exactly the way she gave it to me, too.""

"You missed the mark on that one, Viv. Of course, you classed up my girl's vinegar with all them *fuckin g's* and elocutions." We laugh at Collin's spot-on imitation of the way Val says fucking and then my manners kick in.

"How have you been?" Collin turns to face me, and I hear shuffling from down the hall. *Milla must be checking out her bedroom.*

"I'm good. Missing my girl. She called me last night after you'd gone to sleep. Told me what went down. I called John to see if he needed me to come over."

"Did you?" I inquire while moving away from the window. I catch movement in the entryway from the hall just before Milla steps into the living room. Collin and I turn to face her, and she stops short. Her plump lips are agape and her small hand floats up to the hollow divot at the base of her throat.

What the hell is this? Hello... remember your little birdie, Vera?

He takes in the petite artist from Chili. They watch each other like predator and prey; only I'm not sure which is predator, and which is the prey. His voice pulls me from my revery as he continues our conversation, "Aye. She was a little shaken up and a lot pissed off. She was also horny as fuck..."

"Yeah, John and I will take the blame for that."

"Well, *I took care of her*. Introduce me, Vivian."

"Sorry. Camilla, this is my friend and the co-owner of the artist cooperative collective, Collin."

"Hi. Is nice to meet you."

"Aye. Heard you had some excitement over the weekend at Viv's."

"Yes."

"I'm glad to see you stuck it out. This is quite the opportunity for an artist. I love your work, by the way."

"Thank you." She steps into the living room proper and takes a seat on the funky, gold velvet sofa sitting in the middle of the space.

"We've checked everything, and the apartment is secure." The suited men step into the room from wherever the hell they've been.

I forgot they were here.

The one in charge finishes in his no-nonsense voice, "Instructions for setting up the security system is on the kitchen counter. The leased car for Ms. Fazzini is parked in the second parking space for this unit, keys are on the counter."

"Thank you." Milla stands and extends her right hand to the man. He looks at it like it's a dead fish, but eventually he grabs it and gives it one pump before letting her go. Collin's smirk must mirror the one kissing my mouth.

"Yes, well. Mrs. Ellis," He clears his throat before he turns to me, a bemused expression painting his stoic features with a softness that looks foreign and states, "Your husband would like to have lunch with you today." I catch Collin's gaze just as he gives a terse nod of resignation.

"Aye, John seems to have shit well in hand." A broad smile breaks out on his face. "Why don't you go take care of whatever you need to do with John, and I'll get our artist in resident settled in and over to the collective."

"Are you sure you don't mind?" I don't pose the question to anyone in particular, but it's Milla who answers.

"I don't mind. You baby-sit me for the whole weekend, Vivian. I will see you later, cachai?"

"Yes. And I was *not* baby-sitting you. I enjoyed having you over, even if it was the weekend from hell. Collin is good people and will take care of you."

"Aye." He walks over to stand in front of me, and I know he wants Valery to come forward. I call her from her room but tell her I need to remain up front with her."

"Fuck! You look like the darkest, filthiest fuckin fantasy come to life, Colli. No wonder I was boneless and calm after that goddamn phone sex session." Valery hums an appreciative sound from the back of her throat. "Thank you, baby."

"I'll always take care of you, blood moon."

"Did Viv give you my motherfuckin message and did that white girl with a taco hear it?" Val gives Milla some serious stink eye. I doubt Camilla even registers it with the way she's looking at us like she's watching a traveling freak show.

"Fuck, yeah, she did. Made me so horny for you, Val. And don't be such a cunt. You know I don't have even one extra fuck to give to anyone who isn't you, babe." I feel Valery melt like ice cream on a summer afternoon. Dripping over hot and sticky fingers only too happy to be licked clean.

Well damn, maybe that's my ice cream that's melting. They're hot as hell.

"Not bein a cunt, Collin. But you better believe me when I say this shit," She pauses and swings her whiskey drunk gaze over to Camilla before finishing. "I'll gladly let you fuckin own me as long as the goose gets the same goddamn rights as the gander."

I love how she claims him with her whole being.

"You know you fucking own me. Mind, body, and the entirety of my soul, woman. It's only you, blood moon." Val retreats without another word. It takes me a minute to come back into full awareness.

Jesus-Joseph-ain't-your-daddy! Collin and Val's sexual chemistry is enough to be classified as a weapon of mass destruction.

"Was th-that... did you *switch*?" Milla's luminous eyes are even brighter as beautiful shards of wonderment flash within their depths.

"Yes. That was Valery, she and Collin are together." I collect my things and prepare to leave. "She's extremely... *territorial*." Collin gives an indulgent chuckle and chimes in with his two cents.

"Aye, that's my little blood moon goddess. She just came out to mark what belongs to her." Collin and I share a smile, but Camilla looks like someone just told her that her first born will be a damn cyclops.

"Milla?"

"How is Collin *with* Valery?"

"It's complicated, but it works. I need to run. See you guys later. Collin, use the company card to take care of initial groceries and whatever else Milla may need. Keep all receipts, we'll be able to write them off come tax season." I fall into his arms and accept the bit of comfort he offers before stepping away.

"Mrs. Ellis," The taller man in the black addresses me. "I'll be driving you today and Jameson will follow in the sedan."

―――

"Oh, okay." I turn and wave to Collin and Milla before following the intergalactic peacekeepers into the hall. "Do you know how long this is going to go on for?"

"As long as is necessary, Mrs. Ellis. Your safety is of the utmost importance to your husband."

I know, I just wish he hadn't gotten involved with such nonsense during undergrad. We wouldn't have to worry about all the little gamecocks coming back to roost in our little coop.

~28~
Vivian

Vivian Ellis, 2003

I want it to go back to the way it was before The-all-powerful-Order infiltrated our lives. Sometimes—especially on days like today—I want to pack my bags and leave him to sort this mess out on his own. Like maybe doing so is the kindest action I can take for myself. It feels like every time he has a problem, it automatically becomes 'our' problem. One that disrupts both our lives. One that requires more compromise and sacrifice. Usually from... me.

When these thoughts pop into my head, I feel like i'm failing him and our marriage. He's always done everything he could to make sure I and, by extension, all alters have what we need. He never complained. Never said it was too much or I was not enough. Except in the beginning. After the stay in Washington state. He didn't say it... didn't say I wasn't enough, but he showed me. His actions with Valery shouted it from the rafters that I wasn't enough for him. But that was then, this is now. We're in a better place. On the same page. I know what's going on and he's not keeping anything from me.

I need to trust his love and commitment for and to me. Need to trust that my love is enough for him. Know that he's making similar sacrifices and compromises for us. I want to believe this. Need to believe this... but I don't. Because I can't. He's still keeping shit from me and I refuse to ask him what it is.

I'm willing to hold him down, but like Valery told Collin; it only works if the goose has the same rights as the gander. I know John doesn't see me as an equal. He probably loves the idea of me staying a broken doll, playing dress up in the mirror. Waiting on his love to consecrate my being. Fuck that and the horse his arrogant ass rode in on. (Shoutout to Valery. ;)

It's been a week since the incident at Diane's, and I still have the men in black suits driving me around. I'm kind of over it, to be honest. "Bea," I call out to the cat who's more like a daughter than a pet. "Where's mommy's beautiful girl? My thoughts turn to John and the hired drivers he calls protection, but it feels more like another way to control me.

Bea and her litter of four, saunter into the room like they own the entire house. My heart is not big enough to contain the love I feel for them. I can't imagine how I'll send them to their forever homes in a few weeks. "Hey, girlie. Your snapback game is on point." I praise her while running my adoring hands all over her sturdy body. Her kittens twist in and out and in between my legs. I'm surrounded with proof that we two-legs are indeed the inferior animal among the mammals.

"Is your daddy home, yet?" I give them all one last cuddle before I head upstairs toward the hot shower I've been fantasizing about since lunch today. I covet the barely there feel of my ratty Carolina tee shirt and the comfort of the first pair of boxers I stole from John our freshman year. A frustrated sigh precedes my heavy footsteps as I succumb to the fatigue that's been riding me all afternoon. *Maybe I'm getting my period... that would explain my moodiness.*

My last journal entry concerning John and everything we've got going on sifts through my mind, just as hot water cascades over my face. I didn't share my feelings in the collective journal because I wanted or even needed any feedback. I shared them because I needed to know what I thought about my own thoughts. Of course, that didn't stop either Val or Vera from throwing their two cents into the pot. But it was Vera's scathing response that pissed me off.

How you can began to think such things about that man. He love you in spite of all your short comings and he don't make you feel like you have to carry them on your own, yeah? Maybe put yourself in his shoes and see how uncomfortable his daily walk really is.

***

"Vivian."

Think of the devil and he will appear. I smile as I wait for him to find me in my office. His measured steps eat up the distance that separates us. So confident and regimented, like he's leading an army to march on Zion.

"There you are, lovely."

"Did you think I was lost?" I beam at him from my seated position on the floor in front of the picture window. My shower gave me some much needed clarity, allowing me to see John for the man he's striving to be. Vera was right, I want to give him what he freely gives me. Unconditional compassion, forgiveness, acceptance and love.

"No, but you didn't answer me." He stands outside the open office door, his shoulder casually propped against the casing.

He looks relaxed and understated in his faded 501s, white tee, and leather flip-flops. My own personal all-American boy dipped in hues of hickory, umber, and cinnamon. A beautiful imagining of the American dream.

"Viv..."

"Why do you look like you spent the day on the lake instead of in the office?" I ask to cover my slight embarrassment at being caught ogling my husband.

"I left the office early today. Changed into something more casual for a meeting. So, why didn't you answer?"

"I didn't want to lose my train of thought." I hold up my journal by way of explanation and say, "Besides, I knew you wouldn't stop until you found me."

I stretch my arms up like a toddler, even though I don't need his help to get up from the floor, but I still want to feel his strong arms

---

188

around me. The comfort and security they provide. The moment he pulls me into his body, I feel the tension release from my shoulders and lower back.

"What's got you so worked up? You haven't been thinking about last Sunday."

"Of course, I've been thinking about what happened last Sunday, John." I wince at my shrill tone. "I didn't mean it like that, but *really...*"

"I know, Vivian. I'm not trying to minimize the situation. I know how traumatizing it was for you, and everyone involved. It's just,"

I pull away from the safety of his arms because the dissonance of his tone sounds like internalized rage, grief and disappointment. I shake my head to dislodge the pitchy chords of his self-loathing and say, "Baby, I don't blame you for what happened. I know you think you're in control of everything and everyone, but you're not omnipotent." I expect the weary look to drain away, but his next words give origin to the weight upon his shoulders.

"Vera told me what you wrote in your journal, Vivian. I didn't ask, obviously, but she thought I should know how you felt. Since *you* had no intention of telling me yourself."

Dammit-all-to-hell in a handbasket wearing gasoline drawers!

"You're right, I had no intention of telling you. Because I hadn't worked out how I felt, yet. That's why I wrote in our journal, trying to process my thoughts. I don't know what I'm thinking unless I write what I'm thinking down. Then, I can figure out what I think about what I'm thinking about, cachai?"

John slants a quizzical look my way and I realize I've used the vernacular Chilean phrase Milla often uses. I role my eyes and shake my head, while offering a little smirk in response.

"What does, *cachai*, mean?"

"You know or okay. Milla uses it all the time to make sure I understand. Anyway, I would never come to you with anything until

I've worked out my true thoughts and feelings." I take a moment to steady my breathing.

"If you need to work your thoughts out with someone, then that someone is me, Vivian. Not any-damn-body else."

"John." I drip ordinary beige tones of frustration over the vibrancy of his name before continuing in more muted hues, "Vera had no right to go behind my back, and you had no right to indulge her."

"I don't disagree with you and told Vera as much when she refused to keep your entry private."

I turn around to gage the truth of his words so fast, I'm dizzy by the time my palms collide with his solid chest.

"Y-you told her what, now?"

"Vivian, I would never knowingly violate your trust again. I don't go to counseling just to say I'm going. I go because I recognize I have to sort my shit out not only for our sake, but honestly—and more importantly—for my own." He captures my hands and brings my knuckles to his lips for a soft kiss and states, "I realize every time I hurt you, it's because I'm too chickenshit to turn my pain and anger on myself." Sincerity strengthens the beautiful prosody between his spoken words.

"Thank you."

"Have you worked it out?"

"Yes."

"And?"

"And... even without the girls 'uninvited comments, I realized those feelings were rooted in my ego; therefore, they were rooted in fear. I'm afraid and didn't want to admit it to myself. Didn't want to appear weak. Mmmmm—"

"How does being afraid make you weak?"

"Weak is the wrong word. It's more like—you know when you're a kid and have a nightmare—as long as I keep my eyes and mouth closed, the scary stuff couldn't get out to hurt me."

"Okay. Except ultimately it's the real shit that goes bump in the night that makes every nightmare a goddamn fantasy in comparison." We quietly sink into the truth of his words until he squeezes my hand to pull me from my thoughts.

In gratitude, I explain my fears. "I'm scared of losing you to The Order. Vera hit the nail on the head and drove it through every one of my insecurities, when she brought up my shortcomings and..."

"And, what?" John maps out the details of my face like this is the first time he's been granted the right to do so. I watch him, watching me.

Even after all these years together, he still looks at me like I'm a shiny, new penny he stumbled across on a walk. It's a gift.

I square my shoulders and share my deepest fear. "What if I'm not enough for you? After seeing that video of Cole—an"

"You think I'm bisexual."

"No? I don't think I do... but. You didn't *not* enjoy being in that dungeon with Cole and those other men." I'm ready to retreat but he doesn't let me move even one inch.

His voice is low and serious. "Come out and ask the real question that's been scratching inside your brain since viewing that video, lovely-mine."

I know that tone. I need to pay attention. I double my resolve to face this fear with my eyes open.

He continues, "Would it be a deal breaker if I told you I enjoyed fucking men?"

My heart stops beating for an eternal breath. I deflect, "I never thought you were anything other than straight. Would it change the way I feel about you..." I trail off.

Thinking.

Feeling.

Listening to the rhythmic emptiness between each heartbeat.

The shaky void after each inhale and after each exhale of my humid breath.

I connect with the silent whoosh of my blood as it pools warm and languid in my lower belly.

"Well, lovely."

"I'm possessive of you. Selfish. Voracious in my need for you. It would drive me to murder if I had to share you."

Seemingly satisfied, he deadpans, "I'm not."

"I know. If creating delicate corruption enveloped in controlled anarchy were a type of sexuality, you would be that. And The Order... they could give you *that*."

"The Order can't give me shit that I can't get for myself. I never needed them. Didn't even know they were a thing. How white folk run their world, has abso-fucking-lutely nothing to do with how I run mine."

"How can you say that? These people are part of a larger organization. What they do; what they say affects economies. World trade agreements. Wars. They start and end wars, John." I hear the rising terror in my voice and can't seem to get it under control. On a shaky breath, I question, "How can you fix your mouth to say they have no bearing on you?"

"In my world, they do not. The Order may start and end wars, Vivian, but not in *my* world."

I step back and look at my husband. Really look *into* him, and I think... for the first time, he allows me to see him as he truly sees himself. Behind the mask, the persona, the beautiful lies. This is the countenance of a man who has gathered every fragment of himself—dark and light, powerful and impotent, honorable and villainous—in pursuit of the kind of pleasure only found in the intimate knowledge gained when one accepts themselves.

Sovereign. Poised. Able.

"No, I don't suppose they do. They never could, and that's why they won't give up without a hell of a fight." The feral flash of his white teeth is an entire mood. I respond with a knowing smirk of my own. So damn proud to belong to the man standing before me, my chest feels two sizes bigger than normal.

He smiles—that special one reserved for me. The one that tells me how amazing it feels to be understood and accepted by the most important person in his life. That I am that person, is an honor I never want to take for granted.

As complicated as John is, he protects and provides the simplicity I value. The stillness that cradles me when everything else is rolling and tumbling in my world. He is home. My own private island.

We are the beginning of each other, and there is no foreseeable end to either of us.

~29~

Vivian

Somehow, time continues to move faster than I want it to. We're already twelve weeks out from the kittens making their entrance into the world. The kitties are going to their forever homes today. I decided not to keep any of them, and Bertha is scheduled for spading next week. I'm glad her genes will continue on in her first and last litter. They're beautiful representatives of the majestic Maine Coon breed.

"So, the kittens are leaving today, are you ready to be a one cat household again?" John echoes my thoughts as he walks into the kitchen looking like my favorite snack.

"Honestly, I'm going to miss having them around." I turn toward our kitchen door. "Are you expecting someone, John?"

He shakes his head and motions for me to stay put and stalks over to the door.

I could bite him, he's so damn yummy.

" Jessa?" I recognize the confusion in his voice because my thoughts mirror it. "You're a little early to pick up your kitten." John says by way of greeting. Their relationship has improved vastly since my last horrible episode. It may have something to do with the fact that the girls and I don't depend on her as heavily as we used to. Or it could be that John is really putting in the work to be the best version of himself. Whatever it is, I'm just glad they're no longer at each other's throat every time they're together.

Still doesn't answer why she's here. Something tells me it has everything to do with a certain green-eyed alter.

I watch her placid look turn into a more familiar accusatory glare as she looks up into John's face. He either doesn't notice it or doesn't care enough about Jessa's opinion of him to address it. I step into her personal space to get her attention away from John and say, "Let me guess, Vera called you."

She turns those deep obsidian eyes on me, and my ire rises like a thermostat. The truth sears my thoughts into my brain like a scar. After she drops the cat carrier on the floor and her large tote bag on the island, she nods her head in affirmation.

Jessa rakes those same obsidian eyes over the side of John's head. If she could weaponize her glare, she'd be guilty of first degree murder.

"Yes, she was frantic about sharing something private with *someone*—" She pauses to point another angry gaze in John's direction. He looks at her like all the shits he had to give have been flushed down the toilet and out to the Broad River. Her raspy voice scrapes the rest of her words onto the floor at our feet. "Even though she knew he had no business asking about it."

John's expression darkens, just as frost crystalizes his rich brown eyes. "Look, I'm not sure what Vera said or indicated. Or maybe... you're just assuming you know what happened." As he passes me on his way to turn the kettle on, he presses a quick hard kiss to my forehead.

I'm trapped in his gaze for longer than is necessary. In our unspoken communication, he tells me to *deal with Jessa because I don't want him to do it.* With a quick nod and a small smile, I give him my response.

Consider it done, baby.

"I'm going to head into my office. I'll be back when Daily and Rhyan come to get their kitten. Yell if you need me. Oh, the security detail are aware of who's allowed to come onto the property." He kisses me again before turning a stony look to my therapist and friend. "Jessa." Any warmth from before is clearly missing from his tone.

She nods her head. I don't know what she's thinking, but something about the slump in her shoulders tells me she realizes she's made a huge mistake.

She turns to face me just as she asks, "What the hell is going on, Vivian? You're usually the point of contact, when I heard Vera's trembling voice on the other end of the line, my heart stopped beating for a moment."

"I wrote about how frustrated I am with everything going on with John and The stupid Order. I was venting. Trying to figure out what my true thoughts and feelings were. She read it and ran to John. She thought I was planning to leave him."

"Why would she think that?"

"Because I said something to that affect; like maybe I'd be better on my own."

Jessa studies me. I don't know what she's looking for, but apparently she doesn't find it because she shakes her head. Dislodging the two braids on either side of her elf-like face. The ends wrapped in leather and tied at the end with beads.

"Did she not come and talk to you before she went to John—who, I'm assuming never asked her to spy for him—and blabbed about your entry?"

"No and thank you for acknowledging your gross mistake. You better let John know you worked it out for yourself. He's ready to rip you a new asshole and not in the hot anal sex kind of way."

"Ewwwe, Vivian." We share a laugh, and it feels amazing to experience the tension sluicing away from us. On a peaceful exhale, we end our mutual joviality. Jessa sobers and says, "did you work it out?"

"Work what out... oh, yes. I did. I'm not going anywhere. I just needed to get my thoughts on paper. See what they looked like. How

I felt reading feelings that felt less like my own and more like my ego's. You know what I mean?"

"Yes. The ego is always going to act from a place of fear. Its sole purpose is to protect the body. The ease of physical existence, but you're operating from a higher sense of self and that gives you courage."

"Exactly. I can't kill my ego; I need to hold space for it to fully experience what it feels." I move over to the kettle and make two cups of tea. Jessa climbs up onto the counter-height stool and waits for me to finish my thoughts. I don't keep her waiting long. "It's like having another alter that only lives inside my consciousness. Does that make sense?"

Her eyes soften and smile at me. I've seen Jessa smile with her mouth maybe a handful of times because she mostly smiles with her soul. It's painfully beautiful. She responds in her soft, pensive voice, "It makes more sense than anything we've said this morning."

After placing the tea and breakfast cookies onto the island, I take a seat across from her. We're both quiet. Hands wrapped around our warm mugs, the steam from the orange-turmeric tea wafting in our faces. It smells like a mother's hug and your first real kiss.

Of course, this peaceful moment is interrupted when John steps into the kitchen and asks Jessa, "Was she standing beside Valery when she called you?"

I have no idea what he's getting at, and it doesn't even matter anymore. I look at him like he walked in here with his dick hanging out.

"What?" He asks as he fixes a cup of lemon-ginger tea with honey.

"Fine, John." Jessa states. "I apologize for assuming you were up to your old tactics. I know you would never use Vera like that... or in any way, really."

Adequately assuaged, he places his cup in front of the chair furthest from Jessa, placing me between the giant and the hobbit.

She watches him like he might pull a knife from under his shirt and stab her to death.

John can be such an asshole.

He sips his tea like he's having it with the Queen of England. The playful lines at the corners of his eyes make him look like a naughty imp.

We share small intimacies.

"I'm glad you were able to work that out for yourself. Vivian and I already talked about it and so have Vera and me. I'm good, but Vera may need some guidance in how to clear the air with Viv."

I jerk my gaze to him. This is the first time I'm hearing this. He shakes his head in a dismissive way that makes me feel like I'm missing something.

"Lovely," It feels as if he speaks directly to my discomfort when he continues. "... she knows she fucked up and she's scared you're pissed at her. I told her you weren't, but she thinks I'm just blowing sunshine up her ass."

"Were those her exact words?" He gives me a derisive look and continues to drink his tea.

"I can see where Vera may be internalizing these feelings. She's used to people discounting her when she does anything that goes against their desire for her."

"Yea, but it's me. Surely she knows how much I love her."

"Knowing and trusting are two very different things, lovely."

"Hmmm, I guess you're right."

"Of course, I'm right. When have you ever known me to be wrong, woman?"

"There doesn't seem to be enough room in this mini-mansion to accommodate your enormous ego, Mr. Ellis." Jessa deadpans as she gets up from her seat.

"Where are you going?"

"To get my kitten and go home. This has already been an interesting morning and it's not even eleven o'clock."

"Honestly Jessa, I think you just didn't want to wait to get Petra and used this as an excuse to come over early."

She chuckles softly under her breath. Her eyes giving away her diabolical plan, while also showing concern for the situation. "I wasn't planning to be here before two, but Vera's call was... *disturbing*."

"I'm going to get her out here. I don't like talking about her like she's a nonfactor."

"Vivian, she said she didn't want to come out until after I heard from you and John."

"Well, that's just too damn bad. She was woman enough to call you over, woman enough to tell John what she had no business telling him, and she'll be woman enough to come out here and face the music she so boldly orchestrated."

John and Jessa look at me like I'm overreacting. It's called accountability. And if she isn't held to the same standards as the rest of us, she'll never progress beyond the point she is in this moment.

Vivian

I reach inside the Internal House and call Vera's name like a tired mom yelling down the street for her children.

Veer-ra! Jessa's here and we need you.

She doesn't make me wait long. I'm already back in the driver's seat when she sidles up beside me. Her expressive eyes spill warmed over hurt, and days old regret.

Jessa here already?

"Yes, Jessa's here and so is John."

Oh, y'all already talk about everything, yeah?

"No, we haven't talked about anything, yet. I thought it was important for you to start the conversation since you were the one who initiated everything else, Vera."

I-I... uh, y-you w-want m-me t-to..."

"Yes and stop stuttering. You're an intelligent woman who is more than capable of clearly articulating your thoughts. Now, please tell Jessa what upset you so much you had to call her to come and sort it out. To sort *us* out." Wide, pitiful eyes that belong to a scared child stare back at me, but I can't give into her fear. She knows better than to violate the Seeking Wonderland journal shared between the alters. I let her see my anger, my disappointment, and most of all, I pour my hurt out in front of her like an offering at her shrine of treachery.

I'm s-so sorry, yeah? I didn't think before I reacted, Vivian. I know better, yeah? I do... but—

"Tell it to everyone, Vera. When you're bad-ass enough to do a thing, be bad-ass enough to admit to doing it." She steps across me to get into the driver's seat, while I take her place as the passenger. Nodding my head in encouragement, I relax and wait.

"Morning John. Morning Jessa."

"Good morning Vera, how are you feeling?" *Jessa*

"Like I'm carrying a whole load of heavy on my back, yeah?"

"I imagine it would feel like that, based on your phone call last night."

"Vera, tell Jessa exactly what you did yesterday." *The usual tenderness John reserves for Vera is missing. I peek out from behind Vera's mostly green eyes, because his pain belongs to only me. Just as I suspected, he's crushed.*

"V-V-Vi—"

Stop with the stuttering. Be the bad-ass woman who did what she thought was right at the time, Vera!

"V-Vivian had been wr-writing in Seeking Wonderland, yeah? About last weekend when Camilla Fazzini stayed over and all the things that happened from Friday to S-Sunday, yeah?"

"Alright. I don't know what happened last weekend, Vera, but Vivian may not have felt the need to tell me about it. What does it have to do with what you did?"

"It d-doesn't... not really, yeah? But it kind of does, too. She wrote about how—" She slides her eyes over to me, waiting to see if I want her to say what I wrote about in front of Jessa, and it pisses me right the hell off.

You've already violated the sanctity of the journal, Vera. What does it matter if you tell one more person?

She flinches, I feel the body jerk back like it's been hit with a two-by-four. A tear rolls down our cheek, but I don't change the resting-bitch-face I'm currently giving her.

Go on, finish what you started.

"Vera, do you need—"

"No," John cuts Jessa off. "she needs to say what she has to say. It was easy enough for her to tell me what Viv wrote in their journal and even easier for her to tell me exactly what she thought about it." John has never taken this tone with Vera before. T

201

his may be worse than my RBF.

"He's. John... is right. Vivian wrote how she wasn't feeling like it was worth it anymore and maybe she should leave John to handle his own problems because he's to blame for them coming home to roost—her words, yeah?"

"And you ran to John with the journal you share with the alters to share it with *him*?"

"I w-wasn't thinking straight. I thought Vivian was gonna leave him when he never left her—*us*. He never left us, and he always helps us handle our problems. I couldn't let her take John's love and throw it away, yeah?"

"If she wanted to throw John's love away, Vera, it's hers to do with as she pleases. You get that, right. John and Vivian are in this relationship. John's love belongs to Vivian. End of story."

"I know that Jessa, I'm not stupid, you can stop talking to me like I'm some kind of slow kid riding the short bus, yeah?"

"I don't mean to be patronizing, but it sounds like your concern is more about what you receive from John than the love he has for Vivian."

"That's not true. John never treats me like he does Vivian. I wouldn't want him to, yeah? I don't want Vivian to be unhappy, and she is unhappy without him. You trying to start something that doesn't need to be started, yeah?"

"Vera," John cuts in with less disappointment and a little more understanding. "I think, and I'm not trying to speak for you, Jessa, but I think she's saying that you and I also have a relationship of sorts. And may—"

"We are not a couple. I don't see you like that. You don't... you can't see me like that, yeah"

"Of course, we're not a *couple*, Vera. There are many types of relationships. Honestly, you've become the sister I never knew I wanted."

I watch from the passenger's seat as the tension falls from her shoulders and the breath she'd been holding whooshes from her mouth.

"Okay. That makes me feel better because you feel like my brother, yeah? If I'd had a brother like you, maybe..."

"There's no maybe about it, Vera. None of that shit would have happened to you." A heavy silence settles around the small island.

Vera breaks the silence and challenges, Yeah, but then Vivian and Valery or even Valeria wouldn't be here. John, you wouldn't have the love of your life. Just because the cause of a thing is broken and dirty doesn't mean the effect is worthless, yeah?"

"Of course, you're right. It's profound that you have come to this conclusion, Vera." Jessa sounds impressed.

"Anyway," Vera continues without acknowledging Jessa's comment, "... that's why I wanted him to know what she said... ur, what she wrote. I didn't want her to make choices because she was scared or tired, yeah?"

"But did you have the right to take Vivian's choice away from her like you did?" Jessa sounds like her normal self, not as placating or cajoling as she usually does when speaking with Vera.

"No, I guess not. I just knew I didn't want anything to change. Didn't want to have to start over like we did when John left before, yeah?"

"All right. What about the fact that you violated the integrity of Seeking Wonderland, Vera. I doubt Vivian or Valery feel comfortable writing in there anymore."

It feels like I've been cut away from an integral part of myself. A part I need in order to function in my daily life. I say to Vera. She turns and looks at me and it's like seeing a distorted reflection of myself in a cracked mirror. I don't like it.

"I-I didn't even consider they wouldn't want to still write in our journal. It's been so important to us. It's where we first started to meet each other, yeah?"

"Vera, your actions are akin to rape. You took away the rights of the others to choose; you took their power away. Are you able to see how triggering that is. And you did it out of selfish fear, not for the good of the whole." Jessa doesn't pull any punches with her delivery.

I'm proud of her for doing so. Vera needs this.

John intercedes, "Vera, we're not trying to gang up on you, but I can tell you that I am disappointed in your choice to share information that wasn't yours to share."

Vera slumps into the driver's seat, her entire body folds in on itself. She makes herself as small as possible. I've seen her do this before when she thought she'd disappointed her father when she refused to take the milk and cookies he offered at bedtime.

Vera, I think you've had enough. Come over here, get in the passenger seat, but stay with me, okay?

"Vivian's ready to get back in the driver's seat. I'm sorry, John. I never wanted to disappoint you, yeah? I didn't want to hurt Vivian or Valery, either. I made a mistake." She slides her soft body from the driver's seat and refuses to make eye contact with me as we pass each other.

Once I'm comfortably seated and back in control, I turn to her and speak aloud so the others can hear me. "I love you, Vera. I don't care if you make mistakes because that's a part of living. What I do care about is how you handle the repercussions of your actions when you do."

She straightens a little in her seat and finally meats my gaze. Disappointment floats like Lilly pads on the surface of her eyes. But there's also respect. Hopefully that respect is for herself and how she's taken responsibility for her actions.

"Welcome back, Viv. I thought Vera was very brave for coming out to talk with us on her own."

"That's not being brave, Jessa. It's called being an adult and taking responsibility for one's action. Why do you insist on treating Vera like she's stuck with the mindset of a child?" It pisses me off. The only child in this system, is Valeria and she wasn't much of a child considering all the shit she dealt with.

"I don't treat her any differently than I treat you or Val, Vivian."

"All right, then. Jessa, thanks for coming over early to *sort* shit out." John interrupts Jessa before she can launch into some long-winded explanation. Then he turns to me with a filthy smirk on his sinful mouth and asks, "Viv, are you feeling sorted?" He doesn't wait for a response before he turns back to Jessa and claps his hands together like the gay choir director in a Baptist church and says, "Since you're here, you may as well collect Petra and the new-cat-human pack Vivian made."

I'm doing everything in my power not to laugh at his foolishness. He only spares me a cursory look before standing from his chair to collect the large basket of kitty supplies. I take the hint from the assholery of my husband and push away from the island just as Jessa's small hand comes to rest over her heart. I don't know what she wants to say, but I don't give her a chance. I mumble under my breath, "Yes, I'll go get Petra for you. You have your carrier."

"What's going on?" Jessa steps away from the island, a little flustered and a lot confused.

"What do you mean?" I'm moving away from her like she has leprosy.

"Something got you upset enough to write about leaving John to deal with his own mess. That got Vera upset enough to violate the rules of the journal, and now you and John can't get me out of your house fast enough. What the hell is going on and why aren't you telling me, Vivian?"

This is the problem with having your therapist become one of your closest friends. We don't need her as a therapist as much as we did in the beginning—she should be proud of how far we've come—but she doesn't know how to simply be our friend, either.

"Jessa," I deepen my breathing to find my center before I attempt to explain how some things have changed. "I. We aren't the helpless DID system you and your mother met two years ago. You have done an amazing job helping us acknowledge, work through, and accept the trauma that allowed us to remain separate identities. We are grateful."

John saunters back into the kitchen carrying the large Moses basket filled with all the things a little Maine Coon kitten could ever need and want. This one has silver and lilac bedding with cream-colored ribbons wrapped around the top of the overabundance of sparkly, silver tulle encasing the entire package. It looks more suited for a baby shower than a carry-kitty-home pack.

"Vivian, I thought you were going to collect Petra for..." He stops midsentence after taking the temperature in the room and finding it considerably less warm and friendly than it had been moments ago.

"Yes, I was... but," I hate how awkward it feels to say these next words. "Jessa, you are one of our closest friends. We know for a fact; we would not be where we are right now without you. We also know as we discover more about ourselves as individuals and as a collective, we will need to reach out to you. Dr. Jessa..."

"But right now," She interrupts with a knowing smile on her small face, "You need Dr. Jessa to step back and let the collective work through their own growing pains." She doesn't sound angry. That counts for something.

I check on Vera, who looks better than she did earlier. I think she realizes this was something we could've handled ourselves, if she had only trusted the system and my love for John. I toss a small smile her way and give her a wave. She mouths her gratitude and walks to her room.

"Right now, we need you to be our friend. To see us as we see ourselves. Vera may have been a fragile, childlike woman in the beginning, but the innate strength is evident in the intact identities that remain. If our mind felt safe enough to form one solid identity... if the body were older when the abuse started—had time for convergence—that bastard wouldn't have stood a snowball's chance in hell." The pride in my voice shocks me. "Give her credit for having such strong identities to pull from had she grown up in a loving home."

Well damn. That's an epiphany if I ever had one. I guess I'm going to have to write that down in Seeking Wonderland.

And just like that, I know Vera didn't ruin a damn thing with her actions. We're stronger, wiser, and more resilient than we've ever been.

"Well then, give me my damn kitten and your bourgie ass kitty-care-pack and we'll be on our way." Jessa rarely shows her teeth when she smiles, but this one splits her face in two. It tells me we've all passed another crucible in this beautiful journey we're on together.

"I feel like you guys are kicking me out for some nefarious reason. Am I correct in my assessment?"

"I'll put everything in your hobbit car for you." John smiles at me like an old skull head preacher when the ushers walk by his pulpit.

With a little amusement and a whole lot of lechery.

~31~

John

Of course, there is a reason I want Jessa out of my house. First, I don't need the security guys walking into the kitchen with intel reports while her little ass is standing here acting like my wife is breaking up with her. Second, it's kind of dope that Viv and I are in such a good place that we don't need outside help to deal with inside shit. It's nice to know Jessa's available, but even better knowing the woman I love trusts me enough to work with me. *Why isn't she happy about this?*

"No, Jessa. Nothing untoward if that's what you're implying. It's early and Vivian and I haven't even started our day, yet. Last weekend, we had an unexpected houseguest and this weekend..." I let the words linger, with awkwardness of her showing up unannounced and earlier than was expected. From the pensive expression tightening the smooth skin around her eyes, I'd say the intended point was made.

"No, of course, I understand. Vivian?" She looks over to where Viv is holding Bertha like she doesn't weigh as much as a toddler, before she continues, "If you or any of the girls need me, you know where to find me. I would like to meet with you all to process the breach of trust as well as discuss the relationship between Valery and Collin." Jessa's voice is soft like she talks to preschoolers all day, but there's a core of abrasive steel wool scratching around the edges of her melodic tones. Clearly betraying her sense of self and purpose.

"Okay. I'll speak with the girls. We'll set something up. Oh, and Vera hasn't broken trust as much as shed light on our need to revisit and revise how we intend to use Seeking Wonderland going

---

208

forward." Vivian bends down to place Bertha back on the floor and stands just as I open the back door for Jessa to take her shit and go.

"Is your car open?"

"Yes. Why would I lock it?"

"I don't know, just thought I'd ask before going and discovering I have to come back inside to get keys."

"Oh," The monosyllabic word drops from her pinched mouth while she turns back to my Vivian, effectively dismissing me from my own goddamn kitchen.

I'm almost on the other side of the door when I hear lovely's placating tone as she assures Jessa of her usefulness. "Thanks for coming over and checking on the situation. I'm glad Vera thought to call..." I don't stay to hear the rest of their conversation before I slip out of the house carrying everything Viv got for Jessa and Petra.

True to her word, I find Jessa's little Toyota Prius unlocked and ready to transport her new pet. After placing the Moses basket in the trunk, I quickly secure the carrier in the backseat and shut the door. I tap the roof to say goodbye to the not-so-little furball. I really didn't want to give any of them away, but when Valery called me an *old cat daddy*, I knew I had to let them go.

I walk back and catch the tail end of whatever Viv is saying. "...yes he does, but it doesn't mean he's not also aware of his part in it."

"Maybe and maybe not. Why are you so defensive about it?"

"Defensive about what, Jessa?"

I don't want to know what they're talking about so; I clear my throat.

"Oh," Both women turn and exclaim in unison at my abrupt appearance.

"John." Jessa finds her voice first and I give her my most impassive face. Waiting for her to say what it is she wants to say. Or grab her bag and leave.

"Did you get Petra settled?" My wife, the peace maker, interjects to diffuse the tension that hangs like the scent of magnolia in the air between the three of us.

"Yes." I find that when people are plotting behind my back, if I remain quiet and look disinterested, they usually shoot themselves in the foot trying to disarm the smoking gun. So, I stand in our kitchen with loose limbs and a relaxed posture. For all intents and purposes, I look like my mind's a million miles away. Meanwhile, Jessa's small features are contorting themselves into acrobatic routines as she tries to ascertain how much of their conversation I overheard.

Now, this is interesting. What are you hiding, little hobbit?

"Well, thanks for the kitty care package and for putting Petra in the—"

"Defensive about what?" I inquire like it's the second or third time I've had to asked this question. Interlacing my hands in front of my body, I appear calm as I meet Vivian's eyes. And she knows. From the way she squeezes the back of the high stool until her knuckles turn white; she knows I'm about half a second from losing my shit in our kitchen this morning.

"We were talking about Collin and Valery, their relationship. I *guess*—no, I don't guess—I'm protective of their relationship. I didn't like the direction Jessa's questions were heading and said as much."

"Oh," I make a point of looking at my watch before I look down at Jessa and advise, "Leaving Petra out in an unheated car for any length of time is not advisable. Enjoy being the human to a Maine Coon." I look over at Vivian, tip my head toward my office where the men and women are waiting to give morning reports, and excuse myself.

I haven't even had my first cup of coffee, thanks to Jessa's nosy ass.

***

"Come in." Vivian walks through the door with a trey of morning beverages and vegan pastries with napkins. Rosenburg nods politely as she places it on the coffee table.

"Thanks, lovely. You didn't have to go to all this trouble."

"It was no trouble; I was planning to do this before we were ambushed. Sorry about that, by the way." She leans down to press a chaste kiss on my mouth, and it's hard to stop myself from snaking my arm around her waist. In my mind, she sits her ass on my desk—right in front of me—and I consume what I really want for breakfast this morning. But I digress. I return her kiss, while the security team tries to look anywhere but at us. She flashes a mischievous grin and stands to leave.

"Behave."

"Well behaved women rarely make history, Mr. Ellis." Vivian is the only woman who can get me from flaccid to hard as stone with a few words and a flash of her beautiful sunny day eyes.

Now I'm supposed to lead a meeting with my dick pounding against my zipper.

"Sir, "Rosenburg must read my body language because he struggles to keep the smirk from his face, and he attempts to call the morning debriefing to order.

"Yes," I answer and notice that two of the three women in the room presses their thighs together. I clear my throat and continue, "So, ladies and gentlemen, what do you have for me this morning?" We spend the next couple of hours going over reports from last night. We revise the protocols for the upcoming week. Everything is in place to bring this shit to a head. I can't wait until it's all over. The last thing on the agenda is the house in Savannah. The last of the contractors will be packed up and heading out within the next two weeks. Perfect timing.

***

"Hey. I'm sorry for interrupting, but I wanted to know if you wanted some lunch, or..."

"Yes, we're done. The team was just about to break. I didn't realize how late it was. Have you eaten, yet?"

"No. I was waiting to see what you were going to do. I—" The team stands from their seats and leaves through the private entry door. They move as if they share one body and mind. She's so enamored by their synchronicity, she's stops talking altogether to watch them file out of my office. It's poignant to see her look of awe at the security team, when she's part of the most awe inspiring system I've ever witnessed in my life.

"Viv, you were saying?"

"Oh, yeah. God, they're like a kaleidoscope of butterflies—the way they move as a unit. Or maybe... more like a school of fish."

"They're impressive, that's for damn sure. So..?"

"Oh, I was saying that I just talked with Collin, I think I'm going to call Milla to see if she wants to have a working dinner with Collin and me before the start of her second work week."

"I guess that means, I'm on my own tonight." I sound disappointed, but relief floods my blood stream like a hit of cocaine. I have several irons in the fire that need tending tonight. This is perfect timing. I'll know where she is and that she's protected.

"Only if you don't mind. I really need to check in with her. She's running from something, and I don't want that something to chase her to my front door. You know?"

"You want me to look into her—further?"

"I didn't want to ask. I was kind of hoping she would just come clean and talk with me, but so far, nothing."

"Well, lucky for you, you didn't have to ask me. I offered. Consider it done. I'll have whatever I find to you by tomorrow morning."

"Thank you, babe. Lunch?"

"I'll be right out to help fix it. Are all the other kittens gone?"

"Yep. I have mixed feelings about rehoming them. The King's owner was ecstatic over Onyx. He said he just acquired a beautiful chocolate princess and hopes to breed the two when they're mature and ready."

"Old Larry-la-la is the hardest working cat-pimp running these streets. Show you, right." I sound like Isaac Hayes on the last few words.. Crazy images of Larry Limpshaugh—a fifty-five year old Jewish lawyer—dressed in a purple fedora with a large feather sticking from the side, wearing a purple polyester, bell-bottom leisure suit with a butterfly collar and, white leather platforms with fish swimming in the heels, fill my head.

Fuck, I'd pay good money to see that shit.

I'm caught in a cyclone of laughter that has tears pouring from my eyes.

"Shut up!" She tries to sound stern, but the peels of giggles pour from her like wedding bubbles. It's hard to stop laughing. So, I give up and throw my head back and give into it. I need it more than I care to admit.

Finally I get it under control in time to say, "Give me a minute to make a phone call, and I'll be right out. Oh, and Viv," I pause to make sure I have her attention, "I'm so damn proud of you for sticking up to Jessa this morning. I'm proud of all of you for believing you're capable of handling your shit when it starts to stink."

"God, John." Her eyes turn soft and glassy. I know she needs to hear those words sometimes. They all do, even Valery.

We've all come a long way.

I don't know how any of this is going to play out, but I know I love Vivian Ellis too much not to have her in my life. If that means I have to share her body with Collin or even that Camilla chick—if things work out for Vera the way she wants it to—then, so be it.

"I live for your love, John."

"Lovely-mine."

~32~

Vivian

Even in the winter months, time in the South moves like a lazy, summer day. Sluggish and heavy with oppressive weather that bows heads into the locks of defeated shoulders. Either way, time moves according to its own agenda. No faster or slower than it deems necessary. That was one of the most difficult lessons to learn: I can't control time, other people, or situations. I can only control how I respond to the inevitable changes that affect me.

Collin and I wait for Camilla to make her appearance in our artist's studio staff meeting. She's twenty minutes late and there are no more excuses, this is her third week on the job. It appears her dependency on substances is greater than her love for her art.

"Val told me about Vera..." Collin lets his voice trail away while he doodles on the legal pad with his favorite Micron fine liner in black.

"Yes, Vera is devastated over Milla's substance abuse. She enjoyed their connection because it was with someone outside of the system and household, you know?"

"Aye, but the fact she's not willing to compromise just to say she has a friend or possible love interest is bad ass. I don't know her well, but even my girl's proud of her." He smiles at the thought of Valery. It's like watching someone make cotton candy.

Before I can respond a blur of hair and muted colors streaks across the threshold.

"I so fucking sorry to be late. I find the most beautiful pile of trash on my way in, I had to stop and pick..." Milla stops talking long enough to read the room. She's greeted with a winter storm and scorched summer skies.

215

"You're more than twenty minutes late. We didn't wait for you, which means you've missed the morning meeting for the fifth time since you've been here."

"I-I know, and I'm sorry, Vivian. But I found the most amazing shit to start work on a major piece."

"Good. But I don't think you're going to be working on that major piece as an artist in residence with this facility, Camilla."

"What do you mean, I leave everything to come here and work with you and now... what? You send me back to Chile?"

"Yes. Or you can choose to stay until your three-month work visa expires, but you will have to file for a new one with a new employer. I am not in a position to sponsor a drug addict whose main focus is scoring blow."

Collin's liquid metal eyes are as big as I've ever seen them. He's never heard me speak to anyone like this and if he's lucky, he won't ever have to hear it again. But I will not let this girl destroy what I've worked hard to build, I don't care how damn talented she iso

"You don't have a right to talk to me like this. I can do what I want to on my own time—"

"On your *own time*, yes." I stand up from my chair and walk over to stand a couple of feet away from her. Not trusting myself to stand closer, for fear I'll knock her on her narrow ass. "But you are on my time and your blown pupils, bloody nose, and the fact that you missed another morning meeting tells me that you're doing whatever you want on *my time*.

"It is just a little powder. I'm artist, Vivian. Every artist has their vice—right, Collin?"

Collin's head snaps up at the mention of his name. His luminous eyes go from wide to narrowed in the time it takes him to consider Milla's question.

"Aye. I 'spose we all do, but those of us who take our art seriously don't shite where we eat."

"What does that even—"

"It means," Collin cuts in, "that we don't let our vices destroy our opportunities to earn a living doing what we love. It means we know how rare it is to meet a woman like Vivian Ellis who wants to give talented, underrepresented, up and coming artist a chance to make a name for themselves in the states."

I send an appreciative smile Collin's way before addressing Camilla again, "You've taken up enough time. I've already called the property management company; you need to have your stuff packed up and vacate the premises by the end of the week. I've purchased a ticket for you to return to Chile and you can pick it up from the airport. You will receive full payment for the three-weeks you were here, but your work visa is invalid unless you secure employment elsewhere."

I channel John's no-fucks-to-give attitude and deliver words that wouldn't ordinarily come from me. I'm not a cold-hearted woman. I want to genuinely help artist like Milla, but I'm not a social service program, either. She knew what to expect when she accepted the position. I also told her this was not some kind of artist retreat, she had detailed duties, deadlines, and responsibilities. If she wasn't equipped to handle them, she shouldn't have come.

"Is that all. Just pack the bags and get my ass on a plane to Chile?"

"Yes."

"But you are a woman."

"Yes."

"A minority woman. How can you do this to another minority woman?"

217

"No one gave me anything I have, Milla. I've worked like a slave with no feet to earn my reputation as a renowned curator and gallery owner. Not only in the southern region of the United States, but all over the world. I don't care if you were my blood sister, if you don't care enough about your shit to do what's best for you, then I don't have time nor energy to give a shit, either."

"But—"

"I'm done. Please remove yourself from my property and follow through with leaving the apartment. Everyone else, good meeting. Collin, I'll see you at the gallery a little later. I've got that artist coming in from LA to talk about her photography show at noon."

"Aye, lass. Be safe."

"Thanks." A chorus of goodbyes follow me out the door as I make my way to my truck that's parked behind the studio.

"Mrs. Ellis."

"Hi, Mr. Rosenburg. I'm off to my gallery. Are you driving or following behind me?"

"Driving." He steps to the passenger door at the back of the car and holds it open. Once I'm ensconced in the buttery-soft leather bench seat, he shuts the door and moves like an athlete to the driver's side to slip behind the wheel. "Do you need to stop for a coffee or tea?"

"No, I'm good. Just the gallery, thanks." I busy myself getting my portfolio situated on the seat beside me and pull my cellphone from the pocket of my handbag. It's only after a few long moments that I realize we haven't pulled off, yet. "Is something wrong, Mr. Rosenburg?"

"I'm waiting for you to buckle up, Mrs. Ellis. Safety first." I smile and take care of my seatbelt and he promptly pulls away from the curb onto the main road that'll take us to La Magnolia Nior.

"Sorry, I guess I was preoccupied." As the words fall from my mouth, I'm texting John to let him know about the meeting."

"Is this something Mr. Ellis needs to be made aware of, ma'am?"

"God, Rosenburg. I'm not old enough to be called ma'am, and no. I mean, I'm texting him about it right now, but it's nothing to be concerned with." I hit send on the text and place my phone face-down on the seat next to me.

***

"Lovely." John walks into the kitchen looking like the poster child for every decadent, hedonistic act known to man.

I stop what I'm doing just to stare at him. "How do you manage to look so damn good at the end of the day, when I feel like death warmed over by the time I make it into the house?"

He laughs and shakes his head at me like I'm the hot mess I just described.

"Did I say that out loud?"

"Yes, lovely, you sure did. And what are you talking about? You're beautiful from the time you wake up in the morning, right through the minute I slide into your wet pussy at night." His voice has dropped, become a bit rougher. And his eyes... darken with scorched desire, fiendish smoke sifts through his irises.

Bertha wraps herself around my ankles in her signature figure-eight. I didn't realize how much I missed her doing that until she started doing it again. "Who's mommy's beautiful girl?"

John steps into my personal space but doesn't stop me from baby talking to my pampered kitty or making duck-lipped-kissy-faces. He indulges me, as I shake my head like a demented dog with a bone.

"I was going to try to make that question all about me, but you had to ruin it by adding *girl* to the end."

I lift my duck-lips to him for an appreciative kiss, but of course, Jonathan Ellis does nothing as expected. He combs his dexterous fingers through the locs at the back of my head, pulls them into his fist at the nape of my neck to position me the way he wants, before fitting his supple lips over mine. He sucks so slowly on my bottom lip; it feels like he's going down on me.

"Mmmmm." The moan is low and starts in the back of my throat. He hasn't even breached my mouth with his tongue, and I'm already soaked and swollen for him. God, when was the last time we played?

"Keep making those little desperate noises, lovely, and this will be over before we even get started." John uses the tip of his tongue to give the seam of my mouth a lazy lick. He's not trying to gain entry; he doesn't want me open for him at all.

Right now, he's playing with me.

Warming me up to burn me down from the inside out.

It's working, oh, my God, is it ever working.

"I've been thinking about you all day, Viv. Thinking about you standing from your seat of power in that tight little, red pencil skirt that falls just above your sexy knees. How your see-through silver button-up oxford with its starched collar, is pulled across your perfect tits, showing off the lacy red bra you chose to show off beneath it." He chooses this moment to nibble on my sensitive bottom lip before he licks it to sooth the small hurt left behind.

I'm going to come from this kiss if he keeps at it long enough." I pictured your long," John continues in that sex demon voice that calls to the primordial woman in me. The savage, wild, and wanton beast that lives to spread her legs and be used until there's nothing left. John's rumble breaks through my sex-drunk thoughts when he says, "... elegant legs uncrossing to carry your sylphlike body across the room—like my favorite fucking fantasy—toward your adversary."

He stops talking, adjusts the heavy erection hanging to the right of his groin and widens his stance. He still manages to pull me closer into his strength. "In my mind's eye, you stood over her like Nubia,

220

facing colonizers determined to steal her ancestral lands." John has the most sapiosexual dirty talk I've ever heard.

He doesn't just turn on my sacral chakras, he lights up every last one of those sacred wheels of energy and sets them spinning like newly built whirligigs. Just when I'm ready to take the kiss over, his glorious tongue fills my mouth but then it's gone just as quickly.

"John. Please." I don't know what I'm begging for, I just know he's the only one who can give it to me. The slide of his clever tongue against mine is everything, and still too little of what I need. We set a punishing rhythm as we invite our teeth, lips and fingers to join in this war being waged by our mouths. His maudlin, masculine groans blend with my feral feminine mewls and create a song so harmonious; it could only be composed when two souls become one.

This kiss is just the prelude to the opus we will co-create. Abruptly, he pulls away from my greedy grasp. One lone, tenuous string of saliva stretches between us, obstinate in its refusal to break our physical connection.

John checks in with me, "Where are you in terms of head space, lovely?" His voice flows over me like warm baptismal water, consecrating my sensuality, while obliterating any sense of self-preservation.

Thank fucking god.

"I'm fine, Sir."

"Mmhmm. Then get your *fine* ass down to the playroom. First position. You have ten minutes before I come for you." I'm transfixed by the way he squeezes his generous length through the fine material of his trousers, in an effort to alleviate the pressure of his desire for me. John groans and draws my gaze back to his, just before he whispers, "Lovely,"

"Yes, Sir."

"I won't be gentle."

"Yes, Sir." I accept this condition because it's only through the total surrender of my will that I find my innate power. My submission during play-time frees me to go out into the world and live as the highest version of myself

"Hey girls," I wait for them to acknowledge me. "John and I are getting ready to play, please don't disturb us. I really need this." No reply, just the feeling of acquiescence and that's good enough for me.

Part IV

I wonder how the majority of the world manages to stay sane. The responsibility of being present with, and for others all the time, is inhumane. If I were never allowed to fully immerse into the counsel of my own consciousness, it would be akin to never experiencing the tantric soul connection John and I are cultivating. That's my definition of insanity

~Vivian Ellis

~33~

John

Thinking about Vivian as an Amazonian goddess has so many imaginings floating through my mind, the scene is creating itself.

Head in the game, Ellis. It's play time.

"You're so goddamn beautiful, lovely." She had no idea I'd entered our church. I know this because the moment she heard my voice, she jerked violently. She's on her knees, with her ass high in the air, her hands interlace behind her back and are lifted toward the ceiling. The top of her head presses into the soft mat placed in front of her; she's in a modified rabbit pose.

In this pose, she strengthens her connection to spirit while showing me what's on offer during worship. Her demure white cotton panties indicate purity, yet they rouse my soul's most depraved desires. My need to dirty her up becomes a syncopating throb pumping more hot blood to my horny dick. "Your offer is exquisite, sub. What are your hard limits,?"

"I have no limits, Sir, hard or otherwise." I feel the animal under my skin unfurl like a leviathan waking from its disenchanted world. Savage talons scratch at the surface of my humanity; seeking entry into the civilized world of sinful devotion. I want nothing more than to give him free rein over this service, but he is more fucked up than me.

I reserve his full wrath for sonsofbitches like Earl and The Order.

I'll give her enough of him to sate the unrestrained beast crawling under her scored skin.

Come out, come out wherever you are, lovely. My monster wants to transform yours; be transformed in yours.

"Good, girl. Take the next few minutes to set your intentions for this scene." This is an important step; otherwise, we'll tear each other to shreds. I question, "How do you desire to feel afterwards?

224

What do you need to surrender?" I need to know because our monsters will be off leash, and they're only happy when we give them freedom to seethe. Fuck and transform.

"What will you give me and what will you take?" Standing beside her, I gently push her arms into a more comfortable position.

I caress her exposed vertebra to ease her down into a comfortable child's pose. The sound system is a few feet away and tonight requires something special. I've been wanting to use this song in a scene for a long time.

The extended version of The Doors, *Riders on the Storm* spins on the vintage record player. The snap, crackle, and pop of the needle's first kiss of the night blisters through the admiral blue walls of our most sacred space. Filling it with the tinny sounds of an organ, just before the dulcet voice of Jim Morrison crawls over the floor like liquid sex and testosterone.

I look over to Vivian and I harden in my lounge pants as shivers rack her body.

Her reaction is why I wanted this song. The primal rhythm speaks to the lower chakras, heating them up and turning them on.

Over the years, we've amassed quite a collection of enhancers to bring into our worship. Choosing which ones will be permitted to take part in our sacred practice is always a turn on for me.

A black leather flogger.

A pair of sapphire and onyx clamps.

A pair of black leather elbow cuffs.

A blindfold and a simple ball-gag.

She won't be able to move, speak, or see but my god; she will feel every goddamn thing she hears tonight.

"Are you all right, Vivian?"

"Y-yes," She sucks in air like my fingers have just released her elegant neck. "Sir."

"You don't look as if you're doing *all right*, lovely-mine. Why don't you tell the truth."

"I am, Sir."

"Ass up, now." Immediately, she falls forward and lifts her ass into the air. The gusset of her little white panties are so wet, they no longer appear white. I can almost make out the pulsing of her clit from this angle.

Thwack, thwack, thwack.

"Sir? W-what...?" She cries out after the third hard crack of my hand across the center of her ass. Morrison's voice is a placid lake as he sings, *Girl, you gotta love your man Girl, you gotta love your man Take him by...*

"Not that I owe you and explanation, but since you asked so nicely, I'll give you an opportunity to answer that question." The music is moving into the organ feature, and I'm going to light Viv's ass up for every note I hear. I instruct, "For every wrong response, you'll receive three spankings." I inhale the aroma of her arousal and my monster roars to life because he can smell her fear.

"My panties are wet, Sir?"

Thwack, thwack, thwack.

"I wasn't in the correct position, Sir?"

Thwack, thwack, thwack.

"Um, I-I lied about b-being all right."

Thwack, thwack, thwack. Thwack.

"Sir. I lied about being all right, Sir."

"Good girl. Now why would you do that, lovely?"

The long organ solo hits the part where improvisation and chord runs do crazy things to the torporific chaos pouring from the surround sound.

I want to be inside of Vivian's warm, wet cunt now. But it's not time. She's not ready to give it all up to me, yet.

"I don't know, Sir."

I peel her soaked panties from her body and extend my hand to her. She places her smaller one into mine and rises from the floor to stand at her full five-feet, eleven-inch stature. Once she's steady on her feet, I relieve her of the sodden underwear. The cotton is soaked and infused with the heady scent of her pussy, inspired, I stuff them into her mouth—gusset turned inside-out—now she's able to taste herself for the rest of this scene. With a soft, satin blindfold, I secure the makeshift gag, careful not to cover her nose or tie it too tight around the back of her head.

"Vivian, where are you, now?" She holds up the index finger of her right hand, to let me know she's good and can continue. I walk her over to the newly acquired breeding stand. "I'm going to blindfold you before securing you in the ankle and wrist cuffs. Nod if you give consent, shake if you do not." I watch her carefully and hold my breath until I see her head tilt forward and return to a neutral position.

Once I have her blindfolded, I help her get situated on the heavily padded bench covered in dark blue, vegan leather—just wide enough to support her ass, back, shoulders, and neck. Her head hangs over the edge of the bench, locs the color of cinnamon and honey brush the floor beneath her.

I'm so damn hard for her, this bench takes too fucking long to get her into.

"Your ankles next, lift these gorgeous legs in the air for me, lovely." She obliges.

One at a time, I secure her ankles to the padded cuffs on either side of the crossbar suspended above her body. Now she's completely open and available for my pleasure. The slight spread of her legs gives the most tantalizing hint of her pouting, wet slit. "How is this, lovely?"

Please, give me the index finger. I don't think I could stop if you needed me to.

She holds up her right index finger while she still has control of that hand, as I cuff her left wrist to the underside of the stand. "This is the last check in I'm giving you. Do you trust me, Vivian?" Another finger lifts in the air.

I quickly cuff her right wrist and stand back to admire my handiwork. The breeding stand is brutal, but it speaks to the darkness inside me. Vivian's legs are splayed open in the most lude way; one knee bent at a grotesque angle toward her flat belly, and the other flopping out to the right like an afterthought.

Her weeping pussy leaves an aromatic puddle of arousal on the soft leather. High tilted breast heave up and down as she tries and fails to calm the anticipation of what will happen next.

Surrender your will to me, lovely and I'll give you the freedom you so righteously deserve.

~34~

John

I see I'm losing her to the swirling thoughts inside her head, and we can't have that. "Vivian," Her name is the flick of a snake's tongue; sharp, deadly and exacting. The muscles in her face smooth out and I know she's back with me. "I see the thoughts running on a loop through your mind. Is there something you need to tell me before we continue?" I don't expect her to answer me, so I redirect, "Take two quick breaths in through your nose and exhale slowly." While she calms down, I remove the silk cloth from her face and pull the panty-gag out of her mouth.

It takes a small eternity of seconds before her breathing evens out.

"

Good job, lovely." I whisper as I hold her panties against my nose and inhale her potent scent. I remind her, "Just because your gag is gone, doesn't mean you have permission to speak."

Vivian lifts her eyes to meet my gaze and the trust that drifts through them makes me nearly come in my pants. I lean over her and murmur, "My intention is to fuck your throat, but that dreamy look in your eyes and the slight smile on that mouth, has another need rising within me." Without warning, I swipe my tongue across the seam of her soft lips until she opens for me. The taste of her tongue—with remnants of her own arousal coating the surface—is one of the most erotic flavors I've ever experienced. I syphon the enchanted saliva from her and feel it deep in my balls.

Pulling away is difficult.

How can Viv's pussy tastes even better when I taste it from her own tongue?

"I'm going to fuck your throat. Remember, no talking."

"Sir, is moaning permitted?"

———

229

"That smart mouth is going to get you in a world of trouble, sub."
I don't give her a chance to respond before I slide the full length of
my dick down her throat. Dry and rigid. I didn't let her lick and
lubricate Jughead before feeding every thick inch
to her.

I don't move. She needs time to acclimate to having me lodged so
deep. Vivian—wearing her biggest brat ever panties—swallows and
tightens her throat around my cock head like she begged to have her
face dry fucked.

*Holy mother of sin and shame. Bless her, for she knows exactly
what she does.*

I pull out of her hot, wet mouth to paint her puffy lips with drops
of thick, creamy pre-cum. I know she wants to lick it off; see her
struggle with thoughts of how to ask permission without actually
asking. Before she can come up with a plan, I push myself deeper
into her mouth.

She feels so good, words are spilling from me like drool, and I
don't even try to stop them.

"That's it... fuck." I rotate my hips before pulling out partway,
only to surge back into her warm embrace. "I fucking love how you
swallow me, lovely." I pump in and out of her mouth slow and deep,
rotating my hips when I hit the back of her throat before starting the
pattern all over again. "Baby, if this was your pussy, you'd be
queefing for me."

I drop her head and let it hang at the most delicious angle. It
allows my dick to slide all the way down her lovely throat. Her eyes
are saucers as she realizes that I've completely cut off her airway,
and she'll need to breathe strictly through her nose if she wants to
stay lucid.

Once I'm sure she's breathing, I start to move like I have all night
to fuck her mouth. Long, languid strokes of my body into hers. My
heavy sac, bounces off her forehead with each drive of my hips. I

wrap my fingers around the iron bars that run parallel to Viv's torso to support my weight. I had the table modified with a shock-absorbent neck support because I knew I wanted to use Vivian's mouth like this.

With the strap securing her head to the support, I can fuck her face as hard as I want and do absolutely no damage to her neck. But I'm not interested in fucking her hard and fast— this is where she comes to lay her burdens down—and worship is meant to be generous and intentional. Chris Isaac's, *Wicked Games* is the perfect praise music to set the reverent mood for our service. I hum along to the hypnotic lyrics as Viv baptizes my cock in her sacred saliva.

No, I don't want to fall in love, with you.

I move my body at the same tantric pace as the slide of the lazy, sensual guitar riffs. Slow and meditative. She needs to feel my love for her. My unequivocal appreciation for her willingness to continuously strengthen our connection through the sacred sensual games we play.

Nobody, loves no one.

I come with an audible exhale of my breath, but it feels like I've just transferred part of my soul to Vivian. I pull back and watch her feast on the tattered parts of me that she somehow finds sustainable—even beautiful. Tears drip onto the floor. I don't know if they're hers or the ones trailing from my own eyes.

"How was that, lovely? You may speak if you're able to."

"S—" She clears her throat.

Looks like my girl needs ginger-chamomile tea with honey during aftercare.

"Perfect, Sir." She coughs again.

We'll finish the rest of the scene in the California-king bed. I think my little sub has had enough of the breeding stand for tonight.

"Good, lovely. I'm glad you enjoyed that, now..." I allow my words to trail off as I uncuff her ankles and wrists from the furniture.

Her long, toned limbs flop like Bambi taking her first steps, and I have to bite the inside of my cheek to keep from laughing at her bratty antics. "Come, I'll rub some life back into those noodley limbs of yours." I lift her in my arms. She looks up at me and smiles like a drunkard. Loose-lips and glassy-eyes. *So fucking beautiful.*

~35~

I must have fallen asleep, because I wake up submerged in the claw-foot tub in the bathroom just off of our playroom. John's strong, capable arms are wrapped around me, and my head is lolling against his firm chest. We're covered in jasmine and honeysuckle scented water that feels like the inside of a womb. Healing water falls over my breast from John's cupped hands.

"Welcome back."

I turn my head up to look at him, and he looks damned pleased with himself. *Smug bastard.*

"How long was I out for?" I turn my head back around after he pulls a kiss from my offered lips.

"For a while. I didn't want to move you. You're beautiful when you sleep, but I didn't want the water to get cold."

"Oh. How long is a while?"

"Maybe forty-five minutes or so. How are you feeling?"

"Pretty *fucking* amazing!" I beam up at him and love myself a little more for bringing a wide, toothy grin to his handsome face. I haven't seen it in a while with all he's dealing with. It's nice to have these moments where it's just him and me... being us.

"Good. I'm pleased." He takes a breath that feels too heavy for the light-hearted banter we've been having, and I know he's getting ready to burst our happy-little-post-orgasmic-bubble.

"Out with it, Ellis. I'm listening."

"Shit. I hate that you know me so well. Okay, here's the thing,"

This is going to make all of the other bullshit we've been through seem like a high school cat fight.

"Ellis."

233

"I need us to go away for about a month or so. Just until everything blows over with The Order."

"No."

"No? What the fuck do you mean, *no*?"

"No, I can't leave. I have a million irons in the fire, and I still have to figure out how I'm going to fill the slot Milla left vacant. No, John, I can't go away for a month or even a day."

"I'm not asking you, Vivian."

Oh, my fucking gonads. Not him reverting to his cave-man behavior.

He goes on to inform, "You don't have a choice. Neither one of us do. Oh, and that includes the people you're close to, as well."

"What are you talking about?"

"Collin, Jessa, and—are you close with Tammie—anyone else you may have formed some kind of connection with."

"Are you out of your testosterone-filled mind? I can't ask these people to uproot their lives because of some fraternal order my husband joined when he was a stupid, nineteen year old college freshman. Are you hearing yourself right now, John?"

"I hear myself just fine, Vivian. You, on the other hand, seem to be *hard of hearing*. So, let me break this shit down to you so you get a better understanding of what I'm saying."

He waits a beat for me to turn around and face him before he starts rattling off letters like he's a guest on Sesame Street.

"The FBI, CIA, DEA, NSA—all of these alphabet motherfuckers are relocating us to an undisclosed location until they get this mess cleaned up.

"They all realize that they've allowed The Order to become much too powerful and now they fear they've lost control. So, yes. You *are* going to pack a couple of bags and get your happy, black ass on the private jet and settle the fuck down wherever they drop us, until this shit blows over."

I'm so mad, I can't even form words. My thoughts are moving so fast, I'm afraid they're going to cause my head to lift away from my body. All of those post-orgasmic feelings have left the building and in their place is only one emotion: thermonuclear aggravation to the millionth power. I stand in the tub and start to step over the lip, when John wraps his large hand around my left thigh, effectively stopping me in my escape and further pissing me off.

"Don't touch me right now, John." I seethe through my teeth. I'm surprised the words didn't come out as liquid alphabet soup, my jaws are clenched so tight.

"This is not how I wanted to bring this up and certainly not after what just went down in our playroom. Baby, I—"

"Let. Go. Of. My. Damn. Thigh. I can't have this discussion while I'm laying naked in a bathtub with the man who just blew my back out. No, I need to put on some clothes and find some sense of sanity."

"I love you, Viv."

"I love you, too."

~36~

Vivian

I wasn't tryin to listen in on your conversation, but did I hear that mothafucka say we gotta go somewhere because of this ass-humpin-order bullshit?

"Yes." I keep my answer short because I'm so pissed, I can hardly see straight. I knew something like this was going to happen and I'm still on the other side of *what-the-fuck* about the entire situation.

So, we just gonna pack our shit up and go wherever that bastard tell us to? Like we ain't got shit of our own goin on. What the fuck is wrong with you? You let that man fuck all the sense right outta your stupid head?

"Valery, please just... just shut up. Give me a minute to get my thoughts together and take a damn shower. I can still smell him on my skin and it's messing with my judgement." I admit because I need her to leave me alone.

Fine, you stupid cunt. Don't be makin decisions with your greedy pussy that your brain won't support.

"Goodbye, Val, and stop calling me names." I walk into my bathroom and into the shower. I don't wait for the water to heat up before standing under the freezing cold spray of the showerhead. I need something to jolt me out of my sex-induce haze.

Just when I think things are finally calming down, it goes sideways again.

***

"Hey, lovely."

"John." I move around the small island to stand in front of him. His gray sweats hang in that unfair way that they do, and his white t-shirt stretches in that I'm-your-favorite-mistake way that it does. My mouth waters, then it dries at my nearness to him.

"I know you're seven shades of pissed right now, but Viv—"

"Correction, I *was* seven shades of pissed, now I'm just resigned and slightly irritated." I walk over to the fridge and pull out some sweet-potato and black bean chili I'd made yesterday. "I hate that you pulled me out of subspace, John. It feels like you used the scene to make me more receptive. I thought we were past the manipulation and games." I don't try to hide the hurt in my voice because he needs to hear it.

Acknowledge that he caused it.

I will not hold on to stains that I didn't walk onto my carpet; stains I didn't give consent to be left there. I'm returning John's shit back to him.

"Vivian, *I-I wouldn't*." He stops mid-defense and lowers his head, realizing why I came to this conclusion. "What can I say to make you believe me?" He mumbles, more to himself then to me. He lifts his sorrowful gaze to mine and states, "I promised you I would never intentionally hurt you or the girls again and I meant that."

"I want to say I know you wouldn't, but John the timing is just too... I don't know. It all taste like something you've done before. You know, it leaves the same acrimonious disdain to coat my tongue as in previous times." I pivot away from his burning gaze to stir my chili and reduce the heat on the stove.

"I would never desecrate what love and acceptance has made sacred, to manipulate you, Viv. I couldn't." His large body is close enough to transfer the energy from his skin to mine, but not close enough to actually touch me. I lock my knees to keep from sinking into his warmth.

"Lovely." One word whispered on a single breath. He grabs my hips and turns me around to face the stark burden that dumps sooty ash around the outside of his brown irises. "The timing was shit," John stops and licks his lips, then clears the burnt coals from his throat and starts again, "I'll admit that. And still, I stand by the statement our scene had absolutely nothing to do with what I told you.

"When I received your text earlier today, it aroused me. The thought of you wielding your power... flexing on people who think you need them." His eyes eat away at my mouth before returning to my curious gaze. He digs his fingers into the flesh of my hips and rasps out, "Fuck, it took all of my self-control to stay in that damn meeting. To goddamn make it to the other four I had on my calendar.

"I couldn't wait to get home to my bad ass wife. Break you down in our playroom. Vivian, you have no idea what it means to a man like me..." He nuzzles my neck, just below my ear and inhales like he can get high from my scent. After placing soft kisses in the same spot, he pulls back and lifts a beautifully veined hand to wrap around my vulnerable neck. Immediately my head drops back as my eyes flutter close.

"John, I be—"

His voice is the love-child of a fine dark chocolate and top shelf whiskey, as he cuts me off to confess, "That you—a goddess capable of creating and destroying worlds—would willingly surrender your free will to me. If I lose every cent I have. Become blind, deaf, and dumb. My friends and God forsake me. I get so sick, the flesh falls from my bones. None of that shit matters as long as you still gift me with your submission. Vivian Ellis, I am a lucky and undeserving bastard as long as you love me."

"Okay."

"*Okay?* What do you mean, *okay?*"

"I mean if you keep looking at me like that, we aren't going to have this discussion because I'll beg you to fuck me on this kitchen floor. So, *okay*."

"How about I fuck you on the kitchen floor, and *then* I'll tell you what needs to happen to bring this to a close?"

"Or... "I toss my best bratty smirk his way and suggest, "I fix us a couple of bowls of chili and some red wine, and you can tell me after we eat."

"Chili and red wine doesn't compare to the taste of your pussy, lovely. However, I'll take whatever you offer, because if it comes with your forgiveness. It's priceless."

After I prepare our meal, and we get comfortable at the table, we eat in silence. It took John a while to get used to being quiet and present when sharing meals, but eventually he saw the benefits of it.

***

He clears the table, after which he pours more wine. Once he seated beside me, he takes a breath and starts with, "First, allow me to formerly apologize for springing this on you at such an inopportune time. I really didn't mean to let this bullshit seep into our play time."

"I know that now and thank you for making it clear for me. So, I'm listening."

"I've been advised to limit discussions about the *merger* to need-to-know information only." John looks at me as he brings his wine glass up to his mouth. His eyes are conveying much more than his words. I stretch my eyes to let him know I pick up what he's putting down. He continues in a flat voice, "The board becomes more paranoid the closer we get to closing this deal. I'm only able to share a little about the logistics, okay?" I nod my head, working out his codex to make sure I follow the conversation. He directs, "Words, Vivian."

"Yes, that's fine. I'm only interested in the logistics anyway."

"Right." He throws me an approving smile and continues, "Well, as you know, we've been working around the clock for the last ten months to close this deal. It's been a bloody battle because the board members, CEO, CFO, and COO of the organization don't really want to walk away."

"I guess that's why it's called a hostile take-over." I chuckle like I'm one of the boys in the boardroom, smoking cigars and drinking whiskey while playing with people's lives. John looks at me like I've lost my mind. I shake myself to sober up and give him a nod to continue.

"The hostility is mostly from the other side, Viv. Lives have been changed, destroyed, and even lost."

I know he's thinking about how that tape changed our lives. I wonder if he considers Cole as one of the lost, or if the drive by Camilla and I endured about two weeks ago crosses his mind.

"Is this organization worth all the manpower and sacrifice, John?"

"The organization? No, not really, but the capital and intelligence is more than worth every bit of the resources used in this acquisition."

I know he believes this and in some ways I agree with him.

"I get why you feel this way... I do."

"But?

"But... all I see are a bunch of baby-men shitting in the sandbox to see whose pile is the biggest and smelliest." I peer up at him through my lashes as I deadpan, "That's not even the most disgusting part."

John chuckles softly while shaking his head at me. The look he shoots my way says, *go ahead, lovely. Tell me what the most disgusting part is.*

"The most disgusting part, is when it's all said and done, and the winner has been crowned King Shitter; all the baby-men sit down in their collective piles of shit and start building shitty sandcastles." I wrinkle my nose like I'm sitting downwind from the proverbial sandbox.

John is laughing out loud, now.

"Damn, Viv. Tell me what you really think of men in three-piece suits." His laughter fades to an introspective sigh and his gaze becomes more intense.

"It's not what I think about all men in three-piece suits, John. Only the ones who shit where they play."

He nods his head in either agreement or resignation. I don't know which one. It doesn't feel important.

"As always, you are observant with a keen sense of judgement. You're right to question the worthiness of this merger, lovely. In fifty years from now, the organization and their actions will be nothing more than an urban legend whispered by college professors in hallowed halls to young men and women who'll believe anything."

A huff of air masquerading as amusement falls from my lips and I pivot, "Worth it or not, this merger requires a brief relocation for us. So, tell me the logistics."

Another approving smile before he finishes the wine in his glass.

I watch with hungry eyes as he swipes a few drops of the deep burgundy liquid from his bottom lip with that talented tongue.

I feel the movement between my thighs.

~37~

Vivian

"Correct me if I'm wrong," He pulls his bottom lip into his mouth and the look he gives me heats my skin from the inside out. He questions, "... but didn't you suggest getting a beach house back on our first anniversary trip to Charleston?"

I smile so wide; it punches up into my cheeks. I'm already shaking my head in disbelief as thoughts of that trip float back into my memory. Everything was so simple. Easy and uncomplicated back then. We were living our best lives and didn't have a clue what was waiting for us three short years down the road. The giddy feelings are trickling through my blood like a slow drip of morphine, making fuzzy the sharp edges and loose the tightness in my chest.

"I know you didn't just fly me to Charleston—in a helicopter—only to check us into a fancy hotel and have your wicked way with me." I try my best to sound disparaged, but the way my breath kissed every word broadcast the actual emotion running rapid through my veins.

"Lovely, if your plump lips, and the way your honey-colored eyes glow like a bottle of Greenore Irish Whiskey, is any indication to your injured sensibilities; I damn well could have booked a room here and you'd be just fine with it." He doesn't take his eyes from my face as he studies me like I'm some kind of alien species he's contemplating having over for dinner.

"Yes." He takes a breath I didn't realize he'd been holding and gifts me with his all-American boy smile. The one reserved for me.

With a haughty lift of his right eyebrow, he murmurs, "I didn't think you would, but no. I didn't rent a helicopter, fly you to Charleston just to take you to a *fancy* hotel to fuck you seven ways till Sunday. But—"

"But nothing." I cut him off. "Where are we going?"

"To hell if we don't get right with God." He chuckles as he leans over and drops a sweet kiss to the tip of my nose.

I, on the other hand, am pouting like a five-year-old child who didn't get a pony for her birthday. It only makes him laugh harder... until he's not laughing at all.

"You're so goddamn beautiful." The fact that he sounds so amazed; like he's seeing me for the first time, and he thinks I'm something wonderful to behold. It humbles me that this man would find me *wonderful*, when he is my sun, moon, and stars. Something in me resonates with something in him. He looks at me and I see my feelings reflected back in his eyes.

"I love you, John. So much." I stop to swallow the golf ball size lump in my throat before I can finish my thought. "It scares me, while at the same time it makes me feel safe. What I feel for you is a paradox."

"How's that, lovely?"

I take a deep breath as I gather my thoughts because if he's asking for clarification, this must be important to him. "There are parts of me that believe I shouldn't love you or even trust your love for me, but the biggest part of me knows that you're the only one who can keep the darkness from closing in on me. I love most about you what scares the hell out of me." Up until that moment, I hadn't realized just how I truly felt. By the look on John's face, he hadn't either.

***

"Lovely." John's voice pulls me away from my memory of our ride to the restaurant at the Charleston Marina. It was on our walk from the drop off dock that I suggested we look into buying some property near the ocean. Silly me, John already had property on the west coast, courtesy of Della Richman. AKA Vera's own mommy dearest. "Vivian, where'd you go?"

I shake the disturbing thought away and reply, "I was just thinking about the ride to the marina." I downplay it because I'm not sure how I feel about that anniversary trip—the stunt he pulled on the chartered boat and what it ultimately led to in our marriage.

"Oh. Well, I know we have the house on the west coast, but I know you prefer the Atlantic to the Pacific." He sounds a little strained. I'm sure he recalls the foul play he made back then, as well. "Anyway, I found a sweet deal just off the coast of Savannah down on Sapelo. It needed—"

"You already bought a beach house. Near Savannah, Georgia?"

"Yes. I would like to go there while the board ties up the loose ends of the merger. It's a large home with room for all of us and then some."

"All of us? Are you referring to the girls... or—"

"Collin and Camilla will need to join us for this little getaway."

"Wait, what?"

"The end of this... *merger,* will be difficult at best—things could get dangerous—because the heads of the organization don't like to lose. The board would rather have anyone who means something to either of us, be with us until it's over. It is not a request." His face is as implacable as I've ever seen it.

"What about Jessa, why didn't she make the list?"

"Jessa, as far as anyone is concerned, is your therapist. The only relationship we have with her is a professional one. And besides, she can keep our girl while we're in Sapelo."

"Why can't Bea come with us?" My heart stops beating for a minute at the thought of not having my cat with me. She got me through the most difficult period of my life, after finding out I wasn't alone in this body.

"It will be stressful for her. And it's only temporary, Viv."

"I don't know how I feel about leaving her with Jessa. Not that she won't be taken care of; she will. It's just that she's my baby, John."

"The board feels it would be best interest if there's a plausible reason to come back periodically during our time away." I nod my head as his meaning sinks beneath my skin, causing a phantom itch that can never be scratched.

"Okay." I acquiesce. "If this is what it takes, then I guess I'm... we're going to this mystery beach house on Sapelo. How long before we leave?"

"So, you're okay with this?" He stands from his seat to step over to me. After wedging himself between my thighs and placing his hands on either side of my face, like he can pull the answer from me with a kiss. He rubs his lips against my mouth. "Lovely, I need an answer." Every whispered word becomes the air I need to breathe. I lick my dry lips, while simultaneously licking his. The rough groan that crawls from his throat stirs the banked coals of desire warming my lower belly. "Of course, I'm okay with this. As long as we're together, and there's nothing I need to know that I don't already..." I leave everything else to get trapped between our working mouths. I nip at his bottom lip, needing him to make that sound again; the one that tells me how deep and hard he wants to pound into me. I do it again, my hunger rises like the crashing tide.

I hope that John's ready to surf.

"Fuck, Vivian. I need you again, but in our bed this time.

"On one condition, Ellis."

He lifts his perfect brow in that arrogant way I love.

"You give me a piggy-back ride upstairs?"

Bursts of laughter shoot from his chest and lands straight into my soul. I devour it as sacrament. I glow with his joy because I know, accept, and love the darkness that surrounds it.

John doesn't give me a piggy-back ride; however, I *do* get a fireman's carry and my hands on his fine ass for my troubles. I'm not disappointed because I'll be sure to ride him—reverse cowgirl—once we're in our bed.

38

John

I tell my contact we'll be ready to head out on the following Monday. He's preparing the private jet and an undisclosed flight plan. I can't say I'm looking forward to living with Collin and Camilla, but I know it's important that we find some kind of middle ground if we're going to make this situation work.

Oscar must be a goddamn root doctor if I'm really considering this arrangement as a viable option.

I smile at my own silly thoughts, while simultaneously checking the paperwork I had curried over a few weeks ago.

There's so much shit I haven't told Viv. I honestly believe the only way to let her know... to let them know, is to show them. They've been hinting around about visiting Della's house since I returned home last November. I'll drive them down to Georgetown, but first I want them to see the place that shattered the woman they never had the chance to know.

I don't know why this is so important to me—giving them a reason to show Della a little compassion—but I'm determined to see this through.

My desk phone lights up with internal call. I press the button and wait to hear my assistant's polished voice. "Mr. Ellis, you have a call on line one. Shall I pass it through or take a message?"

"How much time before my next meeting?"

"You have about ten minutes, sir."

"Take a message."

"Yes, sir."

Funny how hearing my assistant call me *sir*, does absolutely nothing for me. Not even a twitch from Jughead, no increase in my heart rate... not a goddamn thing.

***

The rest of my day is a blur of grey and black suits, sensible pumps, and too much ass-kissing to be anything other than a display of the lowest common denominator of the mindless products of corporate America. Sometimes I feel like selling my company to the highest bidder, moving to the coast, and becoming a venture capitalist.

Shit, that's not a bad idea, Ellis. Would Vivian consider staying on Sapelo? Maybe opening another gallery in Savannah...

I'm dizzy with the possibility of change. I don't remember the last time something outside of bullshit and Vivian, got my heart pumping this fast.

"This could be exactly what we need." I murmur. Then I look around self-consciously, like someone else is in my office listening to me have a conversation with myself. "Fuck it. I read an article in *Psychology Today* that said that people who talk to themselves tend to be more intelligent than those who don't. "So, take that to any asshole who has a problem with me doing it." I declare out loud like there really is someone listening in on my conversation.

Jonathan Ellis, you're losing your motherfucking mind. Get your shit and let's go.

The moment I'm free, I slip out of my office and head over to the parking garage. Once I'm on Gervais, I take a right and then a left onto Assembly. I've walked this path for as long as I can remember. Today, I actually take the time to notice the changes that have happened over the past ten years I've been in Columbia.

Ten years... seems like only yesterday I was moving into my first apartment in Park Place Towers.

"Mr. Ellis. You knockin 'off early this evenin'." Jasper, one of the many garage attendants I've gotten to know over the course of my time working downtown, never asks a question. He simply states what he observes as fact. I've learned a thing or two from old Jasper.

"Yes, sir. It's been a long day."

"Yeah, ain't a day gone by in my life as a Black man in South Carolina that ain't last from sun-up to goddamn sun-down." He finishes with a laugh that doesn't even attempt to reach for his eyes. It's a dried-up empty ghost of what was surely a robust and unreserved laugh.

What the hell is going on with me, today? It's like my gut knows something but hasn't sent my mind the memo.

"I feel you, Jasper. All right, have a good evening." With that last exchange, I step into the elevator and press the button to take me to the floor where I pay too much money for my car to sit idle all day. Just before the doors close, a large, tanned hand slides in to hold it open. I don't move to help, it's not my business if this fucker makes this lift or the next one.

Shit. I'm tired.

My thoughts are all over the place. It feels like something is coming to an end. I don't know if I'm sad or happy about it.

"Thanks. Brother." Two words, chewed into alphabet soup and delivered through a fine-mesh strainer.

What in the freshly fucked virgin is he doing here?

"I didn't think you was gointuh 'hold it for me."

"I didn't know it *was*... you."

"Shits fixintuh 'hit the pre-ver-bee-ul fan, if you smell what I'm grillin'."

Only Coleman Whitman could make each syllable its own separate word and get away with it. I look at him like he rose from the dead the morning after Jesus did, and he looks like a damn peacock standing in the corner, cleaning his nail with a goddamn hunting knife.

"*Yeah*?" I utter. Waiting for him to drop whatever bomb he has to blow my life to hell and back.

"You playin 'this shit mighty fuckin 'close to your motherfuckin ' chest, ain't you, Ellis?"

"Mmhmm."

"Fuck! What the hell I gotta do to make you trust me again, John?"

"I trust you fine, Cole. I just choose to trust me more."

"You find some place for you and yours to skedaddle off to?"

"Mmhmm." I raise my eyebrow hoping he's not stupid enough to ask me where that place is.

"I guess you won't be divulgin 'that information to me."

"Nope." I press my lips into a tight frown as I shake my head to drive the point home.

"You need security?"

"Covered. Cole, what the fuck are you doing here?"

"The Order knows their goose is cooked and they scramblin ' 'round tryin 'to find any asshole they can fuck to get outta this shit." He pauses long enough to wipe his knife on his cargo pants and slides it back into one of his many pockets. In a voice he must have dredged up from the bowels of hell, he states, "Ain't no more assholes available. You know what that mean."

I'm so over this cloak and dagger bullshit, but Cole seems to be frothing at the mouth to pull me into his fucked-up world. So, I deadpan, "Let me guess, they're backed into a corner, and they don't know the meaning of defeat. And what... they plan to come out." I pause for effect and step into his personal space before continuing. "*Swinging?*"

"Shit's not a goddamn joke to be takin 'lightly. They comin 'for your black ass, John. It really don't matter where the fuck you go to hide. They don't want to hurt you physically."

"You think I give a motherfucking fuck about anything other than the safety and happiness of my wife, Cole. I don't have a fuck to give about the fuck that fucked the first fuck before he got fucked. Hear me—"

Cole's impassioned voice cuts off my fucking tirade when he hisses, "John. Hear. Me, motherfucker. There are other ways to rape a man of his power."

My spine snaps into a straight line at his last words. "Rape... Cole, look. I know you think you're here to save me—"

"I'm not tryin 'to save your arrogant ass," He cuts me off again. "I'm tryin 'to *warn you*, brother. Those sonsofbitches are comin 'for your company. It's already in the works. They fixintuh 'fuck you hard, no goddamn lube."

"Good." The word falls from my mouth, and I swear I feel this weight lift from my shoulders. A weight I didn't even know I'd been carrying until just now.

Cole looks like I just told him I want us to run away together and adopt a rainbow tribe of babies or some shit. The thought makes me smile. He scrunches up his brows a little more, and I chuckle.

"I'm done with this conversation. You can go play GI-fucking-Joe and get the glory, the metals, and all the pussy you live for. I've got my plot of land under control over here."

"John, why the fuck don't you ever listen to a goddamn word I say to you? I don't want you losin 'all the shit you worked for, brother."

"You know me better than most people. Your sentiment, not mine."

"Fuck you. And I do know you better than any-goddamn-body."

I step away from him to walk out of the elevator and ask, "What's the first thing you learned about me after we supposedly met for the first time?"

We're walking to my car. The security detail waits a couple of cars to the left of my Pathfinder. As soon as he notices Cole, Mitchell's right hands slides under his woolen peacoat. I give a slight shake of my head and he relaxes his stance.

I'm still waiting for Cole to answer, when I notice his hand is inside his jacket, too.

"They with you?"

"Yes, answer the question and take your hand off your gun before you blow your dick off." We both chuckle as we step up to the driver's side of my SUV.

"Wait, what did you... oh! Most men look at the world and try to imitate what they see and like; however," He changes his voice to something darker to imitate me. "Jonathan Raynard Ellis visualizes the world in which he wants to live and makes it his reality." Cole looks over my shoulder at my security detail and back to me. The tension that's been riding him since we rode up in the elevator, finally falls away. Allowing his shoulders to give his fat earlobes some breathing room.

"Exactly. I'm good. We're good. Don't worry about me. Be sure to watch your back and remember that not all friendly fire is meant to keep your lily-white ass warm, *brother*." With one last meaningful look into each other's eyes, and a terse head nod, we part ways. Each of us going to fight in the same war, but on two considerably different battlefronts.

"Mr. Ellis," I catch Mitch's cold, winter-green eyes in acknowledgement. "... do we need to put a tail on him?"

"Yes. Your best, he's a brilliant motherfucker. Advise your tail to be ready to assist and protect to the best of their ability should the need arise."

"Roger." I silently scream, *Rabbit,* because I'm still such a goddamn child.

"I'm heading home. Check with my wife's detail. If there's anything I need to know before I see her, contact me. Otherwise, see you during the debriefing later. Roger. Out."

"Over, sir." These damn jarheads and all their wartime, bullshit protocols.

They do love playing GI-Joe games.

***

Another day, another dollar. That's what the old heads in my childhood neighborhood used to say when they came home from working in the factories or mills. I'd hear them talking on their front porches or while out in their yards cutting grass. I thought that's all I had to look forward to when I grew up. Marry a woman who would eventually become a porch-sitting barracoota, have a litter of children—who couldn't wait to hate and leave me behind, go to work for the man and complain about how little the man paid me. Oh, and fantasize about fucking someone who looked like Della Richman. Those dirty bastards were never worthy of that woman. Hell, no one was.

Myself included.

"Viv, I'm home." As the words leave my mouth I realize how stupid they are. Of course, I'm home if I'm standing in our kitchen yelling like a fool. "Hey. Viv?" I go up the stairs to see if she's in the shower because her car is parked in the garage, so I know she's here. I round the corner from the landing, and run into a large, solid chest that doesn't belong to my wife or one of the alters. I'm reaching back to unload a two-piece combo on this motherfucker when I hear his Scottish brogue.

"Keep the heid!" I drop my arm and step back from the big Scotsman.

"What the hell are you doing in my house?"

"I'm with Valery. Dinnae Vivian tell you Val and me was spendin 'the day and night together?"

"No. Where's Val?"

"She's takin 'a shower and wanted to take a quick nap. I made a real mess of her earlier and she said she didn't want to get that shit— her words, not mine—stuck in her sheets like we did before."

I'm trying not to punch this asshole in his perfectly symmetrical face, but if he continues to talk about *messing Val up*, while she wears my wife's body; I will not be held accountable for my actions.

He must see my murderous thoughts as they roll across my face because he throws both hands in the air like I just pulled a gun on him. My trigger finger twitches on my right hand.

He licks around his entire mouth like a satisfied dog who's just eaten the juiciest steak he's ever had.

I'm going to fucking kill him.

"No. Not like that. It's not what you're thinkin', John—may I call you John? —*Mr. Ellis*?"

I can't say a goddamn thing because I have no idea what shit will come flying out of my mouth if I open it. I stay quiet and wait for him to finish.

"*Right*. I was sayin', it's not what you're thinkin'. We worked on another large art piece today, she was covered in charcoal and glitter. She feckin 'loves glitter," He stops talking and smiles, while shaking his head.

I know that look he wears. The one that tells anyone paying attention, he's completely gone for this woman. Willing to be with her even though she's part of a system of dissociated identities and her body is shared between three other women, maybe more. One of whom is married to the six-foot-five-inch cave-man standing in front of him. Any anger or animosity for Collin, dissipates immediately.

He lowers his arms back to his sides the moment he realizes I've tucked my cave-man back into his cave. An easy smile spreads across his face. I can admit, he's a pretty motherfucker. I see why

Val is so enamored with him. I even see why he's in love with her crazy ass.

Progress is the feast for Lilliputians. Meant to be experienced in small, delicious bites at a time.

"Want to grab a beer while your girl gets her shit together?"

39

John

"I hear we goin 'on a family trip." Collin says this as he spins the metal top of his beer on the granite island top. Like he didn't just cause my beer to slide down my windpipe.

I'm still coughing like a tuberculosis patient when he shoves a dish cloth into my chest. After yanking the towel from his hand, I wipe myself down and throw it on the island. Then I grouse, "First of all, it's not a goddamn family trip. Secondly, because of your connection with Viv and Val, you'll need to come with us. We leave Monday morning, so get your shit together." His ass is on a need-to-know basis, and this is all he needs to know.

"Vivian told me that Camilla is comin', as well."

"Yes."

"She didn't tell me where we're going."

"No."

"For fuck's sake, will somebody tell me something about whatever MI16 bullshit I'm bein 'dragged into?"

He is pissed. If he knows what's good for him, he'll shut the hell up and enjoy this all-inclusive-fully-funded vacation. I take a drink from my long-neck and lift my right brow as I swallow the dark Bavarian ale with an audible gulp.

Hope that answers his questions.

"So, how are things with you and Val?" I ask to let him know the topic is closed for any further discussion. Collin is hot as fish grease. A chuckle escapes my smirking mouth as I finish off my first beer of the night.

"Let me get this straight; only you and Vivian know what the fuck's going on and where the fuck we're flyin 'to; I assume."

"You know what they say, *Scotty*. One should never assume because it makes an ass out of u and me." I laugh a little louder on my way to grab another beer from the fridge. I turn back to the temperamental artist just in time to see him fighting the smile that has the left side of his mouth tucking into his cheek.

"Fuck you, John."

"Nah, I'm good. I would think Valery would be enough for you."

"She's plenty enough, lad," He breaks off and looks into my face like he's searching for a hint or hidden secret. He must not find it because after he clears his throat, he states, "You're really all right with me and Val bein 'together."

"Look, Scotty, I've been in love with Vivian since the first day I laid eyes on her." My mind takes me back to that day in early September of ninety-three. She didn't even notice me staring at her from across the Horseshoe, and I was completely oblivious to the other students flowing around me. "She was standing in front of the little chapel inside the Horseshoe. It looked like she was caught in a daydream; imagining what her wedding day would be like." I say.

Or maybe it was me imagining that day.

I shake the thought away to tell him, "I desired her as my possession. The need to lock her away before anyone else realized what she was, what she could help transform them into. It was... primordial; what I felt ten years ago, and what I feel for her today."

Collin's stares at me with those quicksilver eyes that usually give nothing away, but right now. I know every thought running through his shocked mind.

Good, I need him to understand what Vivian means to me.

Before he can ask that stupid question inching its way up his working throat, I inform him, "Collin, there's no beginning or ending to what Vivian and I are. Our love isn't an occurrence or something that happened to us. We are a state of being. We are consecrated by our unconditional acceptance of each other; the destructively beautiful darkness as well as, our utterly chaotic luminescence.

"Our souls act as mirror reflections; allowing us to see the best and worst parts of ourselves. And there's no judgement. No condemnation. We have the freedom to hold space for one another, and then decide if we want to work through, discard, or embrace whatever is discovered.

"It was our brokenness that brought us together, and our unconditional love is what creates our harmonious lifestyle."

After a brief eternity of looking at me like I have a pair of double-d's on my forehead, Collin clears his throat and takes a sip of his forgotten beer and says, "Aye, I can appreciate what you're sayin', but it doesn't tell me one way or the other how you feel about Valery and me." He makes quick work of his beer before getting up to get himself another from the fridge. I watch him move in my kitchen... like it's his kitchen, too.

I like that he stands about as tall as I am and isn't afraid to look me square in the eye. I respect that and I respect him.

I didn't realize it until just this moment.

"No, I guess it doesn't tell you a goddamn thing, does it?" I ask just as he plants his ass on the stool. I let him settle in and deadpan, "The truth is, you're with Valery. For the longest time, I didn't understand that *they* are completely separate people with their own needs and wants. In my mind, Valery was simply a more sexually adventurous alternate of my wife. Vera was a more innocent, docile alternate, and that little sassy-twelve-year-old, Valeria was a giant pain in my ass."

I shake my head and marvel at how the memory of her trying to slit my throat brings a sad smile to my face. She held so much of their pain and self-loathing. "Anyway," I return to our conversation. "I'm glad she's finally found her peace." I digress.

"What's that, lad?"

"Oh, I was thinking about Valeria. The child alter. She's gone dormant, but she's the bravest little pre-teen I've ever known. Did you ever meet her?"

"No," He barks out a loud, throaty laugh before continuing, "... but Val has stories for days about her—and I quote—*little chicken-shit sister.*" I share this laugh with him because she is a *little-chicken-shit.*

"Yeah, well, to know Valeria is to love Valeria. To answer your previous question... When I saw you and Valery together the first time in the studio—"

"You mean the time you came in like Big Daddy Warbucks and showed your ass?"

Laughing, I nod my head and continue. "It was the first time I'd ever seen Valery as she presents inside the Internal House, you know. Seeing her how Viv and the others see her; it was... *enlightening.*"

We've somehow made it into the family room and are sitting on the sofa together. Both of us lost in our thoughts about the two women we love.

Collin breaks the comfortable silence and asks, "So, how did *you* and Val end up as... fuck-buddies?"

And for the second time tonight, I choke on the beer sliding down my windpipe and fall into a coughing fit that rivals a thirty-year smoker... on oxygen. He could've asked me to whip my dick out and let him measure its length and girth, and I would have been less surprised than I am in this moment.

What the actual fuck?

"Uh," After a series of gruff coughs and hard swallows, I'm finally ready to broach the subject his inelegant ass brought up. "It was when I first brought Viv home from Washington state. After we lost our first daughter, and everything was all fucked to hell." I sink into the morose miasma of rotten emotions that engulfed us during that time.

"When she confronted me about fucking Valery behind her back," I turn my head slightly to the right, trying to assess Collin's reaction. His expressionless gaze tells me nothing so, I keep talking. "Yeah. So, anyway. I thought Viv was batshit crazy for accusing me of cheating on *her* with, *Valery*." The huff of breath is a humorless attempt at levity because in hindsight, that's exactly what I was doing to her. I turn away from Collin because his silver orbs see too much.

"Ye really dinnae see they were different people." His accent is more pronounced than ever.

Viv says it only gets that heavy when he's drunk, pissed, aroused, or all three.

My guess is he's pissed.

"This was before they had their own rooms, wardrobes, and all the other shit. It didn't matter who was in the driver's seat, they all looked like my wife. Subtle differences in the way they moved or spoke, withstanding." Memories of the hurt and sense of betrayal in Vivian's eyes the night I dragged her out of that fucking shrink's office assault me.

Then another memory pushes it aside. This one is more recent, and I'm compelled to share it with Collin because I think he deserves to know. "But I wasn't the only one confused about how the system worked."

He leans forward with his elbows on his knees and offers a grunt in response. I clear my throat, again, before sharing, "No, Valery was just as confused as I was. Her confusion was more than likely the result of my actions. Viv and I were speaking with my therapist, Oscar when she told me about the session I'd come to yank her out of with that motherfucking Irishmen." Taking a deep breath to dislodge the rage coloring my vision black, I tell him, "Viv said that Val was asking questions that finally led her to acknowledge that our *relationship* wasn't healthy for her."

"Wh-what kinds of questions, lad. Did Vivian say what she asked Dr. Wanker."

I flash a knowing smile and share what I know.

"Viv said she'd asked him, *why didn't John think she was as important as her*? And Dr. Dickface told her it was because *I was in love with Vivian*."

"Anything else? I mean, did she ask him anything else?" His voice is an open pothole, filled with gravel and broken glass. He hurts for her just like I hurt for Vivian.

"Yes. Viv said—and this is why I fully accepted them as separate people—she'd looked at Dr. Numbnuts and whispered, but... *I'm her, ain't I*?"

Collin paces the length of the room and pulls at the roots of his hair. I know exactly what he feels. I also know I made the right call to share this with him. Encouraged, I finish with the last thing my wife said about that session.

"Viv said that Dr. Dickless was extremely direct when he told her, *no. Valery, you are not her. You are you, and that makes you a part of a whole. You have completely separate experiences than the other parts of the whole*." I refrain from breaking the tense silence because I know he needs time to digest the shit meal I just fed him.

Collin cuts into the quiet and throws me a bone of sorts. "I guess it was all still new to ye'. And new to my girl, too."

It's kind of him, but I've long since accepted how blissfully ignorant I allowed myself to be after Gayle's passing. I want him to know the truth, especially with him being in love with Valery.

I clear my throat once more and drink the last of my liquid courage, square my shoulders, and recant one of the most profound conversations lovely and I have ever had.

"It was, but that's not why shit went sideways with Val." I scrub my beard a couple of times before I say, "We were sitting inside my truck in our garage, because I wouldn't let her drive her car home.

She was so damn transparent. She pulled her anger around her like the armor of the righteous, and I wasn't prepared when she asked me point-blank,

What the hell is your problem John, for the last four months, you haven't had two words to say to me. You rarely come home from work, and you haven't made love with me in... since you've been fucking Valery."

Collin isn't pacing anymore. He stands in front of the fireplace with his feet shoulder width apart and his large arms crossed over the wide expanse of his chest. But what makes me flip his ass the bird, is the shit-eating grin spreading across his fucking face.

"I see you're familiar with my wife when she's done with the bullshit." We share an easy laugh that cuts through the tension and makes breathing a little easier.

As my laughter fades into the phantom pain sitting in my heart, I continue, "Anyway. I knew she hadn't planned to bring it up, but she did because I'd hurt Valery. And I was hurting her, too. I thought she wanted me to feel their pain but in hindsight, I realize she needed me to acknowledge and feel my own."

Fuck me. How is it that I'm just realizing this after all this time?

Collin bursts the bubble of realization when he asks, "How the fuck did you respond, lad?"

I tuck the epiphany away for later and answer, "Like a goddamn viper who's been waiting for the perfect moment to strike my unsuspecting victim." I give a self-deprecating laugh because I was defensive as fuck when lovely called me out on my bullshit. After I stop laughing at my own stupidity.

I recount how, "I asked her something like, *The fuck did you just say, Viv,* in the darkest, most menacing tone I could muster. I felt righteous in my indignation, too."

Collin is doubled over laughing at my dumb ass, and I can't even blame him.

I continue to regale him with my crack-head antics. "Man, I completely expected her to back down, but she shut my goofy ass up like I was a willful child who'd lost his mind and grabbed the damn switch. She was all," I pitch my voice high to imitate Viv's sultry vocals and say, "*I didn't stutter, John. You heard me and I'm no longer in the habit of repeating myself. Not for you. Not for anyone else, either.*" I stretch my left arm across the back of the couch, cracking up with a man who looks decidedly happy to learn my wife showed her ass when she found out about my transgression.

"Aye, that sounds like the lass I know. Real ball-buster, your Vivian." The pride in his voice is telling.

I guess he sees Viv the way I see Vera. *Interesting.*

"Yeah, well, I wasn't ready to concede my position of power, so I tried for a more... carnal, manipulative approach to thwart her attempt at bringing me to heel." Although I'm smiling, the desecrated remnants of censure for having the balls to ever treat my wife that way, slide over my soul like the devil's fingernails against old chalkboards.

Collin isn't laughing anymore.

Perceptive motherfucker.

I clear my throat before giving the last of it. "I said, *Ooooh,* drawing out the word like I was stretching my arm back to hit the winning homerun for the Braves. I was moving as slow as I possibly could, when I turned around to look at her. With an arrogantly feral smirk plastered over my ruined ego, I attempted to make her feel small. Vulnerable." I maintain eye contact with the man standing across from me.

No longer do we share a bemused smile, rather, he looks forlorn and a lot disappointed.

"So, anyway, she blows up at me and wants to know, *Don't you have anything to say? That's the way communication works, or maybe you don't remember how to have a conversation with your...*

wife. It was the way she paused before saying, wife. When I think back on that night, it's that goddamn pause that breaks my fucking heart." I stare down at my right hand and pull on a loose string on my sock; no longer able to bare the weight of Collin's gaze.

His gruff voice pierces my veil of self-loathing. "It's always the littlest shit that gets your balls trapped between your ass cheeks. The shit that seems so inconsequential in the moment, but in that bitch with twenty-twenty vision, it becomes painfully clear."

It sounds like he's had some moments of clarity to contend with himself.

I brave a glance at him and see the same self- reproach pulling his brows down, as me. Nodding, I inhale forgiveness and exhale the bullshit. There ain't a damn thing I can do about the past except learn from it. And I have... learned from all of it.

"Well, at any rate," I hurry to finish the story before our periods sync. "Viv drove all of her pain into my guts when she asked—with those oil-slick tears that turn her bright, summer sunshine gaze into a soggy, overcast accusation—*You know, the woman you married right after we graduated from college... Vivian. Valery is not Vivian, is she?* Again with that little pause before saying her name. I was so fucking pissed, I decided to give as good as I was getting."

Collin looks like he wants to beat my ass up one side, and down the other. He tries, but fails to hold his peace and blurts out, "Why the hell does that woman put up with ye'. Dinnae why she stay wid ye'. Really, lad." His face is a little red and his fists are balled up at his side.

I laugh loud and hard because I ask myself that same damn question every day. I'm glad when he joins in to help break the heavy tension lingering in the space between us.

~40~

John

I can't remember the last time I sat around drinking with a friend. It's been a long time, but it feels good to be able to do this with him. I answer, "No fucking idea, man. But I'm eternally grateful that she does."

"So, what cave-man bullshit did ye 'pull from ye 'hindparts?"

"I pulled the D/s card on her ass. Leaned in too close and spoke with the devil in my throat and whispered, *Oh, I don't need a reminder of who you are, Viv. I'm thinking maybe...* I may have run my nose up the side of her neck and breathed her in, before growling again, *... just maybe, you're in need of a reminder of the motherfucker that... I am.*"

Collin shakes his head at me with a look of pure disgust and spits out, "God, I hope she hauled off and popped you in your arrogant mouth." He chuckles afterward, but I know he means that shit.

"She got right back in my face and basically told me to go fuck myself." We're laughing so hard; we both have tears running down our cheeks. "She said something about giving me an STD—"

"Wait, what?" Collin interrupts. "Vivian gave *you* an *STD?*"

"Fuck, no! She was referencing me being with Val and—"

"Val? As in, *my Valery...* she gave you an *STD?*"

"Collin, if you would just shut the fuck up, and let me finish. Nobody gave anyone an STD, all right?"

"Oh. I was tryin 'to figure out how the hell that would work. If Vivian had an STD, wouldn't they all have one?"

I stop to look at him for a long moment because that's a good question.

"I don't fucking know, but if any of them was going to have an STD, it would be your girl. No offense, just the way she is... or... was? You know what I mean." Fuck, what the hell were we talking about, anyway?

Oh, yeah.

"No, well, I was saying that Vivian came back to the fact that I'd been having sex with Valery. She sneered in a voice I still have a hard time reconciling truly belongs to her, *You are a motherfucker, but I wouldn't need a reminder if you hadn't abandoned me after I buried Gayle."* I take a breather, because I hate I made her deal with the death of our first daughter alone. Honestly, I didn't know how to handle my own goddamn grief.

Collin's voice is just above a whisper when he states, "You were with Valery after the death of your daughter."

I think he's looking for clarification, so I nod my head. The look he shoots me is one of introspection and... is that *compassion*?

Not wanting to dwell too long on that thought, I continue, "Yeah, so she goes on to say, *I wouldn't need to try and remember the motherfucker my husband is, if he weren't so damn busy fucking Valery but avoiding me like I gave him a goddamn STD!"* I look over at Collin to see if he connected the dots.

He confirms, "Oh, that's where the STD part fits in."

I give him an impassive once over and continue with the most important part of this entire fiasco but not before adding, "I'm glad I was able to clear that up for you."

"What happened next?"

"I choked her out." I sound like a sociopath. No remorse or emotional connection. "My hand was around her throat before she could take another breath. At first, I was just asserting my dominance over her because she needed to calm down. But the more her words worked their way into my conscious mind, the more caustic they became."

I had indeed abandoned my wife and had been using Valery to slack my need to comfort her the only way I knew how. I'm hesitant to share this next part with him but he needs to hear all of it.

"I never saw Valery. Not once did I kiss her. Hold her. Speak softly or kindly to her. She was a means to an end, one that in hindsight, had no real ending and meant absolutely nothing." I hate dredging all this shit up, but he has a right to be confident in his relationship with Val.

Collin walks back over to the couch and sits on the other end before he grunts, "You are a right *motherfucker*."

The spike of anger in his voice, makes me smile. It shows how serious he is about being with Valery, which means he's not fetishizing DID. I'd hate to kill him, but I most certainly would if I needed to.

It wouldn't be the first time I had to get someone away from Vivian and the girls.

"Yes, I am. But never again to my wife or the other women who make up her system."

"Obviously, you didn't choke her to death, what happened?"

"I did lose sight of my initial plan, squeezing harder than was needed to subdue her. I could feel her panic rising as her pulse kicked up under my thumb. I wish I could tell you that her fear brought me to my senses, but it didn't. It made me want to squeeze a bit harder. Ingest her fear and get drunk on the smell of her discomfort." I look up from where my right hand is balled into a tight fist and realize how much of a fucking psycho I must appear.

Yep, he thinks I'm nuts.

Should I tell him I'm on the spectrum for sociopathy?

It's only because of my capacity to love and care for Vivian and a couple of the alters that I'm not deemed a psychopath.

No need to make him shit himself.

"Right. So..." Shit, now he's uncomfortable and probably looking for a way to end this conversation.

Let's wrap this story time up, Ellis.

"Yeah, so. By some feminine instinct, Vivian gave me exactly what I hadn't even known I needed. She just stopped—"

"What,"

It sounds like he asked me, *woot.* He continues and I really have to pay attention to his lips because I can hardly understand a word he says.

"Did she pass out or some—"

I cut in before he finishes his question, "No, she just stopped fighting. Stopped struggling to take in air. She completely surrendered to my dominance." My eyes burn with the memory of that moment, as I recall asking her, *Where the hell have you been, lovely?* I shake myself from the moment when our souls mirrored each other's, and focus on the man looking at me with a sense of... is that *acceptance?* He doesn't leave me in suspense for too long.

"You're a true Dominant. It isn't only a sexual lifestyle choice, it's who you are." He states with certainty and murmurs, "You found your true counterpart in Vivian."

"Indeed, I did." It's all I can say, because the emotions clogging my throat are all encompassing. He continues to paint me through the lens of an artist's eye. I can't imagine the colors his brushes are covered in; but if his voice and words are any indication, they're a warmer, gentler hue.

" In short," He starts again. "You substituted Valery in the role of submissive when Vivian was too grief-stricken to be there for you herself. You dinnae understand why she came to ye 'like she did." The pride in his voice was all for Valery. He gets her in a way I never could, or ever wanted to.

"Not at first," I admit, and then confess, "I thought she was doing it to fuck with Vivian, and I'd rather be in control of the mind-fuckery she did to the others. It wasn't until Viv, and I talked later, that I was able to see the dynamics of how their system worked. It was the catalyst I needed to finally start seeing them as four separate people, sharing one body."

"How did Vivian forgive you and Valery for the affair?" This fucker is coming for my neck with his questions.

"She told me the first thing she had to do was forgive herself for the loss of our daughter, Gayle. She said she didn't feel like she deserved to have my love or commitment after taking something so precious away from us."

"You told her none of it was her fault, right?"

"Of course, I did. It didn't matter how many times I said those words to her, it only mattered when she worked it out for herself. Once she forgave herself for Gayle, and for not being present in our relationship, she was able to forgive Valery and me for the affair."

"It wasn't easy to regain her trust, but she somehow realized that Valery's actions were done as a way to protect her from feeling guilt over not being available in our marriage." We sit in a calming silence, both lost in our thoughts.

"Hmm. Valery said she didn't even realize she'd been fucking you to make things easier for Vivian," Collin's beer-roughened voice breaks the silence, and he continues, "... not until they worked it out with Jessa. She said it was hard to come to terms with the reality that she was *always gonna be Vivian's ride-or-die bitch because that's the only fuckin reason their stupid, motherfuckin brain allowed her fine ass to stay around in the first fuckin place*—her words, not mine."

We look at each other for a beat and then both succumb to the crazy that could only be Valery Denyle's ass.

I'm still smiling when I say, "That's some heavy shit. Now, I have a question for you. Why are you in this relationship with Valery? And before you get started, I don't want to hear shit about the art or painting with the *blooode.*" I do my worst imitation of his Scottish brogue to let him know I really am curious and interested in his response.

***

It felt good to hash everything out with Collin. I realize he's just as gone over Valery as I am over Viv. This is not how I saw my life when I approached a beautiful girl back at Carolina. To the outside world, it'll look like we're in a polyamorous relationship. When in reality, I'm with Vivian and Collin is with Valery.

Two completely different women. One incredibly beautiful body. An what if Vera decides to take a lesbian lover; to the public, Viv will appear to have three different lovers at her disposal. I mean, if Vivian and Valery get to have meaningful relationships, it would only be right for Vera to have the same damn opportunity.

I hope they don't think they're going to leave Vera out in the love department. If anyone deserves to be loved on her own terms, it's Vera. I smile, realizing how important it is to me that Vera gets everything she deserves.

I would've made a great big brother, even if she had half of Earl's genes. Maybe I should talk all of these thoughts through with Oscar. I already know the moment some pineapple-loving-motherfucker approaches me or them, my black ass will be going straight to jail. No passing go and no collecting 200 dollars.

I complete my final walk through the house and head upstairs to sleep in our bed. I usually sleep downstairs to give Val and Collin some privacy, but I'm missing my wife and want to at least have her scent surrounding me when I sleep. I'm not the least bit quiet as I come to the landing. I intend to walk by Valery's door, but the unmistakable sounds of hard fucking pin my feet to the floor. I feel like a damn pervert in my own home, and still, I don't move a muscle. I'm not sure if I'm even breathing, I'm listening to the carnal sounds on the other side of the door... just to my left.

"That's it lass." He Grunts and Val emits a low, desperate whine. "I ken ye can take it all."

My first reaction is to tear the damn door down and pull his Scottish ass out of my wife's body, but then I remember, he's not inside *my wife*.

She's in the Internal House, oblivious to what's going on out here.

I remember that it's Valery in there. With her lover. Doing what consenting adults have the right to do.

~41~

Vivian

We've changed cars no fewer than four times since leaving home. I don't think all of this cloak and dagger stuff is necessary, but I don't say a word. John is completely stressed out about getting us safely to this undisclosed location. I haven't the faintest idea about how he found this place. He just keeps repeating, *When we get there, you'll know everything that I know.* His words don't make me feel any better about what's going on, but I know he needs my full support on this. So, I keep my mixed feelings to myself.

Granted, I was a little excited about the prospect of all of us going away together but as the date got closer, true apprehension settled in. There's no real reason behind my misgivings, I just have uneasy feelings that cast long shadows over any part of my excitement.

It feels like someone on the other side of the veil stepped across my unmarked grave. Pointed a finger at my naked headstone. They don't even try to correct their wrong; they need only bite the offensive pointing finger and step back across the way they came. It's that they're willful and intentional in the act, that's not sitting right with me.

"Penny for your thoughts, lass." Collin's raspy voice breaks into my spiraling thoughts, and I give him a thankful smile.

Hopefully, he will take the hint and let me stew.

"Aye, I know what that smile means. Still, I have that penny at the ready to pry them thoughts right out of ye wee head." He sprinkles an extra flurry of his Scottish brogue onto his words, because he knows how much I love hearing it.

"You're not playing fair, Collin." I fake my ire, even as I laugh at his antics.

"What's got you in such deep waters?"

"I don't know. It feels like. Whatever we left... is ending. You know? Some obsolete thing that needs to end before a better thing can begin." I shake the thoughts rattling in my head around, and try to make sense of them.

It doesn't help. Nothing has, not since this unearthly vine took root in my heart.

"Aye, lass, I know exactly what you mean. I don't know what's about to come to an end, but I feel like it's only endin 'to make room for something *more*. Something bigger than is standin 'in the way."

I turn in my seat to face him as tears fill my eyes. I don't try to hide them, or my emotional state.

Collin reaches out and pulls me into the shelter of his strength and the warmth of his arms.

"Och, sweet lass. Is gonna be alright. I promise ye, just trust the road ye been on and ken it takes ye where ye need to be." The fact that his accent is even more pronounced speaks volumes about his concern for me.

Collin is the big brother I never had. I love him for loving me in a way that feels like family.

I pull back and wipe my eyes with the back of my hand. I give him a wobbly smile and say, "You might want to work on that," I nod my head toward his face and continue to smile up at him.

"Work on what, lass?" He rubs his hand over his entire face, and I know he's wiping away the moisture from his own eyes. *Big softy.*

"When you're feeling emotional, your accent becomes so much heavier, it's almost impossible to make out what you're saying."

He points his index finger at me, and we both burst out in cathartic howls of laughter. We laugh until we're crying again. Only this time, the tears are a form of release.

I release my need to hold on to the way things are, and I open myself up to whatever the universe has for me.

I'm not quite sure what Collin needs to let go of, but from the easy set of his shoulders, he's made his peace with it.

"How much longer," Collin asks. "... 'til we reach this mysterious location your John has found?"

"I'm in the middle car," I deadpan and point out, "With you."

"I know, and?"

"That means I know as much as you know, Collin."

"Why did he stick ye in the car with *me*... not that I mind, ye see? But I thought he'd want to have you up front with him."

"John is obsessive about my safety during times when nothing is happening, he's been on high alert for the past few months. He trusts you to protect me if something should go sideways."

"Of course, I would. But why not have ye with him?"

"Because he has a target on his back."

"Lass, tell me what the fuck is goin 'on wid ye and John. I ain't askin 'to be nosey, I cannae help if ye winnae tell me what's happenin'."

I grab his hand and give it a hard squeeze. I wish like hell I could unload all of this on his broad shoulders, let him help me carry the load, but I won't put his life in any more danger than it already is.

"Valery didn't tell you anything?" I try another tactic. If she's said anything to him, then I will answer specific questions, if not... then he'll stay in the dark.

"She winnae say. She told me the same thing ye just said. I dinnae want to walk into some shit blind as a fruit bat. I'll be no good to anyone."

He's right.

I take out the burner phone with only one number programed into the contacts. I open the texting app.

ME: John, Collin wants to know what's going on.
Can I tell him or do you have plans to share

274

when we arrive? I love you.

I watch as the three dots indicating he's typing dance across the screen. He doesn't keep me waiting long. His message is brief. His tone, terse.

> JOHN: Lovely do not tell him anything. I will
> handle everything when we reach our
> destination. How are you doing?

I shake my head to let Collin know I'm not able to tell him anything before I say, "He's planning to tell everyone what's going on when we get wherever we're going." I type my reply as I watch the muscles in Collins scruff covered jaw clench down. Hard.

Valery, you're a lucky girl.

> ME: I miss you and I'm scared. I want to
> know where we're heading and what we're
> going to find when we get there. I'm doing
> fine.

> JOHN: Don't be afraid, lovely. I'll die to keep you
> safe. Get some rest, we'll be there in thirty minutes
> give or take. Stop worrying. I love you.

I don't bother responding. I relay the news of our expected arrival time to Collin and lay my head on his lap. He spends the next thirty minutes running his fingers through my locs and humming some Scottish pub song. I wonder if he's thinking about Valery or if he regrets the day he came into my gallery. I hope he's thinking of Val, because I'm for damn sure thinking about John.

***

"Wake up, lass. We're here, wherever the feck here happens to be." Collin's voice sounds like a piece of twenty-four grit sandpaper as it scrapes across the surface of my eardrum.

I look up into his liquid mercury gaze and shake my head a little before asking, "How can you be so beautiful, and sound like you deep throat horses for a living?"

He throws his head back and laughs so loud, I hate to think what the security detail is telling John at this moment.

"God, Vivian! You're as quick with your tongue as my Valery."
He pushes on my shoulder to detach my head from his firm thigh,
and I roll onto the floor like a rag doll. "Och, lass! I dinnae mean to
push you so hard. Here..." He holds his hand out to me while his face
splits with a mischievous grin.

Bastard, he meant to see me fall.

"No, I'm good. I'll get myself up. Thank you very much." There's
no bite to my words. I honestly think we've been riding in this little
car too long, and we're finally losing our minds, with the thought of
freedom looming over our heads. With that thought, I start laughing
like a loon and can't seem to stop or get up from the floor.

"Lass, what the hell is wrong with ye?" He admonishes with a
broad grin on his face. "Get ye ass up from the floor before John
finds ye down there and thinks I'm making ye suck my cock." Now
Collin's crazy laughter joins with mine and that is what John opens
the back door to.

"Oh, my god! Collin, could you imagine what John would think if
he saw us like this." I cackle again before I set the scene for him.
"Me, on my knees on the floor and you sitting above me on the
bench seat. These damn tears would be the last straw..." We're
laughing like we're at a comedy show. My head is on Collin's left
knee and his head is thrown back against the headrest. We are
completely oblivious of the voyeur who's been watching us descend
into lunacy.

The moment we realize that John is standing in the door looking
at us like he's envisioning a slow and painful death for Collin, we
completely lose it all over again. There's no stopping the hiccups and
guffaws bubbling up from the backseat of this car.

John must've shut the door on us because we seem to be all alone
at the Mad Hatter's tea party.

"Lass, we need to get the feck out of this car, we're losin 'it.'"

"You think anyone noticed?"

"Of course not. Who could tell the difference with all this shit goin 'on?"

"Help me up, please. Let's go see where we are, shall we?"

"Give me ye hand, m'lady."

~42~

John

The couple who were its caretakers for the last fifteen years, meet me at the door with smiles too bright and eyes too shifty for my liking.

"Good evening, Mr. Ellis, sir. I hope you didn't have too much trouble finding the place." I take his outstretched hand and give it a firm shake before stepping through the door. I've given orders to keep everyone else inside the cars until I look around.

"No. No problem at all. Have you all had the chance to get the house ready for my family and guest?" I ask and stand in the middle of the foyer taking stock of my surroundings. This is a beautiful home.

"Yes, sir," the wife answers in a low, smoker's voice. I turn to look at her then.

"Have you been smoking in *my* home?"

"No, sir. I'm just getting over a bad cough, is all. I... we don't smoke, sir." I nod my head, pleased with her answer.

"The security team."

"Yes, sir. We welcomed them to Sapelo about a week ago, sir. They were busy for the entire time. I put them out in the guest house, like you said, and they had access to the main house, too."

"Good. Were you two able to put away the luggage and set up the guest rooms accordingly?"

"Yes, sir. Everything is taken care of on the list you sent ahead. We even prepared supper for you and your guests, sir. It's in the kitchen and it'd be ready when you all are, sir."

"Thank you for being so efficient and for maintaining the property for all these years." I clear my throat and inquire, "Did you know the woman who owned it before me?" I turn in the opposite direction, feigning disinterest in their response, but my heart is beating like I've run a million miles just to hear what they have to say.

"Yes, sir. We show did know Miss. Della. She was a beautiful soul. I—we were so sad to learn she had passed away."

I give a curt nod of my head and start to walk away as I tell them, "Well, you've been well compensated for your services. Enjoy your retirement. A car is waiting to take you to a private airport where you'll be flown to Boca Raton, Florida to start your next adventure."

"That's exactly what she used to say."

"Excuse me," I look over my left shoulder, to see what the old man is talking about. "What did you say?"

"Miss Della, she used to say that she was off to start her next adventure whenever she packed a few bags and went on her way. The last time she said that..." He holds his head down in lamentation because the last time she went looking for her next adventure, she must have found... *me*.

"Yes. Well, I'm sure she found what she was looking for before she passed." I keep my voice neutral as I turn back toward the guts of Della's childhood home, and what would eventually become her legacy.

***

"John, how on earth did you find this place, it's magnificent!" Viv's excitement is another person sitting at the dining room table with Collin, Camilla, and myself. I almost feel like putting a bowl of Vegetarian chili and vegan cornbread on the table in front of the empty space it occupies.

"Viv, I told you it was a property I acquired some time ago." I won't have this discussion with an audience so, I quickly change the subject. "Um, how are the girls doing? Have they said anything about the trip?"

Collin perks up like a Scottish wolf hound at the mention of possibly hearing a word from Val.

Poor bastard.

"I know what you're doing, John. Fine, we'll discuss this later, and yes. They're both feeling anxious, but for different reasons. But there is excitement mixed in there as well. I don't think they'll have trouble settling in once they've had a chance to get the lay of the land."

"Did my girl give you a message for me?" Collin's hopeful voice is familiar.

Viv turns her attention to him and smiles, "Val is anxious because she wants to make sure the space she and Collin share is set up and comfortable for them. She's also a little on edge because, and I quote, *Bet not one fuckin hair be outta place on his goddamn head from a bitch or a hoe runnin a hand or blowing her funky-ass-breath through it.* Again, her words, not mine."

I watch Collin's eyes spark with heat at hearing Val's crazy ass message to him.

Those two are made for each other.

Vivian turns back to face everyone and says, "Vera's anxious about Val and I having you guys while she's here on her own." Her lids float down over her eyes, and it looks like she's in the middle of REM sleep cycle, which means somebody on the inside is talking to her.

As if to prove my assumption correct she deadpans, "Too bad, you never said not to tell anyone."

"Vera?" I ask, but they're still yapping away from the inside.

Viv nods her head and answers, "Yes." More from the inside and now a look of complete befuddled amusement crawls across her features. Then she smiles indulgently before she drawls, "God, Valery. I never thought I'd see the day..."

The next time her eyes open, they're not her eyes at all. These eyes are the color of perfectly aged whiskey with flecks of mossy green floating around the center. After Val listens to whatever is being said from the inside, she whispers, "Yes, I ain't tryin 'to do some shit to make you and John feel any kinda goddamn way."

More listening and then she turns her tawny gaze on me. "I ain't hijacked nothin 'so, don't get your dick bent outta shape. She sittin ' her prissy ass right here beside me. I just wanted to talk to Collin and then I'm goin 'back inside."

I look at her for a few seconds and realize she's explaining herself to me. When the hell did she get so considerate?

"I figured as much but thank you for letting me know."

Her gaze quickly swings back around to look at the other man at the table. Her shoulders visibly relax when their gazes connect.

"Hey, Col." Val's voice is as calm as I've ever heard it.

"Blood moon." His eyes become the low-hanging mist of early morning.

He's so in love with Val.

"Baby," Val starts and stops, only to start again in a more intimate voice than before. "Are you all right? I know what an asshole John is..."

Collin grins and nods his head, making the messy man-bun bobble around. Because she already called me an asshole, I feel more than within my right to address her surly ass.

"Good evening, Valery. It's the *asshole* speaking, by the way." I chuckle and Val throws a dirty look my way, it makes me smile harder.

She turns back to face Collin and deadpans, "See what I mean. Don't let that fucka get to you, okay?"

Collin laughs like she's the funniest thing he's ever heard. He speaks through the stupid love-sick grin splitting his face in two and says, "Val, baby, don't worry about me and John. I'm here for ye in whatever way ye need and want me to be. How're ye holdin 'up in there?"

"I miss you, and..." She looks around the table and whispers, "... we gonna have to talk later on. Viv can let you know when, okay. 9-1215225-21."

Collin immediately responds, "84."

~43~

Vivian

After the strange exchange of numbers, Val moves out of the driver's seat. She answers my unspoken question with a rueful smile before heading back into her room. It takes me a minute to get myself back into driver's mode; the allure of the Internal House is much too enticing sometimes. With a couple of blinks, I find myself back in the dining room with three sets of eyes staring at me.

"Took you a little longer than normal to get back, Viv." This is John's way of subtly checking to see if it's me or someone else. I flash him with my summer sunshine eyes and watch his shoulders relax.

"Yes, sometimes the pull of the Internal House is almost impossible to resist. It's so peaceful inside."

Camilla's eyes catalogue every nuance of my face like she's running them against her robot brain to verify if I'm on the kill list. Now that she's sober, she's back to being the woman I spoke with on the phone a year ago.

Apparently, the medicinal marijuana she'd shipped here was laced with LSD and cocaine; it had her completely messed up. She smokes to treat her social anxiety and depression. John secured her medical grade marijuana tinctures—whatever that is—and she's been a totally different woman.

I'm glad because I think she and Vera will make beautiful art and poetry together.

"Aye, Val often tells me how much she needs the peace and quiet found inside of the IH. The way she describes it to me makes me fuckin 'jealous that I don't have my own to crawl into sometimes." We all chuckle, but I think everyone would greatly benefit from having their own IH.

I wonder how the majority of the world manages to stay sane. The responsibility of being present with, and for others all the time, is inhumane. If I were never allowed to fully immerse into the counsel of my own consciousness, it would be akin to never experiencing the tantric soul connection John and I are cultivating. That's my definition of insanity.

The low timbre of John's voice drags me from my inner musings as he observes, "You have the mind of an alchemist. Your unwavering desire to stand above all physical constraints of language and delve into the more obscure, shades of sound allows—with complete surrender to creation—for the presence of a purer version of reality." His eyes never leave mine as he shares intimacies as though we were alone at the table. That he spoke to me with such affection and tenderness, even with a small audience, speaks volumes about how much he's grown.

Why am I so turned on?

Part V

I never thought I would come to accept the alters as true individuals with a right to pursue their own agendas and live their own lives, but at the end of the day, nothing else could ever make sense. It's like the universe allows this phenomenon to happen as a way to show human beings a living model of how worlds are created. To explain that every living thing known and unknown, is simply a dissociated identity within a collective system of one conscious mind

~Jonathan Ellis

~44~

John

Everyone is settled in their rooms for the night. Now it's just Viv and me walking around the ornate mansion that sits in the middle of nowhere. I know she has questions—most of which I don't want to answer. I showed her Vera's room and all of her new, smaller clothes that hang in her closet. She's already seen Valery's room because Collin is sharing the suite with her.

"Camilla has been very quiet since we set off this morning." I note as I wrap my hands around hers. We turn a corner that leads to another set of stairs.

"Yes, I noticed that, too." She looks down at her feet before stepping onto the first riser. "I don't think it was good for her to be in a car by herself on the long ride... *here*."

"Why the pause, lovely?"

"John," She stops walking and turns her body to face me. She's two or three steps above me so, we're pretty much at eye level with each other. After a deep breath she continues, "... not that I'm not completely in love with this property, but." Another pause and a twist of her lips tells me she's looking for the right words.

"Spit it out, lovely." I encourage.

"Fine. How did you manage to find this house on such short notice?" I look into her eyes and realize I don't want to lie to her; even though, the truth is going to cause all of them pain. I won't lie to protect myself or them.

I walk up to stand beside her and intwine our fingers. She gives me a questioning look, but follows me when I tell her to, "Come with me. Let me show you our set of rooms, okay?"

286

Her inquisitive eyes drag all over my face like she can discern the information I'm keeping from her. I won't have her look at me with suspicion, we've come too far to allow that shit back into our marriage. "I'll answer every question you have. I prefer to do it in the privacy of our rooms."

I lower my head so that our mouths are almost touching.

Viv doesn't make me wait.

It's not long before our lips are gently embracing each other. I pull away first and whisper the words into her slightly opened mouth. "Trust me, you'll want to be somewhere comfortable when we start talking."

"John?" She queries, "will I need wine for this conversation?"

We're moving again but I give her hand a squeeze as an answer to her inquiry. We come to a stop at a pair of reenforced steel doors covered in beautiful live-oak woodwork. The artist took her time engraving two halves of a weeping willow tree into the ancient wood. It is exquisite. Our doorway is an enchanted portal to another realm.

I know what Vivian's going to see upon entering our rooms, what I don't know is how she'll react. I place my thumb against the bio-scan-lock and wait for the clicking sound.

"Is this really necessary or are you just living out some kind of spy fantasy?" She's amused, but a little flustered too.

Instead of answering her, I push the doors open and stand back to allow her to enter first. I only realize I'm holding my breath when she turns around.

Strokes of humiliated fury paint her features in muted hues of orange and fuchsia.

Solar flares spark on the surface of her flashing eyes.

Then blue-grey rain clouds unleash their torrential down pour.

The air trapped inside my lungs whooshes out through my slack mouth.

She is devastated.

"Say something." I implore her, as I step into the room that will be the first of many things about this house that brings tears to her eyes.

"What do you want me to say, John?" She scrubs the tears away from her skin like they can remove the large mural hanging on the far wall in front of us.

"I-I. I don't kn-kno—"

Her scathing voice interrupts my burbled words. "Hi Della, so this used to be your goddamned house." Venom drips from each syllable.

Fuck, maybe I should've been upfront with her before moving her and everyone else into Auntie's childhood home.

"... like ripping off a bandage." I mumble under my breath like a schoolboy trying to defend himself while the teacher scolds him in front of his friends.

"What did you just say?" She sounds about fifty shades of done with my ass. I can't say that I blame her. There was definitely a better way to do this, I just couldn't think of it in the time I had to get her here.

Clearing my throat, I chance a look at her and explain, "I was... lovely, I had no idea how to tell you about this home. This way, it's like ripping off a bandage." I soften my voice and let my sincerity bleed into my words. "You know?"

"No, I don't know." Her eyes touch every surface they can without her moving her head. She returns that demolished gaze back on me and challenged, "Why would you bring us here and under false pretenses, too? Did we even have to leave home, or was that just a convenient excuse for you to pull this shit out of your ass, John?"

I feel my anger rise but then I remember, I don't have the right to feel attacked because I did keep this place and a lot of other shit from her and the alters. I take a deep breath and hold it for a small eternity, before I let it sift through my closed throat and out of my mouth. With a clearer mind and some compassion, I address her valid concerns.

"No, we *had* to leave. I would never play when it comes to your safety and well-being. And as for why I chose this place..." I turn around to shut and lock the door before walking further into the sitting room. The room with a large mural of a nude, twenty-eight-year-old, Della Richman, painted in all of her magnificent glory.

It's of little wonder I fell in love with Vivian upon seeing her across the Horseshoe, she's the spitting image of Della. Only, Vivian is dipped in the protective elegance of darkly melanated skin.

She breaks into my thoughts with words written in greens and yellows. "I'm listening."

I hate hearing the resigned insecurity in her voice. She should know, I'll never love and want any woman more than I do her.

Why doesn't she believe that my love is strong enough to stick? That's a discussion for another day.

"I've been listening to you, you know?" I explain with an impassive tone. "Listening to you talk about compassion, forgiveness, acceptance, and love. You speak like those four acts are the keys to the fucking kingdom. But I know for a fact..." Viv didn't let me finish my thought before she jumped in with her own.

"You know for a fact... what? That none of us have forgiven Della for abandoning her daughter to the whims of a goddamn monster? That's what you think you know. Am I right, John." What would be a question under normal circumstances, presented as a pointy finger of accusation.

By the self-righteous look on her face, she was just getting started.

Vivian theorizes, "You're trying to get absolution for your dear, sweet, pedophile. Even after she's been dead for almost twelve years, she still holds your cock and balls in the palm of her desiccated hand."

That she has the audacity to bark out a humorless laugh, all while shaking her damn head as she looks at me like I'm the most...

My thoughts come to a screeching halt as her words eviscerate me. If someone had told me this morning that by this evening I would hear my wife hiss,

"You. Are. Pathetic."

If she would've kicked me in the balls, it would've hurt less.

I step back until my back is fully supported by the heavy doors. I don't trust myself to be any closer to her than this. I warn, "Listen, I need to make a few things crystal-fucking-clear for you, Vivian. Firstly, don't even think about interrupting me again. Secondly, coming here was first and foremost about keeping *you* and those who mean something to *you*, as safe as possible. And thirdly, I hoped staying here would bring about a sense of closure for you and the girls..." I point at the undeniably beautiful image of the woman who sacrificed her daughter and corrupted me, because she never realized what an exceptional gift she was. I add, "and if that makes me pathetic, as you've called me, then so goddamn be it."

Contrition never looked more beautiful on her countenance than it does in the dim lighting in our room. The soft glow frames her in what looks like the golden hour just before the sun starts to descend below the horizon.

I won't dwell on her initial reaction... it was absolutely warranted. I walk away from the door and step in front of her. Her eyes dance across my features as she struggles to catch the rhythm and beat of my mood.

I'm transparent energy in motion. I want her to see all of my intentions clearly.

Perhaps I should've trusted her with this part of me before bringing her to the place that will force her to face her own dark energy.

Just as it forced me to face mine.

Vivian must find whatever she was looking for because she asks, "Why is this so important to you? And why didn't you tell me about this property?" Without giving me a chance to answer her questions, she continues, "I'm sure you've known about it since you inherited it along with the rest of her fortune."

"I did. I've always known about this property. I've had it renovated several times since it became mine; always with the plan to sell it or turn it into a boutique resort." If she's surprised, she does a great job of hiding it.

She turns to look at the mural before she continues with her questions. "Why didn't you... sell it, I mean. Why keep it?" She doesn't finish her thoughts, but I don't need her to. She wants to know, but she's also too afraid to hear my answer.

She shouldn't be—afraid, that is. My reasons have everything to do with her and subsequently, the girls.

I start with the hard truth and confess, "Every time I found a buyer or had contractors come out to modernize the place, I just couldn't bring myself to get rid of it. To get rid of *her*." I know my words are fists to her solar plexus, but I refuse to apologize for loving my abuser. I've made my peace with it, and she needs to get over it.

Vivian's voice is a void beneath a hidden cliff when she utters, "Okay."

Oh no the fuck we aren't going to do this shit. Not tonight and not ever again.

I keep talking like she's my own personal wailing wall. I hold her weary gaze and continue, "When I was away from you for those three months, I spent a lot of time down here. It was being renovated for the third time. I wanted it to be more tranquil. Anyway, the contractors called me out because they'd found a secret storage space under the floor in the adjoining bedroom," I point to the right where the bedroom door sits slightly ajar. "Over there. Said they had a box of items that they dug out and didn't know what to do with any of it."

Vivian watches me like I'm her favorite fucking movie.

Bet that got her damn attention.

"What was in the box?" She hates that she asks. Her twisted mouth and the tell-tell 'm 'between her brows gives her frustration away every damn time.

"A bunch of shit." I chuckle and shake my head with affection and reveal, "Articles and newspaper clippings; all with Della Richman bylines. Apparently, she was active in the Black Power and Civil Rights movements. She'd been published in several prominent papers and magazines in the seventies.

"Anyway, there was also a diary. One she'd started back when she was twelve and made the decision to escape the depravity of her... *family.*"

Just thinking about all of that shit, in her goddamned diary, makes my blood run ice cold in my veins. If Auntie had endured twelve years of hell at the hands of her mother and father, there was no way for her to grow up and be anything other than what she became.

Della Richman was shattered from the very beginning.

"Do you have it?"

I looked down into my wife's stricken face and the look of horror mirrors the one I wore on my own.

She clears the thick emotion from her throat and asks, "Is it with you, here?"

"Yes. It's why we're here, lovely. You—all of you—need to accept that Della Richman didn't have a snowball's chance in hell, wearing gasoline underwear in becoming anything other than who she was."

"What do you want to happen, John?"

"I want exactly for you, what you want for me..."

"You want us to be happy, healthy, and whole."

"It's the only way we'll move upward and forward."

"You've forgiven her."

"I never held anything against her, lovely."

"Have you forgiven your own mother, then?"

"I forgave my mother the moment I bashed that fucker's brains in. He was a fucking disease, and she was sick with him. Died because of him. There was nothing to forgive her for. Once I realized she was sick."

"You want us to forgive..." Her gaze snags on the mural before she can finish her inquiry. "Della."

"I want you to forgive yourselves, and yes. To forgive her, too. It's not for Della, it's for you. You told me once that forgiveness benefits those who forgive, not those who are forgiven. I love you, and I want you to have the benefit of forgiveness."

She gives free reign to the dark energy flowing through her; she uses it like cleansing rainwater running through trees. I hold her as tight as I can without causing physical pain. Because right now, I'm her fortress while she sinks into the depths of vulnerability. I hold space and bear witness to the pouring out of what's been trapped inside for longer than she's been in existence.

If I could shoulder her pain, I would. But then she'd never grow stronger, if I did. It doesn't make it easier to watch her break under the choice to let go.

~45~

Vivian

Ain't no need in worrying what the night is gonna bring,
it'll be all over in the morning.

I sit on the edge of a bed I'm not sure I would've slept in had I not passed out last night, and that old gospel song by Anita Baker and the Winans lays itself over my thoughts like a smooth warm whiskey. I always loved that song because it gave me hope for better days when every day was the eighth circle of hell.

There was one part that really spoke to me. I remember writing it over and over on my notebooks, jeans, arms, legs... I wrote the words everywhere I could with the hope they'd somehow protect me from the people who made me cry. Before I can stop myself the words bubble up in my throat demanding to be sang. "Weeping will last, but only for a while, but when the sun shines, you'll wear a smile; it'll be all over in the morning."

In a way, that song saved my life. Gave me just enough hope to fight and keep the others safe and inside. And I survived every horrific night and somehow; the mornings were better. Better because I was strong enough to stand up and move away from the hell I'd been trapped in; when there was no sun to shine its light on the depravity I endured under the cool watchful eye of the moon. I clear my thoughts, but I can't stop singing the damn song to save my soul. "... Ain't no need to worry your mind, no. Every day's a new day—" I hum a few more bars as I place my feet on the hardwood floor and stand up.

After a full-body stretch and standing-forward-bend, I release the resentment for waking up in this... *her*... house and try to prepare myself for what will accost me as soon as I step over the threshold into the sitting area,

I amble from the bedroom and come face to tit with none other than one, Della Richman. It hurts to look at how familiar she looks.

294

It's like looking into a mirror in bizzarro world. She is the perfect amalgamation of all of us, except she could've passed for white if she wanted to. "What made you so selfish, huh?" I whisper like she might be listening in through the walls. I expel a disbelieving huff of humor and walk closer to get a better look.

I can't seem to stop my gallery owner's eye from noticing the exceptional artistic gift with which the painter preserved her likeness.

I wonder who she commissioned to do this mural?

I move closer to find a signature or some other mark that may indicate who the artist was, but there's nothing.

"So," I pause because I think I see something but quickly realize it's nothing, so I wondered, "... who did you get to paint this mural of you, Della? Maybe an old lover. Only a friend, perhaps." I don't know where John is, so I guess I'll talk to *mother, dear*.

I find a tray with my favorite morning tea, scones, and fresh fruit sitting on a Scandinavian coffee table. I didn't notice anything other than the large painting of her last night, but now I see the room in the light of day and can't help but notice how aesthetically similar it is to my sense of style.

Is this where I get my love of all things MCM/Bohemian?

A large curved, burnt-orange velvet sectional is placed away from the wall giving the straight lines of the coffee table a soft maternal hug. At least that's 'how I interpret it. As I continue to admire the design of the large rectangular space. I notice all the feminine curves in the furniture, patterns, and even in the wallpaper on the adjacent wall to the painting. It hangs like a bespoke evening gown.

My greedy eyes devour the two floral-patterned armchairs—more like his and her thrones—floating to the left of the sectional. However, it's the beautiful 1970s rattan chaise lounge with a vibrant Arabic motif-covered cushion that pulls the breath from my lungs. The colors are so close to the ones I chose when I redid our home in

Lake Murray, it's no wonder this place soothes an initial element of my soul.

"Is this your furniture," Because I'm already committed to this one-sided conversation, I prod, "Or did John choose it because it matches *my* aesthetic?"

"No,"

My heart falls into my stomach at the sound of John's voice. And that he caught me talking to *her*, is enough to cause heat to deepen the color of my cheeks to plum-purple. To his credit, he continues as if he didn't see me have a full body flinch like it was Della who answered my damn question.

"This furniture was already here. I know quality when I see it, lovely. I repurposed it."

"I didn't hear you come in," I brave turning around to face what I'm sure will be a smug look before I finish. "I just noticed everything... *else*. The furniture and the decidedly mid-century modern vibe. I guess, I only saw the—" I indicate the mural with a toss of my head. To change the subject I ask, "Who fixed the tea and breakfast?"

"You're cute when you're embarrassed, lovely. You always have been." He strolls further into the room and takes a seat in one of the oversized throne chairs—the one fit for a king—and crosses his right leg over his left to look down his straight nose at me.

He is comfortable in her space. It makes me wonder what he looked like as a teenage boy while subbing for her.

"Are the others awake, yet?" I ask to distract myself from my thoughts.

"Do you remember when we were hanging out in my dorm room?" He asks like I didn't just ask him a question. "I was reading Lord Byron to you like some love-sick fool." John wears a small smile, but only in his eyes. A few lines mar and crease the corners, but they only render him more striking.

"Yes. Are the others awake, John?" I ask again.

Maybe he didn't hear the question.

After a beat, he brings both feet onto the thick, shag carpeted floor and leans forward to rest his forearms on his knees, his large hands clasped together. With a quick glance at him, I know he's not going to answer my question. At least not until he's trotted down memory lane.

I take a seat on the orange sectional and take a sip of my tea. If patience is a virtue, I must be the most virtuous woman walking the planet. I swear this man tries it more than anyone ever has.

Out of the blue, his baritone skitters over my skin. "We had been spending crazy time together since I took you from that white kid... what was his name?" John snaps the fingers on his right hand like a pneumonic device that'll help him remember Kyle's name.

It won't.

I take another sip of my tea, trying not to smile at the memory of him showing his ass just to get me.

"Mmhmm. Probably too much time, looking back." I murmur through a smile when he still hasn't come up with his name.

"Not enough if you're asking me. But something embarrassed you when I was reading that day... what was it?" He's back to snapping those damn fingers again and then he lifts his eyes to ensnare my gaze. The deep ridges between his brows and remembered pain sifts through his russet eyes, and I know exactly what he's going to say next.

I shake my head, totally prepared to beg him to shut the hell up, but it's already too late. John's feet are firmly planted in the soggy soil of the past.

"I had just finished *She Walks in Beauty*, and I felt you crying." There's wonder in his voice, like he still can't believe I cried over poetry. He smiles while pointing out, "Your tears soaked the middle of my t-shirt because your head lay over my heart."

"Yeah, and your attempt to get me to smile again was pretty bad. *What's with the tears? My reading couldn't have been that bad.*" I deepen my voice to mimic his and watch the smile reserved for me bloom like wild flowers across his face.

"You were so overwhelmed that I loved Byron as much as you. I remember thinking that there had to be more behind your tears than the love of old, dead, white poets and flowery words." He pauses and locks our gazes together before he confesses, "You know, that was the moment I realized you were too good for me."

I look closer at him, because I wasn't expecting him to say that.

He nods his head like he's proud of himself, but his eyes are filled with deprecation when he sneers, "Yep. I knew it. And still, I was so goddamned selfish, I could—no, scratch that—would not consider... ever. Letting you go." Sharp anger makes his voice harsh.

I give him a small smile before sharing, "For some reason, I thought you were going to bring up," I place my teacup on the saucer before saying, "... the revelation of my sexual history. How I feared losing you if we *did*, and/or if we *didn't* have sex.

"I was pretty damned embarrassed to admit that I'd never had the pleasure of choosing a lover for myself." I keep my eyes focused on John's somber gaze. I'm much too self-aware to hold onto shame, guilt or any other dense feelings over what I survived.

I own the darkness left to fester in my soul as a result of my abusive past, and yet, I choose to embrace the malignant developments as steppingstones. Childhood trauma is the anti-security blanket I'll never get rid of. It is not a soft and cuddly thing. It gives absolutely no comfort or sense of safety. When—not if, because it always will—it crawls out from the deep recesses of its hiding place; I give myself permission to sink into the awful warmth of its painful familiarity. Taking whatever solace I can, while petitioning my broken soul to fight because we won before, and we must win again.

John's pensive voice pulls me away from my wayward thoughts. "Not quite sure..." His trail off as understanding breaks across his face like the rising sun. "Hmm, it makes sense that you were so... *uncomfortable* talking about s-e-x." He whisper-spells the last word like a toddler is in the room.

Maybe he's scared his precious Auntie will hear him and punish his ass for using such explicit language.

His contemplative mood is portrayed in the colorless tone that whitewashes his words as he admits, "When I finally realized what you *weren't* saying... I remember wanting to steal you away from the world. Hide you. Keep you locked up in a safe and secret place.

"I had to work so damn hard to control myself that day. Hoping to give you some kind of reassurance that nothing like that would ever happen to you again."

I'm sucked into the memory of the conversation that exposed my cracked jars to John all those years ago

"You are a beguiling woman. I know we haven't known each other long, but I think whatever this is between us just might be forever."

"John. I don't know what this is we have, but I don't want to; it's just that... I don't want to have sex... with you. I have never had sex wi..."

"Hey, lovely, where'd you go just now?"

I startle from the past and reply, "I was reminiscing about the conversation we'd had that afternoon. It was raining cats and dogs. The perfect soundtrack for the dismal truth I shared with you.

"I still don't understand what made me feel bold enough to tell you about my abuse. I had never uttered a word about it to a soul before then. I just knew that if I didn't say it, and something... s-e-x-u-a-l," I whisper spell the word out to lighten the mood before continuing, "happened between us, that I wouldn't survive it. And something told me that I *had* to survive."

He levels me with impassive eyes that give nothing away. I wouldn't know if he was board or engrossed in this conversation if I didn't know him so well. John catalogues every minute detail of my face. The inflections in my voice. The tiny trimmers holding my right pinky finger hostage. He's completely tuned in to me, ready and waiting to hold me together at the first sign of a fissure.

It's one of the reasons I love him like I carried him for nine months.

In reality, I've carried him in my soul over multiple lifetimes.

"Do you remember what you said to me after I told you I didn't want to *do it* with you?"

He gifts me with the smile I was hoping for before answering, "Not verbatim, but I remember the just of it. Why?"

"I've always wondered if you recall that conversation the same way I do. Well, not in the same way, but the words—"

"Let's see," He gets up from his throne chair and comes to sit on the end of the sofa. After kicking his shoes off he stretches his body along the deep curve of the sectional; it molds around him like a lover's embrace. "Come here, lovely, snuggle with me like you did that day."

I don't respond, I simply get up and become the little spoon to his big.

"Good girl."

Oh, my god. I love when he says that to me. In scene and especially, out of scene.

"Okay, I'm here?" I settle my butt tight against his flaccid penis, but the heavy thump on my right cheek indicates he won't stay soft much longer.

He squeezes my hip and warns, "If you don't stop teasing Jughead, I'm going to scrunch that little lacy slip you're wearing up to your waist, rip those delicate panties from your body, and fuck your pussy raw right here. Right now. Hard."

Jughead gives my ass another tap in approval, and I reciprocate with a little wiggle.

His voice is smoke and midnight when he whispers, "Keep fucking with me and see what happens." With a smirk he can't see, I scooch forward and attempt to behave.

I giggle and say, "Not sure how I'm supposed to do that with the image you've put in my brain, but I'll try." I want him to praise my effort again.

I'll need a pick-me-up for later.

"That's what made me go against my better judgement and keep you, lovely. You were always willing to try."

His words baptize my frayed emotions, transforming the hurt he brought me last night into reluctant understanding.

John shifts behind me before he commands, "Relax and I'll tell you how I remember that conversation."

"Yes, *Sir*." I earn a squeeze of my belly for being a brat. I pack these stolen moments up as treasures, because I know I'm going to need to revisit them before this getaway is over.

~46~

John

The way Vivian always seemed to be trying on her emotions to see if they fit the given situation, crawls across my memory like a hag's fingernails against my back. Even during her bouts of melancholy, it was easy to fall in love with her and those damn summer-sunshine eyes.

She swore up and down she was fine being on her own, but shadows of loneliness would sometimes pass over her face, turning those lovely eyes the color of aged whiskey.

Ignorance may be blissful, but knowledge and understanding is more powerful.

I also remember how she dissociated—I didn't know that's what was happening at the time—when she tried to tell me how she'd never willingly had sex before. It felt like something had been trying to tear into my soul and consume the best parts of me. If it was her soul reaching out to mine, I'd have been more than happy to give her anything she needed.

The whole time I had been falling in love with Viv, she had been falling apart.

I pull my wandering mind back to the present and attempt to answer her question. "I know these aren't the exact words, but I said something along the lines of, *Vivian, I want us to find what makes both of us happy. With, and within one another.* I promised to never ask you for something you weren't ready to give. If I recall, you gave me a look that said, *yeah, right.*" I slide my hand under her nightgown and rub the silken skin on her belly.

I smile, knowing she'll hear it in my voice. "This next part is a little fuzzy, but I feel like I dipped my toe into the cave-man pool and made you more nervous than you were before."

She chuckles and asks, "What are you talking about? I don't remember any cave-man episode... Oh." She drags out the word until she trails off and thankfully, I hear the lilt of humor traipsing through her sudden recollection.

It gives me the courage to tell her this next part.

"Like I said, cave-man skinny-dipping-fool." I deepen my voice for dramatic effect and repeat words spoken more than ten years ago, "*I won't lie and tell you I don't dream, fuck that. I fucking fantasize about being inside your guts. Finding a rhythm that belongs to only us. You are the loveliest soul I have ever known. I'm going to love you, Vivian Anne Bruno. Let me love you.*" I finish and gloat, "I was a smooth motherfucker if I do say so myself." I lightly tickle her belly and delight in the sound of her school-girl laugh.

How she's retained a sense of innocence after all she... they've endured is a fucking miracle.

Neither of us mentions that this detour down memory lane, is an attempt to weather proof our love against the storms blowing in from the shores of yesterday's abandonment, and its scabbed-over hurts.

We're not delusional, we recognize it for what it is. We give one another permission to linger a little longer in the safety of what has already occurred, knowing it can't harm us here.

Viv interrupts my revery and teases, "Yeah, yeah, yeah. You were a smooth mother—"

"Watch your mouth." I cut her off, pulling another peel of laughter from her, while lessening the pressure in my own chest. She elbows me in the stomach, but it feels like a kid's punch. I know she's stronger than that, she's flirting with me. It's cute.

"No, but for real, though," I'll keep this going as long as I can if it makes her laugh like this. I squeeze her boob and listen to her breath hitch before I entreat, "You can't tell me that the next part wasn't some serious mac-daddy *shiz-nit*, straight from the nineties player's book of mac-daddying. I hit you with some old-funky-ass-philosophical-shit you weren't even ready for."

She turns, so I'm able to see her face, then rolls her eyes so far back into her head, it looks like she's having a damn seizure. That only made me want to ham it up even more.

I lower my voice and let a little of my Dom ride the edges, I needed to remind her of how I'd said what I did back in Capstone. I placed my lips next to her ear and restated, "Most people separate fucking and making love, Vivian. Some say to make love is to create poetry, while fucking is like writing a term paper. Poetry is a living, breathing, growing expression of self, while term papers are dependent on other people's ideas for validation.

"With us, even when we're fucking, we'll still be making love. And not until you're one hundred percent sure it's what you want. That *I'm*... what you really want."

Vivian is so quiet; I can't even hear her breathing in the silent room. I will my heartbeat to remain steady, but my thoughts are flying around my brain at the speed of sound.

I'm startled when I hear her soft voice.

"You know," She starts but stops to turn over so she's facing me before she continues, "I don't remember if those were the exact words, but I *do* remember how your words made me feel as they washed over my bruised heart."

"How was that? How did my words make you feel?" I hold my breath because it feels like I've been waiting my entire fucking life to hear whatever she's about to say next. To know that what I said somehow made a goddamn bit of difference in her life. In her healing.

"I think I said something about not being comfortable with the *idea* of sex, but you stepped right up to the plate and hit another

304

homerun." Viv cups my cheek and rakes her nails through my beard, pulling a low rumble from my throat for her efforts.

"What'd I say?" Her nails feel so good scraping the skin under the course facial hair; I swear I can feel it on my shaved balls.

Fuck, I want her.

"Mmmmm, something like," She doesn't bother deepening her voice this time. No, she's done playing and wants me to pay attention as she breathes life back into me. "If you and I never fuck, never make love, I won't leave you."

I watch her take several deep breaths before she's composed enough to finish her thoughts. It's endearing; that she's so moved in her love and appreciation for me. I'm humbled by her humility, her bravery.

"You seemed shocked to really mean what you were saying. It was almost as if you couldn't believe you were willing to forego sex just to be with me." Her gaze darkens with worried anxiousness, only to lighten once more with interested curiosity. I let her look her fill. I need her to see how impressed I am that she could read me so well, even back then.

Viv nods her head in confirmation but continues with her memory about our talk. "I must've given you dubious looks, because I clearly remember you—pouring yourself over the sacrificial hot stones—searing your sincerity into my head."

Her smirk makes my dick harder and I'm about two-point-seven seconds from slamming my tongue inside her smiling mouth and kissing her to orgasm.

She notices the change. I imagine I look like a demon incubus, ready to imbibe her erotic energy until we're both drunk from repeatedly coming.

Fire and brimstone singe my voice when I reiterate, "Lovely, I already told you... but you're going to make me show you. Aren't you, lovely-mine?" Her spine bows with excitement and expectation.

Oh, so she wants to be a brat right now.

I bring my right hand down on her naked ass cheek hard enough to earn a throaty moan. "Is that what this is, lovely?" I don't give her a chance to answer before I light her ass up again. Another whimpered moan escapes her sinful mouth. I rub my warm palm over her smarting flesh and clarify, "Does my little brat need a spanking?"

A garbled sound scrapes up her throat and lands in my balls, making me shift and adjust my package to the left.

She murmurs, "Sorry. After years of loving and being loved by you—discovering and reclaiming my sexual agency—it's hard cuddling and talking about a time when I was too traumatized to let myself dream about having you. You know?"

I smile and impart, "You asked that same question laying in my arms ten years ago. I didn't answer it then and I won't answer it now. Tell me, what else do you remember?

"Oh, yes. You went into a deeper explanation about your *intentions* with me." She says intentions like it's a dirty word. It brings another smile to my lips. She goes on to repeat verbatim what I said, "Something like, *I'm not just spending time with you because I want to fuck, Vivian. Don't get me wrong, I fucking love looking at you. Love having your lush ass tucked tight against Jughead when we catch catnaps in the afternoons. Even with saying that, it's still only you I want, Vivian. If we get to a place where fucking is on the table, I'm down like four flat tires for that shit, but if we never get there... you're more than enough for me. I want you in my life, that's all. You.*"

I wait for her to make a goofy joke, but she doesn't. I look down into her upturned face and see the shiny pool of sentiment settling over the cloudless summer day of her irises. Sunshine covered by gray skies, shining onto mossy green grass. Still so fucking open and expressive, they make my chest hurt.

——

"How, lovely?"

There is no hesitation this time when she answers me.

"I felt the power of the word, no, in my arsenal. Like I could say it, and people would actually respect what that word meant. For a long time, that word had two different meanings. For me, it meant what I wanted didn't matter, and I had no right to think that it did.

"After you told me that I was enough... It was like your words emancipated me from the chains of mental and emotional bondage. Chains that had kept me stuck in one place. I couldn't move, think, or feel anything. Not until your words freed me. I finally had the right to be heard. The right to be still. The right to simply be... *alive.*"

Any remnants of her previous arousal have dissipated as she lay herself bare before me.

"Your words gave me the freedom to take a breath that wasn't rushed or trembling in fear. One that wasn't forced from my lungs because my body was being pummeled, used, destroyed."

She believes I gave her that. That I—a piece of shit degenerate—was able to gift a galaxy with the stars that make her shine.

With a resigned shake of my head, I whisper-spell, "S-a-f-e." As if saying the word aloud would bring the boogie-man out from his hiding place. Perhaps she always knew that the only thing that could keep her safe from the monsters, was a bigger, meaner monster.

I concede, "And then I took it away from you. Took what made you feel safe because I couldn't—no, I didn't want to be responsible for placing limits on myself when it came to us."

She lifts her eyes to catch my gaze as questions sift across her face like stock prices on a ticker-tape. I have no idea what she's thinking, but I imagine she's trying to figure out what I'm talking about.

Ass Gate or our first anniversary.

She mumbles under her breath, "I wasn't expecting a confessional this morning."

"And yet, that's exactly what this has become."

"Sorry." Embarrassment darkens her eyes for a split second and then she admits, "I didn't mean to say that aloud."

"Don't apologize for your thoughts, lovely. They're just one of the many reasons your last name is Ellis." I give her a cocky smile filled with adoration and a little sadness, too.

"What were you referencing, earlier?"

Guess I do know her better than anyone.

"The ultimatum I issued on our first wedding anniversary— remember when we went to Charleston—on the chartered boat." I watch forgotten or suppressed memories dance like phantoms in her eyes. I feel even worse now than I did back then.

"Yes, now that you mention it..." She locks an accusatory glare onto my face and recants the memory to me, "You were anxious. You told me a crew member would escort me below deck to the bedroom. Undress, completely and wait for you. There were ten items on the bed, I had to choose four that I wanted to play with that day. I was to place them on the floor next to me. You would be in shortly." Her voice is a cup of soda that's been left out overnight.

"I was being a coward. I remember how I kept thinking about all the ways you'd been changing since we'd taken the D/s component from our relationship."

"I guess hindsight truly is twenty-twenty." She offers.

"Everything that's ever happened in our relationship has brought us to this moment, lovely. There is no way in hell, that we weren't planned by something much wiser than us."

"The Universal Law of Magnetic Affinities would agree."

~47~

Vivian

"The universal law of what?"

"The Universal Law of *Magnetic Affinities*. It basically says that we design pretty much every aspect of our human experience before each incarnation."

"Really," Incredulity cools the tone of my voice as I clarify, "Even the bullshit?"

I don't miss a beat.

"Especially the bullshit. The point of incarnating is to learn something, show that you've learned something, pay down karmic debt, and give something to humanity that helps to bring it into harmonious balance."

"So, let me get this straight—and don't think I won't be looking this shit up for myself—I planned to be born to a woman who would bring a lunatic into our home and send my life on a trajectory that would ultimately..."

John's words trail off as his mind connects the dots.

"... a trajectory that sent me to Columbia on a crash course collision with..."

"Me." Silence falls like a weighted blanket over our bodies; as cozy and comforting as a mother's hug. It's an inelegant shell around a vulpine truth.

After a beat or a couple thousand of them, John breaks the silent dissonance and gives voice to my own thoughts, "There's so much to discuss. Valery and Vera need to be on board with this, Viv. Especially Vera."

"It has to do with... *Della*."

I meet his gaze. The breath before he said Della, is heavier than the others taken before it. Usually, his clenching jaw made me hot between my thighs. The tick, tick of his teeth, don't ignite a spark.

It doesn't even make me feel warm and fuzzy.

"It's where everything starts." He finishes like it cost him something precious to say those four words.

My thumb caresses his bottom lip. He relaxes his jaw and avoids cracking a tooth. It works, and I earn a small smile for my effort.

I wonder if that includes The Order.

Before I can ask, John answers it like he lifted it right from my head. "No, that started in my mother's kitchen when she introduced me to Earl Friendly."

Confusion is becoming a constant state of mind around my husband as of late, because he's forever revealing new and strange facts.

"Don't worry about it, lovely. We've got time to hammer all of it out." He leans in to place a soft kiss on my lips, and whatever tension had built up, melts away.

"So, is it time to get dressed and see about the others?" I ask, while praying to anything floating by that he has something else in store for us.

"Or..." He lets that tiny two-letter suggestion dangle in front of me like a damn carrot.

"Or?"

Come on, Ellis. Put me out of my misery, already.

"Or we could take a long hot shower after I fuck you in the filthiest way possible."

John speaks with the posh diction of a well-educated businessmen, which makes me even hotter for him. I thread my right thigh between his legs and press my knee against his simi-hard flesh. A low, sexy moan extends like a lazy stretch from his throat in response to that little bit of pressure.

"Or... we could make love in the shower and kill two birds with one stone." I offer as an alternative.

He grabs a handful of my ass and squeezes so hard; I know there'll be a bruise left behind. John kneads my cheek like he's making bread and I'm so wet for him, I already know we won't make it to the shower or the bed.

"Or." He starts, and his large hand moves between my legs. Dexterous fingers rub the heated, wet flesh at the apex of my thighs.

He murmurs, "... I'll fuck you on this couch to slack my need to be inside your sweet cunt."

A thick finger breaches my entrance, pulling gasps from my parted lips.

He continues, "And then..."

In and out.

Round and round.

Deeper. Deeper.

Only to start all over again. I'm so close to climaxing, I sound like a bitch in heat.

He finishes, "... I'll pick you up, carry you into our bedroom. Lay myself out as an offering to the only god I've ever worshiped, and exalt you upon my phallic altar of servitude. Watch you sink your gorgeous tabernacle down every rigid inch of my sacrifice, until I'm baptized in your essence. Fuck, lovely."

He adds a second, and a third finger inside of me. Then he curls them up to rub against that osmotic spot that soaks up euphoria and transforms it into harmonizing vibrations.

"I'm coming, John."

"Yes. Yes you are. And it's a beautiful fucking thing."

"Jesus-fucked-a-black-woman-on-Sundays!" I scream at the top of my voice as the orgasm tears through my womb like a warm knife through a cold stick of butter; vast, violent, and undeniably vital.

"God, nothing makes me harder than watching you come." John has us both naked before I start to come down from my high. He's inside me before I realize we're naked. He proceeds to make good on every last one of those vulgar promises he made, until we had no choice but to leave the devil's lair and find our house guests.

I honestly didn't think I could experience any pleasure in the rooms that used to belong to *that* woman, but the way John and I worship at one another's altars creates a sacred space regardless of who or what was there before us.

***

John and I walk into the beautifully designed kitchen to find Collin and Milla sitting at the breakfast bar. Collin's in the middle of whatever he'd been saying when he notices our entrance, but he continues with his conversation.

"... lass, I'll have to go lookin 'for her." Both sit with a mug of something steamy warming their hands. Camilla looks like a little girl sitting next to his oversized frame. She still looks a little weary and a lot tired. Hopefully, with time and fresh air, she'll be able to shake the effects of whatever was mixed in with her latest supply of herbal relief.

"Aye, the ye are. I was just tellin 'Milla here that I might have to go lookin 'for ye if ye don't show ye face soon." He looks over his shoulder, flashes a devil-may-care grin before turning back to his coffee.

"That would've put you in an embarrassing situation." John deadpans as he walks me to the breakfast bar and pulls out a high-back stool for me to take a seat. Once my bottom touches the cushion, he pushes it underneath. His eyes swing in Milla's direction.

"Good morning, Milla."

"Buenos dias John. ¿Cómo?"

"I'm freaking amazing. Are you still messed up with that bad bud you were smoking?"

"John!" I give him a warning look that would make most people stand down, but not him.

"What? Stop stretching your eyes at me, lovely." His laughter is as sexy as his dark smirks. "I'm not being rude, I'm genuinely concerned."

Milla lifts her eyes from her coffee cup and replies, "Sí un poco. Tengo miedo de que le haya hecho algo a mi cerebro." (Yes, a little. I'm scared it's done something to my brain.)

I feel bad for her, but why would you buy weed from someone you don't know, in the airport of all places?

"I doubt it." John says and sits a cup of tea in front of me. He turns back to Milla and offers, "Let me know if you want or need an MRI or CT scan done. I have a good friend with a neurology practice in Savannah." John's moving around the kitchen like he's lived here his entire life.

Just how many times has he come to this house?

"I've smoked enough shit to kill an elephant, and my brain is just fine. I wouldn't worry about it if I was ye." Collin brags like he's proud of himself and his accomplishments.

Am I the only one who hasn't gotten high before?

"That explains why you're so hard up for Valery."

"Fuck you, John. Don't talk about my girl."

Under his breath, I hear Collin mumble, *fucker*. It makes me giggle. He cuts his silver eyes to me, and I poke him in his side to let him know I heard him. He shoots John the bird behind his back, Milla and I burst out laughing.

"What's so goddamn funny?" John turns his narrowed eyes back to the breakfast bar and waits for an answer. I can't stop laughing long enough to give him one, even though I try with all my heart.

———

"Fuck, bro, can't a person take a shit around here without ye knowin 'who did it?'"

The heavy brogue makes Collin's question much more comical, but my giggles abruptly come to an end as the last word peters out over the bar. The temperature in the kitchen drops about ten degrees.

Before I can intervene, John beats me to the punch.

"I'm sorry, Collin. I didn't mean to offend you by teasing *my* wife in your goddamn presence."

Lord-have-mercy on Collin's soul. John keeps his voice even while he speaks. Still, the weight of his words sits like an anvil in the middle of Collin's chest.

"John," I hedge in an attempt to pull his attention to me and away from Collin. "... let's all take a minute to calm down. Take a few breaths—"

"I'm breathing, lovely." John cuts me off and pins Collin to his chair before he continues, "Can't say how much longer your boy will continue to if he doesn't tell me what the fuck just happened."

Collin has the grace to look down at his fisted hands on top of the bar. When he finally lifts his gaze to John, contrition shines like a beacon from a lighthouse.

"I'm sorry. I dinnae have a right to take my frustrations out on ye. Please accept my apology, John."

My worry about the two of them fighting has transferred into worry about what's going on with my friend.

"Collin?"

"I'm... Vivian. I'm sorry for lashing out. It's me... my own bullshit."

"We all have our own shit," John turns away from all of us to continue cooking breakfast, but he keeps talking, "but Viv and I have a white carpet rule."

What, is he waiting on me to explain the damn rule or is he taking a dramatic pause?

Before him or I can jump in, Milla blurts out in annoyance, "Bueno, ¿qué es esta regla de la alfombra blanca?" (Well, what is this white carpet rule?) She doesn't bother lifting her heavy head from its resting place on the bar.

I'll have to remind her that we don't sleep where we eat. What the hell?

"It's simple." I start because John is busy making our breakfast and is still probably too pissed to be bothered with an explanation. I clear my throat and dive into it. "We think of our lives as pieces of white carpet. We accept that we'll probably drag some personal shit in on the bottom of our feet from time to time. We also accept that there will be some transference of our personal shit between our two carpets because we're married."

I pause and look at him and Milla to make sure they understand. So far, they're both nodding their heads like this makes perfect sense.

Collin dips his head and says, "Aye, Viv. Keep goin', it's startin' to get inside my noggin'."

I smile and continue, "Sometimes, we may allow other people to drag their personal shit in—making us partly responsible for cleaning it up. However—"

John places a plate of grits, avocado toast and a bowl of fruit in front of me with a hard kiss to my temple before cutting me off, "When someone walks onto our carpets, uninvited, and leaves their personal shit behind... *that shit.* That shit is not ours to clean up."

I cut my eyes at him when he pulls his stool next to mine, noting the smirk on his face. He's seems to have calmed himself down while cooking our breakfast. I turn my attention back to the two artists sitting across from us, interested in what either one of them will say in response.

Collin's the first to speak, just as expected. "Och, Aye. I like that. Sorry for dragging my shitty feet onto your carpet, John."

I bring my tea to my mouth to hide my smile. I thought we were about to have an all-out-dragging-on-the-floor-ass-whipping on the first morning here.

And we haven't even told them about all the changes coming their way.

John's velvety tone pulls me away from my bleak thoughts.

"No problem, just be sure to clean it up before you leave."

~48~

John

I watch Vera as she walks around the family room where a picture of a twelve-year-old Della, posing in a pretty dress with her new white family, sits on the mantel over the fireplace.

"So, this is where Della grew up, yeah?"

"Since the age of twelve. Before that, she lived near Butterbean beach with her mother."

"Hmm, what about her daddy?" Vera runs her index finger along the edge of the poured concrete counter tops. She looks like a little girl talking to her older brother's best friend. The one she wishes were her brother instead of the jerk of a brother she had.

"The man who fathered her half-sister, Callie, was married to her mother. Della grew up believing that man was also her father until her mother told her the truth." I keep all emotion out of my voice. I deliver the information like a museum guide talking to a patron. In a way, that's exactly what this feels like.

And that's the most fucked up thing about me introducing Vera to her mother through artifacts left behind in a damn house of horrors.

Vera's rich molasses intonation drags me back to the present moment.

"How do you know all this stuff about her. She told you when she was *playing* with you, yeah?"

Her words knock the breath from my lungs. It's still hard to hear the truth of what Della did to me.

"No. She never spoke of her childhood." I answer honestly. "In fact, she never spoke about any part of her life prior to moving into my neighborhood."

"But you somehow still know all about her childhood, yeah? How is that possible?"

"You remember when I went away for three months?"

"Yes."

"I spent some time back in my hometown. In the house where Della lived. While looking around in her home, I came across a diary she used to write in when she was a girl." I watch the play of emotions crawl across Vera's sage-green eyes, it's like looking into an enchanted lake. I wait in our silence.

Fortunately or unfortunately, Camilla breezes into the sitting room looking better than she's looked since I met her.

"... I'm so turned on in this damn mansion."

I stifle a grin and wait for her to say more because I know she's got a mouthful left.

"I just want to go to my room. It is too—"

She stops in the middle of the room. Standing in a pair of multi-colored gauchos and a white tank top, she looks every bit the Bohemian artistic genius Viv proclaims she is.

"Uh... sorry. I didn't see you—*Vera?*" Her greedy eyes rake over Vera's face like she's hanging in the Louvre.

Is she checking Vera out?

"Hey, Milla. Yeah, it's me. You need help getting back to your room." Vera doesn't ask as much as she confirms what she just heard Camilla say.

"Yes. I guess I got turned on...wait, I mean out. I don't know how to say... I'm lost." She sighs into her frustration and looks anywhere except at Vera.

Interesting.

"Milla." I watch as her slow lidded gaze swings back to my face with all the enthusiasm of a dead man walking. The smirk that lifts the right side of my mouth is completely unbidden, but it puts her off all the same.

As I watch the color drain from her face, all I can think is how I'm probably fucking up her high. It's that thought that pushes my smirk into a full blown grin. And it's that grin that makes Camilla's shoulders drop away from her ears.

"John. I didn't mean to interrupt your conbersation. Ur. *Your* conversation. I meant to say, your conversation."

"Why are you so nervous around me, Camilla?" I expect to hear her soft voice, but the words are drenched in the thick magnolia-flavored syrupy timbre belonging to Vera.

"Because you probably looked at her like you didn't want her in your house that first weekend... and then we, and by we, I mean Vivian thought she was doing drugs—you are scary when you go all cave-man, yeah?"

A loud bark of laughter leaps from my chest, and it feels so goddamn good to laugh at myself, I do it again.

"Yeah, Vera. I guess I can be. But you know Camilla has no reason to fear me unless she has nefarious intentions toward Vivian, or any part of your system." I say the last couple of words in a deep serious voice; she needs to know I will fuck her up if she ever comes for my wife or any of the alters. Including crazy ass Valery.

"John talks a big game, yeah, Milla? But trust me, you won't find a better man anywhere than the one sitting on that ugly orange and brown couch."

My heart stops, stutters, and starts beating a different rhythm after accepting Vera's words. This feels different from any rhythm I've ever felt before. I'll have to think about it later. *Maybe Oscar can help me decipher what it means.*

"Thank you, Vera. From you, that's a true complement. You know how much your opinion of me matters." I clear the rising emotion away from my throat and notice how Camilla's eyes are swinging from Vera to me, and back again. Her mouth tightens in a straight line, while her brows lower over her shrewd eyes.

What the hell is she thinking?

"Is there a thing with you two... *lovers*?"

Both Vera and I jump up from our respective seats; me from the couch and Vera from the flat brown armchair. Gone is the complementary, but protective younger sister and in her place is a scandalized little girl being accused of poaching another woman's husband.

"What the fuck did you just say, Camilla?" I hear the low, controlled resonance in my voice but right now, I don't care if I'm scaring this little slip of a woman.

"I—I. It seems... you. Vera and—"

"You must be out of your *gotdamn* foolish head, yeah? Must be if you can fix your mouth to say something so horrible about John. About me, yeah?"

I peel my eyes away from Milla's red face and fix them to a version of Vera I've always known was hiding beneath the oversized clothes, too big hair and tightly measured words. She's fierce in her defense, and even fiercer in mine.

"Vera, I—I, ur. I didn't mean anything. I mean Valery has a... Collin. So, it—"

"So..." Vera stands in front of the chair in a pair of slim-fitting cream corduroys. They look great, paired with the deep orange turtleneck and fall-colored crochet cardigan. She's even wearing a braided leather belt around her actual waistline.

She shifts her position from protective to brave and stands as a field of wild dahlias, beautifully committed and steadfast in her righteous indignation.

Desperation sinks its teeth into every part of Camilla while she holds her ass in her limp hands, wondering how she can get out of here without losing any more of herself. If she didn't look so damn pitiful, I'd be laughing my *own* ass off, but she does... look damn pitiful. So, I refrain and keep my thoughts to myself.

Vera hasn't said another word, nor has she moved a muscle. I know she's still in the driver's seat, because her turbulent turquoise-green eyes mist over with a little disgust, some bravery, and a whole lot of anger.

Milla clenches her tiny fist at her sides and licks her cracked lips before she launches into an explanation.

"Entonces, estaba pensando que no sería extraño si John estuviera contigo y Vivian."

Okay, so we're going to get it in Spanish. Does Vera even speak Spanish?

Milla continues, "No sé cómo funciona todo esto con alters y citas y quién puede follar y quién no … es confuso y estoy muy drogado en este momento." (So, I was thinking that it wouldn't be odd if John was with you and Vivian. I don't know how all this works with alters and dating and who gets to fuck and who doesn't... it's confusing and I'm high as hell right now.)

I don't know if Vera finds her response as funny as I do. But there is no way in hell I can hold this laughter in one second longer.

Thunderous howls pour from me. I laugh so hard, tears stream down my cheeks and my jaws start to ache. I have to sit my ass back down on the scratchy material covering this couch, before I fall over laughing at Camilla's stupid ass.

"Woo!" I expel the last bit of humor as I rest my elbows on my spread knees. I can't remember the last time I laughed that hard. Damn, Vivian would've been cracking up right along with me if she were here. And just like that, I realize how much I miss her.

"*John?*"

"I'm sorry, Vera. Do you understand Spanish?"

"Every language Vivian speaks, we speak, yeah?"

"How did I not know this?"

"I guess you don't know everything about our collective."

Smugness drips over Vera's words, and I have about twenty new reasons to add to the growing list, of why she could've been my baby sister in another life.

"Is that right, Vera?"

"Indeed."

"Why were yo. What was so funny, *Jonathan*?" Camilla spits my name from her mouth like it left a bad taste on her tongue. *Someone's hopped their little ass on the D-fence.*

"Alright." I take a breath to find some of that compassion Viv's always telling me I need to give to myself and others. Not finding any, I turn to Milla and answer, "Please know I only address you by your full name because you and I aren't acquaintances, yet. I prefer to keep firm boundaries in place when dealing with anyone outside of my inner circle. I forget that our lifestyle isn't common and not everyone lives with a DID collective system. It's just funny to hear your take on everything and the last bit..."

Vera allows a small giggle to fall away from her smiling lips like autumn leaves. I watch in fascination, as Milla's eyes track the swipe of Vera's tongue as she breaks the sound and returns her mouth to an impassive expression.

What. Is this?

Vera lets another peel of giggles float into the air and repeats in English, "... *and I'm high as hell right now*. It was the last bit for me, yeah?"

Again, Milla sucks in a quick breath.

"Fine. Maybe I don't be around people right after smoking, but I was looking for my room. Not running in on whatever the hell you two have on."

"I told you there is nothing going on between me and John, yeah? He's the brother I never had but always needed."

"The feeling is one hundred percent reciprocated." I level my eyes on Camilla because I already see she's into Vera, and promise her...

like any good big brother, "I'll fuck anyone up who comes for my little sister. I won't see her fucked over because of a sick fetish."

Vera swings wide eyes to search my face. I show her my brotherly love and loyalty, as well as my sincere intention. She nods her head, and we share a smile before Milla's voice breaks the moment.

"I'm sorry, Vera. I don't mean to... imply. I really tried to research DID when Vivian told me her diagnosis. Life got a little," She takes a deep breath and holds it like she's afraid it might be her last one. Eventually, the air whooshes from her thin lips before she finishes her thought. "*hectic*. Life seems to find a way to get so. Fucking. Hectic all the time."

I make a mental note to get the full dossier on Milla from the alphabet agencies.

Something doesn't feel right with this girl.

Vera's sassy Southern tone grabs my attention when she tells Milla, "Well, if you looking for peace and tranquility, you came to the wrong place, yeah? We always got something or other going on. That being said, yeah, we always come together and get through it, too."

Vera is the calmest person I know. After everything she's been through in her twenty-six years, she continues to amaze me.

I check my watch and realize I'm a little late for a meeting with my security team. I stand and stretch my arms over my head to get into the right frame of mind. Pinning both ladies where they stand, yet I only address the woman who looks like my wife's sister.

"Vera, I want to talk with the three of you about this diary. I haven't even had the chance to tell Viv about it, yet." I move around the G-plan Teak and glass round table and make my way toward the entryway.

Before I step over the threshold, I turn back to Camilla, "Your rooms are in the front of the house on this floor. When you come in from the side door where you smoke; you'll turn right and walk pass three doors, two on the right and one on the left. You'll come to another hallway, take a left and pass two doors on your left, your bedroom suite is the third door on the right." I'm not sure she understood a word I said.

Honestly, she looks pretty fucked up right now. I need to talk to Viv about her smoking. "Oh, and don't offer any of that shit to Vera or anyone else in this house. We clear?"

Vera answers, "John, you know we don't do drugs. I'll show her to her room and help her get settled in, yeah?"

I don't like Vera hanging around with the pot-head artist, but she seems to be drawn to her like flies to shit.

"Okay. Well, I'll be in meetings for the better part of the day. Are you driving today, Vera?"

"Yeah. Vivian says she need some time to process... something about a beautiful, naked, pink elephant in your room." I smile because only Vivian's ass would give such vague description without clarification.

Collin's outburst this morning skitters across my mind, causing me to turn and ask Vera, "What about Valery, when's she coming to check on Collin?"

Vera doesn't miss a beat. "She said she'd got some stuff on her mind and she want to talk to Viv about it. Looks like of the three of us, I'm the only one with a clear head, yeah? And why you think that is, John?" A mischievous glint deepens her green and blue irises as she watches me.

I shrug my right shoulder and shake my head, waiting to hear how she responds. If the way the left corner of her mouth is kicked up is any indication, she's about to say something unexpected. And I'm here for all of it.

I'm so fucking proud of her. I need to let her know without freaking her out.

She tilts her head to the side and lifts her right brow as if to say, well, ask me what you want to know.

So I ask her, "I don't know, Vera, why don't you enlighten me?" Quick as a whip, she flashes me a gloriously toothy smile before shocking the hell out of me with her next words.

"I'm the only one of us three who don't have to worry after a man and his fragile ego, yeah?"

She and Camilla laugh like they belong to some kind of lunatic lesbian league, as their raised hands fly by each other's in an attempted high-five.

"You got jokes, Vera?" I ask before leaving them to fall over one another, while they laugh at the expense of the heterosexual alters moping in the Internal House, because of some concern caused by their respective males.

Shit, Vera's probably right.

With that depressing thought, I climb the stairs to head into my office where the security team is waiting to give me a full report.

"Gentlemen and gentle-women, what do you have for me?"

~49~

Vivian

I've been tucked away in the private rooms, of the woman whose diary has been my constant companion, for the last three days. We each take turns reading her elegant script. Getting to know the woman who gave birth to this body. The way she came into the world, and all the hell she endured while surviving her grim reality.

We learn about the chance she took when she was twelve, hoping to carve a better life out for herself. We also find out Della carried the memory of her dead sister, Callie, in her soul for most of her life. So many lies and manipulations, only to fall into the hands of Vera's father.

John—to his credit—has left us to our own devices; cocooned inside this womb-like space. We're armed with each other, food, wine, and a playlist curated to be the perfect soundtrack to our second awakening.

We will either emerge as beautifully transformed butterflies, or as distended deficient dissolutions?

***

I straighten up on the large velvet sofa and stretch my legs out along the curved back. My heather gray sweats bunch around my ankles, the elastic bottoms trap the tops of my thick, yellow socks. I'm cozy and warm in the matching hoodie.

Della's leather journal sits in my lap like a child waiting to be noticed.

The choppy licks on the guitar bounce into the room, just before a breathy staccato blows life through the lyrics of the song. I feel Val's agitation like an itch under the skin of my left foot.

"What, Val?"

What? What the fuck kinda shit you makin us listen to, now? If this is the best your stupid, uppity ass can do with music, get back inside. I'll drive and choose the fuckin songs we listenin to.

I like this song, yeah? It's happy and makes me feel like I can save myself...

I cut Vera off before Val turns her viper's tongue on her. "It's Jewel's, *Who Will Save Your Soul*, and I agree with Vera. It's empowering without being so preachy. But Val if you want to drive, that's fine. I'm good either way."

No, I don't feel like bein out there just yet. Can you just fuckin read more of the... her diary.

"Of course, from where we stopped?"

Yeah, from where we stopped. Thanks for reading, Viv.

"No problem, we all..." I let my words fade into nothingness because I'm not sure what we're meant to get from reading Della's diary or learning about her life.

Yet, I know in my heart that her life and words already exist as flesh of our flesh and bone of our bone. Where she begins, we end; and where we cease to live, she springs into life anew. We are the head and the tail of a self-devouring serpent. Until one of us figures out how to feast on something other than ourselves, we are doomed to consume and be consumed by one another.

The revelation is so shocking, I immediately share it with the girls. "We all... need." The words float away again.

The fuck you keep startin and stoppin for with the same goddamn words. Shit or get your ass off the mothafuckin pot, Viv.

I give Val an internal eye-roll before explaining, "There's an elemental connection between Della and ourselves. It requires this macabre cycle to repeat itself... until we figure out how to..."

How to, what? What do we have to figure out, to stop this repeating cycle, Viv?

Look, bitches. I ain't sign up for no conjurin-hoodoo-bullshit. We readin this fuckin diary cause we nosey as fuck and wanna know what kinda hoe could do what Della stankin ass did, and not give two shits about doin it.

"Think about it like this, Val. We are the reflections of our parents 'deepest fears and regrets. We are also the echoes of their greatest desires, expectations and possibilities. If we are to rise above our shattered beginnings, we must stand over and eventually master what they failed to, while continuing to honor and ascend our own personal mountains."

A sense of stillness settles in my soul, where only moments before, I felt the lingering effects of ages old dis ease. I'm not sure how I came to possess this knowledge, but I trust in the staunch conviction of my words.

With a new sense of ease rooted in my heart, and the beginning of Linkin Park's alternative anthem, *Numb,* burning a hole in my mind, I accept it all as the necessary truth of soul evolution.

I listen to the lyrics and let my body move the way it wants to. A tantric offering to this new easiness bubbling through my blood like Champaign.

And I know I may end up failing too
But I know You were just like me with someone disappointed in you

I pick up the worn leather journal and open it to the page marked with a pink ribbon used as a bookmark. It's so faded and thin, it must have belonged to Della or maybe it belonged to her dead sister... our dead auntie. "Okay, here we go. I can't say I don't love that she titles her journal entries." I mention with a smile.

That shit freaked me the fuck out when I saw it.

Why would you be freaked out by something like that, Valery?

Cause, Ve-ra, we all do the same goddamned thing when we write in our mothafuckin journals. That shit don't make you feel like somebody walkin on our damn graves?

"Really, Valery?" I ask through my chuckle. "When did you become superstitious?"

You ever spend time talkin with Collin when he deep in them damn cups? That mothafucka start talkin bout all kinda crazy shit. Stories his da and ma told him when he was a wee lad. Valery's impersonation of Collins brogue is everything. I hear them laughing along with me.

"Collin ever hear you imitate him before?"

Hell yeah, that giant highlander love when I talk like him. Always teachin me new words and phrases. He so fuckin filthy, the shit he have me sayin sometimes make me blush.

Get outta here! Make you blush, yeah?

Fuck, Vera, you just don't fuckin know how filthy my Scot is. I'm always goddamn here for that shit, too. But enough about all this, get to readin. Stop stallin, Viv.

"That obvious, huh?"

Hell, yeah.

Even to me, yeah?

"Okay. She titled this one, *No Good Things*."

She only write to her dead sister in that journal, yeah?

"Yes. She promised to take her with her everywhere she went, and for the most part, she did." I run my eyes over Della's neat cursive writing. We'd been reading the journal for the past three days. It's getting more difficult every day—with a first-hand account of her life born of lust and greed—to hold on to the initial thoughts about the woman who gave birth to us. It appears she was doomed to repeat this vicious cycle.

Get to it, Viv. We ain't got all fuckin day.

"*No Good Things. Dear Callie,*"

I've been walking on back roads for what feel like weeks but really it only been a couple of days. I tied your satchel around my neck and stuff it inside my shirt. I told Dixon we gotta stay out of sight because the white men is looking for some niggers to kill. They all so angry about changes and Civil Rights and colored people voting. I don't care if I never cast a vote or if I never get to live with, ride with, or eat with white folk. Don't think most colored people really want to be with them so much as we want to have the same rights as them. Anyway, we been sleeping under trees and inside old buildings where seem like nobody lived or worked in forever. His momma sent a lot of dried meats, and canned, pickled vegetables for us to eat. It ain't half bad, except when I have to use the bathroom. I thought the outhouse was disgusting but using the bathroom on the side of an open field with hardly nothin to wipe myself with is way worse. We just passed through Crescent and Dixon say after we make a right on Smith road, we just a few more turns from Sapelo Dock road and then we can hop the ferry in Townsend and that's it. He say some rich, white man own Sapelo, and he hire locals to clean and play with his children when he come here from whatever big city he from. Said with my almost looking like a white girl, he might hire me to travel with his family since I read and write and know my math so good. I'm gonna tell you something, Callie. Don't go whispering what I'm about to say to you to your friends on the other side. You know sometimes, ghost slip up and tell their own living relatives secrets that don't belong to them. I don't want nobody back home to know where I'm headed. Or who it was who help me get away. But, if I don't tell somebody what happened last night during the witching hour, I'm gonna go plum crazy. You have to promise me, Callie. Send me a sign that you promise you won't let a word of this slip from your ghostly lips. If you promise, then make my stomach stop hurting when I finish counting to three. Then I know I have your word. "One. Two. Three." Okay, you prove to me you still the sister I know and love. Listen, Callie. We found an old run down hunting lodge to sleep in. He say it's our last night together because he'll deliver me to Sapelo tomorrow... well, today, but it would have been tomorrow last night when he told me this. After we ate the last little bit of salt-pork and skins, he say he saw a creek a ways off that look like a good place to get clean before we set off in the morning. It was already dark, but I could smell myself, Callie. I don't like being stank. I guess that's one good thing momma instill in me. He said he would come with me to watch out for me. Make sure nobody sneak up and do me no good. I said, "Promise you won't look at me when I'm in the creek." He said something about not belonging to the same fool praise house I do. Mumbled under his breath, "I'm almost twenty years old. You just a little girl, remember? A pretty little girl, but still a little girl." I didn't care if he thought I was a little girl, hopefully that meant he wouldn't look at me. Or touch me. The water felt so warm on my skin. Like being in the bathtub at Nanna's when we would visit her in Eastover, South Carolina. I wish I could walk to her place. I know she don't believe in all that foolishness momma and daddy do. Anyway, I scrub my skin almost raw with a rough-smooth stone I found beside the creek. I used my hands to wash between my legs and some of the soft, spongy clumps of little green leaves floating on the top of the creek to wash my ass. I knew it was dirty, so I was glad to have the soft mat of leaves to scrub around back there. I was just dipping my hair into the water when I heard a crack. Sound like somebody stepping on a fallen branch or twig. I didn't want nobody to see me, so I duck my head in the water and use one of those empty grass straws to breathe. Remember when we hid from daddy's brother that time using them? Callie, you won't believe what I saw when I came up to see if someone was spying on me or if an animal was waiting to tear my flesh from my bones. Dixon Montgomery! Standing naked as the day he was born. His chest so wide and with all kinds of muscles. Even with his short leg and those thick glasses on his face, he look like a man. Not like daddy or Old Man or any of them nasty men at home. He was just standing on the other side of the creek. There was a lot of trees between us, but I could still see his... Callie. Dixon need to start spelling his name D-I-c-k-son. After seeing that dried-up, black turkey neck sitting on top Old Man's rusty balls, I thought all of them looked like that. But Callie, D-I-c-k-son has something so pretty hanging between his muscled thighs. So long and thick, I thought a snake had slithered up between his legs. It look like he dusted it with fresh cinnamon-sugar powder. That was the color of it. Except the big mushroom head. Callie, you remember when Nanna made us that rhubarb-blackberry jam during the summer. That was the exact color of the head of his dick. Can you imagine anything so pretty hanging between a man's legs? He caught me looking at him and I didn't have the will power to turn away from it. I didn't know it could look like that. He must cut the hair that grow around it, because it looked like soft, brown beach sand hugging the wide bottom of it and just a little bit on his ballsack. Gawd, did I tell you that his balls were as big as the tomatoes we grew last summer? So full and ripe. If Old Man looked like D-i-c-k-son, I might have stayed. Anyway, he called me a nasty little girl for being a peeping-Thomasena. I yelled back across the creek, "I ain't no peeping Thomasena, I thought a snake had got hold to you. I wanted to make sure you were all right, is all." I said it like it was the only truth and I guess he believed me. But then he did something I wasn't expecting him to do. He walked his naked ass across to where my naked ass was standing and stood in front of me. just stood there. Eyes locked on my tits. It must have been because we was out in the woods during the witching hour because he grab at my hand and wrap it around himself. Then you know what he ask me, Callie. He say, "Still think a snake got hold of me, Della?" I didn't even know his voice could sound like it was coming from some deep, gravely place inside him. I try to pull my hand back and cover my tits, but he wrap his own hand around mine... the one holding onto him. Then, Callie. The next time he talk to me, he sound even more rough, if that's possible. "Maybe you ain't such a little girl after all, Della. Little girls don't got tits like those. And little girls don't have all that pretty, silky hair covering up their pussy like you do. And you know what else little girls don't do, Della?" He ain't even give me a chance to answer him before he started pushing and pulling my hand along the length of his hardness while he answer his own question. "Little girls don't be out in the middle of the woods, naked with grown ass men and looking at dicks like you been looking at and now tugging at mine. And little girls damn sure don't know how to make a man dick jump like your little pale, buttermilk hand is making mine jump and twitch right now." My heart was beating outside my chest because I didn't know what he was gonna do to me.

I told him, "You and my dead sister, Callie was in the same class. I carry a piece of her soul with me everywhere I go. Don't piss her off, D-i-c-k-son. She won't like you bothering with her little sister." But before I could lift your satchel up and show him how you was still here watching over me, he made our joined hands speed up on himself. It felt like it came to life and had its own heartbeat and could move around in the world without being attached to D-i-c-k-son. He was moaning and growling from the back of his throat like he was in two places at the same time. One of them places must've felt like heaven and the other, like hell. I swear his face was so screwed up and ugly I thought maybe what I was doing was hurting him and so, I squeezed my fingers as hard as I could and kept right on moving up and down, up and down on it. He moved his hand away and grab hold to the tree. His hip pumping like a race horse, Callie, I ain't ever seen nothing so disturbing and entrancing in all my life. I looked into his balled-up, sweaty face and it looked like he was on the verge of passing out, which I decided I wanted to happen so he would leave me alone. So, you know what I did, Callie? The next time my hand went down to and just before coming back up to that big head, I used my other hand to grab his balls! I pulled and tugged and rolled those bad-boys while my other hand—the one squeezing his dick—got to the head and then I squeezed his cock-head and his balls at the same time. Callie! I do believe I broke your classmate, D-i-c-k-son because it squirted something thick and white and sticky. Then he fell to the ground. Holding himself between his legs, writhing and moaning like some kind of downed hog. I quickly washed my hands in the creek, put my clothes on and stood over his naked body and did what I was trying to do before he put his hand on me. I lift your satchel up and show it to him. With all the marks and some of your bright red hair hanging out the side. Guess what? He jumped up from the ground and ran his long-dick-big-tomato-balls right back across the creek and didn't say boo-hag to me for the rest of the night. At least I know when I'm ready, I don't have to settle for a dried-up turkey neck. I guess Dixon was right about no good things happening during the witching hour.

Della, Looking for good things

The silence in the room is mirrored by the silence inside the Internal House. Of all the horror Della had endured before leaving her parents 'home, to be sexually assaulted by the boy who promised to keep her safe and get her away from the depravity of the people in that crazy church. How much damage is one girl supposed to take.

Vivian, she never had a chance—s

"No. She didn't. And because she never had a chance—"

I guess that explains why she ain't know how to make sure her fuckin daughter would have one either.

You can't give what you never got, yeah?

Oh, we read some old ass sad diary and all of a sudden, what? She get goddamn mother-of-the-year. Fuck that shit! She still left Vera's ass with a man who fucked her until she couldn't get fuckin whole.

"I know, and I'm not saying I forgive her, but reading this does give some insight."

Fuck insight! I'm only readin this bullshit because it's here and y'all want to get to know mommy better.

It's not about getting to know her better, or at all, yeah? It's more—well, for me—it's more about maybe learning more about myself.

"In the end, that's the only reason to ever pursue knowledge. The only reason to delve into the soul of the ghosts who haunt our nightmares and run bony fingers over our gravestones. Man, know thyself.

Man... ain't no man here.

"This is an ancient Kemetic proverb born from the spiritual teaching that all of heaven resides inside of the body. If one seeks to know heaven and god, they only need to know themselves."

Right. Like you said, Viv, the more I learn about Della, the more I feel like I understand her. What made her move in her life the way she did, yeah? And because we carry part of her inside ourselves, it mean we have more information about each other.

Shit, Ve-ra. When the fuck you get so fuckin smart?

I always been smart, Valery. You just never took time to notice it, yeah?

Whatever, bitch. I'm done with all this goddamn bondin. You know... Della shit been fucked-up since she took her first goddamn breath and she still somehow managed to leave John a fuck-ton of wealth by the time she was thirty-eight. I got to give it to her, she was a mothafuckin boss-ass bitch before it was even a thing.

The pride I hear in Val's voice definitely mirrors what I'm feeling for the beautiful enigma whose visage looks down on three versions of the daughter she brought into this world.

"On that we can agree."

That might be putting it mildly, yeah?

~50~

John

Vivian and Collin come floating down the stairs clad in matching bright, green t-shirts with a glittery four-leaf-clover emblazoned on the front. Collin has on some kind of dark-green, felt hat with a feather sticking in the side, and his partner in crime is wearing a flowy green scarf tied around her head like she plans to run off and join a caravan of Romani.

What fresh hell is this?

"Good morning, John." Viv goes up on her toes to place a kiss under my jaw, while she snakes her right hand up my left bicep. Just before her soft lips grazes my skin, I feel a sharp, pain at the back of my triceps and I swear, it brings tears to my eyes. She slips away with an impish grin on her lovely face and looks over to the cackling fool and whispers loud enough for the dead to hear, "I told you he wouldn't be wearing a stitch of green."

They devolve into obnoxiously loud fits of laughter because for some reason we're back on the elementary school playground and I'm the only kid who forgot that today is St. Patty's Day. *And of course, no one reminded me to wear something green.*

"Are you two asses nearly done or will this little Tom and Jerry act continue throughout the rest of the day?" I was hot as fish grease and not because they were laughing at my expense and certainly not because Viv pinched me. I was mad because Valery and Collin spent an entire week out in one of the guest bungalows and they thought it would be great if I joined them for dinner.

Seeing him with his fucking hands all over the body that's belonged to me for the past ten years, was the equivalent of watching Vivian fuck a goddamn professional football team. One big motherfucker after the other. I know she's not there. I know Collin has no interest in my wife—at least not in the same way as he's

338

interested in Val—based on how he treats her like his favorite sister, but it still makes me want to commit murder.

"Aye, John. We plan to continue our little—what'd ye call it, lad—Tom and Jerry act until eleven-fifty-nine tonight. So, ye cannae join us, or be a grumpy bastard by ye'self." I can't even look at the good-looking artist without feeling absolute violence leak into my veins from the dark recesses of my soul.

His buddy is not to be outdone, so she chimes in like a damn mocking bird. "That's right, babe. You can join us," I watch as she grinds her hips in a filthy roll, before stepping into my personal space and bracing her hands on my chest.

First, a slow swipe of her tongue across her bottom lip. Next, a deliberate lift of sultry lids to reveal the wickedness held in those damn summer sunshine eyes of hers. Then, a ridiculous brush of her full breasts against my chest as she tiptoes a little to whisper, "Or forget about using that cock ring and those anal beads we ordered."

Like the evil succubus she is, she drags her tongue from my ear to the corner of my mouth and waits for me to take the kiss over. And I know she wants to put on a dirty little show just for Collin. A little piss and vinegar for flaunting his and Valery's sexual chemistry in front of me last week. One look at the twisted smirk gracing that fuckable mouth, and my suspicion is fully confirmed. Debauched mirth and revenge paint a beautiful shade of fuck you across her lovely lips.

"Don't worry, lovely." I tell her as I slide my dominant hand up the back of her neck and into the tightly twisted locs she wore hanging down her back. I fist the spongy roots at the base of her oiled scalp. Tight enough to let her know she's not going anywhere, loose enough to let her know I have no desire to hurt her. It's the sigh that leaves her slightly opened mouth that tells me she needs the reassertion of my dominance more than her next breath. Needs Collin to see *us* together in this intimate way. *This is why this woman is my god, my judge, and my fucking deliverer.*

"I never worry when it comes to you, Sir." Viv's voice is an auditory cunt; deep, open, and squeezing my thick lust until I'm ready to explode.

"I'm more than willing to join in with you and Collin's merriment," I tug on the roots of her locs and watch her pupils dilate, the thrumming in the pulse point in her neck speeds up. "As long as you realize for every action there is an equal and opposite reaction." I drop my face to hover above hers for a fraction of a second before sealing my lips over her sexy smirk.

She opens for me immediately and I waste no time pushing inside the warmth waiting for me.

Our tongues slide against each other's in a sensuous dance choreographed eons ago. This is not a kiss to have in front of company, but I have zero fucks to give about Collin watching me fuck Vivian's mouth like I'll be fucking the rest of her later on.

I want him to know how this feels... how *I feel* every goddamn time I see him with his motherfucking hands all over Valery. I need his balls to tighten up as blood flows into his cock at the thought of what he could be doing with *his girl* if she weren't inside the goddamn Internal House.

I come back to the kiss with an audible grunt and visceral jerking of my hips. It's not until that moment, that I realize Viv and I have come sharing this categorically filthy kiss.

"*Fuck me, aye?*" Collin's low, gravely whisper breaks through the cloud of erotic haze we're cocooned in. Viv—my little shy exhibitionist—buries her sweat-dotted head in my chest and fans her blush-warm cheeks.

I kiss the top of Vivian's head and reply, "No, lad. I'll take a hard pass. I'm going to take my girl upstairs, get us both cleaned up and we'll be back and ready to drive into Savannah to celebrate the drunkest day of the year."

"Aye. I'm goin 'out to my flat to get myself..."

340

"*Off*? The word you're trying not to say, is off, *aye*?" I feel, more than hear, Vivian laughing at my silly joke. Collin, unaffected, belts out a boisterous laugh and nods his head. No shame or licentious intent toward Vivian in any way. And for the first time since all this shit started, I can see how things will be.

When he and Valery are out and about, I'll be a horny motherfucker. Chomping at the bit to be back with the woman I love, only with more appreciation, devotion, respect, and unconditional love. It's the same for him, only he feels this way about, Valery.

I never thought I would come to accept the alters as true individuals with a right to pursue their own agendas and live their own lives, but at the end of the day, nothing else could ever make sense. It's like the universe allows this phenomenon to happen as a way to show human beings a living model of how worlds are created. To explain that every living thing known and unknown, is simply a dissociated identity within a collective system of one conscious mind.

***

St. Patrick's Day in Savannah, GA is not to be taken lightly. Collin, Camilla, Vivian and I look like a pair of couples who decided to come to downtown Savannah for the sole purpose of getting shitfaced with about a million other people. All of us dressed from head to toe in various shades of green.

I wonder what Milla, and Vera got up to when I left them alone.

She must feel my gaze on the back of her head because Milla turns to look over her shoulder with an inquisitive glint in her eyes. I decide to play nice and flash a smile with a curt nod.

"John, when's the last time you heard from the alphabet people?" Viv pulls that question from her ass because nobody was talking about the foolishness that brought us down here.

"It's been a few days—maybe three—why?"

"I was just wondering if it's..."

"Of course, it's safe for us to be out in the open. I wouldn't have us out here if it weren't. Are you feeling okay, lovely?"

"Yes." I thread my fingers through hers and pull her body closer to mine, before dropping a kiss onto the top of her head.

"Talk to me."

"It just feels... strange. Being out here in this party atmosphere while people are looking for you with intentions to end your time on the planet."

"I don't think they are actively looking for me, anymore. They are more than likely, scrambling to save their own asses from the firestorm that's raining down on them from all of those alphabet people you asked about." I place another kiss at her temple and breathe in her jasmine scent. I hope the smile in my voice eases some of her tension, but I know she won't be able to fully relax until we get an all-clear from my contacts.

"Change of subject," Viv doesn't give me a minute to switch gears before she's on to the next thing. "You read that diary in its entirety."

"Are you asking or confirming?"

"Confirming."

"Yes, I did. Why?"

"What parts stuck with you the most?"

Oh, now I see what she's getting at.

"Honestly, lovely, the entire thing was fucking disturbing. Every part of her story crawled inside me. Hooks buried too deep to ever relinquish their hold on me. Why?"

"I don't know." Viv turns her beautiful face up to look at me, and I can't stop myself from placing a slow kiss on her mouth. No tongue or teeth. No heat or suggestion. Just a pressing together of her lips and mine. Just enough contact to ground both of us in this moment.

"Tell me, lovely."

———

342

"It-it just seems so *unfortunate*. Her life... and how she never found whatever it was she sought."

"She found some of what she was looking for; although admittedly, much later in life. At least she believed she did."

"With you." It's not a question but I still feel compelled to answer her.

"It's not as black and white as her finding what she was looking for with me. Not really... it's more like she found a reason to hold on." I lock eyes with Viv while I attempt to gather my thoughts. "It almost felt like the only thing she wanted was someone who would put her needs before their own selfish ones."

"If she was looking for that in you—a sixteen year old boy—I'm sure she was sorely disappointed. I mean, teenaged boys are notoriously selfish when it comes to sex and relationships."

I couldn't disagree with her because I was a selfish asshole in the beginning of my abuse. I remember feeling like I'd hit pay dirt when Auntie called me onto her wide, wrap-around porch that hot day in June. I didn't have fuck-all to do until football practice started. I couldn't stand to be in the house with Earl and the woman formerly known as my mother.

I didn't have a job or a bunch of guys whose houses I could crash at. It was either wander the neighborhood looking for shit to get in to or pray that Auntie would take a liking to me and make me a man.

"So, tell me about the shades of grey you and Della found yourselves playing in that summer." Vivian's low, soft voice pulls me from my musing, but her question sinks me into another memory from that amazingly horrific summer.

I had been outside in Aunties backyard, butt-ass-naked, pulling weeds and whatever else didn't belong in her garden. I was hot as hell and thirsty to the point of dehydration, but I didn't have permission to do anything other than work and work some more.

I can see her standing on her back porch, looking like a damn wet dream come to life. She'd been telling me all about the damn freedom riders and Black people getting sprayed with high-powered water hoses. She had asked me something like what would I do if she gave me permission to fight back. By that time, she'd been spraying my naked ass with ice-cold water from her backyard hose, all I wanted to do was take the hose away from her. Use it to assert my own power. My right to tell her to stop doing what she had been doing to me.

I snap my gaze to my wife's rapt expression and attempt to pull her into the shades of grey Auntie and I got lost in that summer.

"We had just come inside from when she turned the water hose on me and dared me to take it away from her. It was hotter than the devil's ball-sack that day. We'd both been sweating profusely, so I brought her in and ran a warm bubble bath to take care of her. It was the strangest thing, Viv. Seeing her behave in a way I'd never witnessed before. Della was a strong, powerful force to be reckoned with, and to see her behave so... docile."

"What do you mean?"

"I was putting her into the bathtub, and she wouldn't look at me or talk to me. Mind you, I'm sixteen years old and scared shitless, but I couldn't let *her* know that."

"Why not, wasn't she your Domme?

" That's where we fell into our first shade of grey. After subduing her with the water hose, she immediately fell into a submissive head space. She needed me to be something more for her.

"I remember telling her as she sat like a child in her bathtub, *Auntie, you can look at me.* My voice was strong and sure. I watched with fascination as Auntie's head swept up and she stared at me. I may have whispered, *What's going on Auntie? Why are you behaving like this?*

"Although I had been enjoying the sudden change of power dynamic, it also made me nervous. I'd known that I would never be able to be what she had been to me. I can still see the blank way she stared into my eyes. Like she was waiting for something. Then it hit me in the face like a wet rag...she needed me to give her permission."

"Permission? To do what, John?"

"To speak to me."

"Did you think she'd lost her mind?"

"No, not really—maybe a little. I was sitting on the side of the tub just cupping water in my hand and pouring it over her shoulder. The only thing I was thinking was, *what was going on in her fucking head?*" I chance a look down at Viv, but her face is pensive and facing forward. I don't know if I should continue, but she's the one who brought it up.

"So, you were scared... at least a little bit?"

"Understatement of the goddamn year." She lets a huff of laughter slip through her glossed lips as she shakes her head. I think she might be trying to dislodge all the fucked-up shit she's learning about Della., or about me.

"Well, how do you know she believed she'd found what she was looking for? I didn't get a sense of that from reading her diary. The last entry was when she left Vera behind with her father." Viv could be talking about the weather for all the emotion missing from her smooth voice.

My hand tightens on her right hip at the mention of the tragedy that befell that little five-year-old girl when Auntie walked away from her. I breathe deeply and relax my grip on Viv's supple flesh.

"That entry tore a fucking hole into my heart." Shit, I sound like I smoke three packs a day. After clearing my throat, I add, "It quickly filled with fire, rage, and malice. The only problem, I didn't know who deserved it. Della. That spineless, gutless motherfucker, Bruno. Or... *myself.*"

"Della and her baby's father, definitely." Viv's voice leaves no room for challenge of any kind. She goes on to explain, "You had nothing to do with the choices either of those grown-ups made. You were trying to survive your own sinking ship. Della took advantage of you and that's it."

"That's the thing, though, lovely. Intellectually, I know what we had—" I stop our forward momentum to look down River Street at the happy, drunk people moving as one nescient, writhing organism with no care for where they end up.

I turn us so we're facing one another and continue, "... I know it wasn't. Healthy. It probably fucked me up more than I already was, but still—" I look to the right and observe the crowd once more. Needing a moment to take an intimate assessment of my feelings before laying them at the feet of my god to be judged.

This conversation is more difficult because I know she's comparing our experiences—because in her mind they're congruent—as if we were both delt identical shitty hands in different card games.

I reconnect our gazes and admit, "Still, I believe it was one of the most beneficial relationships I've ever had." I gently pull her to restart our walk. "Come, lovely." I want to be done with this conversation

Come on, baby. Let's become one of the happy, drunk crowd with no cares.

~51~

"Help me understand, John." Her voice is full of curiosity.

Okay, so we're not going to be a part of the happy, drunk crowd. Good to know.

"Like I said, we were sitting in her bathroom. She was in the tub, and I was on the edge beside her. I guess something finally clicked inside my head,"

"Oh—you realized she was waiting for permission? Was that when you knew she was behaving like a sub?"

"Yes and no. It wasn't until she started talking that I fully understood what she was offering me, you know? She... Della. She looked so young sitting in the tub filled with bubbles and water. Looking up into my face like I was the one she had been waiting for her whole life. In fact, she said as much."

We continue walking down River Street, behind the serpentine caravan of green and silver partiers too inebriated to care whose hand or tit they're grabbing.

Maybe there's hope for us—the ancestors of slaves and slave holders—modern Southerners.

Viv seems lost in her thoughts, and I don't fight the tug on the strings connecting my present to my past. I'm pulled into the memory of Auntie sitting in that bubble bath, with her heavy hair floating around her beautiful face. The longer strands were clinging to the soft skin of her rounded shoulders. Even her hair knew to worship her because she was a goddamned goddess. Or maybe Auntie was a demon—a deceptively beautiful and disarming one—and more destructive.

I can still hear the words she was whispering as she looked at me like I'd just saved her soul.

"J-Jonathan. I have searched all my life for you. One so young and beautiful and passionate and strong. Strong enough to command my submission."

Her words echoed my own thoughts. I always wondered how she was able to do that. And if I stayed in this role, would I develop that uncanny ability, too.

Pay attention, Ellis. Now is not the time to fuck around.

"Do you know how difficult it is to always be in control of everything and everyone around you?" She asked, but didn't give me a chance to respond before continuing, "Do you have any idea how badly I have wanted to submit to a man? This is usually the part in my summer relationships where I tell the young boys goodbye."

She paused and locked her violet gaze on mine, inviting me to see inside her soul. To see her pain. Her fear and, was that *loneliness*?

"Jonathan, if I ever have to say goodbye to you, I do believe I will die...on the spot. I will die without you."

Once she was done talking, she lowered her eyes and turned her head towards the front and waited for whatever I had to give her. I wanted to run screaming and yelling from the house and never return. I had never felt so needed, so desired.

And it. Scared. Me. Shitless.

Auntie had shared herself with me in a way that she claimed to have never shared herself with anyone else. The responsibility that came with being with her in this new way made me question myself. I didn't really believe I could do what she wanted me to. If I could really be who *she* thought I *was*.

What the fuck do I know about controlling her...hell I can barely control myself. I needed her...but, now she seemed to need me even more.

Droplets of green water splash against my arms and serves to ground me in the present moment.

Vivian is so quiet, even surrounded by all this noise, there's a sense of stillness wrapped around us. Somehow we've become impenetrable. I don't offer to recount what was said during that bubble bath, rather I choose to convey something Auntie shared with me afterward.

I squeeze her hand to get her attention, she returns the gesture but doesn't look away from the giant pineapple fountain spewing gallons of green water into the sky. I'm relieved I don't have to look at her when I reveal, "Della told me—sometime later—that in her first relationship she was forced to submit, and it was such a relief for her. Not having a choice in how it happened. She said that she couldn't tell him no, and there was nothing anyone could do to change her circumstance."

I pull Viv away from the crowd because I need her to hear this next part of what Auntie revealed. I cup her left cheek in the palm of my hand and place a soft kiss on her forehead. When I pull back to look at her, a bemused expression greets me, but she doesn't say a word.

I pressed my lips together and preface what I'm about to say. "I need your full attention, all right?" She nods her head and I proceed, "Della talked about her first relationship like it caused the sun to rise and set. She admitted that she'd walked away from everything—her lover and the father of her child, and even her only daughter—to search for him. To *beg* him to love her again; however, she said it was too late."

"She... she left, Vera wi—"

I watch Vivian try and fail to understand what she just heard. There is nothing I can do to make this easy for her. It's why I didn't want to have this conversation in the first place. At least not in this setting.

I squeeze her hand and pull her into walking. The crowd has moved on and we were being left behind. Vivian moves on autopilot. One foot in front of the other.

I interrupt her internal processing and ask, "Would you like to continue this conversation later. Perhaps, once we're back on Sapelo?"

She turns determined eyes on me, and I already know her answer so, I give a slight nod and continue to spill Auntie's blood and guts all over Forsyth Park.

"You ask me about the shades of grey, Della and I played in... she was more broken pieces than anything else, lovely. She told me that she'd given up hope that someone could do what he did."

"She was talking about her adoptive brother, Ethan."

"Yes. I didn't know it at the time, but yes. He groomed her from the age of thirteen and made her exactly what he wanted her to be."

"Do you think maybe if Della had ever been allowed to grow up in a safe home, she would have been more careful with Vera?"

"It's hard to say. Della's entire life was a lie. Even when she thought she'd made her own way, she learned that her biological father had already planned to take her when she turned twelve."

"Yeah, but maybe if she'd had a chance to be a child. It's like she never experienced childhood so, she recreated one with you."

"It sounds like you're not in the same I-hate-that-woman-camp you were in before."

"That's because I don't hate her, anymore."

"You still think what she did with me—"

"Hell, yes. It doesn't make her predatory ways any less harmful because she was prey first. She took advantage of a vulnerable boy. Just because you have a dick and had some bass in your voice, doesn't mean she didn't sexually abuse you. Nothing you ever say or do will convince me otherwise. Della Richman was a pedophile, and you were her last victim."

~52~

Vivian

John and Collin have formed some kind of bro-mance and I'm not sure any of us are used to seeing them laughing together. I can't say I don't like it because it makes things that much easier with Valery's relationship. So far, things have been going well, yet I still feel like there's another shoe waiting to drop and shatter the tentative peace we've established.

Milla slaps her feet against the hardwood floors like she's testing its strength. I don't have a chance to tell her I'm outside before she starts rattling off her list of demands.

"Vivian, I. To talk Ve. Her poe. Lk it. See my head. Me please?"

On the best of days, Camilla's English is difficult to understand. Everybody speaks Spanish and say it's fine if she wants to use her native language, but she insists on speaking English.

"Camilla, I honestly only caught about four—maybe five at the most of the words from your run-on sentence." She stumbles out onto the patio wearing a pair of cut-offs with more holes and threads than actual denim, and an oversized long-sleeve Henley with paint splatters covering most of its surface area. In other words, she is a hot-ass-mess.

Milla want to talk with me about some of my poems, yeah?

"What?"

You didn't hear her just now? She say she wants to talk about some of the poems I let her read. You must be off somewhere inside your own head, yeah?

"Uh, how in the world did you make sense of that garbled—"

"There you are—"

Milla's easy to understand, you just have to...

351

"Wait." I shake my head to get Vera to shut the hell up and inform them, "Both of you are talking at the same time. Please, just give me a moment to figure out what the hell's going on." I pinched the bridge of my nose and take a few deep breaths to stave off the impending headache. After a couple of long seconds, I look over at Milla, who for lack of a better description, looks like a jacked-up chihuahua waiting for its next hit.

"Milla, what were you yelling about?"

As expected, they both start talking in tandem, Vera's honey-suckle voice inside my head, and Milla's scratchy musical voice beside my ear.

I already told you she need to talk to me about my poetry—

"Vera and I were up late one night talking and... you know, just—"

Wait a damn minute. What did Milla just say?

"Just, what?" I cut both of them off and somewhere near my right boob, I feel the warmth of embarrassment like someone's cheeks are blushing. "Milla, what were you and Vera just doing.... *late one night*?

Vera doesn't give Milla a chance to answer before jumping in with her own vague response.

It's fine, Vivian. We were just spending some time together, yeah?

"Spending time together doing what, exactly?" I ask because I have a sneaky suspicion that a hell of a lot more than reading poetry happened between them.

This time, it's Milla who jumps in to answer my question. I feel Vera's agitation as if it's my own. What is this?

"We up late talking about art and then Vera read me some poetry. And we fuck... wait. No, not we—as in us—no, we—"

Wait, what she say? We did not do that, yeah? We just read—

"Vera, I don't think she meant to say that. Did you, Milla, mean to say that you and Vera—"

"Oh, Dios mio. No. I—we did not. I would never do that to. With Vera... I mean not unless she wanted me to do. It. Does she want me to do the things with her?"

Vera has gone completely silent. I look at Milla like she's some new exhibit in the UK's *Royal Human Zoo* that would've been on display in Wimbledon Park.

"Okay," I start because I don't know how we've gotten so far off track, and I don't know how to get us back on. After a deep breath I clarify, "... so you're reading her poems and..."

Camilla looks so damned relieved to have an out, she quickly asks, "Have you read any?"

"Vera hasn't shared any of her poetry with me, yet."

I write erotic poetry about women loving other women. You don't want to read about that, yeah?

"You're missing out my friend. Anyway, she give me one of her notebook to read. I read everything more than once and now..."

Now... now, what? What is she saying, Vivian?

I want to tell Vera to shut the hell up and listen, but Camilla's throaty voice pulls both of our attention back to her.

"I have whole sketch book full with art pieces inspire by her words. Image after image after image after image after... well you get what I saying. That make my fingers itch... to make them to real life. I need her, Vivian."

Vera feels like a hot-air-balloon with no sandbags to weigh her down. I can't stop smiling, and it's not my feelings that make my lips turn up into this goofy grin; it's hers.

I turn my gaze on Milla and question, "Vera's erotic, lesbian poetry has inspired you to create your installation?"

Why do you have to say it like that? Like my poems can't be inspirational to an artist.

"No that's not it at all, Vera. It's just that I haven't read any and I'm curious about how the two work together."

"Are you talking to Vera?"

"Yes."

"Can she please come out; I need speaking with her... alone."

"Milla, I was in the middle of something."

I want to come out and talk with Milla, yeah?

"Fine. Let me call John and let him know what's going on in case he comes looking for me."

I'm going up to my room to change. Tell Milla I'll be right back, yeah?"

"Milla, Vera's going up to her room to change. She said she'll be right back down so, wait for her here."

"Thank you. Vivian, you need to read her shit. Valery would paint sexy as fuck pieces. Collin, too. Oooooh, them painting together."

"Yes, I think I will ask to read some of her poems." I pause before turning to face her. I pin her where she stands and reiterate, "Milla, don't take advantage of her..."

"Shit you don't know Vera well do you? She's sharp and knows what she will and won't do and I'd never take advantage of her. Not ever."

"I'm holding you to it. John will probably be around to check on you guys—he's protective of Vera."

"That's fine."

When she isn't nervous, her English is really good. But she's always so hyper and keyed up; most times she sounds uneducated at best... developmentally delayed, at worse.

"See you later, Milla." I walk into the kitchen with my head full of questions. I'm not sure when they've had a chance to spend so much time together, but Vera has always been sneaky with her time in the driver's seat. I wonder what else they've been getting up to.

Well, at least Camilla finally found inspiration for her art installation. Hopefully she'll get started on it sooner rather than later. I plop down on the scratchy sofa in the family room and take out my phone to call John. I can't wait to get a real phone again; I hate this burner.

"Hey, lovely." John's smooth voice is even sexy over the phone.

"Hey, you! I'm giving the driver's seat over to Vera for a little while. She and Camilla have been collaborating, and they need some time to hash some logistics out."

"Hmm. All right. Is Collin still down in his flat?"

"I think so, I haven't seen him at all this morning. Honestly, I haven't seen you since you left our bed."

"I know. I'm in Savannah. I can't talk right now. Just know..."

"Know... *what*?" The hairs on the back of my neck stand in horripilation.

"When I come home tonight, we're good."

"Are you serious, John?"

"As serious as a heart attack, lovely. Take some time inside the Internal House because when I get home, we're going to a room you haven't seen, yet."

"Really? Has anyone seen or used this room before?"

"No. I had this room custom finished to my specifications. It used to be a game room."

"And now..."

"And now, it's our own private *Playroom*."

"Hurry home."

"I'll be there as soon as I can. I'll call Collin to come up into the main house and keep an eye on Camilla's freaky ass. I still don't trust her, especially with Vera."

"I know, but Vera insist she can handle herself, *yeah*?" We both snigger at my horrible imitation before saying our goodbyes and hanging up. "Vera?"

Hmm?

"We're standing in front of your door. Get in the driver's seat, I'm going inside. John is calling Collin to come up and stay in the house while he's away."

I don't need a baby sitter, Viv. You and John act like there's something wrong with me in the head, yeah. It ain't. I'm as sane as the rest of you... probably more so.

"Take it up with your *big brother*. He's the one insisting on calling Collin."

He such a good man, John is, yeah?

"Whatever you say. I'm leaving you to it. And Vera?"

Yes.

"Don't feel pressured to do anything you don't want to do. Milla has a lot more experience than you when it comes to relationships so... be careful."

You worried she might try to take advantage of me, yeah? Well, you might need to worry about me taking advantage of her.

"I don't even know how to respond to that."

Then don't. See you later, enjoy your time inside. You can get one of my notebooks from the desk in my room. Some of my poetry is there if you and Valery want to read it, yeah?

"Thanks." I watch Vera pull out a pair a slim red slacks and a long-sleeved, silk blouse in the palest shade of gold. She's going to blow Milla's thick wool socks off.

~53~

Vera stayed in the driver's seat longer than I've ever known her to. When she indicated she was ready to come back inside, Valery gave me a knowing glance that said she suspected the same thing I did; neither of us are quite sure how we feel about it.

Now I'm sitting in the extra-large soaking tub, trying to get my head in the right space to play once John returns from Savannah. I keep thinking about the look in Vera's eyes when she came gliding back inside. I know for a fact I've never seen her look like that before. Valery kept hitting me on the back of my thigh, like I wasn't looking at the same damn thing she was. I'm giggling like a school-girl as Valery's brown-liquor voice coats my memory in its ignorant oil.

"What the fuck got that bitch lookin like she been smokin on some kinda mothafuckin hippie-lettuce?"

"Val, be quiet. She might hear you. And besides, we'd know if she were high. We would, *right*?"

"How the fuck would I know, bitch. If she ain't high on the puff-puff-pass, her ass is fucked up on Camilla's puff-puff-puffy-pussy."

"Jesus H. Christ and his seven dwarfs, Valery. Must you be so vulgar?"

"Vulgar? I got your mothafuckin vulgar, bitch. It's called Vera eatin out some spicy Chilean kitty-cat and suckin some even spicier Chilean asshole."

The sound of the door opening brings me back to the present, while the elemental awareness of my husband brings desire crashing through my veins.

"Lovely." I release a breath, and it feels like the first one I've taken sense *The Order* ordeal started. I hadn't realized how on edge

I've been before this moment. John must have taken his shoes and socks off before coming into the bathroom, because his footfalls are as silent as butterfly kisses.

"Hi."

"You mind if I join you, lovely-mine?" He doesn't wait for my answer; he's already stripping his fine wool slacks and organic cotton boxer briefs from his long, muscular legs. Absently, I wonder where his belt is. I continue to watch him undress, in that languid way he does, when the only thing on his mind is how many ways he can fuck us into higher versions of ourselves.

I want him to fold me in half and love me nice and slow. Long and deep... for the rest of the night.

"Keep looking at me like that, lovely..." He tosses his silken grey dress shirt to the floor like he didn't pay hundreds of dollars to have it tailored to fit his stunning physique. "... and see what happens to you."

Darkness swirls in the depths of his eyes. Deep enough to drown me a thousand times over; but is it considered drowning when you feel recreated every time you're allowed to resurface?

"I haven't seen you all day."

"I know, I missed you. But—"

"But... I have a right to adore you as I choose." He gifts me with a small lift at the corner of his sensuous mouth. His molten gaze devours me as it slips beneath the jasmine scented water to stroke fiery glances over my nipples, leaving me panting and impatient for whatever he has planned for us tonight in this secret room.

"You're not wrong, lovely, not at all;" He steps closer to the tub before he says, "However, it would behoove you to refrain from poking the tiger right now."

Something about the way he phrases that last part, makes me sit up and take notice of more than my lust-filled brain allowed me to before.

"What's... w-what's going on, John?"

"Let me get in the tub behind you, baby, and then we'll talk."

"Careful, the water's going to spill over the si—"

"You forget we're in a wet room, it'll just drain away. No harm done."

"Right. I keep forgetting you had work done on this house when I thought you'd left me alone for three months."

"That still hurts, doesn't it?"

"Yes."

"I apologize. After the first time I had to redeem an IOU, I promised myself I would never do anything to you that could be absolved with your selfless gift."

"Sometimes, we don't get to choose how, or when we avail of other people's selflessness. Hopefully, we can simply be grateful it was extended to us in the first place."

He doesn't acknowledge my comment, I didn't expect him to. He runs his nose down my neck and caresses my left shoulder, all while breathing in my scent like he'd forgotten what I smell like.

"Your skin feels like silk under my palms. I shouldn't even be allowed to touch something so goddamned luxurious. As fucking exquisite as you are."

"Mmm."

"Yet, you let me. Every damn time I reach for you. For these proud titties tipped with plush, tourmaline nipples. Just perfect for pulling and squeezing, and sucking... you fucking let me defile you, lovely. Why would? Why do you let me do these things to you?"

"*Baby.*"

"The first time I saw your naked thighs I almost came in my basketball shorts. You know why?" He runs his fingertips across the raised marks on my thighs and whispers, "These."

"My scars."

"I was instantly hard. Violently aroused at the sight and feel of them. The intricately raised skin in such precise patterns—I wondered who loved you enough to take the time to mark you in such a profound and permanent way?"

"No one loved me, John. Not even myself."

"I loved you and I *loved* these. They tell the epic story of your resiliency. Each puckered, braille- like intention reveals the story of your creation. I wanted to rewrite it; you know? Use a language that only *we* can understand; only we can read and decipher."

"John. Baby, what's... what's wrong?"

"And then there's the treasure nestled at the apex of your thighs. Once abused, misused, and destroyed—even by my filthy hands—and still she is the most worshiped altar in all of our kingdom.

"For the first time, I understand something that you, Della, and even my soft-headed momma have been trying to teach me my whole life. Not just me, either, but every stupid male to ever stand and walk on two feet.

A Black Southern woman knows she will always have to fight to own any part of herself. But especially the crown of her head where she's tethered to all of divinity, as well as the soles of her feet, where she's connected to the natural world.

Y'all know—in that way of knowing passed down through mitochondrial DNA—that once you own all of it, there is no one or group of things in this world or the next, as fucking powerful as you. Guess who else knows it, lovely? Men. You damn-well better believe we know it. And that's why we work so hard to claim you as our possessions.

"We work like slaves with no feet to mark you. Stuff our DNA inside your cunts and fill you with a part of us. We hope to keep you so damn busy with our children and so damn high on endorphins from coming on our dicks, that you don't have time to remember that you have a right to own your divinity and your physical experiences in the world."

He cups my heavy breast, and it feels like he's preaching his sermon on the mount. Like this is the start of his ascension back into heaven to sit on the right hand of god.

John speaks directly into my ear when he continues, "And if you choose to share a small piece of yourself with a man, it is a gift. An allowance because you know he has absolutely nothing to offer you that could begin to replenish the divine feminine energy you leak into the world.

"And we—the greedy, undeserving men—take whatever you're willing to give us and more than we could ever repay, because we know. We fucking know—maybe even before you—that just a tiny piece of you is enough to bring this entire world into harmonious balance. Can you imagine how that world will be, lovely-mine?"

"It is done." He doesn't respond, just continues with his oration. His ministrations. Tugging on my nipples and rubbing tight circles against my clitoris. He's driving me out of my mind.

"That's why inferior men try to assert their false claim of control. Why they lie and say that *god* is a man and that *he* placed men in charge of everything and everyone that isn't male. But you know what?"

"God, John. If you keep touching me like this, I'm going t-to... Mmmmm. I'm going to—"

"You're stronger than that, Viv. Don't give it up so easily to me. Where was I... oh, yeah. You know what, Southern Black men know—have always fucking known—about you, Southern Black women?"

"I know... yes, like that. Just. Like. Fucking. That."

"We have always known who you were; we may have lost knowledge of it when we were ripped from the breasts of our homelands, then forced to drink the devil's milk of damnation and forgetfulness. But we've always known that Southern Black women are sacred portals between this world and the eternal one."

"Oh, I can't stop it. I'm c-coming."

"Yes. Yes you are, lovely. Thank you for giving me pieces of your eternal favor. You're so damn beautiful, squeezing my fingers like you don't want me to pull them from the warmth of your honeyed walls. That's it, use me. When we're done in here..." He doesn't finish his thought, or if he does, I certainly don't hear it.

I'm drifting on memories of myself as a primordial flower. Fragrant and tantalizing, my supplication flows from the base of me, attracting the probing mouths of harried honey bees.

The perfect symbiotic exchange between two imperfect, but willing partners. Each giving no more than they take, ensuring everyone is fully sated once the bee takes flight and moves on to the next willing flower. I shiver with the simple beauty of knowing this gift that John gives me is the same gift flowers and bees have given to each other since the beginning of time.

"Thank you for... that."

"Where'd you go, lovely?"

"I'll tell you about it some other time. Can we get out of this bath?" He looks perplexed but doesn't push me to tell him.

"You're anxious. Come," He stands from the water like a forgotten lover of Yemaya, virile and potent for having lain with the goddess. "I've kept my first promise to you, and now it's time for me to fulfill the other one as well.

***

"Tell me. Before we play, or I won't be able to get in the right headspace to give in to your dominance." We lock eyes and he bears witness to the severity of my need.

"I've been with pretty much every alphabet this corrupt government has sanctioned to police and entrap its citizens, and any other country's citizens, too. All day—back and forth between little boxy windowless rooms with microphones and cameras and pasty ass white men wearing ill-fitting suits and more bags under their tired eyes than you bring home after a day of shopping with friends."

"Damn," I chuckle over a smile. "That's a mouthful, and you hardly stopped to take a breath." I throw him another affectionate smile to assure him I'm teasing, and just as happy things are finally over.

"Again, you stay with the damn jokes, don't you, lovely?"

I nod my head because his answering smile plants a garden of sunflowers in my heart.

"Yeah, well... basically—there's a lot of shit I will never be able to tell you or even Jesus—I can tell you that The Order was so much more than just a secret society at the flagship state college of South Carolina."

"How much more?"

"You know how in the Matrix when Morpheus was training Neo in the simulation program?"

"Of course, I do. Wait, are you saying The Order are the *Agents*—like they're everyone and no one."

"You're the biggest, goddamn nerd I know. And you have the nerve to be sexy as hell when you nerd it up. But, yeah, to answer your question, that's exactly what I'm saying. I've been extricated from their clutches and so has Coleman Whitman."

"Cole Whitman? I thought he was d-dead. Didn't he get shot outside of our... *house*?" My brain spins into overtime. Then it dawns on me, just as John opens his secret-keeping lips to tell me it was all part of the plan.

Who the hell is this man I married, anyway?

"I promise you, lovely, I'm done. No more covert bullshit. No more running around playing GI John.

"Okay so, when can we go back home?"

Silence is a pair of strong arms thrown around an out-of-control-child, meant to calm and reassure them, but only ends up restricting the little air they're able to bring into their deflated lungs. I know what this kind of silence means. I've stood within its misleading embrace, hoping against all manner of truth that for once, it will comfort me.

He watches as a shiver of awareness works its way through my body. One. Two. Three deep breath cycles before he opens his beautiful mouth to let deceiving words drip from his golden tongue.

"I love you."

"I know."

"I want you to keep an open mind about this."

"We're not going back to Columbia."

"It's not in our best interest."

"My gallery. The artists 'studio. My life... our life."

"Whoever and whatever we were—"

"*Were.*"

"Yes, were. We can never be those people again. None of us."

"If we aren't those people, then who are we?"

"We are who we were always meant to be. I'm not explaining this right. Listen, on paper we're still John and Vivian Ellis. Our names are still the same as before, it's just our pasts have been redacted and replaced with something new. Different birthdates, socials, upbringings, colleges... everything about who we were, no longer exists. Only our names."

I stumble backward and my right arm recoils from the dueling force of my need to both get away from John, and climb inside of him to prove he's still the man I love.

He reaches for me and cautions, "Vivian, dammit—stop before you hurt yourself. Calm dow—"

I'm safe. I'm with my husband. My name is...

I try to repeat my mantra and fail miserably. "M-my name i-is..."
The words of my mantra are sharp teeth eating through the taunt
string tethering me to my sense of self. I want his silence, but if I
can't have it... I'll take his lies. But he continues to masticate my soul
with the consecrated bite of truth.

~54~

The room blinks out and comes back in like a bad connection on my cellphone. Or when the radio picks up two different stations at the same time, and I can only hear a part of each song coming through the faulty speakers. One minute, I'm standing in our bedroom in the Sapelo mansion, and the next I'm a crumpled mess of blood, cum, and snot on the heated wooden floors of our old Playroom.

John is standing over me, trying his best to remain calm after realizing he's just raped and sodomized me for his own selfish, egotistical needs.

"Fucking hell. Vivian! On your hands and knees, now!" He yanks my hips towards him and places his left forearm in the middle of my back, forcing my torso onto the floor. I push my ass higher in the air; I'm wet and swollen for him. I almost come again.

He growls in my ear, "Vivian, this will not be an easy ride for you."

My sex sucks him in and clamps down so hard, I see stars as my breath whooshes from my lungs.

"J-John...I. Can't. Do."

He doesn't stop or check in with me. He just continues to fuck me like he wants to ensure that I will never want another man to dominate me. Then his thrusts become punishing and that's when I realize I'd made him question himself.

I try to get up and away from him, but John won't allow it. He lays most of his 220 pounds onto my back and wraps his right arm around my waist for leverage. His knees force mine even wider. Giving him more room to get deeper inside of me.

He prays to a god he doesn't believe in as he pounds into me like we could become one filthy legion of depravity.

His prayers continue, *God, I need to stop. Help me gain control, I don't want to hurt her. I want her ass…What if she lets some other man claim her ass. It's mine…I have a right to it. She won't dislike it…I won't give her an option.*

I hear a loud, sucking pop before he slams it into my back entrance. I'm breaking apart. Shattering into shards of jagged little pieces of unidentifiable parts. John's voice feels like sandpaper against the gaping wound in my soul.

He thinks I want this.

He believes I'm enjoying this assault.

"Baby. You feel like fucking heaven."

I'm descending into the bowels of hell.

"I knew you'd love this."

You're giving me every reason to hate you, John.

"Yes, Vivian. Your ass is so very fuckable."

Fuck this mothafuckin asshole. Go lay your weak ass down, I got somethin for his monkey-ass.

"Every hole in your body is mine. My cum filling you up. In every hole."

I got somethin to fill up every goddamn hole your fuckin ass got, too, mothafucka. It's called hot lead pumped into you from the barrel of a shotgun. Pussy-ass-coward-dickless-fucka.

"Feel what *you* do to me, how much you make me want you."

Don't hurt him. He doesn't know what he's doing. Please, I love him. He doesn't understand what's happening to me.

From a far off place, I hear John's frantic voice calling my name. I feel him rubbing my back, while he peppers kisses all over my face.

Baby, please come back to me. You're safe. You're with me. I love you. No one will take your name from you, baby. Please.

My eyes flutter open. I feel like I should be somewhere different, but no—I'm still on the floor with John's growling words ricocheting off the walls like filthy bullets, while he continues to fuck my ass off.

It was too much for me to endure, but I couldn't leave John alone with *her*. She hated him. He didn't have a clue of the danger he was facing, but I knew.

"I own your ass. You love it, don't you? You want me to pound this sweet little puckered hole until it's stretched and wide open."

John, she's going to kill you as soon as you're done. Please, stop. Come to your senses. You're breaking me and I can't keep you safe from her. Please, John. Stop what you're doing.

"Holy shit, Viv. I—I I'm coming. Yes! Sweet-baby-Jesus, your ass is fucking perfect."

He don't deserve no kinda warnin from your silly ass. He gonna get what the fuck he deserve. Soon as he get the fuck off me, I'm gonna cut this mothafucka to the white meat. Watch his black ass bleed like a goddamn pig.

I know the moment he realizes something isn't right. I feel fluids flow from my body that cause my face to heat with shame. I look up in time to see the horror etched on his beautiful face.

It's okay, John. This is nothing that hasn't happened to me before. Don't be put off by the blood and...

"Vivian. I'll give you aftercare and we'll go to our bedroom and talk about..."

I lay there and let him bear witness to the desecration of my body. When it becomes too painful, I follow a little girl into a house I don't visit often. I know I'll find safety and comfort inside.

That's right, bitch. Take your funky ass on in the house. The fuck make you think you was strong or brave enough to handle this goddamn demon from hell. But I am. I'm the mothafuckin demon slaya comin to open up a can of whip-his-ass-back-to-hell on Mr. Big-dick-John.

I peek out of the open door, catching snippets of his rushing words to see if they feel true in my heart. They don't. The other half of my soul is now the mirror image of the depravity that created me.

***

My bottles tumble from the shelf where they've been neatly resting for the last seven years. One by one they fall and shatter, spilling the Others from the safety of their hiding place.

"I'm sorry. I tried to protect y'all. I didn't know he was a monster." I cry out as one by one they come to stand around me. Two of them I don't recognize, but one looks exactly the same.

"Who... where are Vera and Valery?"

They don't answer, but the pretty, plump woman extends a hand to me. Her soulful green eyes with their blue skies, tell me I'm safe. The little girl wraps her arms around my waist and places a kiss on my shoulder.

The dark-whiskey-eyed woman with the desperate scowl on her otherworldly face, turns to me and a sinister smile spreads across her mouth.

"So, that mothafucka finally show you just who the fuck he is. I been waitin for his chocolate, covered, hillbilly, ass-fuckin self to fuck shit up so I could get out and fuck his monkey ass up.

"You were already out there. Please, don't harm him. He doesn't know about any of this. Let me talk with him..."

"Go sit down somewhere, slut-whore. You too stupid to be out in the goddamn world where grown ass men like to fuck and destroy soft-headed little fools like y'all. Me? Imma a bad bitch. Ain't no mothafucka ever gonna get shit on me. Now, y'all take her uppity ass inside and let a woman handle this thimble-dicked-bastard."

***

I'm in a bed. A weighted blanket covers my body from neck to feet. The lights are dim. The smell of lavender and bergamot perfume the air. I'm alone. My head is quiet, like the room. My face is relaxed. Shoulders are flat against the mattress. My breathing is normal and calm; my heartbeat... slow. My belly is calm and easy. My sex and butt are relaxed, unaroused. My right thigh is straight and the left one is bent so my foot is touching my right knee. I breathe in for three counts, hold it for six counts, and blow it out for a count of nine. Finally, I open my eyes.

"Lovely."

"I'm all right, John."

"Don't."

"Don't, what?"

"Don't absolve me. I fucked up."

"Yes."

"I apologize for springing this on you like I did."

"There was another way this could've happened?"

"Ye-I knew it was a possibility that we'd be required to change... to give up our old lives."

"You didn't mention it."

"No. If I had, then——"

"It would have gone that *other* way."

"Yes. You and the others would have at least had time to consider the possibilities."

"Well, that's not the way it went so, we need to get everyone together."

"No, Viv. Not yet. I-I need to." John steps away from the shadows but he doesn't come close to the bed. He hesitantly implores me. "I. Please, lovely. I need to hold you."

"That bad, huh?"

"Flashback with dissociation. Acting out."

———

370

"Hmm."

"Do you remember anything?"

"Mmhmm."

"I had to pick you up from the floor. You were on your hands and knees. Screaming, crying, thrashing around."

"Yea."

"I'm so goddamn sorry, baby. I-you still haven't forgiven me?"

"I have. It's not me who needs to forgive you, John. *You* need to forgive yourself."

"Forgive myself? For treating you like a fucking animal. How does that even work?"

"I had to forgive myself for loving a man who could treat me like a *fucking animal*. Forgive myself for getting pregnant with two of that man's babies. Forgive myself for submitting to that same man and willingly letting him take my ass after he treated me like a fucking animal.

"I had to forgive myself for going down a road I knew would break me. Forgive myself for being too scared to walk away from you when my soul screamed and begged me to. Forgive myself for thinking I knew better than them who created me.

"John, I'm still learning how to forgive myself for choosing your joy over mine. For choosing your peace over mine. For choosing your pride over mine. For choosing you over me."

I search his soul, which he doesn't hide from my prying eyes, and see the smudges of self-loathing and the viscous slags of recrimination lurking behind his foolish pride.

I offer him a small smile and remind him, "Forgiveness is an act of compassion, John. It's an act of kindness and it's also exactly what you, me... huh, the whole damn world deserves to give ourselves."

His voice is cracked plaster, crumbling and breaking into chunks.

"I can hardly look in the mirror sometimes without feeling sick to my stomach."

"Guilt and shame can be quite gassy, so I've heard."

"Are you trying to make me smile, lovely."

"No, I'm serious." I say even as my lips turn up into a slight smile of their own volition. I clear my throat before continuing, "We internalize feelings of guilt and shame... it's the shame that causes digestive and central nervous system dis-ease."

"You're deflecting, Viv. Talk to me."

"No. I don't need to talk to you. I had a flashback. I dissociated. And now, I'm sitting in our bed. There's nothing to talk about unless you want to tell me about our new histories."

He stares into me for a long moment before crossing to the small writing desk situated in the corner of the room. The placement is thoughtful; a perfect place to sit and journal in front of the large picture window. While he's doing whatever it is he's doing, I climb down from the bed and smile when I see I'm wearing one of his long-sleeved t-shirts and a pair of my fuzzy socks.

That's when I notice John's dressed in gray joggers and a black Henley. His feet are bare.

I don't know what it is about bare feet, but I utterly adore when his are.

He swaggers over to me carrying a large envelop with all sorts of papers escaping from the top.

"Who did you secure new backgrounds for?"

"You, the girls, Collin, and Camilla."

"You're shitting me, right? Collin and Camilla aren't even American citizens; they're both over here on work visas, John."

He tosses the envelop onto the bed and deadpans, "They're still not American citizens." The heavy package sounds like two or three telephone books hitting the bed.

I peek over my left shoulder to see what falls out, when John mumbles, "They just have permanent work visas and diplomatic immunity."

I stop my back-and-forth stutter steps and screech, "Diplomatic immunity—why would they—"

"*We*." He cuts me off and steps closer to me. He moves like he's facing a coiled snake ready to strike at a moment's notice. When he's only a couple of feet in front of me, he asks, "Why would we need diplomatic immunity? Because *we've* all benefited from my association with The Order."

"Oh." I sink down into easy pose because my wobbly legs won't continue to hold me up much longer.

"Ready to hear about your life?" John has the good graces to share his shy smile with me.

Poor bastard, I wouldn't want to be the one burdened with telling everyone, who they were, doesn't exist anymore.

"Do I have a choice?"

"No." He starts but then says, "Yes, maybe. You'll always have a choice, lovely." He knows how much I needed to hear that, even if it's not possible in this situation.

"If my only other option involves us going our separate ways, then I don't really have a choice."

"All right, here's yo—"

"Wait." I throw my hands out in front of me like I'm trying to stop a speeding bus from turning me into a grease spot on the highway.

Once he starts reading this new past, he'll effectively invalidate every horrible traumatic experience we've faced and overcome.

My thoughts are on a collision course with a thick wall of rejection until John's soft touch under my chin, calls my attention back to him. He's sitting in front of me in easy pose, two fingers tilt my face up to meet his calming gaze.

"Lovely," I'd follow that voice into hell without blinking an eye. "Think about it as a reset button."

The words feel like sawdust in my mouth. "A reset button." I lick my dry lips and wrap my mind around the words. With an unenthusiastic nod I whisper, "... would start everything from the beginning. I don't want a reset."

He looks at me with understanding. I watch a familiar cocky gleam set fire behind his dark eyes and my favorite sexy smirk kisses his lips. With a quick lean forward, he kisses me and speaks against my mouth, "Okay. Fuck a reset button, how about we call it a, *if-I'd-had-fuckall-to-do-with-anything-this-is-the-way-shit-would-have-happened-button,* then."

I kiss him on his smiling mouth. Before long we're both laughing and rolling around on the floor like a bunch of drunk teenagers. It really is all about perspective, sometimes.

He sobers enough to ask, "You know the space that exist between one great idea and the next?"

I nod my head and answer, "Yes, of course I do. Why?"

"What do you call it?" He stares at me like my response contains the keys that open all the doors in the world.

"I don't know. It's," I chew on my bottom lip and gather my thoughts. I consider the space between one idea and the next... what is that space filled with? What can happen in the space between thoughts, breaths, heartbeats... I shake my head because what comes to me sounds completely ludicrous. Ridiculous, even, but I open my mouth and blurt out, "... possibilities. Anything can happen in the space between one thing and the next thing."

John looks like he's sucking on electricity and it's lighting his soul up to full wattage; his eyes are so bright. On the tail end of a bark of laughter, he exclaims, "Ex-fucking-actly, lovely."

Vivian

There is vulnerability in erasing the beginning of one's self. A reckoning of the soul when tissue and flesh and bone and blood of your creation are torn asunder; and done so with your willing permission, too.

John and I had shitty foundations. Our contractors were a collection of inbred, unholy indecencies who were determined to raise hell and rule with iron-clawed fists.

They poured confusion and chaos into a mixer with wrath, shame, and fear. For extra fortification, they added a touch of depravity and a sprinkle of hopelessness. Our foundations cured for seventeen years... and then we found each other.

I grapple with the strangeness of shedding my old life and pulling my new one on. It's a tight fit because it hasn't been stretched by my ego's insecurity and fears. Not, yet.

I'm not the only one trying on a new life. Valery and Vera are standing in solidarity with me. Looking into the mirrors of our souls, trying to make heads or tails of what has been offered up as their origin stories.

"I'm glad to see they didn't make either of our lives perfect." I say aloud with a smile in my voice. "There's no way our minds would've accepted a perfect upbringing. At least I don't think so."

No. I don't know if I can accept that my momma died at thirty-eight, but had been a loving parent up until then, yeah?

I guess they tried to keep shit as close to the fuckin truth as possible. Shit, Della did die when she was thirty-goddamn-eight years old. They ain't lie about that shit.

"No, but I see Vera's point." We're all quiet. Attempting to process this new reality and what it means for each of us— individually and as a collective—going forward.

"Wait," I turn my attention back to John. The girls pay attention, but they don't interrupt. "How did you get the alphabet to create complete identities for the alters, including Valeria?"

Val and Vera are nodding their heads in unison, wondering the same thing.

"I thought you'd be happy." John's voice is guarded, but he continues, "When I explained to my handlers about you and DID, they thought it best to give each identity a credible history profile so that it's easier going forward—"

"I get why you did it," I cut him off because I need to clarify myself. "But I don't get why *you* did it."

"Hmm?"

"Why would *you* want that for *them*? You've been very vocal about them not really being separate and complete identities from me. What's changed?"

Understanding casts a golden halo around the rich brown of his irises as he considers my question. "Me. My perspective. The incessant need to be in control of everything around me. I couldn't—in the beginning. I had no idea what you were experiencing as a collective.

"Even when there was a switch, it was still your face, your body, it was still you that I saw. I didn't get how they could be completely separate *people* with different needs, talents, and wants."

I realize while the collective and I have been busy embracing our darkness and learning to trust our collective light, John has been just as busy with his own shadow work.

"I'm so proud of you, baby." I extoll and hope he hears the love in every word.

He offers a reluctant smile framed in confidence, and it makes him look like that nineteen-year-old boy who stole my heart in the middle of the Horseshoe so many years ago.

For fuck's sake. Think about dead puppies or Vera and Milla fuckin—just stop with the goddamn sappy feels.

I would thank you very kindly if you didn't bring Milla and me into your hedonistic conversation, Valery. Mind your business, yeah?

I chuckle at the amount of crazy I share head space with. John looks just as amused as I feel.

"Val and Vera going at it?"

"How did you guess?"

"It wouldn't be a conversation if they weren't adding their two cents."

We share an artless smile as a soft silence falls into the crevices to make a cushion for our thoughts and emotions to land safely.

I jerk my head up so fast, I hear my neck crack. But I don't have time to think about it because I need to ask, "does this mean you're okay with Valery and Collin?"

John doesn't answer me right away. He's pensive. Taking time to ruminate over his words and how they may be received by me, and probably Valery as well. A few beats later he replies, "It means I think Collin's exactly what Valery needs and yes, I'm fine with their relationship. Absence makes the heart grow fonder and helps Jughead grow longer."

I shake my head and laugh at his stupid joke. His smile is more assessing than whimsical, and I know he has another bomb to drop on me... Not quite sure how to avoid getting hit with the shrapnel.

He hadn't said anything about the studio and gallery, yeah?

My face falls as tears sting the corners of my eyes. I already know I'm never going to step foot in my gallery or artists 'studio again. Not as the owner, anyway.

He reads my face like today's newspaper and confirms Vera's unspoken question when he says, "Tammie purchased both of your spots and my partners bought me out of our partnership."

I blink away the nostalgia and although I'm no longer willing to sacrifice or compromise myself—in any way, shape, or form—for John's happiness, I'm also not willing to live without him.

Is it really a sacrifice or compromise, Viv. Especially when you know that man will move heaven, hell and even this rock we live on to put a smile on your face, yeah?

I nod my head, accepting the wisdom Vera often imparts when my ego reacts in fear. She's right, but now I'm standing at the intersection of unlimited possibilities and a bird in the hand beats two in the bush. How do I take the first step onto this new path, when my shoes still have dirt and grime from the old one.

John's fake British accent pulls me away from my meandering thoughts. "Heavy is the head that wears the crown... My Queen, what doth burden thee?" He sounds ridiculously sexy. I'm glad he only whips it out when I need cheering up, because we'd never leave our bedroom otherwise.

We lock eyes and I am inspired to expose the manic sense of insignificance, painting my soul in muted tones of reactive rage.

He acknowledges my ambivalence but refuses to let me sink into the heavy pool of incongruity I'm currently wading through. With an arrogant lift of his brow and a filthy smirk on his lips, he answers my unspoken question in that decadent British accent, "If you're worried about not having anything to do..." His lips twitch and then he deadpans, "You can most certainly do me, lovely"

Instead of giving me another reason to crotch check him, he admits, in his normal voice, "You know me well. But, no, that's not what I was going to say—well, it wasn't the *only* thing I was going to say."

Damn-it-all-to-hell. My throat feels like John just released a week's worth of giggles in one giant ROTFLMAO ejaculation. As soon as he reads my face, a deep, sexy chuckle rumbles from his chest.

"Fine," I agree through reluctant amusement before I clear my throat and order, "so, the rest of it." I say with as much piss and vinegar as I can muster hoping to get a little of my dignity back.

He sobers and the serious man I haven't seen a while straightens and stand before me. Without preamble he announces, "We're the founding partners of Brunellis Therapeutic Artistic Center for Adult Survivors of Childhood Sexual Trauma."

Silence spans the width of our combined lifetimes before I blink out of the serenity of dissociation.

"Did y-you say," I take a deep breath and try again, "Brunellis, as in the combination of Bruno and Ellis?"

"Yes. I thought it only fitting since both our beginnings were shattered all to hell and back by childhood sexual trauma."

Emotions flow through me and quiet the cacophonous silence of stagnate momentum.

"A therapeutic center... is that what you said?" Apathy spreads from the depths of a black well of what-the-fuck, to splash my words in its viscous skepticism, "Since when do *you* push therapy?"

As expected, John rises to my unprovoked attack.

"Therapy saved our lives, Vivian. Of course, I'm a fucking *pusher* of therapy. I'd be more than happy to cook that shit up in a burned out pot on a raggedy ass stove and give it away with a pipe and a goddamned lighter, if it was the only way to get it to people who look like you and me."

His retort yanks me from the high court of indignation, after which, I chance a look in the direction of a man who deserves no less than a nomination for the Nobel Peace Prize yet; for his efforts, I feel perfectly vindicated giving him my ass to kiss. My ego is well and truly chastised. It backs away and leaves me responsible for our atonement.

"Contrition doesn't taste nearly as divine..." I stop and catch his eye before saying, "after consuming an entire hubris pie."

Three minutes. One-Mississippi. Two-Mississippi... 59-Mississippi

Just before I get to the four-minute mark, John breaks the white sheet of silence, it reeks of degradation and strange fruit.

"Imagine the number of adult victims out there." His tone, a bitter wreath made of ordered chaos, singes the outermost edges of his words. He burns more of his corrosive truth into my flesh as he elaborates, "Victims because they haven't learned to heal from the trauma of being sexually abused as children." Another laborious pause and he declares, "They deserve to be... goddamned *survivors*."

John's passion cracks *ors,* leaving them clinging to *survive.* They do, but just barely.

"John, I—I hear you, but."

"Think about how fucked up *your* life would be right now, if—"

"If y-you. If you hadn't taken me to get... help." The words are tender clumps of wet beach sand embracing vulnerable exposed flesh of an inner thigh. I gentle in the arms of this intimate awareness.

"Exactly." He exclaims, but there are no more scorched edges.

Soft brown eyes kiss a path down the length of me but not in a heated-I-want-to-split-you-wide-open way. It's more of an I-will-always-in-all-ways-forgive-you way. I'll take the latter over the former, any day of the week and twice on Sunday.

I watch as he tastes the corner of his mouth, and I wonder how he doesn't invest more time in licking his own skin.

"Remember how you thought you were the only broken one in our relationship?" He huffs a spent breath, pretending to be amused. "Well, at least in the beginning." He finishes, and now his voice, body language and mood are in alignment. *Convicted.*

I quickly match his pensive tone and query, "Are you thinking of a *specific* monster that broke you, even while she fed you a diet of mind-altering pain pills?"

Without hesitation he says, "Yes. I recognize that not all monsters are ugly or even malicious. Some had good intentions, but we both know where those lead."

My heart gathers all the wet beach sand and erects a statue in John's likeness, to commemorate this timid joy his admission ignites within me.

Epilogue

Vivian

The weather outside doesn't reflect the warm feelings percolating throughout the hearts of everyone who now calls this place home. Surprisingly, Collin and Milla were both fine with the way things worked out.

John explained that Collin's family had been notified and given explicit instructions concerning the non-familiar relationship status with their son and brother. It's a bit confusing, but nothing that can't be handled with time and attention.

Milla was an entirely different can of worms. Apparently, she was on the run from one of the most notorious drug lords in South America, for her part in exposing his involvement with an international sex-trafficking ring. Her art installations brought so much attention to her cause; his empire lost millions in revenue.

Milla turned out to be exactly who I thought she was; her art is how she brings awareness to and disturbs the patriarchal systems designed to oppress and marginalize women all over the world. She was more than happy to be given a permanent work visa and diplomatic immunity.

I take a minute to gaze out the large window overlooking the backyard, enjoying the sultry, jasmine scented air that circulates inside my office. I've been inside for the past two days, and am chomping at the bit...

I'm an evolved, Black, Southern woman who knows better than to use expressions like that—

Vera adds her two cents as if I was talking to her.

Well, energy can't be destroyed, and can't nobody make new energy, yeah?

"Vera, I appreciate your attempt to answer me, but I really was just talking to myself. I didn't mean to pull you from whatever you were doing."

I ain't doing anything important. Like I was saying, everything is made of energy. When slaves died, they energy didn't die with them, yeah? No, that energy get recycled back into the universal soul and become part of everything and everyone.

So, that expression is part of slave energy and that mean you may not know how it feels to chomp at a bit, but you know how it feel to want something to stop hurting you so bad, you willing to chew through iron to make it so.

In that way, you and a slave woman forced to wear an iron bit know what one another experience, yeah. All this politically correct nonsense is mainly to remind white people they not dealing with the same turn-the-other-cheek-we-shall-overcome-negro as before.

We know more about white folks, then they know about themselves. But they don't know even the tip of the ice burg about us, yeah?

"For clarity's purpose, what you're saying is it's perfectly acceptable for me to use that expression because it's part of a collective experience of Black people?"

Kind of, but not really. I'm saying that it doesn't really matter what you say, as much as why you say it. If you say chomping at the bit as a way of healing a wound, then say it all you want. If you say it to further cause dis ease, then shut your mouth, yeah?

"Vera, I swear to bobcat, you stay sharing pearls of wisdom and insight, don't you? I wouldn't have come up with that thought in a million years, but I appreciate the different perspective."

Well. So Vivian, can I ask you something?

"You just did."

Yeah, well can I ask you something else—and don't say you just... you know what—forget it—here's my question. Does Camilla ever say anything to you? About. Me... and her. About us?

"She talks about your poetry and how amazing your writing process is. She's shared that you all have *kissed* a few times. And she's always gushing about how exquisite and beautiful you are. Inside and out."

You're not just saying that to spare my feelings, yeah? Because I really like Milla. I know she the only woman I've known in that way... but still I don't have to know a heap of other women to know she special, yeah?

"Vera, when you say *know,* do you mean in the biblical sense of knowing or just the-hey-I-know-her kind of knowing?"

I know her, know her. In every sense of the word, Vivian. We do a lot more than kiss when we share intimate time with each other. She said I was the best lover she ever had.

"What did you say when she said that?"

I laughed and said how could I not be the best she ever had; I've been self-pleasuring my whole adult life. There ain't no part of a woman's body I don't know how to make feel good. I wanted to experience what good touching felt like, yeah? I didn't trust nobody to do it but myself. So, I invested my time and energy learning to love and tease and honor my own sexuality.

"You always act so shy and reserved when the topic of sex comes up. I thought for the longest you were a-sexual."

I might be a little a-sexual, but that doesn't mean I don't like sex or that I don't have a sexual identity. My relationship with my sexuality is deeply intimate, yeah? For the most part, I don't have a connection with the abuse because... y'all took such good care of me.

Protected me from the horrors of it all. It kind of left me on my own to learn about sex and what I wanted from it.

Valeria never told me what happened after I ate my half of the cookie and drank the milk. She just said that my daddy loved me the only way he knew how. Then when you showed up, you were even more quiet about what you did when Jr. Eli would come around, yeah?

But I could feel my body sometimes when y'all were sleeping. I knew my privates were being touched, but there was always so much pain. Every time I work up the nerve to look down there at myself, my pussy look like an angry wild animal waiting to tear the next thing come near it... Asunder.

I was scared of her. She never smelled right or looked right or felt right. I-I thought she was broken, yeah.

"God, Vera."

It's fine. I ain't scared of her no more. She always clean and fresh, look like she worth millions of dollars and I know exactly what to do to make her act right, yeah?

"Vera, you sound so much like I imagine Della did when she wrote that diary. Same sense of smart humor with a pinch of and-what-you-gonna-do-about-it thrown in to round out the rich, hardy Southern flavor."

You speak fondly of Della. What changed?

"Me. My perspective. I gained an appreciation for the cards she'd been dealt. But mostly, I realized that there is no *me* without *her*. And there is no we—John and I—without her, either. And in a profoundly strange way, when she abandoned you, she made room for me.

"And when she took advantage of John, she forged in the image of her god, the only man who could acknowledge and make us aware of our brokenness. He recognized ours because it mirrored his own. It's like she knew we would find each other and that our love would consecrate our wounds, and bring us into the harmonious alignment she sought but was never able to realize."

You think she knew what she was doing, yeah?

"Maybe. In the same way every soul knows what it came here to do, even when the ego can't be bothered to remember. Della knew in this lifetime; she was meant to be a conduit of sorts.

———

"Designated to bring three daughters in one birthed body, one son created in misguided sacred erotic practices, and a legacy of healing wounds inflicted within the soul of the feminine divine."

Seems like we didn't do so bad in the momma department, after all, yeah? She come here and do what her soul vowed to do, and we can't turn up our nose at that.

"No, Vera. We most certainly cannot. So, what's up with you and Camilla? Is this something we need to bring to the collective and let John and Collin know about?"

Oh, lord no. John don't need to know what Milla, and I get up to behind closed doors. I can't imagine what he would think of me if he knew all the ways I make her...

"God, Vera. I don't mean tell everyone the details. I mean... because Collin and Valery and John and I have a schedule for time invested in our respective relationships and other things. That's what I'm talking about... Will you and Milla need to get on the schedule?"

Oh. Okay, that doesn't sound so bad. I'll talk to her about it, yeah. I'm pretty much already in love with her, but I don't know how she feel about me, yeah? If she just passing time, then I don't want to take anything away from you and Valery. But—

"I get it. Just have a talk with her and let us know. You can write it in Seeking Wonderland if it's easier."

Yeah. Okay. Well, I've taken up enough of your time and anyway... I just got inspiration for another poem. We'll talk soon, yeah?

"Okay, happy writing." *Happy writing?* What the hell am I saying? I feel her smile and shake her head like she's wondering the same thing.

The little, square orange clock on my desk says it's already after two in the afternoon. *How long were Vera and I talking?* Time is the best illusion I've ever seen. It doesn't exist, yet all anyone is concerned about is how to use it wisely. If I had my way, I'd be as free as the animals in the forests. Moving with the sun and following the patterns of the seasons.

***

It looks like the defected hospital we purchased at an auction is in a prime location and will serve as the perfect space for the Brunellis. I make a note in the margins to discuss provisions for clients who aren't able to afford the exclusive cost of treatment with the board of trustees.

If St. Jude can offer no cost to all their families, then we can surely offer it to those with the greatest need for our services.

"Shit, I need to get a headhunter to reach out to Jessa. She needs to get her little patootie down here to head up the holistic psychological counseling department." I mumble to myself.

And I need my damn cat.

"Who're you talking to, lovely?" John's voice startles me out of my chair.

"Jesus-jumping-jack-flash, John. Don't you know how to knock?" He stands in the doorway; strong fingers grip bent knees. The muscles in those wide shoulders jumping like frogs under his white tee. Even though I can't hear a peep, I know he's close to peeing himself at my expense.

"Baby—I d-didn't..." I watch John through slits as his head drops back into the locks of his shoulders. It looks like he's praying to every god he knows and doesn't know, to please help him stop laughing at his pissed-off wife.

Undoubtedly, his disingenuous prayers go unanswered. I ignore my desire to hurl the little teal desk lamp at my husband's head and pull my ass back onto my vintage fried-egg chair and glare in his direction.

"Shut up, John. what do you want, anyway? I'm busy."

"No, you're embarrassed and it's fucking adorable." He takes a deep inhale and blows out an audible breath before sauntering into my space like he owns it.

I'll show you how adorable I can be when I kick you in the balls.

"I'm sorry, Viv. I should've knocked, but you looked too sexy in those glasses with your locs in that messy side ponytail." He shakes his head and a dirty smirk slashes across his mouth. If smirks could speak, this one would say, *I want to wrap that fucking ponytail around my hand and make you choke on my dick.*

Yes, please and thank you for the privilege.

Once I'm comfortable again, I stare at him waiting to hear why he interrupted me. He doesn't keep me waiting long.

"There are a few things we still need to discuss, lovely." He pauses to ensure he has my full attention before moving on. "It's been roughly two weeks since everyone received their new back stories and we seem to be settling in with them, for the most part."

My eyes crinkle in confusion. When he doesn't attempt to clarify I ask, "Is there a question in there somewhere, or are you simply stating what we already know?" I smile to let him know there're no hard feelings and I'm *sort* of teasing him.

His eyes change only slightly as he takes me in but doesn't engage otherwise. "What do you think of the market analysis so far?"

Hmm, okay. I guess we're moving on to the business side of things.

"I'm glad you had the foresight to grab the old hospital and the surrounding land and buildings. The analysis says it's perfectly situated to attract the high end clientele we *should attract*." Although it's an obvious statement, the lilt at the end conveys my implied query. I watch for his reaction to my subtle probe. If he has one, I don't catch it.

Bastard. He thinks he's so much better at the businessy shit than me. Hello. I did run two successful businesses, dickhead.

"So," John scrubs his beard like he's come to an important decision. "And stop looking at me like I just called you a stupid bitch. I'm processing." He returns that same hand to his pockets and *processes* the hell out of my face. Not sure what he's sees, but when he's sure it is whatever it is, he offers, "You don't like the wording about the ideal clients. Hmm, I see. Too easy to leave the people who will benefit most from our facility out in the cold, sort to speak."

A soundless chuckle leaves me shaking my head at just how well John gets me. "I'm all for attracting wealthy clients; however, there needs to be provisions for people who can't afford the cost associated with our treatment." I challenge and wait for his response.

"What?" He looks down his straight nose at me and says, "Were you expecting me to argue that point? I'm a firm believer that those who can afford to pay top-dollar for our services, will and should do so. But I also believe that everyone has a right to live as the highest version of themselves, and if our center can assist in making that happen... then I'm all for it."

John looks a little upset that I would think otherwise about him, but he quickly blinks the irritation away and waits to hear what else is on my mind.

"Okay. Well, I've made some notes throughout the document. Um, things I'm sure you've noted as well. We seem to agree on pretty much everything so, what else did you want to talk about?" I ask as I shove the report back into the manilla folder.

"So, lovely I wasn't sure if we'd be able to pull this off," He shifts his weight from one foot to the other before announcing, "but I want to establish the charity at the same time as the business. Because they kind of feed into—"

"Charity?" I cut him off and jump up from my retro orange chair, to stand in front of him.

"Yes. The Brunellis CSA Advocacy Foundation." The name rolls off his tongue like he's been saying it every day.

I'm so confused, I couldn't come up with a question if my life depended on it. So, I just stand there gawking at my husband like he has another head growing from the top of the one attached to his neck.

He continues like he hasn't just blown my mind for the millionth time since I met him ten years ago. "Yea, it's kind of brilliant because the clients of the center, will donate their therapeutic artwork for ongoing auctions that will funnel capital into the foundation, intern, providing monetary support to other charitable organizations with the same focus as ours."

I know my face is wearing an obscenely wide smile because my cheeks are higher than Tupac when he freestyles.

John stares at me like I'm the most enchanting thing he's seen in a long time. He must be crazy or delusional, because there has never been anything as captivating as this beautiful, intelligent, Black man.

"God, that's sexy." I sigh and shake my head again.

"*What?*" John's voice is a shade of opaque grey, murky and saturated with confusion.

I put him out of his misery and explain, "The way your mind works. How intelligent and focused you are. It's one of the sexiest things about you, John. One of the reasons I love you so."

"My big brain? That's why you love me. Not my big—"

"Jonathan Ellis, please don't reduce yourself into some *Mandangalo* caricature of maleness. You are more than what hangs between your thighs."

"What would that—the thing hanging between my thighs—be called, Viv?"

"I've heard it goes by many names. Some are quite vulgar, and others seem more endearing."

"Which do you prefer, vulgar or endearing?"

"I'm from a good family. My mother and father raised us girls to be exemplary Southern women, you understand. I abhor vulgarity, but I find endearments too childish for my liking."

"So, where does that leave you when referencing my dick?"

"I rather like the euphemism, *member*. But again, I could be persuaded to call it a *ding-a-ling,* or even a *shlong*. But honestly, I think the best name for what hangs between your thighs is, Jughead." Peals of laughter pour from my soul, and I take off running around my office like I can ever escape him.

I know there is nowhere I'll ever run where he won't find and catch me. I'm on the other side of the room, laughing so hard, I can barely stand. Before I know what's happening, John wraps his arms around the deep indention of my waist and pulls my ass flush with his rather impressive *member*. He gives me a filthy grind and I sigh, before melting into the only man strong enough to anchor me, while setting me free to fly as high as my soul takes me. I rest the back of my head against his shoulder as the last of the giggles fade into the erotically charged tension surrounding our bodies like a death shroud.

"I love you, lovely. Regardless of your back story or maybe because of it. I love every-fucking-thing about you. Mostly, I love who I am, when I'm with you. You make me fall in love with myself. I don't know if that makes sense. Maybe I'm a narcissist."

Another lazy dribble of amusement falls from me before I reply, "No, it makes perfect sense. Like I said before. We're all just acting as mirrors for each other. Mirrors to show us our own broken pieces so we're able to give *koruna*—compassion and forgiveness—to ourselves.

"My love for you is reflected in my love for myself and vice versa. People have it all wrong, John. When they say we're here to find someone to fall in love with. It's not that we need to find someone else to fall in love with. Not at all. What we're searching for—what our souls are searching for—is someone to help us fall back in love with ourselves. If we had gone into this relationship with this kind of knowing, could you imagine where we'd be now?" I gaze over my shoulder and notice the golden firelight dancing within his deep, brown eyes. Love and affection burn with an intensity I never knew he was capable of.

"I wouldn't change a goddamned thing about how we got here. Not a damn thing, lovely-mine."

He turns me so we're facing each other and wraps his arms around my waist, placing butterfly kisses on the tip of my nose. My eyelids. My forehead and cheeks. Then he snakes his right hand up my back, wraps my ponytail around his hand, and pulls my head back before leaning down to brush my lips with his own.

John doesn't attempt to deepen the kiss and neither do I.

This is about connection. Simply being with each other. Sharing one eternal sacred moment of love and sensuality. With his lips still massaging mine, he whispers a benediction into my soul.

"I love you, Viv, and in our consecrated love, I'm finally in love with the man I am."

I press my lips hard against his and in the brattiest voice I can muster I whine, "Glad we got that out the way so, can we please go to this special room you promised to show me."

The End

Acknowledgements

I would like to acknowledge myself. I would like to thank me for putting in countless hours out in my writing cottage working like a slave with no feet. I want to express my gratitude to myself for going without food, sleep and other important things—wink, wink, nod, nod—for the sake of getting this final book in my Broken Souls series written, edited, revised, proofed, formatted, book cover designed, and published on the day I said it would be released.

I would also like to thank my partner, best friend, and the most patient and sexy man to ever take on human flesh... Joe, baby. Thank you for loving and supporting and encouraging me through this entire Broken Souls series. You are Me. I am You. We are One.

Next, I want to thank the Blythewood Critique Chapter and the virtual Romance Critique Chapter members of the South Carolina Writing Association for all of your input and lending me your big brains and keen eyes. Kasie Whitener, I didn't know what I was agreeing to when you invited me on your podcast, Write On, South Carolina.

I'm grateful for your acquaintance and friendship. When you promised to get me out of my writing bubble, and into a writing community you more than made good on it.

More recently, I joined the international Women's Fiction Writers Association and I have to mention how fun and supportive the writing dates are. So far, I've attended three writing dates. The act of sitting on Zoom for an hour and a half, with my camera and mic off with about 15 other women's fiction writers who are all working on whatever they're working on... is everything. Can't wait to get more involved in this virtual writing community.

I'd also like to thank one other writing community I belong to. The Prolific Black Writers Support Group was founded by new author, Kimberly Powell. This collective started on TikTok. Our biweekly Sunday Zoom sessions are where we come together to share our expertise and help each other with the business of writing. Our GroupMe chat is where we meet to support and encourage each other as we continue our individual writing journeys. I'm all for diversity and meeting and working with everyone, but in the end; it feels amazing to be around people who look like me. Who stand over similar experiences and realities as me. So, thank all of my ancestors and spirit guides for leading me to this melanated group of writers. Where you direct my feet, my soul will follow.

Last and in no way, least. Readers. Thank you to everyone who purchased or downloaded and read my books. If you read them and left reviews, double thank you. If you read it, left reviews and posted about it... you better be on my email list and receiving freebies, coupons, and exclusive content.

I will miss writing on this series, but there are always Vera's poems, the DID system's journal, and enough Internal House moments for an anthology of short stories. Who knows? Maybe I'm not quite done with these guys after all.

About the Author

I knew I wanted to be a writer from the young age of ten or eleven. I'd just finish reading Flowers for Algernon and had completely fallen in love with words; how easily they swept me away to places I never even knew existed. I decided then and there that I wanted to be a magician and use words to create different worlds where other people could travel and discover new parts of themselves.

But then I grew up and accepted the notion that magic wasn't real and I traded in my dreams for a steady paycheck and summers off. Thankfully, the Universe saw fit to release me from my poor decision and gave me the freedom and time to pursue my first love of writing again.

In 2013 I was diagnosed with systemic lupus as well as a host of other autoimmune disease. I won't lie and say it's easy living in a body hell bent on attacking and destroying healthy organs, tissue, and systems but it did change my perspective on what it means to truly be alive.

After getting a handle on managing my health by assembling some of the best doctors in the Southeastern USA and making some difficult lifestyle changes, I was free to write the books I wanted to read, but couldn't find.

It's because of the love and devotion of my best friend and soul mate, that I'm able to stay at home and do what I love instead of what I have to. Together we have three beautiful daughters who constantly inspire me to strive to be the highest version of myself and live my most intentional life as I embrace my sacred womanhood..

Other Books By Ella Shawn

The Broken Souls Series

Broken Souls Book 1
Mirrored Souls Book 2
Consecrated Souls Book 3

Companion to Broken Souls Series
Shattered Beginnings: The Diary of Della Richman

Made in the USA
Middletown, DE
11 June 2023

32083860R00221